Other titles by Howard Ingram:

Fiction

Nnyaa Leina
Fiona's Head
Korean Revenge
Two Harriets

Non Fiction

Reminiscences at Sixty

Dear Jane,
I hope you enjoy (you might recognise a few places!)
Love,
Howard

Nnyaa Leina

by

Howard Ingram

authorHOUSE®

AuthorHouse™ UK Ltd.
500 Avebury Boulevard
Central Milton Keynes, MK9 2BE
www.authorhouse.co.uk
Phone: 08001974150

First published by AuthorHouse 9/20/2007

ISBN: 978-1-4343-2511-2 (sc)

Printed in the United States of America
Bloomington, Indiana

This book is printed on acid-free paper.

For Athena
always

and for my daughter Nicole from whom
came much of the inspiration for this story

Pardus maculas non deponit

The leopard doesn't change his spots

BOOK 1

England and Africa

1965

1

From the Harris family home, the narrow roadway to the church gradually ascended, climbing a long, gracefully winding hill. A road built for slow-moving, careless, lighthearted pedestrians or donkey carts heading for country markets. All that now irrevocably altered as the motor car had long come into its own, destroying the tranquility of the countryside. The enchanting grace emanating from Kathy and her mother recreated that sylvan symmetry if for only a moment, on this their special day.

Following the early morning rain, the village of Arlaston sparkled. May, the month of renewal, re-birth. Tiny yellow and shyly apologetic light blue wild flowers peeked timorously from beneath the hedgerows. Spiders' webs shimmered oblong droplets of rain, priceless necklaces of water diamonds proudly accepting the strengthening rays of the morning sun, destined never to see the afternoon. Springtime buds everywhere, on the branches of Cherry Trees; on the Oak and the Beech, the grand old trees of rural England. Golden and orange marigolds competed with deep blue and yellow pansies for an aesthetic first prize. Both won. Both wore sparkling morning rosettes. The narrow tarmac road steamed as the sun's strengthening rays dried the morning rain that lay forlornly in tiny puddles along its length. A gentle steaming.

Kathy slowly walked on, her mother her only companion. They could have ridden to the church in her Father's new white 1965 Bentley, but Kathy preferred to walk. It was her village and she wanted to feel it, she wanted to hold it to her, for it to be an integral and permanent part of her, especially on this day. She knew every lane, every pathway. She had walked every yard of every narrow road and narrower lane as a child with her mongrel dog, Whisky. Now dead. She had ridden along every bridle way of her quaint small village, galloped over every field on her wonderful thoroughbred chestnut mare, Winnie. Now dead. As Kathy walked, she remembered her youth with clarity. An oppressive family life when all the times should have been happy times, but few were. She glanced sideways at her mother walking beside her. A mother who had never said no to anything or to anyone, especially not to her domineering husband. Few people disagreed with Ian Harris, fewer people said no to him, publicly or privately, even when they knew him to be wrong. Ian Harris was a man whose god was work, whose every driven emotion revolved around the ever smoother running and the even greater success of his business. Ian Harris was a strong man, physically, mentally, morally. He had been a very handsome man in his youth and still retained most of his good looks although his body had become stockier, more substantial, harder. Like a roughly hewn dry stone wall, immovable, resolute, pugnacious. He had few friends, didn't need them. He curried no man's favour, witheringly professional, constantly honest, always fair. Except for the way he treated his uncomplaining wife and unappreciated daughter. His wife could not remember if she still loved her husband and, if not, when had it ceased, and if she did, what else was it that they still had between them? She knew what it was to love her daughter, what it meant to love her son and to forgive him, time and time again. But she was no longer sure what it was to love her husband. Somehow it no longer mattered. The love element in their relationship was no longer important to either of them, or so she forced herself to believe. They co-existed in a calm quasi-contractual relationship, without the necessity for loving phrases to bind them. Both knew they would always stay together, that there was sufficient of a comfort zone remaining. They had procreated successfully, he worked hard, came home to rest a little before sleep, sometimes to eat if he had not snacked that afternoon in his office as he chased the piles of paper around his enormous desk. She was an excellent cook and home-keeper. Together they entertained as necessary, always successfully. She looked plainly pretty with her full figure enveloped in long shapeless dresses or modest sometimes well cut suits. Always chosen from the peg. No need, he said, to go to the expense of having them made. He believed it his prerogative to approve any new purchase, so that she felt, (not really any more for she had become accustomed over time), that all her clothes were but an extension and a reflection of the current uniform distinguishing the Arlaston Hydro Hotel from others. His hotel. Ian Harris regarded not only the building, but also the employees and everything in its environs and estate as his property, including his wife. She no longer objected. It had never been worth it, never would be. If not kicked against, then life was sufficiently comfortable, sufficiently calm. But she worried about Kathy, especially today.

The hill took as its base a tiny two-platformed station. Platforms heading eastwards to the industrial Potteries, westwards to the rural market towns of Stone and Stafford. A station with one astonishingly aged official, combining the roles of porter, controller and administrator. He had been there since the station opened. There as a youth ensuring that middle-class passengers disgorging from their steam trains were able to find carriages to take them for their rest cure at the Hydro Hotel. For those keen to begin their cure immediately he showed them the pathway up the hillside for their short but invigorating walk. Sometimes he was handed threepence or even sixpence for his trouble. But these days the Hotel limousine with white-gloved chauffeur met many customers not arriving by their own transport, driving them the few hundred yards to their destination. Today no one walked up the hill. The curative role of a disciplined hydropathic establishment now replaced by the pampering luxury of a five star hotel. The apparently gentle yet deceptively demanding hill stretched from Arlaston station to, at its crest, the central village green. Few houses lined the road. Those that did retained a studied, roof only in view, seclusion. For they were the homes of the wealthy of Arlaston. Purposely hidden from prying eyes by high dense hedges and almost continuously blossoming trees planted in serried rows to catch the southern sun. Cherry blossom, Horse Chestnut, Apple Blossom, Holly. So the year turned with the trees as the bored occupants soberly peeped unobserved from their curtained upstairs windows. Today those occupants peeped through lace to watch the bride go by. Mrs. Godfrey with her opera glasses hanging on a cord, her blue-rinsed hair captured in a black string net and her puffy gin-and-tonic face bearing traces of the previous evening's thick white cosmetic packing. Kathy and her mother knew they would be there, especially Mrs. Godfrey, but they cared nothing for these people. Kathy not caring overtly; her mother, because of her husband, covertly. In this communal non-caring they fused into a positive union, neither mentioning their thoughts to the other. Neither needing to. As she walked with Kathy to the church on that special day, Mrs. Harris peeked shyly sideways at her beautiful young daughter, the May Bride; wishing her a life of love and peace. Not the life she had herself experienced. But she was not sure about Robert Castle.

Kathy slipped her left arm into her mother's right arm, saying nothing, simply exerting a loving pressure, seeking a return of love, of confidence. Of course he would be there! With his long brown-black hair and his low sideburns, both disapproved of by her upright conventional father. Had he never had a youth of his own? Was he always too busy pleasing his own father and running the business to be able to express his own individuality, his own abandon? Robert's hippie dress created an absurdity of passion in her father. Didn't he understand it was simply a statement against the prevailing conventions? Didn't he understand it would pass as it always did, generation to generation, each making their transient statement against the prevailing mores, rebellion dissipating in time? Yet she remembered the discussions during her foray into philosophy at university; the recognition that all progress is made by unreasonable men. For those who are reasonable conform to the social requirements of their surroundings, eventually fitting in. It is only those who refuse to fit in that take the human race forward. Was it as simple as that, or was there a necessary compromise somewhere along the way? Reasonable progress amongst reasonable thinking men? Would it be possible one day for Robert to sit down with her father and agree on what was reasonable? Certainly that time was not now, but, she wondered, would it one day come?

Robert had insisted upon The Beatles' song 'Love me do' for her entrance into the Thirteenth century church rather than the conventional 'here comes the bride'. Initially the vicar had refused, not wishing, in his view, to lower the tone in the House of God. Then he had acquiesced because of her mother's special pleading, assisted in no small measure by her donation. Sufficient to repair half the aging church roof. Apparently God had been mollified. Ian Harris did not know about the donation, Kathy Harris did not know about the donation. Her mother had wiped out her private life's savings in one single act of love for her daughter and, completely in character, had told no one.

2

Kathy hoped the children would be there. The children taking their morning playtime break in the old schoolyard. Would they stop in their play to watch her go by? She hoped so. Would they wave to her, wish her well on her way? Kathy loved that school. Her school until she reached the age of eleven; then having to travel to the abhorrent senior school far away from her own village. The senior school at Stafford, the all girl's school where every girl was anonymous and alone. She had hated that girl's grammar school with a passion equalled only by the love she had felt for her junior school in the village.

Kathy had timed this special walk to be sure to pass by the playground at morning break. The rain had lifted; there was no reason for the children to be kept inside. It was ten minutes to eleven; they would be there by eleven. The same break time she had when she was a pupil there, with Mrs. Titley as headmistress. Now dead. But the break time lived, just the same. Always the same. Kathy plodded sedately but firmly in her sensible black patent leather low-heeled shoes up the increasingly wearisome hill. But her mind, her emotion, her soul, were not weary. Her mother was not faring so well. Despite her daughter's wise advice, Mrs. Harris had determined to remain in her high heel shoes. She had been told she could easily change at the church porch, or before if she wished, but she was adamant. She wanted to walk in proper style beside her only daughter, beside her Kathy, beside her bride. So she suffered, silently.

Resting for a moment as they reached the village green, atop the long graceful hill, Kathy gazed around at the old cottages semi-circling the Green. At one time they had all been tithe cottages belonging to the Gladbrook family. Their surrounding estate providing much needed agricultural work for the men of the cottages, sometimes for the women too, or jobs in service up at Arlaston Hall itself. The work was simple, honest, like the people of the village; most of them. A good life, a friendly life, a peaceful and rewarding life. Until the machines of the late Nineteenth century began to appear from the furnaces and the vast black engineering works of the industrializing Midlands. From Birmingham came the threshing machine that took away the work of twenty men. And their family's food. But it was progress; they were told it was progress. There was no stopping progress. The Gladbrooks, kindhearted though they were, had to move with the times. Compete or die. So they competed and the occupants of the cottages, many of them, died. Not always in body but always in mind, as they travelled to the grinding dust and searing heat of the pot banks of Stoke-on-Trent, seeking work in the hell of the kilns. Or to the dank and often deadly coalmines of Wolstanton and Hem Heath. There to die. Then their sons, their daughters too followed this burdensome existence. It was a sad time for the declining village of Arlaston.

Just in time, before the death throes were quite upon the village, Ian Harris brought it back to life again. The Second World War over, he borrowed, cajoled, schemed, sold family shares and finally succeeded in raising sufficient capital to re-build, re-furbish and re-open his family's hitherto fading edifice. Breathing new life into the Hydro just as it in times past had breathed new life into its customer patients. Employment, income and new hope returned to the village of Arlaston and by the year 1950 this tireless man, yet to reach his thirty-fourth birthday, had offered employment to three hundred villagers. The occupants of the tithe cottages were loaned money by the Hydro to buy their homes and were no longer tied to the land and to the Gladbrooks. They had a new master, fearsome but fair. He gave them work, dignified work, not that of a coolie in the pot banks or a mule in the mines. They had money to live, even money to save. He had a princess for a daughter and the village loved her. Loved her independent ways, the epitome of what they wanted for their own children. But she was loving and caring too, genuinely so, unselfish. Today was her wedding day and the plump well-fed women of the village remembered the hard times as they sat on their front steps in the rising sunshine to watch her pass. They waved to this lass of the hard times, this lass who with her smile and her charming wayward ways had always given them fun, something to chat about and something to laugh

11

at or to scold. Impossible to be grey about, always black or white, mostly white. As Kathy stopped to allow her mother to rest for a moment on the bench at the side of the Village Green, they waved a fiercely friendly wave to her. She was theirs, they hers.

Kathy momentarily drifted away from her resting parent to the concrete cross, situated in the exact centre of the green. A twenty-foot high concrete cross that had always held a morbid fascination for her. Not really morbid; adventurous. A memorial to all the men of the village and the surrounding farms who had fallen in The Great War, a memorial to the great folly of man. As a child she had woven fantasies around these fallen heroes. Who was Percy Bullock and was he handsome? Henry Buxton, was he brave? Geoffrey Bricknall, was he rich and would he have become a great man, a Prime Minister or a Lord if the war had not taken him? Often, as a junior schoolgirl, she had sat under the imposing grey monument wondering if her own man would be handsome, rich, and fearless? And if he were all these things, would death have to claim him early too, because he was just too good to be allowed to live? And if so, would even the short time she was able to spend with him, be sufficient for a lifetime? Now Kathy had her own hero. A man who resolved never to go to war, a man strong in his convictions, tough in his ideals.

And in this bearded man-youth Ian Harris had met his match. Stubborn, unbending, sure of himself, simply informing his future father-in-law of his intention to marry his only daughter, recognising no conventional compulsion to ask for Kathy's hand from her father. Robert Castle had stood, in the Harris's pristine living room drinking his beer directly from the bottle and talking his nonsense about the need for love, for environmental protection from the irreversible damage caused by industry and by the crassness of man. He stood in this citadel of success and decried materialism and the virtue of hard work. Abruptly Ian Harris left them, he could take no more of the appalling scene, the public touching, the embracing and the damn foolish gazing soundlessly into each other's eyes. Grim faced he marched back to his busy haven of peace. A world he understood, the hectic Managing Director's office. Security. Back to deal with the problems only he could manage, to a place where people were waiting for him to come and manage them. People who needed him, respected him, obeyed him.

With delight Kathy saw that the children were indeed there in the playground, running, skipping, fighting. She and her mother came abreast of the school. Kathy's heart lifted with pleasure as she saw the children stop for a moment in their play to watch her white apparition glide by. Then the girls realised that the apparition was a bride and they knew that one day it was preordained that they would become one of these and the bride looked nice and she waved to them so they ran to the wire fence separating the playground from the road and gaily they waved back to her. All wavers felt pleasure and pride at their wavings. Pleasure to give, pride in receiving. The boys shouted something, at first unintelligible. They had grins on their little round innocent faces as one boy in particular shouted something dirty, something he had heard at home about what happened on wedding nights. Something his father had said to his mother about Uncle Ben and his new auntie Ruth and his father had laughed and his mother had told him to shut up so the children wouldn't hear. But he had heard the words and now he shouted them and giggled and his friends thought it was great. None of them really understood the forbidden words, especially that one, but it was fun to shout them all. The boys, hands to mouths, laughed a knowing, childish laugh and one of the older girls said, 'dirty Jimmy!' and turned away in disgust, which made the boys laugh more. Then Kathy began to laugh with them and it made everything clean, acceptable, and she loved them all. Her mother pretended not to hear, but smiled inside at her daughter's childish pleasure. Her own childhood momentarily flashing in front of her. She was young again, and pure, and unoppressed. She was her own little girl again, before the world came to possess her, to take her from herself, to take what she was, what she could have been. The moment passed with the ringing of the handbell, the incontestable summons back to sanity and sums. Miss Brown was the ringer, a sterner woman than Mrs. Titley had been. Much sterner, for Mrs. Titley had lost her husband in the Second World War and so her family became her children. She never remarried; her husband substitutes walked and ran on many ten year-old legs. Good or bad, she cared for them all. Miss Brown was different. She did not love her charges. They were with her but half the day and she looked for fault rather than actions to praise. Miss Brown went home after school and forgot the children, purposely drove them from her mind. Sweet dead Mrs. Titley had taken every one of them home with her in her head and counted the hours until they would be with her again. That was a mother indeed and a best friend. A protector to beat all comers.

A tall, shy girl, the last in the line snaking back into the classroom, turned and waved a final shy, beguiling wave at the figure in white, then hurried into enforced boredom, following her now silent classmates.

It had been her mother's wedding dress, Kathy was proud to give it the second airing of its long life. She had always loved the long satin dress hanging protected by old muslin cloths in the main family wardrobe. As a young girl she had peeked at it, this special dress and imagined her mother inside it and herself inside it. Then one day when she was twelve years old and there was no one in the house, she had taken the dress from its hanger and stepped into it and pulled up its zipper and stood in front of the mirror in shimmering satin like a young queen. She had taken flowers from the garden and like Ophelia, for she was doing *Hamlet* at school that year, she had pretended to die for love, clutching her flowers to her young unformed breast and lying luxuriously sadly on the new-mown dew-dappled lawn. She knew she had lain but for only a moment on the grass. But then, oh God! The dress had a stain on it and she worried how to remove the green grass stain and she dared not wash the dress and she cried. Hastily she stuffed the dress back onto its hanger and ran from the room. She did not sleep that night and, for many nights thereafter her sleep was disturbed by her dreams. Dreams of her mother finding the dress and somehow the stain had grown since she replaced the dress in the wardrobe. It grew daily and now covered almost the entire back of the dress and it was the ugliest stain imaginable. Then her father found out about the stain. She knew her mother would never have told him because of the repercussions her only and too much loved daughter would have to face. It must have been Edward, he must have told her father and her father beat her and made her wash the dress every day and still the stain grew and in her dream the dress withered as the stain grew and she awoke sweating. Then, for years she forgot about the stain. It was only as the dress was brought out in preparation for this day that she worried about the stain once more. And there it was, if you knew where to look. For it was so small it needed the practiced eye to find it and she remembered all the pain of her dreams and she could not believe the smallness of the stain. The dress was cleaned, but still the tiny stain remained. A stain only Kathy could see. She loved that dress. And now she loved that stain. For the memory. The dress fitted so perfectly, without a single tuck, without the slightest alteration. Wearing the dress made Kathy realize how excellent her mother's figure had been on her wedding day, for immodestly she knew her own to be impressive. Twenty-six years ago her mother must have had thirty-six inch breasts, high and proud, a twenty-four inch waist and long well-proportioned legs reaching to firm thirty-three inch buttocks. For she had all of those and the dress fitted perfectly. Little trace of all that sensuous splendour in her mother now. Not fat, simply rounded. Kathy looked at her mother, at her mother's shape and wondered if that was what life had in store for her. Another twenty years, even less before she in her turn became, yes, matronly. Would Robert love her just the same then? What a wedding-day notion, she thought, smiling to herself as they came into sight of the ancient grey-stoned church, waiting for its new roof. Kathy squeezed the arm of her matronly mum and loved her.

Arm in arm they rounded the bend in the road at the northern edge of the Village Green. A new life now in prospect for Kathy, frightening. The small church somberly beautiful in the soft morning sun. Creeping geraniums fell lopsidedly over its southern facing wall encompassing large aged gravestones proudly proclaiming their departed occupants. There was no room left in the graveyard now for more bodies. Kathy wondered where the people of the village were buried today. She supposed a lot of them would be cremated. She wondered whether she would decide to be burnt or buried when her time came to depart. It was something that Robert and she should decide, should know about one another, just in case. Her morbid thoughts expired as her gaze rose from the mossy gravestones, from the serried ranks of the dead, upwards to the uniquely eight-sided spire reaching majestically above the surrounding pine trees. How, without modern tools, could that spire possibly have been constructed? She would never know. The Doomsday Survey of 1086 recorded that the village of Arlaston, unlike many other villages in England at that time, possessed its own priest. Further documents, now held deep in the chancellery, gave witness to the Pope having confirmed a church at Arlaston in 1146. Into this slim slice of history where she had been baptised as a babe, where alone and weeping she had prayed for her dog Whiskey and her beautiful mare Winnie, now walked this upright, proudly bearing, terrified young woman. But no one could see her terror. She believed that her man would be there waiting for her. He just had to be.

Ian Harris stood at the Thirteenth century South Aisle porch, the only entrance to the church that was open for public access. A semi-circular arched doorway flanked by pointed blind arches. An architectural transition from Norman to early English style. A little forbidding. But nowhere near as forbidding as the scowl on the face of the man standing there. Kathy was happy to see her father scowling as she approached him, for it confirmed that Robert was truly there. Had Robert not been waiting for her in the church there would have been a pretend sympathetic fatherly face, an attempt not to break into a smiling face. But now, this moment, it was a scowling face. Thank God! It was her day, her day of freedom! She walked, almost a strut, the almost strut becoming a triumphant march; her mother forced into step bedside her. They marched towards her waiting father. Ian Harris nodded to his stunning satin-encapsulated daughter and, for a long moment, a suspension in time moment that might have lasted a second or a hundred years, Ian Harris saw the mother again. Saw his young wife once more. Despite himself, but the world could not see, could not feel, he felt the lump in his throat and the tears smarting behind his eyes. But he displayed nothing. He did not attempt a smile; never a hypocrite. Always and simply and absolutely honest.

The Beatles began to sing ' Love me do ' and Kathy Harris entered the full church with a radiant bridal smile that carried all the way down the narrow aisle to her waiting man.

3

Robert Castle wanted her from the first moment his deep set and experienced, some said lecherous, eyes had sight of her. Neither to possess exclusively nor to own, that code of morality belonged to his parents, to the generations before current enlightenment, not to the questioning, caring liberated youth of the 1960's. He simply desired to carnally acquire her, at least once.

It was the night of the Fresher's Ball, to which, being an *ex*-university student, he was not entitled to attend. But he still had friends in the second and third years, especially the small select group calling themselves 'the Animals'. A name appropriate to their academic discipline and in reverence to their favourite pop group. A name also befitting the group's behaviour. Through them an invitation was effortless. It was essential, the Animals postulated, to initiate the wide-eyed immature Fresher girls into university life and university morals. More than essential, it was their duty. At the Ball and beginning to lose their initial shyness, most of the Fresher girls soon gravitated towards the Second and Third year men. They wanted to know how the university really worked, what would be expected of them. They wanted to learn from experience. In time, most of them did so, but they learnt little of the academic activity Glasgow had to offer, and afterwards, most felt ashamed and cursed men and vowed to dedicate themselves to work. Until the next time, the next Ball, the next social event, or even the next drink.

For the First year Fresher men, life was usually disagreeable at the Fresher Ball. There were never any First year, let alone Second or Third year, female students looking for first year men. They would have to wait their turn until next year or the year after. They had first to become 'interesting'. Robert Castle knew that he excelled in the 'interesting' stakes and made much mileage out of that knowledge. Intellectually capable, he had become bored with the theory of his subject, leaving the Zoology course in the middle of his second year. He left to follow in Darwin's footsteps. To take a practical self-taught course in the Galapagos Islands. There to study the marine iguanas found only in those islands. The strange animals that were one of the major keys to Darwin's evolution of the species arguments. He studied the odd beasts, staring them in the eyes for hours, without movement, unblinking. He gave many of them names and met them every day as they clumsily exited from their watery home to enjoy a little of their God's sunshine. He swam with the creatures, astonishingly graceful in their natural habitat, but they always swam too fast for him, too far. However, frequently there was the renewed pleasure when they returned the following day for him to make his notes and to take his photographs. He rode the

Giant Tortoises, older than his own Grandfather, probably much older. Had Darwin seen the same ones that Robert now sedately rode to the water's edge, seen them perhaps as babies? It was possible; it was only a hundred years before. The thought was stunning and exciting. He caught and studied the flightless cormorant, admired the blue-footed booby and loved, most of all, the graceful gloomy albatross as they parried their beaks in ritual courtship. The birds that could fly the world, effortlessly. Evolution in reverse. He paraded with the penguins and body surfed with the friendly dolphins in his nine months of blissful, contented and practical study. He read again all the works of Darwin he had carried with him in his meagre luggage and he not only found the animals, he began to find himself.

But there was absolutely no opportunity for sexual relief and Robert Castle was a young man and the juices flowed healthily and frequently. He returned to Scotland with a mission. Kathy Harris became, within twenty-four hours of his return, the embodiment of the possible achievement of that mission. He saw her, wanted her, knew intuitively and at once that he could have her. And he did, that very first night. Three times before they slept, twice before a late breakfast. Robert Castle was satiated, but Kathy Harris was in love.

Kathy bedded three other men during her three years at Strathclyde University but only once each and always out of pique, when she knew that Robert was carelessly offering himself to the impressionable first and second, even third year students. He was readily accepted every time he tried. She hated the balls, the Fresher's ball especially, for it held too many bittersweet

21

memories for her. But he always came back, always returned to her bed when her flat mate was out or invited her to his, to his tiny warm sensual studio apartment in Sauceihall street, distanced from the noisy traffic below, walls and tables festooned with trophies from another world, far away, yet ever present. Fossils of animals long dead, tiny bones of mammals only he could distinguish and photographs, so many photographs of his time in the Galapagos Islands. He promised Kathy he would take her there one day and she believed him. But Africa was his next quest. He spoke of it continually, of going there to work with the animals, especially to study the preservation of the big five; the elephant, rhino, hippopotamus, buffalo and lion. To spend months there, even years, on conservation projects, on protection of the species as man continued to encroach ever closer to the natural habitat of these great beasts; driving them to hunger, displacement and death. These were the best times for Kathy, when she could lie in this strong sexy man's arms and listen to his passion for the animals, herself transported with him to the wilderness. She knew she would go anywhere with him, travel to any continent, accept any hardship. He was such a thoroughly exciting man. Perhaps in his inexhaustible energy, she rationalized, he really needed the occasional change of partner in his bed; but he always came back. She vowed to herself that she would ensure that he always came back.

Robert remained an unofficial university student. Using the facilities of the university, especially the research library, attending an occasional lecture, especially when a visiting authority came to lecture to the Zoology faculty. Sometimes he heard nonsense from these lecturers, his own research and practical experience exceeding their own knowledge, but sometimes he learned. Then he would work even harder. He was deep into a thesis of which any post graduate would have been immensely proud, but without possessing a first degree, the rules of the day could not admit he was capable of higher work, original research. But his detailed study work was authoritative, in patches brilliant and the professor of Zoology knew it, could not admit it, did not like the renegade. Was jealous of the renegade. Robert took Darwin's work and further extended his own studies into the origin of the marine iguana. Had it indeed come from the mainland of the Americas? Was it evolution in reverse; having once been a land creature, now adapted for the sea? Or had it always been a sea creature? If so, why, unlike its land-bound cousins, had it not also taken to the land; preferring to remain in the sea? What had it been, what was it today and what would it be in a million years time? Where was its link in the chain of evolution, was it a key or was it an aberration? These and a hundred other questions were explored, answered, re-answered and questioned again in the well-researched original work, complete with unique and vivid photographs of the animal, or was it a reptile, a fish? An authoritative study, at the front-end of leading anthropological research of the day. But officially unrecognized by the university he had scorned. He realised the university could never accept his doctorate, knew they needed him to take a first degree, but he was beyond that now. Both parties stood on their principles and thus, both parties lost. But he gave it to them anyway, sent it to the Professor of Zoology with a loose hand-written note. The Professor had never, in all his time at the university, seen a better piece of work from a student. Lengthy, interesting, well-argued, scholarly, practical, thrusting with its questions and conclusions, beautifully illustrated. A work that deserved the highest distinction. A work that deserved to be published and made available to all students and academics in the zoological world. He put it in his bookcase. To gather dust.

Now Robert was finished and Africa beckoned. He enjoyed Kathy, but he enjoyed others too. However, he wanted Africa more than he wanted any woman. Kathy clung to him, feeling him leaving her, even when his strong arms were wrapped around her in the reflective moments after their lovemaking. For those were the moments when he left her, gone somewhere with his animals and his studies, not needing her. Then Kathy, in due course, completed her own studies and Robert, no longer having his own work to demand his time and with her examinations over, they made love more frequently, steering adroitly away from discussions of the future, of any future together. Was there indeed a future together? They made love on the eve of her graduation ceremony and she felt him inside her all that day. She could smell and taste him as she walked with her father on the vice-chancellor's lawn. She tasted him in the champagne and in the salmon sandwiches. She saw his naked body lying prone on the bed as she stood by the lecturers who were telling her father how well she had done. She ached to return to him. But when she did, when all the ceremonies were over, when all the drinking had finished, when the celebratory meal with her mother and father in the very best restaurant in Glasgow had been consumed, when she ran laughing up the stairs to his tiny secure, loving apartment clutching her diploma in one hand, a bottle of the best champagne in the other, when she stood outside his door quivering with delightful anticipation as she remembered the magical ways they had pleasured one another, when she flung open his door in her eager anticipation of the love, the warmth, the delight they would now share, and saw her in his bed, so young she looked no more than sixteen, wrapping nubile white arms around his wonderful body, freely enjoying him, Kathy died. Anger transcended grief and she flung the bottle of champagne at his head and hoped to God that it would kill him. But it exploded on the wall just above his head and drenched him and that bloody girl. Drenched them in cold expensive champagne and tiny slivers of glass.

'Try fucking her with that glass all over you, you bastard!' She shouted at him as she slammed the door. On her way to find a man and a bottle. Any man. Any bottle.

For long moments Robert Castle looked down at the glass on his body, at the champagne dripping from his nose and chest. He hardly heard the hysterical screaming of the eighteen-year-old girl shaking beside him. Her very first time, she had told him. She would probably be traumatized against sex for the rest of her life, he thought, abstractly. But he cared nothing for her. He cared for Kathy. The realisation hit him hard. Fully hit him hard, for the first time. He'd previously admitted he'd liked her well enough, he'd enjoyed her.

They'd enjoyed each other. But this deep? Did he really feel so deeply and absolutely about one woman, about Kathy? He looked again at his body and felt shame. A unique emotion for Robert Castle.

'You'd better go.' He instructed the frightened, sobbing girl, forgetting her damn name. 'You'd better go.' He said again. She sobbed, quietly now and tried to brush the glass from her tiny, almost immature breasts. He did not help her. She did not think of taking a shower, she just wanted to be rid of this crazily attractive man and the madness. She dressed, not looking at the motionless man. Queer with his extra long hair and the glass lying untouched on his face and chest and his dark eyes staring like the eyes of the actor who had played Christ when they pinned him to the cross, and she thought of home and safety and she hated university, and it was only her first week there. She had no idea where she would go now, she had no friends. She was waiting for the allocation of a flat; she had a small room in a bed and breakfast boarding house, with commercial travellers and gas men who were laying pipes or something and she was afraid to return there, but she must leave this crazy room and its occupant with the staring, piercing far away eyes. She stumbled out of the room, vomited twice in the stairway, had nothing to clear it up with, raced guilty and sobbing across the green and into the quasi safety but certain anonymity of the ladies' toilet on platform one of Glasgow Central station.

Robert Castle lay for a long time, unmoving, remembering, regretting.

26

What to say to her, he wondered. He had been too long with her to simply say sorry. It had been her special day and he had totally fucked it up for her. Three years from that first Fresher's ball when they had first met, when they had first lain together, three years to her graduation of today. He had watched her grow, in stature and intelligence and experience. He had observed the slowly developing then well deserved and authentic respect she was afforded by staff and peers alike. He had felt pride in being with her and loneliness without her. He rose from the bed, shameful. He showered, carefully picking the many tiny shards of glass from the thick hair on his head. He remembered the times they had showered together. Her large firm breasts cupped in his strong hands. Her long brown hair cascading in a halo of spray. Her generous brown eyebrows puckered in delight as her beautiful green eyes remained closed. Her buttocks grinding into his erection as if in a dance of delight, indeed, that was what it truly was. Always. Then turning to him, accepting him. Standing firm and taking him, right to the very end and supporting him when he came. Taking, giving, loving.

Robert loved the girl and now he admitted it. In the shower picking her glass from his hair. He loved her. But what the hell could he do now to keep her?

Kathy's pretended wildness hid her real conformity. He knew there was only one way to keep her. Did he really want her that badly?

Yes!

That is why he now stood there waiting. In the Chancel of that aged church, gazing up at the medieval style paintings that graced the roof. He stood before the

High Alter staring unseeing at the beautiful stained glass windows commemorating the rededication of the church in 1240. Robert Castle felt very frightened. Alone and frightened. God, he thought, as he looked around him at all the artifacts belonging to the house of the supreme being, how I wish it were all over!

4

Too soon they came. He didn't want them to come so soon. He was not yet ready. He had been in the church for forty minutes but he was not yet prepared. He thought of that stupid Beatles' song he'd demanded and felt ashamed. He looked down at his ludicrous Indian shirt and baggy trousers and then around at the demure Thirteenth Century church set in the small traditional English village and he felt foolish. And the damn sandals too! She deserved a suit; he should have worn a suit. Not for convention or for her family, but for her. To compliment her dress and to show respect, to her. And he should have played the Wedding March instead of the damn Beatles. For her. She deserved better than he was giving her on this her only wedding day. The girl of the champagne deserved better than this. She was coming towards him now, fearsome father on arm, but her lovely face beaming a radiant smile, transforming the entire church, bringing it alive, imbuing it with happiness. Please God give me time to change into a suit and order the correct music so that she can have what she deserves on her wedding day. If this were a film I could freeze the action, step out of the set and return with the right clothes for her and start the correct music playing. Freeze her smile and her progress; I need only a few moments! But it was not a film and the procession was almost upon him. A procession headed by the biggest smile and the biggest frown he had ever seen in his life. And he felt so very small, and so afraid. So pure and fresh she looks and she wants to be mine. She must be the crazy one, not me. I don't even want to be mine most of the time. Then he saw nothing other than her smile. It filled the entirety of life. She held his hand firmly. Two frightened unsure people instantly became certain, courageous and assured, feeding directly off one another's loving physical presence. And the music and the garments mattered no more. They could have stood naked or clothed in furs, the music could have been traditional jazz or Handle's Messiah, it was no longer relevant. A cloud enveloped and protected everything and made everything soft and fluffy and warm and good.

The ceremony was a blur to both bride and groom. Ian Harris frowned throughout, his wife cried quietly into her embroidered lace handkerchief, observing the obvious joy of her only daughter, praying continually for her happiness through her tears, for Robert to be the good man her daughter deserved.

The small family congregation, no-one from Robert's family, so all had to be scattered on both sides of the church, was swelled within seconds of her entering the church by the ladies from the cottages and even Mrs. Godfrey in her florid pink hat and florid pink face, hiding at the rear of the church so to be sure to see all, to be able to report back over supper that evening and coffee the next morning. But who could she report to, she thought with dismay as, in glancing around the church, she saw her coffee morning partners, in equally florid hats, attempting equal anonymity and failing as manifestly as she. The ladies from the cottages wanted to be an integral part of the day, the ladies from the hidden houses desired only to be able to observe and carp afterwards. Robert provided grand material for their small minds, small worlds. Most of the women of the cottages cried a little, it was expected, and anyway they couldn't control it, wouldn't have wished to do so. None of the women from the hidden houses had recourse to a handkerchief. They sat stoically in the pews of the nave, peeping behind the tall cylindrical columns that reached to the lofty arcades.

Kathy smiled directly at her man for the entire world to see and in that smile there was defiance and strength for all the world to see. Her proud square chin became squarer, prouder, lifting him with it as her intuition brought to her the realisation of his initial lack of confidence. She leaned over to him and whispered 'I'll look after you my darling, always.' Pretending not to hear as she knew he must, but betraying himself with additional pressure from his hand to hers, he stared steadily ahead. But she could feel his body thanking hers and for this she was grateful. It would not be a one-sided marriage. He might lead, but she would be right there beside him, and he would need her. Always he would need her. Today for the first time she was in the driving seat, in charge. There would again be times when she had to take this role, this she knew and was truly happy in the knowledge. No need to discuss it with Robert, it was implicit in their relationship. Unsaid, but very real. A torrent of love, of warmth, of strength, washed delightedly over and through her body and all her fears subsided.

The satin-bedecked white Rolls Royce awaited them at the South steps to the church, but the obligatory photographs came first. Robert did not complain as she had thought he might; he stood demurely while she arranged it all then told the photographer they were ready. The photographs were taken with her radiant smile, her husband's almost sheepish grin, her father's scowl and her mother's genuine love shining throughout her beautifully plain face. After a minimum of fuss they were sinking deep into the soft black leather upholstery of the White Rolls Royce. Again she took the initiative, leaned over, held her man's face in both her loving hands and kissed him fully on the lips with an intensity of love and passion and completeness neither before had truly felt. It coursed through their emotionally charged bodies like a galloping racehorse.

'I love you, my husband.' She announced with a strength brooking no denial.

At last he could relax. Waves of relief washed over him. He was out of that intransigent church, away from her fearful father and it was just the two of them again. Would always be just the two of them. He regretted all those other women, especially that last one, but he should forget that now, Kathy said she had forgotten. But some things can never really be forgotten, never really forgiven. However, today was the first day of the rest of their lives together and he would make everything perfect for her, for both of them. Weights lifted from his body, he felt joyous and young again and noticed for the first time the radiant May sunshine and how it complemented his radiant May bride and he was totally in love and completely happy. Wanting to be one with the woman, one with the sunshine, one with the land.

'Stop the car,' he instructed the driver, 'We'll walk'

The driver did not object, he had been paid to drive the Rolls from the church to the reception at the Hydro Hotel. If they didn't want to be in it, fine with him, he'd still drive it there anyway. He stopped the car to let the young newlyweds dismount. They alighted from the vehicle with a childlike glee and gaily romped together down the hill that Kathy had ascended, it seemed to her, such a very long time before.

'What the hell are they doing now?' Asked Ian Harris of his wife as they followed in his new car, leading the procession of vehicles that was following the Rolls.

'They're walking,' replied his smiling wife. Kathy was always an original, she thought cheerfully to herself. 'We'll walk too.' She finished.

'The hell we will!' Replied her husband.

'Then I'll walk alone. Stop the car!'

Never had she ordered him, always she had acquiesced. But it was her day as much as her daughter's and she would enjoy it as much as her daughter was enjoying it. Ian was dumbfounded, unable to cope with this new wife by his side, preparing to leave the car even whilst it was in motion. It was a management problem he couldn't manage, one beyond his capabilities.

'Stop the car!' She reiterated.

He stopped the car. Mrs. Harris opened the door and on foot began to follow her daughter and Robert Castle.

'Bloody hell!' Exclaimed Ian Harris. He realised he had no choice. Parking the car by the roadside, he slammed the door shut and went to join his wife. She, knowing what must happen had walked slowly enough to enable him to catch up to her without the indignity of having to try to run with his life-time limp. To the occupants of the following cars, she had made the event seem almost together, almost natural.

Then, confusedly, all the cars stopped. Had to, for they could not overtake the walking Bride and her parents. They too were forced to walk, many didn't mind, thought it fun on that lovely May day, others were simply too bemused to question the activity. Two by two the cars disgorged their occupants and it became a joyous parade. The young married couple laughingly leading the procession, almost skipping in their joy. Completely at ease with themselves and the day, no false embarrassment lurking in their newly purified souls. They waved at everyone, at people in their gardens or at their windows, they waved behind them to the entourage following them and everyone merrily returned the waves and it was a glorious day; many becoming younger in thought and feeling just by being an integral part of the parade. The pageant grew with bystanders and gardeners joining in. It was such unaffected fun. 'Where are we going and why?' But it didn't matter; to simply be part of the parade was sufficient. A horse and its young rider joined the parade and two village dogs joined the parade and everything that enjoyed life joined the parade. Kathy's parade. And Mrs. Harris saw the look her husband gave to those around him and saw his grim face soften until it broke into one of his rare and beautiful smiles, and his step became jaunty and his missing right foot became jaunty too and he said with pride to those joining the parade;

'That's my little girl up there, that's Kathy Harris.' And he said it loud enough for all around to hear him and he put his arm through his strong wife's arm as they walked gaily together.

Robert, some one hundred yards ahead, swooped and picked up his bride, literally sweeping her off her feet, he carried her for a further one hundred yards, staggered, pretended to drop her, amidst her screams, then held her to him and kissed her long and hard. And Ian Harris didn't mind a bit. They sang and he could hear the melody of 'Love me do' drift back up the hill to where he walked with his wife, and he didn't mind a bit. The children were coming out of the school and they flooded into the heart of the procession and they added youth and even more joy and even more fun and laughter and Ian Harris could not remember when he had ever felt so young, could not even remember a childhood in which he had felt as carefree as he felt today. The little girls ran to the newly married couple and raced in circles around the young bride, a trail of fairies encapsulating her. A little boy asked Robert to carry him and so the strong young groom picked up the little boy in his long muscular arms and perched him high above the road securely upon his shoulders. The little boy squealed with delight. Kathy's mother smiled and laughed too. And now she worried far less about Robert Castle, began to see what her daughter saw in him. She squeezed her own man's arm and received a reassuring squeezing return. Ian smiled with real affection at this round woman who walked beside him and he recognised once again the true intensity of her beauty. It had never left her; it was just that sometimes he had failed to recognize it. He would try harder in future, he resolved to himself. He said nothing to her, but he made the pledge to himself and knew that somehow she would know too. And Mrs. Harris, for the first time in many years, knew she still loved the man she had married twenty-six years before. Loved him dearly and truly. Mrs. Harris's day was complete.

5

'You must be stark raving bloody mad!' Shouted Ian Harris at his new son-in-law.

Robert said nothing for a moment. 'I've decided.' He said at last.

'*You've* decided! - What about Kathy?'

'She agrees.'

'The hell she does!'

'That's right,' replied Robert, completely and frustratingly calm. 'The hell she *does*.'

Kathy, standing square beside her husband, nodded firmly.

'Then you're both mad! Don't expect me to provide for you, or to bail you out when it all fails.'

I don't expect that.'

'Good!'

Mrs. Harris watched the young couple, looked at her son-in-law standing up to her ever threatening husband and liked what she saw. She looked at little Kathy, now no longer little, married with a good and strong and seemingly caring man. She looked at them and thought they were right. They would have plenty of time to make house and children and career, let them discover the world and themselves first. But she said nothing. Indeed, there was little need to do so; together they were stronger than her well-meaning but blinkered husband.

'But you've saved enough for a good deposit on a house.' Ian Harris would not let up; 'And I'll find a job for Kathy in the business. You can teach or something.' He loomed at his son-in-law, never addressing him by name. 'The WEA are always looking for tutors, or there's Keele University or Stafford College. I'll put in a good word for you, I know most of the decision-makers there, I'll find you something.'

Kathy shuddered inwardly, wondering if her husband was finally going to lose his temper at the insensitive attitude, lack of understanding, even crass stupidity of her father's suggestions. Amazingly he remained calm in the face of the onslaught. She had believed that one day he might be able stand up to her father, to be the one to provide her with the escape and the strength she sought, but she never expected anything as profoundly competent as this performance. Neither did Ian Harris.

'I'm not ready for that, Mr. Harris, not yet. Neither is Kathy.' Calm, collected. In control.

'But Africa for God's sake! Africa! Every day the blacks are killing the whites or wanting to. The place is hot and stinking and dangerous and..black!' Ian Harris had run out of epithets to throw. He sank defeated into a large armchair. He couldn't fight forever. The argument was now into its third day. His wife came to him, sat on the arm of the chair, unobtrusively and as if by accident, slipping her arm around the top of the chair, almost but not quite touching his irate shoulders.

'Why?' He asked in resignation, sinking ever further into the well-padded armchair. Ian Harris had travelled beyond Britain, actually to France and Germany, and there but once only. He loved England with its green fields and quiet manners and decent discipline. He couldn't do with foreigners and their food and their language and their dirty toilet habits and their bad breath and their untidiness. Africa! For God's sake! Would they be safe?

Robert began to try to explain. Again.

'In the Okavango Delta in Botswana,' began Robert patiently, 'and in Chobe nature reserve in northern Rhodesia.'

'That's where the fighting is, isn't it?' Broke in his father in law.

Robert was tempted to ignore the interruption, but couldn't, so he endeavoured to explain further;

'Not really. Movements towards own rule, black rule, are taking place all over the continent of Africa. It is only as it should be. In Rhodesia the first stage is to achieve independence from Britain. Then to get Ian Smith out of power. It will all happen, but it will take time. I'll keep my wife and myself well away from the pockets of unrest. Don't worry Mr. Harris, I love your daughter and would never wish harm to come to her.'

There was nothing Ian Harris could say in reply. He felt a tiny but sure pressure on his shoulders and was glad of it.

'In the Delta and in northern Rhodesia,' continued the tall young man, warming to his theme, painting a picture into which his new family, despite themselves, were forced to enter, to become an integral part of;

'Are to be found some of the rarest and most beautiful species in the world. The bird life alone is astonishing in its variety and beauty. The splendid Fish Eagle hovering above the water then swooping to smoothly capture its prey; the Goliath Heron, one of the largest and most majestic of all birdlife, like a king of the skies. And the animals! The triumphant yet tranquil elephants continually threatened by hunters for their ivory tusks and displaced by man's uncaring use of natural resources, need a protective management programme to ensure their survival. The white rhino is now almost extinct. Gracious and strong beasts which must be cared for because man is, collectively, even stronger and smarter and better equipped than they are. We can't allow these and other animals to perish. At least I can't. I want to do something about it. Someone has to care; someone has to do something, Mr. Harris!'

The room fell silent as the young man's passion hung in the air. Ian Harris looked at his son-in-law through new eyes. He believed the boy was wrong, but there was no denying the boy was enthusiastic and strong and held by his beliefs. He was a man one might be proud to know. A man with a mission. How he wished Edward had some of these traits, even one of these traits.

'Do *you* really care, Kathy?' Demanded her father of the young woman who no longer feared him.

'I care because Robert cares, and I'm learning too!' She was defiant and strong and Ian Harris loved her.

'But your education, all wasted!'

'No education is wasted, father. Anyway, what would you want me to do with it? You'd have given me a receptionist job or an account's clerk role or a typing pool supervisor or maybe a position as second assistant to the recruitment officer or something such. You still don't recognize that I could better contribute in a management role in the hotel. Just because I'm a woman, you don't think I can do all the things that Edward can do and more much more besides. You have to wake up father and realise my potential and that of other women!'

She had never ever stood up to her father like this before. Could only do so as she clung tightly to her protector, but she meant every word, although her body trembled with emotion and concern.

Ian Harris knew that what she said was true, for he had in his mind prepared a role for her in the Personnel department, much as she described. He could not admit it, but at the same time he did not rebuke her. The very lack of a rebuke was in itself an admission for those who intimately knew the man.

'Well, that life is not for me, father. I'm going to really *live* a life. I'm going to discover what exists outside Arlaston and Glasgow, the only two places I've ever been to. Then, when we're ready, we'll return and like everyone else we'll settle down and have children, your grandchildren, but we'll have had our time of discovery together, in the world, with each other. Just ourselves!'

She was exhausted; her mother could have applauded, her father did not move a muscle. He had absolutely no rational or credible argument to offer his headstrong daughter and her headstrong husband. But something in him understood. He was a man who had never in his life sought for or been allowed any real freedom. Always working for others; in essence achieving what he had always been told to achieve, and then placed on a merry-go-round which would not stop to let him off. Something deep inside him struck a sympathetic chord with the daughter he loved, and he sat there quietly looking at the young couple. His wife could detect through her husband's tightly controlled shoulders and body what anguish was going on inside her man's mind and she squeezed his shoulders once more, reassuringly. He did not respond, but he did not want her to take her arm away, to stop the gentle squeezing.

'If,' interposed Robert, 'we decide to return.'

Kathy had never considered that. For a long moment it shook her to her core. She attempted not to show any emotion, but those death knell words of Robert's stopped any further verbal tirade. His words, as they had often done before, created a profound silence amongst the four people. Mrs. Harris felt her heart tear. Never return! She averted her head; her husband wished he could touch her arm, her hand, but he could not reach without the whole world seeing. He did not move.

'What will you live on?' He asked at length, breaking the ominous silence; Ian Harris, ever the practical man.

'I've saved enough for the fare and our first two month's costs,' replied Robert, 'I expect that within that time we shall find a way to support ourselves.'

The money that could have been a deposit on a house, thought Ian Harris, but he said nothing.

'And if you don't find something?' He asked.

'We will!'

The young man was emphatic; it would have been churlish of Harris to question or comment more, but he was unable to restrain himself from making a final cheerless comment.

'You'll be back,' he said quietly, unthreateningly. 'Within two months you'll be back.' Ian Harris declared with a certainty born of experience. His own experience.

'No.' it was simply but firmly said. 'No, we will not.'

There was no more to be discussed. Ian Harris escaped to the only peace he really knew and fully understood. As he sat behind his heavy oak desk, inlaid with polished maroon leather, covered neatly in separated piles of paper from Accounts, Reception, Back of House, F and B, Sales, Personnel, Maintenance; his thoughts dwelt further on his daughter's words. Kathy was right. He *had* already lined up a lowly job for her. Did she really believe she could become a manager, *the* manager! Did she really believe she could handle the job? Would she be as good, as competent, as Edward?

'Hell! She'd be much better!' He said aloud to his empty office. The admission attacking his long-held beliefs. The world is changing, he admitted to himself as he sat staring at the scattered piles of paperwork, but not seeing them. There were even women getting into boardrooms these days! Could Kathy, his Kathy be one of them? If he went to her now and offered her one of the Assistant Manager's jobs, would she stay, not continue in this madness to Africa? Would she remain and give them joy and grandchildren? So they could all remain as a family together. Was it too late, should he go to her now?

But Ian Harris's prejudices were too strong. It was too early for him to enter the new world which was so fast developing around him. He needed to keep his self-imposed life's shackles upon him to preserve his own security. For just a little longer. He gazed around his office, beginning to see familiarly dependable things now that his mind was clearing. He saw the awards for excellence and quality that adorned his walls and the picture of Knypersley Lake, which he loved so much and the bookcase with so many tomes to advise him of best management and business practices and so few of them actually read. He reached to the second shelf of his bookcase, taking down the large World Atlas. He found the continent of Africa on page 21 and began searching for Rhodesia and Chobe and the Okavango Delta.

They had little to pack, their possessions were few. Their most important baggage yet to be purchased. The best camera they could afford, a mini tape recorder and plenty of batteries to power them, for batteries were a very scarce commodity in Africa. They borrowed the Hotel's new Hillman Minx and drove into Stafford some fifteen miles away along the A34, there to begin their meagre shopping. Mrs. Harris had advised them that there was only one shop to visit for their major purchase, Bullock's the photographers. She and the hotel had used him for years; he was dependable and would give them a good deal. Kathy knew the shop, had met the owner before.

'Good morning, Miss Harris, I've been expecting you,' said the cheerful, balding, middle aged and middle spread proprietor as they walked through the door with the jingling chimes. Kathy did not correct the eyes twinkling, upper lip moistening owner who was peering warmly at her with eyes hugely magnified by thick National Health black-framed spectacles.

Expecting us?'

'Yes, I have a package for you.'

'For us? Who from?'

'Can't say, I'm afraid.'

'What's in the package?

'The very best camera I sell. A German Leica with 20 to 70 millimeter zoom lens. A professional's piece.'

The young couple looked at the camera. Kathy had no idea what she was looking at, in all her life she had only ever used a Brownie 127 camera, given to her on her seventeenth birthday; but Robert knew what he was holding and he felt a kind of awe. In the past he had only been able to admire such a precision piece from afar, only ever in wild dreams had he dreamt of owning one. He fondled it as one would fondle the breasts of a new woman for the very first time and he was unable to express in words that Kathy would understand, what contribution this special camera would make to his research. He allowed Mr. Bullock to lead him.

'My job is to explain all its workings to you, to ensure you can achieve the very best results this excellent camera is capable of.' As he and Robert locked themselves in greater appreciation of the equipment, and as Kathy saw the intense pleasure on her husband's face, knowing, despite his not telling her, what this present would be able to achieve, she came instantly to the realisation of what had happened. Her mother recommending the shop, her mother calling Mr. Bullock, her mother ordering his very best camera. Her mother doing all this alone. For Kathy knew her father would not have approved, would never have given his permission for such an expensive and, in his eyes, frivolous present. But what it must have cost her mother! She loved her more; she hoped one day she herself might prove as generous, as thoughtful.

'Mother!' She exclaimed aloud.

Mr. Bullock said nothing.

Kathy explained to Robert and he too loved Mrs. Harris for what she had done for them, for the start she had selflessly given them. He asked Mr. Bullock to confirm.

'The purchaser demands anonymity.' Reminded Mr. Bullock, pompously.

Their return to the hotel with their purchases was joyous, albeit a little subdued on Kathy's part as she realised yet again what it must have cost her mother to buy the camera for them. How to thank her while maintaining her wish for anonymity? They parked the Hillman in its reserved lot and walked hand in hand into the house. Mrs. Harris sat alone, sadly anticipating the moment of their departure. She would miss them so, both of them. Kathy went immediately to her, kissed her, hugged her.

'Thank you mother,' she said, 'thank you so very much.'

And Robert Castle hugged her too, saying nothing other than thank you; more words would have been superfluous and maybe, just a little bit difficult. He was choked.

'What for?' Asked Mrs. Harris, a bemused smile playing on her lips.

'Just thank you, that's all.' Replied her daughter, respecting her mother's wish. Not wanting to embarrass her further, not wanting the purchase to somehow leak back to her father.

'Go and pack,' instructed her mother who could not trust her emotions to be held in check much longer in their company. Hugs and kisses were infrequent in the Harris household and always led to much embarrassment and considerable emotion. The young couple left for their bedroom, feeling that honour had been retained but appreciation given.

Within an hour they were ready for their departure. Their adventure would begin with a brief ride down to Arlaston branch-line station at the bottom of Arlaston Hill. The two-carriage train was still driven by one of the very few remaining steam locomotives which dragged the carriages to Stafford, returning via Stone and Arlaston to Newcastle, Hanley, Burslem, Tunstall, there joining the loop line around the city of Stoke-on-Trent. The famous train called 'the Knotty'. This was to take them on the first leg of their journey to Africa. Through meadows of grassland, hills rising either side, then over the canal used more today for pleasure crafts than for conveying clay and finished products to and from the pot banks and the pits. A canal that would soon silt up and die unless remedial action was taken. There are environmental protection needs everywhere, thought Robert as they chugged through the countryside on their way to Stafford, to meet their connection to London. There are enough in England to get my teeth into, he realised. So why the hell Africa? Inside, but admitting to no one, not even to his new and lovely wife, Robert Castle was apprehensive of the future. He had only enough financial resources for the fare to Africa and one month's costs, although he had pretended two when questioned by his father-in-law. What the hell would they do if he couldn't find work within that month? What would they use to buy food or medicine if one of them fell ill? What the hell *would* he do? He had two to care for now, not just himself. And his palms sweated and he felt afraid. Why Africa? Simply because it was more alluring and romantic than England. And far away.

Kathy's palms did not sweat. She was a little sad to be leaving her mother but she was escaping. Escaping from maybe being a receptionist, from being a housewife and a mother, not yet ready for those roles. This was to be the greatest adventure of her life, with her strong and competent husband who would always protect her from everything, and who would teach her so much. She had not the slightest doubt of their future, of their happiness, not the slightest doubt in her husband.

They changed trains at Stafford station, waiting on platform one. The London bound train from Birmingham arrived twenty minutes late, but it was warm on the platform and they had love and excitement and adventure, and just a little concern, to keep them company.

As they were stepping onto the London train and into their new life together, Mr. Bullock was picking up his telephone. He dialed a number and spoke;

'Mr. Harris?'

'Yes, Ian Harris here.'

'Mr. Bullock here, sir.'

'Yes, Bullock?'

'I gave the young couple the camera, sir.'

'Good, no names?'

'No sir, not at all sir, Shall I send the invoice to you now, sir?'

'Yes, to me personally, marked private. Goodbye.'

Ian Harris replaced the receiver, shook his head, scowled, paused for a moment's reflection, glanced at the World Atlas now returned to its proper place on his bookshelf but now with two bookmarks prominently designating specific pages. He blinked his eyes, refusing to wipe them and pulled the problems of the day back to his slightly shaking hand.

6

The BEA Trident began its descent into Windhoek airport, the plane they nicknamed 'the three and a half' aircraft. Three Spey engines boosted by one RB162 just to ensure the areoplane actually took off from the ground. Robert was tired, Kathy exhausted. Her first long-haul flight. She had not wished to miss anything so remained awake. But there had been nothing to miss. The constant monotonous drone of the turbofan engines maintaining one hundred and three passengers in the air at speeds above four hundred miles per hour; never quite reaching the published potential of six hundred miles per hour, was annoyingly soporific. She had read the newspapers and her mother's *Good Housekeeping* magazine that the latter had stuffed into her bag at the last moment. What a preposterous magazine to be reading, thought Kathy, on her way to live in a tent or a mud hut! The absurdity came home to her, she giggled.

'What's so funny?' Asked a sleepy Robert, head momentarily resting on his wife's shoulder. She quoted: *'A sweeping damask rose counterpane contrasting with the opaque blue fitted brushed nylon sheets is seen to its best effect on this late Nineteenth Century four-poster bed.* - Will it fit into the tent darling?'

Robert looked down at the photograph of bedroom opulence, creased his eyes and replied, 'If you want it to, anything can be arranged, Mrs. Castle.'

They laughed together, holding hands. He would have liked to caress her breasts but an insurance agent from Hampshire occupied the window seat next to Kathy. Robert, controlled by convention! He brushed them anyway, but only with his arm. She smiled at him, wanting more. Both wanting more.

'Soon,' she said, 'soon.'

He nodded, and loved her.

Their departure from the ever mushrooming airport at Heathrow had been exactly on time. Baggage relinquished, seats secured. Camera and tape recorder safely in hand, they had mounted the steps to their plane clutching insubstantial guides to Rhodesia, Botswana and South West Africa. The guides were rather more of a potted history of the area with a few unreliable maps than they were guidebooks. Another possible project, thought Kathy, just before she called home to announce their impending departure from the island of Britain. Perhaps, in time, if they lived there long enough, she could put together a definitive guidebook on a least one of these countries. It would give her a project and an interest in her own right. Her mother, a little tearfully, wished her daughter well, 'Whatever you do, Kathy, have a happy life. Health and happiness are more important than anything else, Kathy.'

'Bye mum,' said her no longer frightened daughter. She went back to her man as together they were abducted into a confusing whirlwind of directions, of tickets, of boarding passes, gate numbers. Of squeezing into their allocated seats in the rear cabin, two out of the six abreast, aisle in the middle. Then the rumble along the tarmac, the catch of the heart as she rose above the earth for the first time in her life, vainly trying to remember the safety instructions they had been given. The immediate thrill of fear rapidly being displaced by the joy of looking out of the window and seeing the snaking Thames greyly meandering below, into view came the Tower of London, sitting proudly and forever on the solid bank of the Thames, then Windsor Castle, the eternal bulwark against invasion. All in an English cloudy grey but wondrous morning. Then the sweep round to the East, Kathy clutching Robert's arm really hard as the right wing dipped with her stomach and fell away. They were truly and at last on their way to Africa and there was no fear of the future in the young bride's thoughts. None at all. Robert lit a cigarette, it seemed that all the men around and some of the women too, were all lighting up. Perhaps it was the relief of actually being in the air after the interminable wait, perhaps it was a mounting excitement that led them to all light up at the same time. The air conditioning system was effective only in moving the smoke around the areoplane, not diluting it. Kathy's eyes smarted. She coughed, but no-one cared. Robert studiously rolled himself another cigarette for when the current one was finished. Thin cigarettes filled with Old Holborn tobacco. She hated him smoking, but then everyone else did, almost everyone.

They had been told that the range of the aircraft with full fuel tanks was 2,500 miles. Would that be enough? How far was Africa anyway? Where was Windhoek? She looked at the maps, especially that of South West Africa and read the historical notes accompanying it. A country whose first inhabitants of record were nomadic bushmen, displaced by the Hottentots herding their goats from poor grazing land to better grazing land, dependent upon the seasons and the rainfall. Then came the Europeans to claim the land, as they had throughout all of Africa. First the Portuguese mariners, then the traders and the missionaries who truly opened up the interior of South West Africa. And then, just as England was eyeing the territory with the intention of making it yet another of its colonies, it was beaten to the post by its arch rival Germany, whose ignominious last minute scramble resulted in the annexation of the country. The local people although strongly resenting the foreigner's laws and taxes and the theft of their historic water rights were not strong enough to do anything about it. In 1904 the Namba people launched an ill advised and ill fated full scale rebellion against their colonial masters, only to be almost wiped out by the superior armed and much better disciplined European fighting force. The First World War shifted the balance. Great Britain pressurised South Africa into invading South West Africa, which they successfully did, and they, in their turn, annexed that country. White South African settlers took the land, stole the land, refusing to release their grip despite mounting pressure to grant independence from both local inhabitants and the United Nations. Not only was the land important to South Africa, but also what was under the land. A fabulous richness of uranium, copper, lead and zinc, but, best of all, it was the world's foremost source of gem diamonds. The South African government was not about to relinquish such wealth. SWAPO, the South West African People's Organisation formed in 1960 was now preparing for war. But for Kathy, on that day in 1965, when the sky surrounding the plane was sea-shell blue, when with every minute she was miles closer to her new life, she worried not about the politics. She was aflame with anticipation. To see her first elephant, even to ride one! It was possible to do so, Robert had told her. To be in a country where the sun almost always shone and there was no snow or ice, unless you went out of your way to find it on the highest peaks. She had no worries about the unrest in South West Africa as she ate her mother's egg sandwiches and drank the beer provided by the airline and she was happy. Robert dozed. She thought of their future together, revisiting the plans she had made. She would make him a good wife, in a tent, in the bush, wherever. Together with the animals he so loved. And best of all there would be no first year students or second year students or third year students, or white nubile graduates. Only black women, not for him. She alone was for him. Other than her there would be no temptations. She harboured few illusions about her man, but her aim in Africa was to prove irrevocably to him that he would never need another woman, ever. She had faith in herself that she would be entirely successful. His passion for her and for his work would transcend all other needs. She would ensure it!

Their short transit in Windhoek was welcome for it gave them time to stretch their legs and begin to feel the continent that was to become their new home, at least for a while.

The twin-engined Cessna 310 lifted easily into the late afternoon African sky, heading from Windhoek to Salisbury, the capital of Rhodesia. Within an hour the honeymooners would experience the glory of their first African sunset. When the grey purple sky reached down to the land, momentarily kissed it and was suddenly gone. Everything occurring as if in an instant. When the unpolluted clarity of the dying sun made an orange acquiescence to the stark blackness of the night, a night sky in which the stars to be viewed were bigger, the planets larger and the moon brighter than anywhere else in man's world. Where the brash yet soundless nocturnal animals and their insect fodder took over nature's responsibilities from the gentler bird song of the earlier and purer day.

Africa!

Their hotel in Salisbury was an orange juice and a bed; that was all they remembered, all they required, sleep immediately capturing both of them. Within two days they had forgotten the name of the hotel, it was of no consequence; unlike the jeep hire and the tent purchase, those were vital, their life-lines. A better than expected two-seater 1955 Land Rover with plenty of room in the back for all the gear they would be carrying was available for them. Plus two spare wheels.

55

'You'll need them both,' was Steve's comment. A young, thrusting, arrogant Afrikaans. Unpleasant. Treating his black workers like slaves, worse, like dross. Striking them at will, shouting at them, kicking them like dogs when he felt they required kicking, or simply when he wanted to. The young English couple kept quiet with a tightly controlled effort, Kathy reigning in her man and his temper. Steve was the only hirer they could find, they had to work with him. So they looked the other way. They did a lot of looking the other way during their first few days in Africa.

At last gear and provisions were all loaded, rental agreed for one month and paid in advance. It was a little less than Robert had budgeted for as he had based his estimates on British prices; so, pleasantly surprised, he realised there was enough budget remaining to splash out on one or two nights' accommodation in the best hotel for his deserving new bride. He knew where that would be, where to take her. He had done his homework.

The somewhat arduous drive to Victoria Falls would take two full days, for the roads and tracks were irregular and worn, treacherous for those not taking sufficient care. They were in no hurry so Robert decided to take all the necessary care, and hopefully the opportunity, also, once outside the centres of population, to see a little of the wildlife along the tracks. They set off Southwards, through the townships of Hartley and Que Que. Then onwards, joining the half-track road through Gokwe to the burgeoning town of Livingstone, sitting on the edge of the majestic and imposing Victoria Falls. Their journey taking them through the lands of the once great Ndebele tribe, defeated time and again by the British under the leadership of Cecil Rhodes, the man who forced his name upon the raped country. An entrepreneur, a warrior, a politician, a plunderer, a pirate.

The year before Kathy and Robert travelled the roads of this violated country another political pirate was at its helm and seeking independence from Britain for the illicit white government of this black country. A government that imprisoned dissenters and the natural leaders of the oppressed people, Ian Smith made his Unilateral Declaration of Independence in the very month Kathy and Robert arrived in Rhodesia. A country whose then leadership stated that 'never in a thousand years' would Rhodesia be ruled by black Africans. As the young couple carefully drove the unknown tracks, in the hills and the black homesteads the outlawed ZANU and ZAPU parties, the then terrorists of Rhodesia, were regrouping, drawing their battle plans. A determined Robert Mugabe at their head. However, for that moment, travel by whites in that white managed black African country was still relatively safe if normal care was taken. Robert Castle knew all about the politics, knew where the pot was boiling, where to avoid. He would not be taking his woman there, would not expose her to risk. They were destined for other places, where the companions were animals and the natives unmilitant.

Kathy slept the sleep of the exhausted pure while her husband struggled with maintaining wheel adhesion to undulating rough terrain. Her body succumbing to the fatigue occasioned by the worry and joy of the wedding, the confrontations with her father, the length and the excitement of the long trip from England. The adrenaline finally having burnt out, Kathy responded to her body's craving for sleep as the vehicle bounced over the rutted road, skirting displaced boulders. Missing it all as she lay cuckooned in her sleeping bag, scrunched into the foetal position with their tent bag as mattress. Robert joined her as dusk fell, it being too dangerous to continue driving on the unlit track. Exhaustion hit home in him also. Too tired to drive another mile, he sagged down beside her, entering his opened sleeping bag. Too wearied even to bother making a drink on the primus stove. Too spent to hear the animals of the night. Too debilitated to be afraid.

His final waking thought was that it was their third night of marriage and they had not yet actually consummated it! It had not been right somehow to do it in Ian Harris's house and before didn't count.

That was all to change when they entered the opulence of the old colonial Victoria Falls Hotel. They did not delay to watch the spitting Chacma Baboons throwing shells of nuts from the slanting roof on to unsuspecting diner's heads and into the tall multi-coloured cocktails and clear consommé soup of the couples relaxing on the bamboo terrace overlooking the grandeur of a sissored lawn, reclining in studied opulence as they delighted in the evening's gloriously crimson sunset. The fall's hazy water spray in the middle distance encouraged sweeping sensuous emotions heightened by the rutting grey mongoose on the lawn who was constantly switching partners, inexhaustibly. As if he had a quota he must fulfill before nightfall. Shameless on the pristine lawn.

Kathy and Robert saw none of this for they were seriously involved in their own shamelessness; drinking as if it were wine, the bountiful love each felt for the other, basking in the afterglow of ecstatic lust. Careful each to please the other. That pleasing being a greater need to both than the snatching of their own gratification. A continual climax of body, of soul and of spirit. Their feelings for one another now subtly different for the commitment had been made, the commitment for life.

The following day they went to view *Mosi-oa-Tunya*, - the Smoke that Thunders, - the African's name for the spectacular Victoria Falls which belches up to five million cubic metres of water every minute onto the gradually eroding rock faces. A volume governed by earlier rainfall in Zambia and Angola as tributaries join the fourth longest river in Africa, the Zambezi, forming for some six hundred miles of its length, the border between Zambia and Rhodesia. A border often bridged, illegally.

As they watched this inexhaustible power, Robert thought of the explorers before them and especially of the first white man to discover the falls. David Livingstone, the Scottish missionary and adventurer who despite his own considerable erudition, ran out of adjectives to describe the wonder he saw.

Kathy and Robert stared, trying to assimilate it all, failing as countless others had failed before them. They stood drenched in the wet smoke spray that gave life to the exotic rain forest springing up around them, constantly replenishing itself. It enveloped them and although totally wet through, neither wanted to move.

The day was warm. It would have been a shallow unworthy act to move on.

'It's like a cascade of sifted icing sugar.' She said.

'Or cotton wool, continuous cotton wool. A wall of cotton wool.' He replied.

Neither had seen anything that bore comparison. In energy, in grandeur, in magnificence, in excellence.

They walked the mile-long gorge, viewing the Falls from the Rhodesian side. Then, by traversing the bridge separating Rhodesia from Zambia and relinquishing passports and five American dollars for the stamper's 'expenses', taken with a smile of welcome and childlike innocence of the theft, they viewed the falls from the Zambian side. Naked and soaking they made gentle love on a small grassy island above the fifth set of rapids, aptly named 'The Stairway to Heaven' and they enjoyed their own heaven. Life had nothing better to offer the two lovers.

That night they soaked together in the huge hot tub in room 208. They drank too much of the wonderful South African Stellenboch white wine. But what is too much when you are in love? They soaped one another. They knew the luxury could last but a few hours longer but they did not speak of the future, they lived only for that glorious moment. Sheer indulgence, beautiful. Tomorrow would be the tent and the jeep and the bush and the animals and the mosquitoes. But they still had tonight. They rose from the tub, glasses in slippery hands, laughing together. They did not even bother to dry their soap-sudded bodies.

They merged.

For hours.

7

Robert awoke with terrible griping pains in his lower stomach. The night was as black as pitch, the curtains drawn. At first he was completely disorientated, forgetting where he was, his head muzzy from the wine. Which direction was the bathroom? He tried to quietly slip from the bed so as not to awaken his exquisite wife, sleeping the sleep of the satiated. He was in the bathroom for a long time. Until the pain subsided, until the contents of his bowels were voided. He returned to the bed weakened but no longer in pain, the small crisis over.

He lay awake, sleep now denied him. He gazed at the slumbering woman beside him, so adolescent and so innocent in her slumbers. Again he fell in love with her as if it were for the first time. The night was too hot for covers, even a single sheet. She lay there naked, her chest gently and rhythmically moving, as if in slow motion love-making. Vulnerable, childlike, except no child ever possessed such fabulous breasts. Wonderfully firm, proudly round, graciously nippled. A wispy brown fringe of hair drooped over her right eye, covering it as completely as would an eye patch. Beautiful one-eyed Kathy. She gave a light moan in her sleep, squeezing her legs together, a moan of pleasure. He hoped she was thinking of him. He traced his hand from her thighs, over her blonde pubic hairs to her firm flat stomach and then upwards and across those wondrous breasts. Never quite touching her skin, just tracing. Then along her strong chin and her little too angular nose, freckled, young. Up to the uncreased forehead and the delightfully springy, unmanageable hair. Robert Castle loved this woman with an intensity of passion he had never believed himself capable of feeling.

At last the dawn starkly broke, not a gentle seductive appearance. It intruded unapologetically into the stillness of the night. The yellow fronted Barbets called their *oh oh oh's* to the waiting world, reminding everyone they were here to stay, immortal. The Nomaqua doves began their noisy morning courtship and Robert realised that humans were of little consequence in this world. Intruders.

'Good morning my darling husband,' she said from her prone position on the bed. She had been watching her naked man as he stood with his back to her, gazing at the rapid lightening of the day. Someone should draw him, paint him, she thought. Thick black hair resting on broad muscular shoulders. A triangular back merging with a neat waist leading to firm buttocks and thick muscular thighs. Not one ounce of unnecessary fat. If there had been, she thought ruefully, it would have been worked right off him over the past two days! She smiled and greeted him.

He went to her, held her, cherished her.

Their drive from the tumultuous power that was Victoria Falls to the quiet sanctity of the officially protected game reserve of Chobe in Botswana took a little less than three hours, border formalities surprisingly few, aided as ever by the gift of a few dollars. Chobe was to be their first taste of the real interior of Africa. Robert's plan was to take two or three days to explore as much of the reserve as possible, then to meet with the Game Wardens and through them to determine whether some form of employment could be offered him which might tie in with research into or protection of the big five animals he wished to study and support. It was on the poorly finished road to Kasane that Kathy saw her first elephants. She was totally entranced. Robert stopped the car to allow the herd to cross the highway. Without fear or concern the imposing beasts plodded steadily from one side of the road to the other, leaving a trail of such forestry destruction behind them that Robert immediately understood some of the claims of the anti-elephant lobby. The majestic beasts created a wasteland as they moved along their surprisingly narrow pathways, one treading directly behind the other. They tore palm trees to the ground, unearthing their roots in order to fell them so they could feed on the higher leaves and bark. They stripped bare other well-formed trees which had hitherto lived as long as they. Now, no more. They were vandals of the forest, but still, they were magnificent.

'Aren't we a little too close?' Asked a somewhat apprehensive Kathy.

'They won't charge unless we threaten them. As long as we sit here quietly, we are no threat to them.'

She believed him. Then she saw the little ones, the babies. She wanted to go to them, to hold them. Robert smiled as he could see what was in her mind, he knew the dangers.

'Now, that's just the way to get ourselves killed.' He laughed. 'Don't mess with their children!'

She smiled ruefully at him. Perhaps another time, perhaps when they had worked long enough with a particular herd to be accepted by them. They had all their lives ahead of them. She no longer worried about when or even whether they would return to the UK. Africa had taken only a couple of days to capture her.

From Kasane, a township sitting at the confluence of four countries, Botswana, Zambia, South West Africa and Rhodesia and of two rivers, the Chobe and the Zambezi, they headed for a river-front strip along the northern tier reported to have a perennial water supply, consequently attracting many animals to its banks. At Ngoma Bridge they made camp.

As he was erecting the two-man bell tent, Robert experienced the pains again. He rushed for the bushes at the water's edge. Squatted. His bowels opened and opened. He felt sick, disgusted, dirty, but above all, for those long moments, too feeble to move. In time the spasm passed. He cleaned himself with broad leaves from a Sycamore fig tree growing by the water's edge and with handfuls of water from the river.

'What on earth's the matter?' Asked a concerned Kathy as he returned visibly weakened to the campsite.

'Something, I ate, I think. It's passing now, darling, don't worry.'

And in time it passed and was forgotten.

They completed their camp preparations then took a long afternoon's walk by the river. Camera, compass and tape recorder poised. He photographed, she recorded.

'Along the riverbank,' she began, initially rather self conscious but soon substituting that emotion with one of enjoyment in the creativity of her activity. And the companionship with her man.

'The most obvious feature is the trail of damage made by the traversing (good word that, traversing) elephant herds. (Or should I have said migrating? I'll ask Robert later) Wreaking havoc as they wantonly flatten the undergrowth and uproot trees. Massive criminals of the forest.' Perhaps, she thought, she could copy her words down later and send them to her mother, to give her a little taste of her adventure. And, I suppose, to that monster of a father too! She loved them both, but she did not miss them. She had everything she wanted, everything she needed, right beside her.

'We're looking for lions or cheetahs,' she continued 'but they will be difficult to spot. We've been told to stand absolutely still if we encounter one of the big cats, if we run from them they'll believe we're just frightened ordinary game, on two legs instead of four. Everything but the elephant runs from the big cats. So we have to stand absolutely still. The chances are that unless they're terribly hungry they will, after a little investigation, go on their way.' She hoped they would never meet a terribly hungry lion.

'Elephants are different, however,' she resumed. 'If they flap their ears, paw the ground, bellow at you, then you are too close! You are infringing upon their territory.'

Robert smiled as he listened to his woman repeating their scant knowledge learned at a bar, at a coffee shop, at a wayside provisioner. What would really happen if a lion emerged from the bush, right now?

'Get out quickly,' she continued, speaking of the elephant, 'Run like mad in a zig zag pattern down wind. The hope is they'll soon give up the chase, no longer feeling their territory threatened, returning calmly to their quiet and steady destruction of the environment.'

Which way is downwind? She thought.

'Oh! A herd of buffaloes just across the river! Staring at us with such sombre looks you'd think we owed them money. And if the river was not between us I think they'd be over here to collect!

Behind them is... I think.... a small herd of Zebra, probably just a family of four or five. I can't see them too well. They look from here like striped ponies or small horses, so I think they must be Zebra.'

And so Kathy filled her tape, while her man consumed his roll of film, both delighting in each sighting. They saw giraffe and impala, wildebeests and warthogs, hundreds of baboons and one crocodile, on the far bank, basking in the warm afternoon sun. A goodly distance away, and that is where she wanted him to stay. Kathy did not like crocodiles; she feared their repulsive indiscriminate teeth.

They saw all that and more, and it was still only day one in the bush.

They returned to their campsite flushed with excitement, but they were not alone. Disappointed to find another tent erected within one hundred yards of their own, their enthusiasm for the night ahead was considerably dampened. However, those feelings soon passed as they met the young couple occupying the tent. From Holland, their third visit to Africa, rich parents, but not spoilt children. Old hands in the bush and interesting to talk to, to learn from.

'The birds of this region are quite fabulous,' said Daniel, in rather quaint old fashioned stilted English, very proper. He was a tall young man of about twenty six, sunburned, clean, strong, happy. 'You'll see the flashy Lilac-breasted Rollers and white-fronted Bee-eaters. The Bustards, the Secretary birds, the Marabou storks and of course the bloody vultures.'

Kathy smiled at his pronunciation. He had made bloody a really dirty word, it was glorious.

'In the water you will perceive the African Jacanas and snakebirds and herons. But savour the most beautiful of all, the Fish Eagle, a flash of whiteness overhead as it commences its dive of precision to the unfortunate fish in the river. Splendid! Just splendid!'

The two couples talked through the dusk and well into the night. Tired, convivial, enjoying one another's company.

'It is now the hour for sleep' announced Daniel, in the blunt but not unfriendly way in which every Dutchman makes a statement. As if it was an order.

'The fire will become extinguished within two hours,' he advised, 'after that' he ordered, 'do not venture outside your tent, for everything here roams freely. Everything. Nothing is likely to attack the tent however, unless we are unlucky enough to experience a poor elderly blind elephant,' he joked, 'but do not exit your tent once the fire has extinguished itself. Goodnight. Excellent dreams.'

'I'm too tired to move an inch, never mind exit the tent,' declared Robert as they crawled into their sleeping bags, zipped together to provide intimacy.

'Oh!' She responded with mock disgust, 'what sort of a man do I have for a husband and me, a poor young girl only married but a week!'

He pulled her to him, forgetting his tiredness, earnestly displaying to his taunting wife exactly what sort of man she had married. Exhausted, absolutely exhausted, they slept.

'Shit! The pain!' It seared through his stomach like a long sharp machete, tearing at his gut in desperate determination. He moaned. He did not cry out, not wanting to awaken Kathy, not wanting to worry her. Whatever the hell he'd eaten a day or so ago had returned once more with a vengeance. 'Christ! It must be one hell of a bug! I have to go outside, I can feel it building up, I've got to release it, I can't stay and do it in here, for God's sake!' He peeped out of the tent flap, the fire was completely out. 'But I can't stay here and do it!' Quietly and very cautiously he crept from the tent. He remembered the way towards the riverbank, to the place he had visited earlier in the day. There was no moon but the stars were bright enough to guide him and there was some reflection on the water to give him distance perspective.

Spasm after spasm grabbed him. He held tightly to his stomach as he walked the few hundred paces to the riverbank, as if fearing his stomach would drop between his legs if he did not support it. God! The pain! Soon he reached the riverbank, squatted and the pain immediately exited with the mess. 'Thank you, God!' He remained squatting for a minute or two, just to be sure. He looked around him, his eyes becoming accustomed to the dark, the tree shapes and the water and those wonderful stars and he thought how lucky he was with the night and Africa and Kathy and how ridiculous he was sitting squatting in the African night, and he chuckled quietly to himself. Then he saw the slightest of movements. An eye flickering, nothing more. Not twenty feet from where he squatted was the enormous Nile crocodile they had seen that afternoon. Then it was safely on the far bank, now it was with him. Only yards away! 'What the hell to do? Try to move quickly away, or remain still? Which one? Shout at it? But then I'd wake the others. The absurdity of his thought struck him. Don't shout and die or shout and wake them! But shouting might not be the right thing to do. He can probably move much quicker than I can. He can certainly move much quicker than I can with my friggin' pants round my friggin' ankles! I'll have to pull them up first. To hell with the leaves, I can clean myself up later. But will the action of pulling them up precipitate the monster into action? Bloody hell! What to do?' He remained most perfectly still. Then he heard a light rustle behind him. Slowly turning his head, hating not to be able to watch the crocodile, even for a split second, he saw the small Impala. Upwind of his own position, upwind of the crocodile. A lost Impala making its timorous way to the river to drink. 'Was the alert crocodile now watching it instead of me? How to tell with such unmoving eyes?' For in the starlight of the night he could see its bloody eyes, its wicked, deadly eyes. 'Was it deciding which to lunge for? Him or me? Both of us? I can't friggin' move! I daren't friggin' move! Come closer little Impala; let him want you more than me.' But he knew he would not be as fast as the Impala. Could he get his pants off rather than pull them up, would that be simpler? Still he dared not move. Dared not blink. Only the eyes of the crocodile blinked. Slowly as if winking a secret. Robert felt, rather than saw the Impala coming closer to his position. 'Please come closer still! Him or me? Him or me? Please God make it him, he's only an animal!' And as he thought it he felt mean, but he could not stop feeling it. 'The Impala is the one that should be eaten, Mr. Crocodile, not me, not me! If the Impala will come down just a little further then it will be between the crocodile and me, then I'll jump up and run, and the crocodile can go for him. But if it goes for me instead!' Fear caused what little was left to exit his frightened body, fortunately quite silently. 'Would the smell of it repulse or excite the crocodile, and what action would the Impala take when it came level and the smell reached it too? The smell of man. Let him still come on, just a few more feet now, not too much to ask, is it? Come to your death, little Impala, so that I might live!' He wanted it to die, he willed it forward. 'Him not me, him not me, come on further, now!'

Then everything happened at once. The Impala smelled him, the crocodile lunged. Robert jumped up with a jerk, smashing his head bloodily open on a stout low branch of the Sycamore fig tree. As his inner

70

blackness enveloped him, as if in slow motion, he saw the huge jaws of the crocodile immediately in front of his closing eyes, reaching with its grey serrated teeth in that heavy ugly head, claiming him, and he knew he was facing death.

8

Kathy awoke with the dawn. Her contented and gentle semi slumbering state slowly registering the fact that Robert was missing. But he always rose early, especially now in Africa, to listen and to be a part of the sounds of the morning. She knew he would be along soon with the tea he was brewing. The loving care he'd displayed since their wedding had been absolute; rather, specifically since the girl with the splintered champagne. Poor girl, it wasn't her fault. Robert constant caring for Kathy, a warm and lovely thought for the young bride, ensuring she had tea when she awoke. That's where he will be, she thought, making some tea. She melted back into their joined-up sleeping bags, awaiting his return, turned over, felt the desire for his body rise as she dozed a little more.

She awoke properly and became completely alert some twenty minutes later. Still he had not returned. Probably sidetracked. Perhaps a photo opportunity had presented itself or a beautiful animal to watch. But he would have wanted her to see it with him; he would have come back for her. Where the hell was he? She saw the camera still lying by the side of the bed. She arose, dressed hurriedly, then went to find her man.

Daniel and Isla were emerging from their tent.

'Have you seen Robert?'

'No.'

'OK, thanks, I'll go and look for him. Robert!' She shouted into the morning's eerie misty stillness. Where were all the birds?'

'Robert! Robert! Robert!' She shouted louder.

The baboons replied to her shout, squeaking at her, mocking her call.

'Robert!'

'I'll come with you.' Said Daniel. 'When did you last see him?'

'When we went to bed.'

Momentarily their frenzied lovemaking flashed across the screen of her mind. Abruptly she changed channels, it was not the time.

'When did he arise?'

'I don't know, I was asleep.'

'After dawn?'

'I don't know!' And now she was becoming a little ragged, her concern mounting.

'In the night? Not in the night!'

'I don't bloody know!' Now she felt the panic rising. She tried to hold herself together. She remembered Daniel's words of the previous evening. 'Oh God, I don't know.' She said more quietly, more distressed.

'We will find him.' Said Daniel resolutely, realising he had panicked the girl. 'We will find him.'

But they looked for over an hour, shouted until their voices became hoarse and they did not find him.

'I'll go for the wardens.' Decided Daniel. 'They'll help us. They can track him. Do not lose hope, Katherine.'

And he was gone and she was in a blind panic. She held her shoulders with opposite hands, scrunching her breasts between, literally holding herself together, and she tried not to cry, not to scream. Isla could not comfort her. She didn't want comfort; she wanted action for fuck's sake! How to control, how to think logically? What, what? She remembered some training from somewhere, it didn't matter where. She jumped into the jeep, ground into first gear and drove along the river bank into the open veldt. She quartered the ground, her own hunting area. She drove the eight points of the compass for exactly five minutes in each direction. Slowly, constantly sounding her horn, returning after each five minutes exactly to her starting point and trying again. Nothing!

'Dear God, Robert! Where are you?'

And when the points had been completed and when there was no sign of her man she collapsed onto the wheel and rocked slightly, like a baby being rocked in a cradle by loving parents. Her father! Her father would know what to do.

'Oh, Daddy, tell me what to do!'

Then Daniel came with the wardens and together they searched again. They questioned her while they searched, but she had nothing to tell them. She didn't know when he'd left the tent, or why. Where he'd gone or why. Nothing, nothing, nothing! She cursed her ability to sleep through anything, through thunderstorms, through loud music. Through her husband's departure!

Then the wardens called to her, they had found what appeared to be his tracks, down to the riverbank. They discretely pointed to his bodily waste. She nodded, realising.

'He had a stomach upset,' she said, ever so quietly, ever so eerily calm while the skin on her wrist was abstractedly being chewed by her teeth, seeing it as if it were being performed by another person on another person's arm. 'He must have come here in the night. Oh God!' She turned from the scene. From what had belonged to Robert.

The tracks had been much disturbed, not only by themselves but also by the earlier searching of the campers treading this area but not knowing what to look for. Yet despite the disturbance the wardens could discern where the crocodile had flattened the grass as it lay in wait for its prey, could see where the struggle had occurred, could see the dried blood of the man on the ground and in the grass, could see where the body had been dragged to the water's edge, into the water. All of this they could see, but they did not want to tell the young woman. Did not know what words to use to her. So they motioned to Daniel to join them. He began to walk towards the two wardens, but Kathy would not allow herself to be distanced in this way. She had to know everything, directly, herself.

'Yes, what? *What?*' She demanded, reaching the wardens at the same moment as Daniel.

'Well, miss...... '

'Mrs.! Mrs. Robert Castle!' She shrieked at them. 'I am Mrs. Robert Castle! Mrs. Castle!' Then her shrieking subsided, her adrenaline gone as she saw the look on their faces and she sank on her knees before them. 'What?' She whispered.

Daniel stooped to pick her up, he held her to him. 'What have you found?' He asked.

One warden, the older one, looked kindly at Mrs. Castle. The other turned away. He had never had to do this before.

'I'm afraid, ma'am, your husband has gone.'

'Gone... 'Her voice trailed into Daniel's shoulder.

'Has been taken, ma'am.'

'Taken?' Her voice distinguishable only to Daniel, who held her tight for her own support had gone.

'By large crocodile, ma'am. See here it took him. This is where it dragged him ma'am. And he showed her and then he stopped showing her. It was unnecessary; he had shown her too much. But she could see the tracks as if they were great furrows in the ground. She could see where her man's feet had tried to gain purchase in the wet mud, she could see his brave face as he screamed at the crocodile, and his strong shoulders and arms as he fought the crocodile and then she could see exactly where he had entered the water, see the ripples still, see his black hair lingering in a halo on the water just for a moment, then she saw it disappearing. Saw the bubbles forming at his mouth; saw where he took his last breath, his last look at the world. Her body sagged in Daniel's arms and she didn't know who was holding her, but she knew it wasn't Robert because she'd seen him in the water and now he was gone.

The older warden had experienced it before. Twice in his long career. Green campers, wouldn't listen, wouldn't abide by the rules, thought they were immortal. Dearest God!

'We'll make the report,' he said. Then they left the scene, their job done. The older warden went home, the one who told her, and he remained drunk for two days. His younger caring companion covered for his absence. He thanked God he was not married, that he still played the field, that he was not the one to make the explanations. But he awoke shaking from his dream of death and crocodiles and water and drowning. He dreamt of death and crocodiles and water and drowning for more than a week.

Kathy wanted no one, could not be comforted. Stood alone, unaided now. She did not cry anymore, she stood and looked constantly at the spot where the ripples marked where her husband had gone. For hour after hour she stood there. The young Dutch couple did not go to her, she did not want them. She needed to deal with her grief alone, not with these unknown foreigners. 'What did they know of Robert anyway? Why don't they sod off back to Holland, with their stupid English, and take this bloody fucking blistering country with them and the damn baboons shrieking and the bloody bloody bloody crocodiles and the fucking, fucking, fucking ...... something. Oh Daddy! Daddy!...'

Then she ran. Ran directly to the spot where her man had entered the water and she threw herself in and the water took her as she shouted at it, as she shouted fearlessly at the crocodile that waited for her. 'Take me, take me too, come on you scaly bastard, take me too, come on come on!' And she shouted until her mouth filled completely with water and she was glad it was filling and she tried to drink the river and it wouldn't all go in but enough went in and she went under and she was smiling and soundlessly shouting as she went under and she was going to see Robert again and then she met blackness.

Daniel and Isla finally pulled her to the riverbank, the water poured from her body, alive just, but unconscious. Daniel pumped her body, put her head on one side, opened her mouth, pulled out her tongue. Pumped her chest, pumped and pumped, breathed his own breath into her and pumped again. She vomited water, through mouth and nose and the vomit saved her. Alive. A life of sorts, an unwanted life. An existence.

They were marvelous people but Kathy did not realise it until many weeks later. They packed her and her gear into the Land Rover. Daniel lay her down in the rear in her sleeping bag, and she slept the sleep of the dead and of the damned as he drove her all the way to Maun, through the night, without a stop. Isla followed at a safe but fast distance in their own vehicle. Kathy murmured in her sleep, indistinguishable words. She never coherently spoke until she made her phone call at the airport.

'Mummy, I want to speak to Daddy, to Daddy! Where is he? Get him! I want him *now!*' She waited, but really nothing now had any time associated with it. Perhaps he would never come to the phone and it wouldn't matter. But he did and she spoke very quietly to him. As a child before sleeping speaks to its loving parents. 'Daddy, my Robert's dead. I'm coming home!' It was all she could say, for when she'd used that word, she knew what it meant. She had said it about Whisky; she had used it for Winnie, now it was Robert's word too. She could say nothing more.

Ian Harris looked at the dead black instrument in his hand thinking that his daughter had never called him Daddy since she had been eleven years of age.

Daniel bought her a ticket home, asked the crew to care for her kindly. Kathy said good-bye to them at the gate, but didn't know who they were anymore. Didn't care. Didn't care about anything in the world at all. Everything was too raw.

Africa had taken her man.

9

But not the child within her.

For weeks Kathy hardly spoke to anyone. Responding blankly to questions, her concentration immediately drifting away. Into the water. She sat alone in her room ceaselessly gazing at the photographs they had taken in Africa. In one, Robert was standing beside the Land Rover, right foot on the door sill, arm resting on the top of the door, left leg dangling in space. A broad yet impish smile consuming his entire face. She remembered him shouting, 'Off on the adventure of life!' as she had taken the photograph. How short an adventure, how short a life! Then there was the shot of them together at Victoria Falls taken by a friendly passing tourist. Then another of Robert. Shirt off, banging oak tent pegs into the ground with a large wooden mallet at their final campsite. His final resting place. These and three more which had captured him. All the others being of the scenery or the birds and animals. Those she tucked deep into the bottom drawer inside her wardrobe. She never wanted to see Africa again. She added the wedding photographs to her pitifully small reminders of her husband and although there were more than twenty wedding photographs, most were of her. Alone, with her bridesmaids, with her friends and relations, with her parents. There were only three she could find with herself and Robert. Uncomfortable in his baggy pants and silly beads, his sandals and his brocaded Indian shirt. Trying to put on an appropriate face for the camera, and failing. Oh! How she loved that man! Not had loved. Loved. *Always* would love.

Her mother despaired as she watched her daughter's face become whiter; the black bags under her eyes become bigger. Watching her rapidly aging until the twenty-three year old became thirty and now might be mistaken for forty. The doctor could do little, it was not a sickness he was trained to cure, not a sickness of the body. He prescribed sleeping pills, Kathy sometimes took them, sometimes forgot to take them. It didn't matter. Nothing mattered any more. If she left her room at all it was to exit the house by the rear patio doors and to walk slowly down to the gazebo at the bottom of the long narrow garden. There to sit alone. Alone with her photographs and her few, too few memories.

It was beyond the capabilities of Ian Harris to cope with the situation presented to him by his daughter's distress. Always in times of difficulty he had picked himself up and got on with his life, no matter whatever the difficulties were that assailed him. He expected the same in others. Indeed, he had yet to come to terms with his own emotions. Only to himself could he admit the initial relief he had felt at his daughter's news. Thankfulness at the death of Robert Castle. Not the thankfulness of seeing a comrade die in battle, that it was him and not me, no, rather the thankfulness that his daughter's life would not now be wasted with a penniless Zoologist! She was still very young; she would soon get over her grief and find another. Hell, it happened all the time in the war years. Didn't seem to take them long in those times. Then came the confusing emotion of wishing that Robert were still alive so that Kathy would not have to hurt so much, not have to suffer, not have to accept so much pain. Ian would embrace Robert willingly and invite him into his family if he would just return and take away his little girl's pain. She had not yet told them how he had died. Could not bring herself to tell them. Sometimes she cried out in the night and Ian Harris was ready for the cry. He slept little, just as in the war years, waiting for something. Waiting for his daughter to cry out and then rushing to the door of her room but she was in some pretence of sleep and so he never disturbed her and she never knew he had been to her. He wanted to hold her, to comfort her, but always stood rooted at her doorway, unable to make the step over the threshold, the step he had not taken for more than ten years. He stood and watched and listened and his heart bled for his little girl.

He had tried to hug her to him at the airport on her forlorn return but his wife had rushed to her and held her and continued to hold her and he had seen Kathy's eyes looking over his wife's shoulders at him and they were unfathomless eyes, dead eyes; eyes of darkness. The moment was missed, for both of them. Since the airport she had not come to him for the hug and he had not gone to her. But the eyes had remained the same. And in both father and daughter their old walls had gone up again and it was too late now for hugs. The bedroom door trapping her solitude within; an unfriendly, infinite and unapproachable ghost, remained firmly closed to him.

Then Kathy realized she had missed two periods. The first miss she had ascribed to her body's reaction to the anguish, to the waves of emotion battering her flimsy hull. But not the second. She could not do the same and so easily dismiss the second. She was always so regular. Robert's child was inside her! She knew it, she loved it. And some of the hurt began to slowly fade away. There was again a purpose to life, but she would tell no-one. Not yet a while. Her emotions raced with her plans and she began to live again. She had to live again, Robert was still with her!

Ian Harris had made up his mind. It was the only way he could determine how to support his daughter, and he would give her special assistance. He could not bring Robert back to her but he could give her something that might help to relieve the pain, at least for a little while each day. It would test her, try her. He was surprised how easy it was to lay his prejudices aside once he had come to his decision. He would see it through, he always did.

'Your father would like you to join us for dinner, Kathy.' Said her mother quietly as she sat beside her sallow daughter on the damask rose counterpane, the only thing Kathy had requested to be acquired for her since her return. She put her arm around her daughter's shoulders, held her. But somehow tonight something was different. Kathy seemed stronger. The photographs were in a neat pile on the dressing table, no longer clutched in her hands as they had been for weeks, part of her everyday apparel. And her daughter's hair had been washed and combed and she smelled fresh, feminine. There was a definite change. Thank God, but why?

Kathy so wanted to tell her mother. This strong round lady who would make the world's best grandma. But not yet. Not just yet, she needed to savour it a while longer for herself alone. She didn't want to share the joy just yet; she had known so little personal joy for so long, she was jealous of giving it away.

'I'd like that, Mother.' She replied calmly and there was a light in her eyes that had not been there, for ever.

Save for simple scratch meals, often untouched by Kathy, it was the first time the Harris family had sat together for dinner in more than two months. Mrs. Harris did her very best to make it special, to remember her daughter's favourites. Home made country tomato soup with real homegrown tomatoes from her garden at the side of the house, not in view from the road. Spring onions from there too and stock. Kathy ate it, ate it all. Chicken in mushroom sauce with roast potatoes and garden peas. Kathy ate it all. Apple crumble with custard and Cheddar cheese and digestive biscuits. And Kathy ate it all. She knew whom it was that she was now eating for.

Her family had not seen her eat like that in weeks, had not heard her voice in conversation for weeks. Her father watched her, a weight beginning to lift, her mother watched her, her despair began to lift, she looked at Kathy's face and the black drooping creases seemed to be lifting too. Her brother Edward watched her and he didn't know what he felt. The two children of the family had never been really close, even as infants. Her mother caught her husband's eye, smiled, nodded.

Ian Harris realised with astonishment that his wife was giving him permission, nay instruction, to speak. His wife had changed since his daughter's wedding, since that walk down the road. Almost imperceptible changes, but changes nevertheless. She had purchased her first hand-tailored dress, not bought off the peg and she had not apologized when he complained. She listened to some of the modern music in the morning when he was at work. Twice he had returned home unexpectedly and discovered the Beatles and Gerry and the Pacemakers blaring through his hitherto Beethoven sacrosanct house. And she had not apologized. Ian Harris was not at all sure he liked the changes he'd detected in his wife. But neither was he sure he disliked them.

'Kathy.' He began.

'Yes father?'

'I have a vacancy for an Assistant Manager and I would like you to fill it.'

Kathy was astounded. There were but three Assistant Managers in the hotel. Above them was the Deputy Hotel Manager and above him, her father. These positions had always been held by men, never had there been any consideration given to a woman. It was so like her father just to blurt it out! Not to lead up to it gently, not to explain the background, the rationale behind his thinking, the relationship to her qualifications and ability. No explanation of the reason for the vacancy, what had happened to the previous incumbent, the justification for this momentous decision. So like him! And she could have hugged him and she could have kissed him. But she didn't. Now she had something to live for as well as someone. She was facing a career, a major responsibility. An opportunity reflecting, even meeting her qualifications, her ambitions. She would make the best damn Assistant Manager the hotel had ever known.

'But father...!' Began Edward.

'Yes?' And Edward was too slow witted to pick up the tone in his father's voice.

'But that would put Kathy at the same level as me!'

'Yes...?'

'But it's not right! I know you want to help her and all that, but after all... '

'Yes! After all, what?'

Edward should have known by the look and by the tone. He should have had the sense to go no further. If he felt more discussion to be necessary, he should have had the intelligence to take it outside the dining room and into tomorrow's office. But Edward was not endowed with that element of sense; jealousy pervaded his soul, the jealousy of incompetence.

'Look Dad, no one will respect a woman. She can't get the job done in the same way that a man can. And it'll be even worse for Kathy. Everyone will know she's only been given the position because she's your daughter, not achieved it on merit. It won't work, it can't work!'

Quietly, very quietly, Ian Harris turned his full attention to his son. Like an iguana lizard he stared at him. Unflinchingly. Calmly, very calmly, he spoke to him. Ian Harris was at his most malevolent when he was calm, when he was quiet. Totally fearsome.

'Edward, one can only earn respect, by example, by ability. It is not something that can be given by one person to another as responsibility or authority can be given, nor is it something that can be bought or demanded. It must be earned. If anyone at all in this hotel has been given a job due to family relationships, it is you, Edward Harris! You do not have one quarter of the qualifications your sister has to perform the responsibilities she is being offered tonight. You have wasted your educational opportunities, frittered away your time at college, exited without any formal qualification whatsoever! Thank God you have some street sense, burning ambition, even ruthlessness and inherited strength. But you have little feeling for people, little in you that makes anyone respect you. You have to realise that we need our employees much more than they need us. You must respect them in order to have any chance of engendering their respect in return. I want you to watch your sister, to learn from her. From her style, her understanding, her behaviour towards others. She can help you, perhaps more than I can, to be successful. But do not try to compete with her, Edward, for you will fail!'

Ian Harris sipped his claret, sat back and watched his vapid son's blood red face as he began to bluster; attempting to collect and synthesize the pieces of the damning criticism and Ian Harris momentarily wondered if he had gone too far. But for once, for this time at least, the truth had been told. Even if hitherto he had never even admitted that truth to himself.

The twenty-two year old youth looked at his father with unqualified hatred. Stared at his sister with loathing. Did not even bother to glance at his mother, she was insignificant. He had nothing reasonable to say. He had a singular moment in which he could have grown in everyone's esteem by accepting the situation, realising he was powerless to alter it. He could have done so by laughing, by kissing his sister, shaking her hand, wishing her well. But he did none of these things.

This was his greatest opportunity to be a man, to display maturity and with it they could have become a team. A new and effective team born at that dinner table that night. The house would have been a happy one and he would have immediately gained that elusive quality, respect. Not only from his father, but from them all. The hotel would have become a zone of increasing efficiency, a learning ground for all. The Harris family's next generation would have become unbeatable, the team for the next decade, and well beyond.

But he was not that kind of man.

'Well, I won't bloody well work with her, and,' he ranted, 'I'm not staying here in the same house with her. I'll move out and take staff quarters in the hotel from tomorrow. From tonight even! She won't get any bloody help from me! And when you fall on your dirty bloody nose, sister dear, you can pick your own bloody self up, I won't!'

Before his father could reply to admonish or control him the man who was still a boy had slammed his cutlery on the table, spilled his glass of red wine which spread like a bloodied wound over the cream crocheted tablecloth, tumbled his chair and rushed from the room.

No-one said anything for a long moment. Eventually Kathy broke the silence, calmly and authoritatively.

'Thank you for your confidence in me, Father. Thank you also for your supportive words. I will not let you or the hotel down. Ever.'

He nodded at her, believing her. She paused for a moment. Maybe it wasn't the time. She'd wanted to save it. But there never was a good time, never a bad time.

'And neither will your grandchild!' She said, gazing from one to another, her smile and her heart both in her mouth. Then, feeling a little foolish, she gazed down at her empty plate. Mrs. Harris began to cry, but she was smiling as she cried. She clapped her hands together as she cried; she rushed to her daughter as she cried. Ian Harris turned his head away. Just for a moment, just to dab his lips with his napkin, just to blow his nose. Nothing more.

'But this changes everything,' He said. 'You can't work now. You must rest.'

Kathy Harris looked lovingly at her well-intentioned old-fashioned father, the bulldog look he so remembered from her tempestuous childhood. The look any boy would have been proud to own. She faced her father down.

'Hear me, Father. Hear me say this once and only once. I shall be the best bloody damn Assistant Manager this hotel has ever known in its long and distinguished history. And when I have my child, I shall take leave of absence for one month. For one month only. Then I'll arrange for it to be cared for while I'm at work and I'll be back at my desk. Do not, for one moment doubt what I say!' She stared long and hard at her father. His scowl became a flat-lipped line. The line became a grimace, the grimace a smile. He looked at this strong woman who should have been a man and he smiled.

Not for a moment did he doubt what she said.

Ian Harris's smile became a grin,

'Well, just make it a boy, then,' he said; he hesitated for a brief moment, then he continued more quietly, his voice breaking, 'just as strong as his special father, and his special mother.'

And Kathy went to him and Kathy hugged him.

BOOK 2

The Arlaston Hydro

1885 – 1979

1

It was in June 1883 that twenty-eight years old Dr. Edward Harris made his first visit to Scotland, thereafter to become an annual event until his death. It was a long journey that first time, by horse carriage and steam train, but the results and ensuing friendships were worth it. Edward had completed his studies in the conventional medicine of the time in the city of London, qualifying as a doctor at the age of twenty-five. He went on to practice in a city partnership before returning to study once more, but this time in the rapidly developing field of Hydropathy. London was, for him, a long way from his beloved Arlaston Downs in Staffordshire, where he rose at dawn to ride alone, preferring the white biting hoar frost of the winter bracing his skin to the balmy mornings of a sheltered summer. He found London a grim place, a place as far removed from his experience as could be imagined. A place full of thieves and prostitutes and disease and poverty and distrust, a bleak and unpleasant city. Dark alleyways leading to death. There was never any shortage of unclaimed corpses available for students studying anatomy and yet, London was also a place of magnificent buildings, of unqualified economic and political power, of distinguished, intelligent and sensitive men and women, a town where new ideas arose with daily frequency. Often too many, often too quickly. For seven fascinating years the young man tasted all around him, returning infrequently to his country home. He swallowed some of what he tasted and relished it, he spat out much more. Then the art of Hydropathy began to intrigue, to consume him.

In the second half of the Nineteenth century it became increasingly popular to treat many diseases by the application of copious quantities of water in various ways and at differing temperatures. Edward knew that water had been used from ancient times in the treatment of acute and chronic diseases, particularly where fevers were involved, but as he studied Hydropathy in London he learnt that it was a Silesian farmer, Vincent Priessnitz, who had developed the 'science' of Hydropathy, using water alone to cure disease. Edward's fellow students were a little dismayed to learn that Vincent's cures also recommended a rather ascetic way of life; alcohol, tea and coffee and other stimulants being forbidden while pure air and exercise was to be encouraged. Edward watched with interest the construction of Hydropathic establishments throughout the length and breadth of the UK; some extremely professional establishments, others riding the wave of that current medical fad, making quick money for unqualified staff who shamelessly and erroneously offered life-giving spring water treatment to terminally ill patients. Edward realised the potential that existed for him, especially in being able to combine his burgeoning talent for business with a deep interest and developing skill in curative medicine.

Edward was an impressively tall and heavily built man. A man requiring a large horse, anything too small would have collapsed under his weight. Yet it was a weight of muscle and latent power rather than uncontrolled and uncomfortable flesh. On first acquaintance it was the plentiful black bushy eyebrows and epic sideburns that one was drawn to. Not quite apelike, nor entirely human. Somehow apostolic. Undressed, he was a most magnificently hirsute man. And heavy. Everything about Dr. Edward Harris was heavy. And reassuring. He could be any age from twenty-five to fifty, he never altered. But he was never young either, never had been. He seemed to have been born that size, to have been created for the world to appreciate him as he was, unchanging. Edward walked with a ponderous gait, never obviously in haste but always covering more ground than his frequently lagging companions. He wore a long black woollen coat, almost touching the ground as he effortlessly swung his generous frame along the footpath. He was one of the few men in those crowded London streets that the prostitutes never bothered to halt; intrinsically aware he was not for them. His voice was a deep rumble, flowing as a river in flood, as unstoppable, as powerful, as positive. He could knock any man he wished to the ground, but he never did. And no man ever tried to rob him. His unruly thick black hair swept from his broad forehead and waved around his head as it moved with a life and an endlessly changing style of its own; always clean, always unbrushed, always disarranged. But it was the only aspect of Dr. Edward Harris that was in disarray. This man who could silence a room simply by entering it was totally organised. Time was infinitely precious to him, he had much to achieve in the one short lifetime he had been allocated. He should have been granted at least two; the world has much need of such men. When he believed in an idea, he would immediately and unstintingly give it his backing, often not working out until afterwards how to make the project successful. Invariably it would prove so, for there was no negativism in the man. He was a formidable opponent, an unflinching friend. He was also a staunch Methodist, which was to have a major bearing on his life's work.

Edward visited the Loch Head Hydropathic in Aberdeen, established and managed by the austere but kindly Dr. Alexander Munroe, one of the founders of the study and practice of Hydropathy in Scotland. Together they discussed and compared scientific evidence of the day suggesting proof of the efficacy of Hydropathic treatment. They dismissed skeptics of the water cure, railed against extremists and charlatans who suggested that the cure had quasi-magical properties. They realised, even before the recognition of psychosomatic activity, the importance of this aspect of patient recovery. But above all and fundamentally, they held firm in their belief that it was the submergence into and the consumption of copious quantities of crystal pure water that would prove successful in the treatment of patients.

From Aberdeen Edward travelled to the beautifully hilly town of Freith, some hundred miles to the South West and close to Perth on the Firth of Tay. A sleepy town brought alive by Dr. Hamish Thomas Carmichael who, after studying with Dr. Munroe in Aberdeen, had decided to create his own Hydropathic establishment in that beautifully romantic countryside. A neighbourhood studied with gothic mansions and solid castles where the sparkling purity of the water cried out to be employed to assist humanity. Dr. Carmichael was more than a medical doctor, more than an avid follower of Christ. These he combined with an enterprising business competence that would not suffer fools gladly and incompetents not at all. It was an instant fusing of common attitudes when the two men met, mutual respect coming immediately. They conversed long into the warm pre-summer nights, Dr. Carmichael offering advice and experience associated with the successes and failures he had experienced in the Freith Hydro during the fifteen years of its existence. The essential support necessary from local businessmen, ways to attract and retain key qualified staff, the importance of continual training, the necessity for discipline, the inevitable conflicts with local authorities and the farming community concerning the usage of the sometimes scarce commodity of water, the cost of water, the deals that had to be made. The older man shared unstintingly with the younger; seeing much of himself in the large reassuring Englishman, thrusting, no nonsense, capable in both medicine and management. A man willing to make mistakes, to learn from them and to move forward.

'But as well as a positive attitude, excellent water, nutritious food, discipline, your patients need Christ,' he told the younger man. 'Spiritual, as well as medical and therapeutic treatment is essential. Couple that with a quiet and peaceful atmosphere in the house and grounds, - no children, you understand; and you have the foundation for success. But you will have to work very hard, young man.'

Edward Harris sat and listened, said little, occasionally probing a point new to him.

'Firmness with sympathy, discipline in all things. No alcohol, no smoking, Godliness!'

The young doctor's English Methodist upbringing saw no conflict with these dictates and the business he was about to embark upon.

'Do not spoil your patients, cure them!' Instructed his mentor.

The two doctors drank water together, late into the night. It was the beginnings of a friendship, albeit at a distance, that was to last until Dr. Carmichael's death in 1914.

Arlaston Hydropathic Establishment opened its doors to its first customer patients on the third of September 1885 with the bull-looking, young yet mature-minded Dr. Edward Harris at its helm. It had taken him almost two years of painstaking toil to raise the capital required to build the magnificent turreted edifice comprising of one hundred bedrooms, a separate male and female bathhouse, capacious kitchens with concrete meat safes and dining and assembly rooms. He leased sixty-five acres of land from Lord Gladbrook for a twenty year period in order to construct a vegetable garden, provide grazing for pigs and cattle and for the team of horses used for the carriages which conveyed guests from Arlaston station to the Hydro and for carts bringing materials. He had twenty-five acres of woodland and downs, some areas landscaped and set with trails for the aesthetic appreciation of his guests, as well as allowing them the opportunity for tranquil recuperative walks in the countryside, picnic baskets and water jugs provided by the hotel. The cost of the building and landscaping came to twenty seven thousand five hundred pounds which Dr. Harris split into three thousand pound units, creating nine shareholders each possessing ten per cent of the stock of the hotel. He put five hundred pounds and his own abilities into his ten per cent share. The shares were all accepted and the money made available by local industrialists and landowners. But Edward Harris made them all sign a paper that the shares would revert to him if he was able to offer them cash of one hundred and fifty per cent of their initial outlay within a four year period of time. All shareholders willingly signed, none believing a virgin business could, in the increasing austerity of the times, realise such a potential. Edward then negotiated with local merchants to provide foodstuffs, kitchen and bedroom supplies on six months credit at two per cent interest. The arrangement to last for one year. Within four years, Dr. Edward Harris had repurchased the full one hundred per cent of his Hydro shares and was paying all his suppliers within one month. He had astounded all his critics and gained the everlasting respect of the county's businessmen. The first two years had been bleak, profit lower or just a little in excess of expenses, but the year 1887, the year of Queen Victoria's Jubilee Celebrations changed all that. The Arlaston Hydro, with its risk taking manager, sunk all its money into a glamorous week's entertainment. And the crowds came. They came for 'the cure', they came for the garden parties on the lawns, for the hunting and riding on the Downs, or they came just to be seen to be in the company of the county's nobility. They came to stand in the vicinity of Lord Gladbrook and the Countess of Chell. They came to see the industrial and agricultural exhibits set up in the grounds of the hotel, they came to listen to the lectures from the theorists on life and religion and art and science and literature and so much more. Edward had learnt much from his years in London. He knew about marketing and public relations, he knew how to draw a crowd. And a large proportion of that crowd stayed in the hotel, becoming members of the Hydro's fast swelling family. Some taking the water remedies, some just taking the air, but all contributing to its success. Edward never looked back from that day, his success assured. Soon the establishment was entirely full during the summer months, then also in the spring. Then in autumn too. And Edward Harris had to build more rooms, appropriating land from his landscaped garden, filling that land with the new South Wing, accommodation for a further fifty guests. And soon those rooms were taken too.

Marjorie Lockhead was among the first guests of the Arlaston Hydro and among the revellers in that heady week of June1887. She returned two or three times each year until she took up permanent residence there. Marjorie was a singularly attractive woman, one inch short of six feet tall. She was strong boned, long fingered, sallow cheeked. Her hair was so brown it appeared to be painted, her eyes as green as round balls of freshly crushed young clover leaves. Her nose angular, but neither too angular nor too long for her strong face which mischievously possessed inappropriate dimples bedecking both blanched cheeks. An unblemished forehead and an uncompromising will. Thirty years old and wealthy from a prematurely dead, ship-owning and trading father, lost at sea when she was but twenty five years of age. Marjorie Lockhead was searching for the right man with whom she would spend her life. Time was passing her by and as yet, she had found no one to match her spirit, to compliment her style, to stretch her intellect, to challenge her ambitions. Until she met Dr. Edward Harris; the only man ever to make her world stand still on first acquaintance. And in time, when she had moulded her excellent body to his, her exceptional mind and powerful will to his, they became an unbeatable team. Soon Mrs. Marjorie Harris had taken control of all the back of house staff. The cleaners, cooks, pantry maids, gardeners, livery and livestock men became her domain and she was as feared and as respected as her capable husband who now focused on the finances, front of house, marketing the Hydro and future strategic development of the business.

Meals were served with clockwork precision in Arlaston Hydro in the late Nineteenth century and guests were fined one penny if they were late for meals. Cleanliness and Godliness vied for superior recognition and prayers always followed dessert. Often guests were unable to distinguish whether they were in a healthy boarding school or a quasi-theological college. At seven in the morning the wake-up bell would be rung, at seven-fifteen a tin jug with hot water would be presented at each guest's door. A major social event of the day would then occur as the female guests in their prettiest and the men in their most elegant, dressing gowns, would parade together to their appropriate bath houses, ladies to the right, men to the left. The baths were separated by curtains so that although no one would be able to see another, conversation was possible through the curtain. At eight thirty everyone would sit down together at long tables for a hearty breakfast of oatmeal porridge with milk, no cream except on Sundays, bread, marmalade, bacon, eggs, jam, coffee or tea. At nine in the morning prayers would be said and hymns sung. The guests were then free to partake of the cure and the invigoration of the strong Staffordshire air until tea at four in the afternoon, held always in the Winter Garden, everyone enclosed in glass like goldfish, reclining on green wicker furniture. At eight p.m. precisely dinner would be served, followed by prayers. At ten thirty the front doors would be securely locked and at eleven all the lights of the house would be switched off. Mrs. Harris would do her rounds carrying a brass lamp to light her way. Hot water would be provided for those requiring it. Many, especially on their second visit, had the foresight to bring along a little additive with which to enjoy their curative nightcap. Dr. Harris turned a blind eye, it was good for business.

In time and as his business flourished, Dr. Harris found himself in high demand, not only as a businessman but also as a leader in his community. In time that community was to take him into their bosom as county Justice of the Peace, Chairman of the Staffordshire County Council and of the Staffordshire Gas Company.

He became an ardent Liberal and was solicited but not prevailed upon to stand for a seat in Parliament. His refusal related to his memories of London, his love of Arlaston and his new son and daughter. All combined to keep him at home. In time the dutiful daughter was married off into the Gladbrook family. The son James became a different issue entirely. One that would task the old man beyond his abilities, even beyond his comprehension. A problem that would see him into his grave. James Lockhead Harris went out with the first wave of hapless recruits to the horrors of the First World War trenches, there to discover a nature inclined more to the company and the love of men than of women. There to recognise the terrible grief and insecurity of life as his friends were taken one by one until he was the only quivering breathing body remaining in the mud blocked trench, unable to bring himself to move. It was there they discovered him three days later, under the rotting bodies of two fallen comrades and they sent him home to his dismayed parents. From that day James cared little for the business, drank to forget the war and found men and boys who would be with him, love him for what he was and never criticize him. His father despaired.

'But the business must continue!' She demanded of her wearily slumped husband, never before had she seen him so broken. He did not move. "Do you hear me, Edward Harris; we've worked too hard to let it die. It will continue!'

'How? He contributes nothing. He just spends.'

'Stop his allowance then!'

And he thought of his only son in the trenches and the stories he had heard and he could not stop the allowance that offered some relief to his son's tormented soul. He could do nothing.

'He's just bought a sports car for himself and his.... his....'

'Boyfriend, for goodness sake woman, his boyfriend!'

'His friend,' she admitted. It was all she could admit, 'For himself and his friend to enjoy. It's disgraceful!'

For Edward Harris it was difficult to hold his head high any more and he was thinking of resigning from the bench. How could he punish anyone when he condoned the actions of his son by his own lack of personal action?

'We will marry him to someone and get a grandchild.'

'What! You're mad, woman!'

'No! We'll find a good country lass, she just has to be with him until they produce a son. Then we shall bring up the son and he, our grandchild, will take our business forward.'

'We will not live that long.'

'I will. I damn well will, Edward Harris!'

And it was the very first time in all their years together that Edward Harris had ever heard his wife swear.

She was a mild healthy lass and a good lass and she understood her task. Thank God she had only to sleep with the drunken wretch eight times before she managed to conceive. And again thank God it was a boy. Her work successfully completed, she was gently moved on; for three further generations her family never needed to worry about their financial security. She had performed her task well and been well rewarded and now had to go away. She went in sadness but in security. Her son, Ian Harris, born in 1919, was a fine boy, a tough boy, a boy who grew up following the dictates and the love and the guidance of two strict and ever protective grandparents. A boy who rarely spent any time with his own father. A boy who did not wish to spend any time with his own father. Ian's grandfather, the founder and owner of the Arlaston Hydro died in 1928, no longer able to face the shame his natural son had brought to him, the Chairmanships he had to resign, the loss of public office he had to accept, the countless humiliations he endured. When all of that happened, the boy, Ian Harris, hated his father the more. The disgust turned to revulsion and then one day to fear. He found the two of them together. It was his twelfth birthday and he went to his father's house to receive his present as was required of him. He entered the room and there they were, naked on the floor together in front of the roaring log fire and the semi-kneeling boy with his father mounting him seemed no older than himself and his father was drunk and Ian could see what he was doing to the boy and immediately he vomited and the vomit struck his father. His naked father smashed his own son's head against the wall, then grabbed his hunting shotgun and threatened him with it and the gun went off and the young Ian Harris lost his foot that day. And James Harris lost a son. They never met again until, at the tender age of twenty-one, Ian Harris became sole heir, manager and owner of the Arlaston Hydro as he put his father into the ground. The family and some close friends knew it was untreated syphilis that had killed James Lockhead Harris, but a riding accident was blamed. It was so sad that Dr. Edward Harris could not stand beside his eighty-five year old wife and proudly welcome in the day she had so well planned for and so constantly believed in.

2

Despite the powerful will customarily displayed by Marjorie Harris, her world came to a standstill when the rock that had been her husband for forty-one years gave up life in utter despair. A flame had been suddenly and utterly extinguished in her. There was not a strong enough life-giving oil available to her anywhere to make it ignite again. Edward Harris had lost his positions of recognition, of responsibility and of trust in the community. Worse still, he had lost pride and status even in his own eyes. And he had lost his son. A son who would have been better off dead, but still lived. Edward Harris could no longer live in a world that also accepted his son. Only the responsibility she felt burning so strongly within her for her nine-year old grandson and the course she had charted for him gave Marjorie Harris the strength to continue. She watched with dismay as James bled the business, spending frivolously rather than reinvesting the dwindling profits. She attempted to fight him when he decided to cut all employees' salaries by twenty per cent at the height of the terrible economic depression of the mid thirties whilst he, uncaring, increased his personal take from the business to finance a new motor car and more horses. But she was over seventy by then and much of the fight had gone out of her. Moreover, she had to garner all the strength remaining to her to fight for Ian, a boy loathed by his father, a boy loathing his father. She had to bring all her energies to bear to ensure the boy had access to the best schools, would be well positioned and capable to enter college or university when the time came. She also and even more importantly had to re-imbue him with pride in his heritage, to make him truly believe in the family name and the importance of family honour, to fill him with tales of his grandfather and the early days of the Hydro, the legacy which, if not totally ruined by his father, would be his one day. She had to prepare him to follow his grandfather and to rebuild the business, the family honour and the family pride. It was a heavy responsibility for a young boy to accept. But every time he saw his father, usually from a protected distance, he resolutely embraced the obligation she expected from him. He both feared and loved his grandmother; but it was a gentle loving fear, a fear of disappointing her, of not being able to accomplish the requirements she was imposing upon him, and that he, in his boyhood pride, was acknowledging. Marjorie Harris had long accepted her son was irrevocably lost to her and that she could not fight him whilst expending her energies on developing her grandson. She had to choose where that energy would be spent. She made the only possible choice; any other would despoil her poor husband's memory. It was all she could do to hang on to her seat on the board of the fast diminishing company and veto her son's worst excesses. That is what she did, for ten long, heartbreaking, debilitating years. She never met with James save around the monthly boardroom table, his social world being so alien to her own, so different from what it should have been. It was as much as she could achieve to prevail upon him to restrict his peculiarities to a very private world; for public disclosure would lead not only to further family disgrace, but also to further loss of trade. James cared little for her feelings or for her reputation or even that of the Hydro, but he did not want to lose his source of income and prestige in the eyes of his friends and so was as circumspect as his nature would allow. His mother had to sit back and watch the occupancy of the hotel slump from eighty-five to thirty-five per cent. In just four years. She had to stand by the rear door of the establishment and say good-bye to long-serving dependable staff that refused to remain under her son's squalid regime, and often they wept together. They so visibly, she so wretchedly and privately, her heart tearing apart inside her tall but sagging frame. She had to remain mute as James, her sad son, lavished more care and expense upon his twelve thoroughbred stallions than ever he did on a hotel full of guests. She tried hard to come to terms with his need for male rather than female companionship, but she failed. However, she did accept one reality, the demise of the world of Hydropathic treatment. In that her fatalism was absolute and at least, it was not his responsibility. A medical experiment, some argued even a fad that drowned in the blood of the First World War and sank under the advances in medicine occasioned both by the war and the inevitable march of time. Water was still good to drink but in truth, even she had to admit, it cured little save thirst.

James Harris did not rebuild as the rest of Britain did after that awful war, did not build for a bright new tomorrow, did not care about that tomorrow, living only for the day and what that day could offer him in terms of his own personal pleasure. He and his establishment decayed together. So, when the young Ian Harris limped into the General Manager's office at the tender age of twenty-one, having laid his dissolute father in the sodden ground of a windy rain-filled Staffordshire Sunday, he inherited a business with debts in excess of three year's current income, buildings that had received little repair or renovation in the past twelve years; an overgrown, unmanaged vegetable garden and a poorly qualified, demotivated staff of sixty-six souls employed to service one hundred and fifty shabby rooms. Then, six months after he held his twenty-one year old worried head in his hands, wondering what to do, sitting in his beloved Grandfather's chair, remembering a vague gigantic sad black figure also sitting there, a chair Ian never admitted could ever have belonged to his own father; an ironic release and a positive challenge came through the mail. The letter informed him that by the end of that month, the Arlaston Hydro was to be requisitioned by the Home Office as a recuperation unit for wounded servicemen back from the fighting in the new war that was never supposed to have happened. The war that Chamberlain promised would not occur, the war that Churchill must win for the British people. But the winning had not yet begun and the soldiers and the sailors were returning with parts of their bodies left in France. The airmen came too but there were fewer of them and always somehow so much younger and more distant than the others, more fatalistic too, as if they had seen more death, dealt more death. Ian thought of his grandfather and how that singular man would have risen to the challenge and he knew what he, despite his youth, had to do to re-establish the family pride. He remembered the stories of how his grandfather had created the Hydro, secured then repaid the loans, gained local support, built quality, built pride, given jobs to a failing community, become a wealthy and respected man. This was his opportunity now and he would not let his Grandfather down, nor the woman who had been both mother and grandmother to him, the woman who had told him her task was now over and that she would soon be going to meet her man again. And he was happy for her, for her life had been joyless without him and she truly believed she would soon be seeing him once more and be in his arms and sharing his love. Ian Harris was happy for his grandmother as she prepared to leave.

And he knew what he had to do.

He gave himself to the hotel, tirelessly. In his first five years as General Manager, Ian Harris took only one day's holiday from his responsibilities and that was to get married to the remarkable woman who was to become his life-time companion. A woman who, despite the difficulties of living with this driven man would selflessly bestow all her strength and energy in support of him, every day of their steady and curious marriage.

The Second World War made a profound and abiding impression on Ian Harris. Much as he wanted to serve his country, to kill the German aggressor, the loss of his foot precluded his ability to serve. So it was with happiness that day in 1941 he received the information that his hotel was to be immediately requisitioned. He was now enabled, in his own way, to contribute by fighting in his own trenches of Arlaston and Staffordshire, fighting for food and blankets and succour for his men, and his boys, many even younger than himself. Helping them to live again. Recruiting, at his own expense, newly qualified physiotherapists, liaising with Chapman's of Hanley in the innovative construction of artificial limbs, finding them the materials, the finance. He gave all those in his care that were capable and wanted to work the opportunity to do so. He turned privates into cooks, sargeants into gardeners, warrant officers into cost clerks. With his indefatigable and youthful leadership, the men began again to find their pride and their purpose in life, the elements of their lives they had often believed irretrievably lost on the fields of France and in the seas off Europe. They discovered latent talents and abilities they were hitherto unaware of. And pride returned to them. Then, as an unlobbied bonus, came the information from Churchill's Government that all debts of the Hydro were to be frozen until the end of the war by order of the Home Office which also promised reparations for any damage and disarrangement caused by the requisition of the establishment as a recuperation unit. With regret, the letter continued, no recompense could be offered for loss of business.

But Ian Harris did not falter. As much as he gave, soon it was returned. His men wanted to contribute, as much for themselves as for him. Soon the gardens were cleared and new vegetables planted, bedrooms were painted by his one-legged, one-armed maintenance crew. Electrical repairs and plumbing repairs were made, the lack of proper materials simply stretching innovation, but never failing, themselves. In one three month period, the entire roof of the main building was re-tiled by twelve men who between them possessed nineteen legs, seventeen arms and twenty-one eyes. And the camaraderie was marvellously memorable in the mess room that had been the Hydro's dining room, now designated by Ian as an all-ranks-together meeting place, transcending status. For the first time in Arlaston Hydro's history both alcohol and smoking was permitted on its premises, even encouraged. A reward, a further companionship, a healing. Most of them, young and old, called Ian Harris 'sir' despite the fact that he told all of them, young and old, to call him Ian. Still they called him 'sir'. And when two-year-old Kathy Harris was so dreadfully ill and not expected to live, the wounded men held a service in the ballroom of the Hydro for the little girl lying helpless in the boss's house on the hill. Every single one of the wounded men attended the service, some had to be carried there on stretchers by their mates, many failed to suppress a tear that day. And then, when she lived, she was instantly granted the pleasure, the privilege, of three-hundred new uncles. There was peace and serenity in the Hydro on Arlaston Hill in Staffordshire in the early 1940's. An oasis of calm and competence in a madly disarranged world. And it was all Ian Harris's doing. His and that of his gentle, kindly, shadowing wife.

Few men remained longer than four or five months in the Arlaston Hydro during the years 1941 to 1946, when it once more reverted to civilian control, but none ever forgot their time there, or the man who had helped them live again. After 1946, Ian rebuilt his hotel with painstaking attention to detail. Many of the previous inmates returned to seek employment and some, better heeled, came as paying guests to support its recovery. Ian Harris's benevolent rule, his competent firmness, his strict attention to quality, his no-nonsense leadership, was respected by all, and with it came the re-establishment of local respect for the name of Harris. All debts were repaid by Ian Harris by 1951 and occupancy for that year reached seventy-eight per cent, the highest it had been since before the First World War. Then Ian built his own addition and he called it the Marjorie Harris Wing. Thirty bedrooms, all with ensuite bathrooms, all with pastel drapes and original water colour pictures of Arlaston Downs and views from the Hydro. So his debt was repaid. Everything was built and supplied by local labour, local materials and local toughness. The toughness of miners and steelworkers and kiln workers, returning to their village from the smoke and grime of the Potteries, returning to be offered pride in their work, in their lives. In that year of 1951, the Arlaston Hydro gave work to three hundred villagers, maintained three hundred families, more than one thousand people. In that new decade, the first after the dreadful war, most people in the Arlaston Hydro and all people in Arlaston Village called Ian Harris, 'sir'. And Ian Harris deserved it.

3

For Kathy Castle, her first day at work was terrifying. In her grey shirt, black jacket, white blouse and grey and white company neck scarf which she wore as a cravat, she was positioned in the correct colours, but it would take much more than a uniform to make her feel well-at-ease. What a drab uniform, she thought to herself, but said nothing, for it was her very first day, so she wore it in silence, with consummate distaste. The corridors she had run along as a child and been suitably strictured by her father and more kindly admonished by Mrs. Smithers, the head housekeeper, with their twists and turns and secret hiding places, no longer seemed so long, so full of enchantment. They were now an integral part of her new responsibilities. Were they clean enough, well-painted enough, were the pictures hanging straight? There was a breakfast tray outside room 119, should she pick it up to make the corridor tidy again and take it to the kitchens? Or would she be frowned upon for performing the role of a room service staff member? Her father had not told her what to do in that situation. In fact, he had told her little.

No job description. That, for him, would have been an unnecessary waste of paper and time, he had never needed one. 'You will find your way, Kathy.' He had said, 'Each of us discharges our responsibilities in different ways, but if you can always remember that everything you do must be in order to maintain our standards of service, increase our efficiency and please our guests, then you won't go far wrong.'

Remembering these words over the dinner table of the previous evening; words delivered with uncustomary warmth and accompanied by an encouraging peck on the cheek, which in his fashion passed for a kiss, she picked up the tray.

She had been given Back-of-House as her very special responsibility. There were three Assistant Managers; each had his, now his or her, own specific area of responsibility as well as the overall role as Assistant. Back-of-House included the responsibility for Housekeeping Department, Maintenance and Engineering Departments, standards of fire and safety prevention, in short, the general cleanliness of the hotel and its safety, performed by staff who were, or should be, almost invisible to the guests. But essential. Kathy had wanted Front-of-House; felt it would be easier for her in her first management position. In that role she would have been responsible for meeting the guests, for the Reception area and the bellboys and for public relations. However, her father, knowing that would be the easiest for her, knowing she could competently handle that role, decided not to give it to her. 'She wanted to become a real manager, so, she will get a real manager's job! I don't expect you to question my running of the hotel!'

And his protesting wife had reluctantly accepted. It was indeed an area she could not question and she realised that if she continued in her special pleading for her daughter, it would not be good for the girl. Kathy was tough, highly motivated, she would survive. Still that night, she prayed for help for her Kathy.

But Kathy felt on that first day that she had no-one to help her. The longest serving Assistant Manager retained Front-of-House. He was a relic of the war, a kindly man but one who knew only how to order, not how to assist, how to support. He had a false leg and walked with a stiff unhurried gait. At first, in his position, he had elicited sympathy, but his pedantic attitude soon developed antipathy amongst his staff. Why should they work so hard if he simply ordered, never tried to understand? He was one of the very few blind spots displayed by Ian Harris. Mr. Harris had taken Tony Carter onto his permanent staff just after the war. Tony had been an inmate, recovering from his awful wounds at the Arlaston Hydro, wounds both physical and emotional. His entire family save himself was wiped out by one bomb during the London blitz, as they all met together for his Grandmother's birthday. A direct hit. The entire family. Tony had never wanted to go back, never wanted to see where the house had stood. So a young Ian Harris had taken him in. There has never been a man more fiercely loyal to another as Tony Carter was to Ian Harris. But the job had outgrown him. It had been easy in the early days as they were rebuilding together, everyone took orders then, without question. It was different today; his staff questioned his orders, even disagreed with him. It was beyond his ability to control. All he could do was order and bristle and try to maintain standards and be there whenever Ian Harris needed him. A man working out his time. Increasingly lost, but for ever protected.

Kathy's brother, Edward, named after the original and dignified founder of the Hydro was inappropriately named. He held, as his Assistant Manager's responsibility, the sports and recreation facilities, gardens and grounds, the nursery, farm and livestock. She was only a few hours in her new position before Kathy began to hear disturbing stories of how Edward would initiate young new female staff as he gave them a tour of the sauna, steam bath and sporting facilities during their first days of employment in the hotel.

The Deputy Hotel Manager was working his time, two years in the hotel, three to go to complete his contract, but already looking for his own hotel to manage. A cold man, intellectually capable, financially very competent, loving and living figures. An excellent back-room man, who ensured the books balanced, ensured the company was profitable. Completely honest and, to Ian Harris who hated to look at a line of figures, absolutely indispensable. The Deputy Manager was obliged to complete his five-year contract but was already positioning himself to leave. Recognising his own capabilities, not enjoying any social role, not relishing meeting the guests, he maintained and improved the accounting practices and the beginnings of a computerization system. Searching and inevitably finding, through his extreme thoroughness, the programmes that would place the Arlaston Hydro at the leading edge in the development of information technology. To his Assistant Managers he was of little help in their everyday tasks, constantly demanding more statistics, more measurements from them. In his turn returning to them expanded information he had personally processed, concerning customer turnover, customer spend and preference, staff and departmental costs. And with all the statistics and all the analysis came his uncontestable advice of where to spend, where to cut back, how to invest. He felt that anyone could walk around a hotel giving orders; few were blest with the ability of really being able to *run* it. So, he made himself indispensable.

But for Kathy, feeling alone, lonely and practically helpless, the moment for her to meet with Mrs. Smithers had come.

Kathy had not met her for more than ten years. Her vague recollection was of a rather dumpy woman, sturdy with big red arms and big red cheeks, warm and friendly, particularly when her father was nearby. She remembered being allowed to play with the Hoover and to run it up and down the corridor, pretending to be a maid; and she remembered how she would 'borrow' small pieces of soap to take to her own bathroom and how Mrs. Smithers wagged her finger at her when she did so but was smiling while she was wagging. She remembered being allowed to take the old flowers from the previous day's displays to her own bedroom after they had been replaced. For her the flowers were still fresh and often lasted a further two or three days. She remembered all these things. She felt small and insecure again as she approached Mrs. Smithers' domain. The domain of someone to whom she now had to give orders. Mrs. Smithers was waiting for her and she was not smiling. Nor was she dumpy, nor did she appear old. She was smart, slim and competent, confident in her own abilities. She had managed the Housekeeping Department for more than twenty years. She needed no one to tell her how to improve her standards and controls, not even Mr. Harris and certainly not his twenty-five year old daughter who had never got her hands dirty by cleaning grubby bathrooms or changing fifty beds in a day. So she stood erect behind her desk, resolute, grim, waiting for the new Assistant Manager. A woman for God's sake! A woman who was now her boss. She was not about to give one inch.

'Mrs. Smithers,' began Kathy, remembering advice from the management guru of her latest-read management book as she was confronted by the intransigent figure, 'I am here to learn from you. I have had the good fortune in my life to have received a good education; I would like to follow in my father's footsteps and become, in time, probably a very long time,' she paused and tried a smile, 'a proper and competent manager of this hotel. But I know I am a long way from that at the moment. I'm willing to work hard and to learn, but I need help from experts such as yourself. Will you please give me that help?'

A long moment passed and then the old dumpy warm and red Mrs. Smithers began to reappear. She sat down behind her old familiar desk. She had seen all of them come and go. Mr. Harris was the best but he was tough, Master Harris was the worst but God would give him his reward, or the devil would. But Kathy was different, always had been different. Loving, gentle, tomboyish, fun, no double standards, a bit like her old man. No, a lot like her own man. She was a mother too now and she was here working at one of the most difficult jobs in the hotel and she didn't need to work because there was enough money in the family to look after her and her child. She could live anywhere she pleased, never work, have maids. But she chose to be here, to work, to contribute, to learn. She looked at the young girl standing in front of her desk and she remembered a small figure in ringlets running along her corridors, pushing a heavy Hoover with a determined face, bursting with the vitality, innocence and naughtiness of youth.

'Would you like a cup of tea, Kathy love? I've just got one on the boil.'

It took Kathy a little over two years to become the best manager, other than her father, in the Arlaston Hydro hotel. She soon realised it was a mistake to try to charm her staff. They were not looking for a charmer nor accustomed to one. They were looking for a person who could lead with humility, a person who would listen to their problems, give them time to explain their problems, their challenges; then do something about the systems and methods that had grown stale over the years and created many of the current difficulties. To change those that were now so antiquated and mediated against efficiency and interest. They were looking for someone who would really care for the grass-roots contribution they were willing to offer.

Kathy was soon working twice as hard and almost a half again more hours than her brother, Edward. With her avid desire to learn and to succeed, especially in a male management world, she was rapidly approaching her father's capability, exceeding it in modern management theory, devouring each new book as it appeared on the bookshelves of the ever increasing business management section of Webberley's book shop in Hanley. Her staff meetings were primarily discussion groups, rather than meetings simply designed to deliver orders. Her methods went against tradition, against the prevailing management style of the Hydro, but Ian Harris wisely turned a blind eye, accepted that progress and modernity must come to his hotel. Unprecedently, he visited one of her staff meetings. He entered the room and sat down, quietly and wordlessly, and after some initial confusion in his employees, merged soundless and forgotten into the far corner of the room. He said nothing at all at the meeting, holding his nature carefully in check when a management decision was questioned by the staff. Ian Harris listened to the suggestions of the cleaning staff and the maintenance men, watched how his daughter deftly controlled the meeting without the need to be authoritarian, noted how they recorded action points then went on cheerily and with high motivation, back to their diverse responsibilities. He watched it all. Unspeaking, he returned to his own office, looked at his traditional piles of papers, reviewed the traditional decisions he would be making that day, recognising the traditional manner in which he would undoubtedly make them, and wondered. Imperceptibly, to everyone save his astute daughter, Ian Harris's management meetings began to take on a slightly different shade, an emphasis that had never been there before, the beginnings of a listening rather than an instruction emphasis, at least for a small section of the meeting. Neither said anything to the other, but both knew. And the hotel prospered.

But Kathy Castle still experienced her own nightly hell. Alone in her bed after the joy of her life, Robert junior, Bob to everyone, had been cuddled and washed and fed and loved. For two years she had slept little, failing to accept the loss of the only man she had loved. The only man she had taken inside her with love and longing. Her emotions and her sanity tested and retested every single night. The responsibilities of the following day barely pulling her through, taking her out of her hell. Every day she worked herself almost to the point of exhaustion just to be sure to sleep that night. She would sleep from the moment her head hit the pillow and then, within an hour, two at the most, she would awaken again, and think of him. Then she would take her management books and try to wipe him from her mind as she read on and on into the early hours, and, perhaps as dawn broke, she would sleep or snooze for an hour or so before she had to be at her desk. The winter nights were the worst for dawn never broke before she had to be at her desk. Sometimes she did a night shift at the hotel, filling in for one of the other Assistant Managers, or when she wanted to see and support her few staff remaining on duty throughout the night, and that was even more difficult. For then she must try to sleep during the daytime, when it was light, when Bob was awake and she wanted to be with him, when the sun shone and peeped through the blinds, no matter how tightly closed she tried to make them, and it was the same sun as that which shone in Africa, over the unknown grave of her husband. She remembered that sun so well.

Sometimes the curly black hair of a guest in the hotel, or his stance or his broad shoulders would remind her of Robert and then sleep that day or that night would be impossible for her.

The first time she relieved herself as she lay in her bed thinking of Robert she cried for an hour afterwards. She thought it crude and disgusting and in some way disloyal. For he was dead. But the second time was better and she did not cry. It was as if she did it in veneration to him, in appreciation of him, of what he had been, of what he still was to her. Although infrequently pleasing herself now, but when she really needed to, she felt only joy that she could remember him so well and still be able to feel him and to bring him so close to her once again. Even for a short time. Afterwards on those nights, she always slept so peacefully and so well.

Kathy did her crying in private. The outside world did not suspect that the hurt remained so deep, so raw. She made herself appear emotionally tough to the world outside Robert, outside Bob and, occasionally, outside her mother too. She fought frequently with her brother and his flagrant crassness in dealing with his staff. Yet somehow he always seemed to charm the guests, to bring them back time and again, especially in families where healthy nubile teenage girls had influence over parents. Sometimes Kathy stood against her father when she felt it essential to do so, often winning more than she lost. Her reputation for fairness and for firmness after a decision had been reached was absolute. She was challenging to her staff and equally and warmly, challenged by them. Accepting generation gaps in thinking and styles, Kathy Castle was utterly her father's daughter.

4

Bill Stanway had been employed by the Hydro for thirty-four years and he had loved almost every day of his employment there. He had been on nights for the last twelve years and, with his wife gone, it was the best place for him to be. He could be with his grandchildren during the day, after he'd had a few hours sleep and in his allotment when the weather was good enough. He believed this year he would have a good crop of cabbages, maybe a champion one, the frost had not got at them. Bill's life was simple, but, in an individual way, complete. He wanted for nothing, had children who loved him and he them. He had a job he cherished and it would see him through to his retirement in four year's time, then Mr. Harris's pension scheme would kick in and he would be financially independent in his old age and another life would begin for him. Bill Stanway was a very contented man.

He rose for his security rounds a little stiffly. Indeed, the stiffness was becoming worse on the colder nights, a little more rheumatism than before was now in his legs. Still, he was not too bad, much better than many others of his age. He had no right to complain. He had to do six security walks within and around the entire building during his shift from ten at night until six in the morning when the day staff began to appear. As Bill performed his tasks he carried a small clock with him and on reaching a particular station during his tour, he would insert a special key which was fixed on the wall there and that would activate the mechanism to stamp the time on a paper disc inside the clock. That way he could prove and the management could check and record that he was faithfully completing his task.

But that night he had forgotten his clock. He knew exactly where it was; he always kept it safely on his mantelpiece at home and, without fail, he collected it as he left for work. But that night he had failed, for he had not left from home. His daughter was sick in bed with some sort of Asian flu, damn Asians; and so he had to collect his grandchildren from school, take them to their home and prepare their teas for them. He had stayed afterwards, watching a bit of tele with them; he enjoyed the puppets, and then he had looked after his grandchildren until bedtime. So he had departed directly from his daughter's house to his work that night, not returning home. He supposed it wouldn't matter too much, just this once. He could not remember ever forgetting the clock before. Anyway, the clock system had only been in operation for eighteen months. He could easily, and just this once, revert back to the manual system and record at what time he had done his round as he visited a particular location. He was not unduly worried. He would explain to young master Harris in the morning. He didn't like Edward Harris much, but that didn't matter, as long as he fulfilled his tasks. He would do his job, but that young man was another thing entirely, not at all like his father or his sister. No-one liked it when the night management shifts rotated and their turn came around to be managed for the next three months by Edward Harris. Anyway, as long as he did his job, the little snipe couldn't touch him. But, he didn't do his job, not completely, that night.

It was a calm night and Bill had already completed two of his tours. His next one was due at one thirty. He had taken a note-book with him, recorded exactly at what time he had visited each station. Ten twenty and twelve twenty-three the kitchens, nothing to report, all equipment switched off, no naked flames. Boiler house at ten forty-three and twelve fifty, all working satisfactorily, door locked. Car park at ten fifty-seven and twelve thirty. All quiet, no movement except one car departing at ten fifty-eight, registration CAD199A. And so he continued his rounds and recorded his checks in his notebook, which he slipped into his jacket pocket. It was a calm night but Bill was in pain from his rheumatic legs as he rose for the third tour of his shift.

Then the calm was shattered. An alarm bell screeched somewhere in the South Wing. Furiously he raced to the location board to find the source of the alarm. *Ground floor corridor* it showed on the board. Was it a break-in or a fire alarm? Damn, they sounded both the same. He rushed to the South Wing. He should have telephoned the Duty Manager, Edward Harris, before he rushed. Those were the instructions. But Bill didn't. His natural inclinations driving him to save the life or to catch the intruder, to solve the problem. When he reached the corridor there was nothing, except the bell, the incessant bell. People in night clothes were all around him and what was the problem and should they evacuate and had he called the police or the fire brigade? Then, all of a sudden, there were children screaming; it was coming from room 102. Bill did not hesitate, he kicked the door in, and there they were. Two nine year old twin boys. They had been trying their parents' cigarettes, had stolen one each and were coughing uncontrollably. They had dropped one, it had caught the curtains, the flame resistant material was doing its job, smoking like mad but not yet burning. The smoke detector alarm was screeching in their room and they were hiding in the bathroom. Both boys were shaking from fear of the smoke and fear of their parents who now appeared from the next room along, bemused and trying to shake off the effects of too late a night and too much good wine. They were not entirely sure what was happening. Then there were the bells of the fire engine that someone had summoned. Bill reached for the quaking youngsters who were about the same age as his own grandchildren and they were cold. He took off his jacket and wrapped it around one of them as best he could. Then the firemen entered and someone had put the hose on too soon and the jet swept the boy off his feet and the jacket was soaked and everything fell out of its pockets and was washed with the water under the bed and towards the smoldering curtains. Then, all of a sudden there was Edward Harris standing beside him and he shouted above the hubbub of the boys crying and the mother crying and the firemen shouting and the father bullying and the guests querying and the jacket lying soaked and forgotten under the curtains that would be gathered and disposed of at daylight.

'What the hell's going on?' Shouted Edward Harris. Bill Stanway had no satisfactory answer, he stood there knowing no-one had been killed, no-one really harmed and he just said.

'Nothing to worry about, sir. I'll get it all cleaned up in a jiffy.'

'Leave it, leave it, leave it!' Shouted the too young, too out-of-control, too hung-over Assistant Manager. 'Why the hell didn't you call me?'

And Bill Stanway had no answer.

'Get out of my sight! I'll sort this bloody mess out.' Growled Harris at Stanway. Then the Assistant Manager remembered his role and he put on his public face and he smiled the guests back into their rooms. He convinced them that all the excitement was over and he was there to reassuringly solve the mishap that had occurred. He would like to apologise on behalf of the hotel and he would charge them only fifty-per-cent of the normal rate for that night's accommodation because they had been so disturbed. They all loved this competent comforting young man and especially his promise of a fifty-per-cent reduction for the night. They wouldn't mind being disturbed like this every night if they could stay here free, quipped one wag. They all returned to their rooms with a story to tell for tomorrow and when they arrived home. What a great and fun place this hotel was and how able they were to look after their guests. It was all that we deserve of course, but how many other establishments would be as

130

quick to offer us a half-free night immediately? We shall certainly come back again. Edward Harris had done his job well. And Bill Stanway had not.

'I want him sacked!' Demanded Edward Harris at the following morning's postmortem Management meeting attended by his father, his sister, Tony Carter and the Deputy Manager. 'I want him sacked! He forgot his time clock, says he recorded his rounds in a notebook, where the hell is the notebook? I believe he sat on his lazy arse all night, allowing the fire to start. Then when it did, he didn't follow procedures. He didn't call me to the scene. He tried and failed to deal with it himself. He is lazy, forgetful, incompetent and old. He has to go!'

There was silence for a moment, Ian Harris waited, knowing.

'But he's been with us for more than thirty years, Edward,' she said. 'We can't just sack him like that. I do believe he did the rounds and that he recorded them. He told us how he lost the notebook. It was in his jacket pocket that was lost or destroyed in the fire.'

'Huh! Bloody convenient that.' Her brother replied, unconvinced. Wishing to remain unconvinced.

'I agree it was remiss of him not to call you,' she continued, attempting appeasement, 'but on the other hand, he got to the scene quickly, ensured no-one was hurt, broke the door down to get the boys out. He made minor mistakes, not major ones.'

'I demand he goes!' Said Edward again. 'He is in my departmental responsibility at the moment, I have no faith in him. He should be fired, and today.'

'But Edward, think about the effect on our other staff, think of how demotivated they will be if we fire some one who has been with us for so long, a man everyone likes. Think what it will do for morale.' Kathy appealed to her brother.

'It'll do a damn load of good, if you ask me. It's time some of these decrepit old stagers were weeded out. It'll set a good example for discipline. I want him out, now!' He looked to his father for support.

Ian Harris inwardly groaned. Again he was forced into the arbiter's role between his warring children. Again he would have to support one at the expense of the other. Again, as so many times before, he knew it would be his daughter he would support. She was right. They couldn't fire Bill. He deserved a disciplinary lecture, even a short suspension, but not dismissal. Punishment had to be tempered with sensitivity and correctness. Fair but firm. Think always of the business first. But Christ! Why did Edward always have to set himself up for the fall, always have to be black and white, no shades of grey? Always his own worst enemy! How many times had he ruled against him in the past two or three years? Oh, so many. Kathy's idea to reduce the livestock in the farm because it was no longer economically viable to keep all of them, especially the cows. Edward's fierce opposition to the plan, but the economic sense of it winning the day and his storming from the management meeting, again. Then her plan to replace most of the in-house tradesmen by sub-contract labour, no-one to be fired, the reduction to be by attrition; then Edward's arguments against taking such action and Kathy's sensible, totally convincing arguments for reduction in overhead costs, supported by the Deputy Manager who had also done his sums. Edward had done no homework at all. It was pure emotion he offered that meeting, that was all and, as it must be, reason prevailed over emotion. Again he had set himself up for a fall. Ian Harris realised that the time was already nigh when he could no longer, for the sake of the smooth running of the business, keep both his children working under the same roof, in the same establishment. He had his plans, but he could tell no-one of them, not yet awhile. Meantime, almost daily it seemed, he had to come between them. And, almost always, the detailed preparation or the intrinsic intuition of his daughter won the day. And Edward's bitterness reached new bounds.

Ian Harris paused, pulled hard on his Senior Service untipped cigarette and looked at no-one, but saw everyone.

'Bill Stanway will be disciplined by me. I will see him directly after this meeting.'

'And you'll fire him?' Asked Edward in triumph, caring nothing for Stanway, simply wanting to beat his sister.

'Kindly do no interrupt me, Edward!'

Edward sank a little in his chair.

'After I have spoken to him, he will be transferred to the gardens for a six-month period. His pay will not alter nor will his pensionable benefits. We will review his case after the six-month period to determine whether he remains in the position as gardener or whether we will return him to his post in security. A post in which he has served us very well for so many years.'

'But that's no damn punishment at all. He even likes bloody gardening!'

'That's enough. Edward, and kindly refrain from such language at our meetings.'

Edward paused on the brink of making another damning remark, wisely thought better of it, and, as was his wont, when unable to give verbal vent to temper, stormed from the room.

Dear God, thought his father for the umpteenth time that month; he has to go.

Kathy said nothing, looked at no-one, shuffled her papers, mentally preparing for her day's work. She thought for a moment of old Bill, knew the decision to be fair, to be correct. Disciplined, but with sensitivity. Everything in the best interests of her hotel. Everything.

5

Increasingly, Ian Harris was feeling tired as his day progressed. He still arose early, was at his desk by seven-thirty, ready for the first reports of rooms sold, problems expected in supplies, the takings of the day before, functions needing his presence that day, external meetings he had to attend. But increasingly, come around three in the afternoon, the lethargy came calling. He had to fight it away. Sometimes he was not successful and then he would wake to discover himself slumped on his desk, having fallen asleep at his post. He had never suffered from anything like this before and he could not accept that it was happening to him. Was it age, was it sickness, what the hell was it? Then one day he completely collapsed. His secretary found him crumpled on the floor of his office as she came to him with his afternoon tea. He was hospitalised for three days after they had told him it was sugar diabetes; that from henceforth he had to inject himself three times every day and he must go to the North Staffordshire Royal Infirmary for a check-up every month and he must not work so hard or he would kill himself within a few years. He told no-one what they said to him. Only his wife knew about the injections but even she did not know what the doctors had said to her husband about his work. Ian Harris realised how desperately he wanted to live and to live a very long time. How desperately he wanted to see his wonderful grandson grow and blossom and maybe even enter the business one day. How desperately he wanted to be with his daughter whom he respected and his wife whom he loved. Could he finally admit that, even to himself? Realisation of personal mortality suddenly brought him up short. Yes, she had always been a good woman, he mustn't leave her now. He had to survive and do what the doctors said, for he really, truly, absolutely, wanted to live. For ever.

He used the recuperation period to announce the purchase of a new hotel in Buxton in Derbyshire. He knew that in so doing it would divert attention from his own situation and he did not want attention. A four star establishment with two hundred rooms. An upper-class holiday resort for trampers and motorists viewing the Dales. Explorers of a countryside embracing such magnificence and charm as to make them stop, stand and drink it all in. An already successful hotel business but dependant upon returning clientele; popular with all age groups, competently staffed. He would simply put in his own manager to run it.

They all lined up for the job.

The Deputy Manager knew that it would be his, not only because of seniority but also because of his financial acumen and general competence. He knew he could make this new jewel in the crown even more profitable. He had sneaked a quick look at the provisional accounts and could already see what initial moves he would make to improve turnover and reduce costs. It was his, absolutely and justly and he waited for Ian Harris to call him.

Edward Harris knew he would be appointed as manager of the new hotel. It was his birthright. He had done his four year's apprenticeship at the Arlaston Hydro. Customers loved him, he had frequent letters attesting to that fact. They returned because of him, because of the way he made them feel, and wasn't that what the new hotel would be all about? His father had more or less said as such. It must be his. That would show the stupid bitch of a sister once and for all. And so, Edward Harris waited for his father's call.

Kathy Castle knew that the new hotel would be hers. She deserved it. She had proven time and again her competence in management. She had displayed innovation, firmness, fairness. She had worked damned hard; all the hours necessary. She had come up with some good, even some excellent, innovative marketing schemes to increase occupancy rates. She understood the finances of running hotels. Hell, she was also the most academically qualified of all of them. She knew the new hotel was earmarked for her to manage. She waited, as calmly as she could in her small but cosy office, waiting for the call from her father.

Ian Harris first called Edward to his office to explain his decision. Then he called the Deputy Manager and finally his daughter. They were difficult meetings.

He guessed correctly what his Deputy Manager would say. The man was eminently easy to read.

'If that is your decision, Mr. Harris, I hope you will allow me to tender my resignation prior to the completion of my contractual period. I feel I am ready for my own hotel and if it cannot be with you, then I must move on.'

It was a pity, the man was right, he was ready. But family considerations came first.

'I shall be very sorry to see you go, but I do understand, you may leave whenever you wish, whenever you find a suitable position.'

'Thank you, Mr. Harris.' He left the office, always controlled, always correct. Ian Harris was sad to see him go.

'But why, father, why? You know I can run the new hotel better!'

'Yes. But I need you here, with me.'

'Haven't I proved myself to you, time and time again?'

'Yes.'

'Then why?'

'I've told you. I need you with me.'

'You don't need anyone! You've never needed anyone!'

'I do now, and it's you I need. You have to remain.'

'Is it because I'm a woman you won't give it to me?'

'No. It's not because of that.'

Kathy slumped in her chair. Momentarily the fight had gone out of her. She had tried so hard, and now, when the moment had come, she was denied it. The new hotel had been given to her brother for God's sake! The least competent of them all! She might just have accepted the decision to give it to the Deputy Manager, but not her brother! She rose to leave the office. In despair. She felt tears coming, she had to fight them, she could never let her father see her cry. It was the wrong decision, it was so unfair, but she would not let him see her cry. Nor give her brother the satisfaction of knowing that she had cried. He would probably be outside the door, waiting to gloat. The little bastard.

'Sit down again, Kathy. I haven't finished.'

She sat, but she felt as if her whole world had perished.

'Edward has the new hotel because I want him away from here. Away from you. During the past two years the fighting between you has become intense, something I can no longer bear.'

'But..'

'Don't interrupt me until I'm finished, then you can have your say. Please listen.'

And Kathy sat, sadly rooted, and listened.

'The new hotel can more or less run itself. Edward can do his hail-fellow-well-met routine, at which, you must admit, he excels.'

She said nothing. Her world crumbling around her like a dried out old scone.

'I have been able to retain the Financial Controller there on a salary and bonus scheme which, if he's clever, which he is, will pay him more than Edward. He will become a Director of the new company, answerable directly and only to me. Edward has the day-to-day management, really the PR of the place, because you and I both know he has no interest in Back-of-House and no real ability with figures, other than those belonging to young girls.' He forced a smile. Kathy had never realised until that moment how much her father truly knew about his own son.

'The Financial Director will keep it on track. He will inform me in good time if there is any problem. I will be Chairman of the company, Edward will be General Manager and you my dear will also become an Executive Director of the new hotel.'

Small reward, she thought to herself; an olive branch, but she said nothing.

'In addition Kathy,' He paused, a long pause, as if he were on the brink, deciding whether to jump or not. He jumped.

'I am appointing you General Manager of the Arlaston Hydro.'

He waited. She knew she had misheard. It was a bombshell, a wonderful bombshell. It was a bloody great bombshell!

'Fuck!' She said. And her father laughed out loud. A deep belly laugh heard far beyond his office. A laugh heard by and totally confusing to his son who was waiting in the Secretary's office, waiting smoking, smiling. Waiting to see the look on his sister's face when she emerged from his father's office, when she had been given the news of his success. Why the laugh when there should have been tears? Why?

'Sorry father,' she said, modestly. They smiled at one another. She tried to look professional, tried to look managerial.

'I shall become Chairman of both hotels. The other directors of the Arlaston Hydro will remain as now with one exception, Lord Gladbrook, Reverend York and Mr. Simmonds.'

'Not Edward?'

'No, I shall explain to him that he has enough to contend with in running the new hotel.'

She paused, she had to ask the question.

'Does Edward know?'

'Not yet. He only knows he has the new hotel.'

She paused again, it was the big one.

'How much of a free hand will I have Father?'

'My dear tough Kathy, I might have known that would be your first real question.'

She looked with love at this man who daily was becoming closer to her and to her son. And it was an agreeable closeness.

'I want more time with my grandson, Kathy, and I want more time with your mother.'

Kathy's eyes widened. She had never heard her father speak with so much affection for the woman he had married.

'I'm not getting any younger; I want a change of pace.' It was the closest he would ever come to admitting anything concerning his illness to her.

'You will have the freedom that a General Manager needs to have, and trust me, I know what that is. You will be accountable to the board of Directors only. You will have the independence you need Kathy.'

She could have jumped the desk and hugged the man. But General Managers don't jump desks and they don't hug in offices. Do they?

Ian Harris looked at his daughter for a long moment, saw all the competence and forced composure in her posture, saw all the ability in her eyes, felt all the love of family. He held her gaze for long seconds then said,

'And if you don't come here this instant and give your old man the biggest hug he's ever been given in all of his life then I'll instantly change my decision!'

She did, and they were one.

6

It was a brisk October morning as the two figures breasted the small rise on the long open downs. A gently dispersing dew dampened the well-shod hooves of their chestnut stallions, best of the breed, sure-footed and strong. They reigned in their mounts, sat square and firm gazing at the scenery they both loved. Two generations apart but as close as two people can be. Loving the land, loving their horses, loving each other. Wispy cirrus clouds raced above them, heading further inland, seeking moisture from the earth as the sun rose to bless another day.

'Do you know how he died, Grandpa?' Asked the boy, innocence and searching in his eyes.

Ian Harris did not immediately reply. He looked at his twelve-year-old grandson, knowing he too would have asked the same question. The boy was calm and patient, he would wait for a reply but, like the father Ian barely remembered, he would demand an answer. He would not be satisfied by pretence. Was it time to tell him, would it ever be time to tell him?

'What did your mother tell you?'

'She told me to ask you, that you would tell me honestly; but that she couldn't. That is what she said'

Ian Harris knew that those were Kathy's exact words. The boy had no guile, none at all. Honest, straight, pure, but as tough as his mother, as tough as his father. As tough as his Grandfather? Not so tough these days, reflected Ian and better for not being so tough. He sat astride his stallion and thought of his life and despaired how little he could tell this young boy about the father he so loved, so admired, but had never known. He drew in a deep breath. Kathy had understandably delegated the task to him. Still, he realised with some wonderment, still she could not bring herself to talk about the death of her husband. What could he say to the boy? What words could he use?

'Your father was a very strong man, Bob, he was fearless,' Ian began hesitatingly. The boy's eyes lit with pride and he sat straight backed in the saddle, wanting to reflect the father he had never known. Wanting to be as strong as the father he had never known.

'He was strong and he was kind. He loved animals as much as people, just as you do. He was his own man, do you know what I mean?'

'Yes, Grandpa, he wouldn't take bullshit.'

Ian Harris tried not to laugh but he failed. He loved this boy, but Kathy had to do something about his forthright language. But today Ian did not admonish his grandson.

'He went with your mother to study the animals of Africa,' he paused 'and he died there.'

'I know that Grandpa, but how did he die?'

Ian Harris had been given a job to do, he didn't like it, but then, he had given Kathy so many things she hadn't liked in her life. Payback time.

'He was taken by a crocodile, Bob.' He said gently, not looking at the boy.

There was a long desperate silence.

'A crocodile killed my father?' Said Bob Castle, so quietly that his Grandfather barely heard him. There was an intense stillness that lasted for minutes. Both gazed at the horizon, distance and objects not registering. The boy's eyes were a mist, his Grandfather's eyes saw long hair and an Indian shirt and a small boy sitting on a young man's shoulders.

'And ate him?' Asked the boy, softly.

Ian Harris did not reply.

Minutes passed.

'I would like to ride for a while on my own Grandpa,' said the small boy at last. Quietly, so quietly. Ian Harris said nothing.

The small boy guided the large horse as it walked slowly away from the older man who no longer saw a small boy. He saw a proud man sitting astride a large stallion fighting a strong emotion. A man anyone would be proud to count as a friend.

7

In Kathy's fifth year as General Manager of the Arlaston Hydro, occupancy reached ninety per cent and remained at that astronomical figure for more than nine months. Her Leisure Break long weekends, although at cut prices to the families and therefore rather low margin, meant people came flocking to the hotel. The phenomenal success soon began to show dividends, weekend occupancy soared, overhead costs that had previously been unrecoverable, especially on Sundays, soon became a problem of the past. Kathy had followed her instincts and built a complete family package of three or four days, all managed by and under the auspices of the Hydro. On arrival the family would be met by a charming, non-threatening non-pushy bright young hostess, who would personally check them in, take them to their room and explain the workings of the hotel and the activities planned for them. If the children were very young and not to be included in the family outings away from the hotel, their personal nanny would be introduced to them and the child placed into her care. At a mutually convenient time during their second day of occupancy, the family would be offered tea, coffee or cocktails with the General Manager of the hotel, who would be interested to hear if they had any suggestions on how she might be able to improve the facilities in the hotel in order to make their stay even more agreeable. Following their initial introduction they would rest for a while, become acquainted with the hotel and its comprehensive sports and leisure centre before departing on their first excursion. Groups of ten, no more, would join their mini bus and driver, the same person who would be looking after them during all their excursions. A person steeped in local knowledge and trained well by the Hydro on how and when to invoke the guest's interest concerning the places they would be visiting, and how to gauge when they had had enough and simply wanted to be left alone to view the passing countryside. Tour one would take them to the new Wedgwood factory; there to see the hand paintresses at work, displaying skills taught by that company over countless generations. The visitors would view the manufacturing process, browse for a while in the company shop. From there they would travel to Longton to visit the Gladstone Pottery Museum, the only remaining traditional working pottery employing the same labouriously unmechanised manufacturing techniques that were prevalent in the industry one hundred years before. Thus, in one tour they would be able to see, understand and appreciate the distance travelled by mechanization of the pottery industry and yet the exquisite workmanship still remaining. Tour two would be water bound on one of the Hydro owned barges, taking guests on the Trent and Mersey canal, allowing them to experience the tranquility of a bygone era, now, for the lucky few, once more returning. A day of quietness, with only the reassuring throb of the boat's diesel engine to fracture the spell, very soon becoming an integral part of that charm, as did the welcome labour of working the lock gates as the barge moulded with the canal. Neither operations disturbing the curious and varied wildlife arriving to investigate the transient invasion of their territory. Tour three took the family to Chester, just over one hour distant, there to view the ancient and portentous wonders of Elizabethan equanimity, of narrow-laned shopping and distinguished tea houses.

Kathy's programme was designed to ensure that the family's time was so productive that they would find themselves with insufficient time to fully enjoy or even to sample all the delights the Hydro had to offer; horse riding, tennis, swimming, fishing, fencing, squash, bowls - so that they would have to return for more, and if they booked during their current stay, their next visit would include favourable discounts or room upgrades. So it was that the Hydro remained almost always full with new and returning guests, even in the winter months. For then Kathy would have the programme altered to create new excursions and fresh in-house events to guarantee the satisfaction of her patrons. The Hydro was fast becoming a large club of well-known friends, of clientele both young and old. A weekender's club, but also well worth going there for the new mid-week breaks or the specially priced holiday weeks.

She employed a bright young business graduate and made him responsible solely for wooing the business conference trade, visiting the key large companies of Staffordshire, and building a specialty conference centre inside the hotel. Wooing even beyond Staffordshire and into the heart of the Midlands of Manchester and Birmingham. His objectives included discovering what was the targeted company's business and employee benefits strategy, to familiarize himself with their products, their modus operandi; then to discover what his competitors were offering and with all this data to determine how the Hydro could do it better, do it differently. How he could offer something extra, some greater value and more attractive benefits. He went further and created a spouse's programme as an integral element of a comprehensive conference and seminar package and did it all at a cost that was no match for the quality on offer. Soon, Kathy had an important non-seasonal business clientele ensuring fifty per cent hotel occupation for every weekday of the year.

Ian Harris watched from afar, even further afar these days, and was glad he was not an hotelier in the county of Staffordshire attempting to compete with Kathy Castle, for she was unbeatable, unstoppable. Yet somehow she too had found sufficient balance in her life to ensure she spent two or three quality hours every day with Bob. Ian admired her for that. It was something, he realized, that he had never managed with his own children. And weekends too she was always on call; never able to travel far afield, but somehow always available for Bob.

And now that Thomas Hendry was in her life she seemed calmer, yet somehow stronger than before. Ian approved of Thomas Hendry; he was a good man. Perhaps not as strong-willed as Kathy but kind, gentle, understanding, generous. An intellectual man of some depth. A solid man. Bob seemed to like him too. Ian found himself wryly admitting, if only to himself, the odd pang of jealousy when he saw them talking or laughing closely together. It was high time the boy had a father; he shouldn't really be father and grandfather to him all the time. Hell, he couldn't keep up with him on the tennis court any longer. No, it was good for the boy. However, he admitted some feelings of regret, even of envy, only to himself. But everyone who knew Ian Harris well, knew it too.

Tom had been the only once since Robert. There had been a few one-nighters over the years, but that had been purely for relief. A relief that had never happened; for always Robert's strong arms had returned to hold her and his thick dark hair tugging at her fingers and his broad shoulders to hold on to and his infectious laugh to hear. His laugh! But Robert seemed to become dimmer each time she had taken another. The picture was fading. It was like losing a life. It was losing a life. And then Tom came along and he was dependable and he was kind and she could speak to him about Robert. Tom knew he could never replace Robert, accepted it and got on with life. Tom didn't mope. Tom was good with Bob and helped him with his collection of butterflies; to pin them, label them, segregate them, identify them. They would walk for hours together across the downs or into the streams and Bob would return with his trophies of the day. With the small torn mouse that incredibly somehow had escaped from the talons of an owl that weeks later, following intensive care, he had released in a hedgerow, and with a collection of new frogs and tadpoles to join the other frogs and tadpoles in the pond outside Kathy's back door. The delight was palpable when Tom bought Bob his first microscope for his thirteenth birthday, and the way they first devoured the sights of illuminated and enlarged insects under its powerful magnification was magical. Then there were the three dogs and two cats that kept her son company when she could not be with him, and the terrapins and the tortoises and the grass snake which she loathed with a passion but that slept guarding its master at the foot of his bed.

Tom was.... comfortable. He could never evoke the passions in her that she remembered, thought she remembered, with Robert, but he was comfortable. Always there when she needed a friend to talk her business worries away with, and, because he thought business a game and not worthy of intellectual exercise, he was easily able to diminish the worry in her mind; not to belittle it, rather to dispel it, to place it in proportion to other more serious affairs of life. In that, she realised, he was much like Robert had been. Would Robert have stayed with her, she wondered abstractly, had he lived to see her become a General Manager? Or would he have gone, seeking new adventures to appease his peripatetic soul? Or would she never have returned to take a job in England, content to be chasing the animals of Africa with the man she loved, having his babies, enjoying his love? She would never know and it was pointless

151

to keep asking, to keep on remembering, to attempt to relive a life now gone, now dead. Tom was good and he had asked her now for the third time to be his wife, and why not? He was good for Bob; he was good for both of them. They could be happy together. Comfortable. She hated the word comfortable; it was such a middle aged word, such a giving up on life word. She would not think 'comfortable' again. But what to replace it with?

'I think I will marry Tom,' Kathy said to her son as she visited him to kiss his sleepy forehead goodnight. It was good timing; he had returned from a hike with Tom over the fields close to the canal and they had collected a wondrous bag of insects, - now safely stowed in the insect box in the garage.

The boy who was fast becoming a man said nothing for a while. Always like this, she thought, pensive, never prone to wasting words, to unnecessary shows of emotion. She waited.

'Will Daddy mind?' He said at length.

For a moment she was too choked to speak.

'No, Bob, he wants the best for you, for me, he wants us to be as happy as we can be.'

'Will Tom make you happy, Mum?'

'I think so.'

The boy looked at her, as if searching for something. A solemn searching, nothing superficial about the look.

'I'll try not to be jealous of the new man in the house mum, the new man who will be taking you away from me.'

She looked at her son and questioned, as she did so often these days, from where his maturity had so suddenly appeared.

'No-one will ever take me away from you, Bob, no-one.'

'We'll see, Mum,' he said. 'We'll see. Goodnight.'

It was almost as if she had been dismissed. Not in an arrogant or jealous way, nor out of pique or anger. More out of resignation. She began to close his bedroom door.

'Mum,' he said quietly as she reached for the light.

'Yes, Bob?'

Again the look, long and pensive and powerful.

'Will you do one thing for me before you marry Tom?'

'Anything.'

His eyes were magnetic, unflinching, irresistible.

'Will you to take me to Africa, to show me where Daddy died.'

She could do nothing to stem the flood of emotion. She didn't know whether to rush from her son's bedroom and to throw herself onto the bed in her lonely room or to rush to her son's bed and hold him while she shook. She didn't know what to do and so she remained rooted. But Bob Castle knew. He lifted his strong tall thirteen year old body from his bed, walked over to his mother, held both her hands in his, looked directly into her misted eyes and said,

'It will put the ghosts to rest Mum. For you, for me. Then we can begin our new lives more easily, here with Tom. The three of us, an entirely new family.'

She hugged the young man who used to be her thirteen-year-old boy. Then she wondered whether he would be proven correct.

8

Ian allowed his daughter to drive him to the board meeting in Buxton. She was a good driver of her new white Austin Cambridge and he would be able to take time to gaze at the undulating countryside he so loved, consuming it, knowing he was fully alive, really living. Kathy drove her solid sensible car for the benefit of her passengers, not for her own pleasure, rather to ensure their comfort, their lack of fear. Not at all like her crazy brother, thought Ian. Why the damn fool had to buy that Jaguar sports car as his company vehicle, God alone knows. Edward had taken the step of telephoning to check that the purchase of a Jaguar would be OK; his second year's profits quite excellent and so, he argued, the car would be a fitting reward. His father had assumed it was to be a saloon car and felt, although perhaps a little excessive, he could stretch a point this time. But the point had been stretched to breaking when Edward appeared in his flashy red sports car. The ensuing row was pointless; it was too late by then, so Ian had let it go. He rarely travelled with Edward in that damn car anyway, the boy drove as if he were attempting to emulate Stirling Moss on the Brands Hatch circuit, without any modicum of the latter's skill, without any of Stirling's anticipation. He'll kill himself in that damn car one day, thought Ian Harris.

Today the journey with his daughter was delightful. She had allocated two hours for a calm drive and thirty minutes for coffee after they arrived to ensure they would be internally composed before beginning the meeting. They would need that composure today. For the past eighteen months, almost from the day that Edward had purchased that damn car, his hotel's results had been showing a disturbing negative trend. Occupancy was down, fewer regulars returning; staff turnover was now more than twice that of its sister hotel in Arlaston, and now, the final blow had come with the resignation of the Financial Director. The man Ian had really depended upon. He had written to inform Ian that he had secured a more senior position in Manchester and wished to leave by the end of the month. Ian and Kathy suspected other motives. A part of their objective that day was to discover fully the true reasons for the resignation, to redress them if possible and to try to get the man to remain with the hotel. Edward needed him, the hotel needed him. Kathy had helped her father to prepare the agenda for the meeting and the questions he would need to ask. In truth she had prepared it all. Is Edward measuring not only occupancy rates, but more telling, is he also measuring the daily average of first time guests and, what is that daily average? What should it be? Does he have realistic targets? What is the turnover of employees by department and by section? Does he conduct termination interviews to try to discover the real reasons for their resignations? Are his social and long-term benefits sufficiently competitive for his staff? How does he benchmark them? Does he have a professional performance management scheme with defined and measurable objectives? Does he conduct a regular training needs analysis of his staff, determining requirements for months, and in the more senior positions, years ahead? How much of his gross profit does he allocate to continuous training of his staff? What is the current morale level of staff, how does he measure it? Is there a successful suggestion scheme operating; a fair employee of the month scheme? Is there any emphasis on Total Quality and a recognition that standards not only have to comply with British standards but will soon have to look to European and even American as the world shrinks? How much food wastage is there per day, per meal, per course? And why? So Kathy's list went on. For every question she had prepared for her father, Kathy could have provided five more on the same theme. The salutary thing that Ian realised was that none were academic questions, not one of them. His competent thrusting daughter had detailed answers at her fingertips or in her memory for every one of those questions for her own hotel. He doubted if Edward would be able to answer more than a handful of them with anything approaching authority for his Buxton hotel. Although Ian's thoughts were flitting in and out on the meeting ahead, they became increasingly abstracted as his greatest enjoyment for the moment, the shared intimacy in that sensible car with his levelheaded daughter, transcended them. An intimacy all too rare these days. For Kathy's time, when not consumed by her business responsibilities, was all too frequently demanded by her son and Tom. Nevertheless, Ian was happy at her decision. It would be a good match. They fitted well; it was time for her to have a man permanently in her life. She was still a very beautiful woman, a competent master of her business, sitting bedside him with a skirt displaying long firm legs and far too much thigh. But Kathy was Kathy and would always be Kathy and he loved her.

'I don't think Africa is such a good idea, Kathy,' he said.

'Oh?'

'No, what's the point? It was so long ago, it will only bring sadness back to you.'

'No Dad, I'm fine now, I really am. At first I agreed because of Bob, his wanting to lay the ghosts. Did I tell you he'd used that expression?'

'Yes, astonishing.'

'But now, I want to go for myself too. I want to see Africa again so that I don't continue to hate it. I'm quiet secure with Tom, Africa can't change that. But Bob is right, I have a ghost to lay too. We must go.'

Ian Harris said no more. He rarely challenged Kathy these days; she always had an answer, and a good one. She was a formidable presence, a will even stronger now than his own. Roles reversed, and he didn't mind a bit.

'Thanks for saying you'll look after everything for the ten days we're away.'

'Not at all, in fact I'm quite looking forward to being General Manager again. You won't recognize the place when you return.....' He grinned.

'Dad! Don't you dare... '

And they both knew he wouldn't.

Their route was almost due north; through Stoke-on-Trent and Hanley, then out of the increasing affluence of a brightening city, in which the City Fathers had at last began their long overdue campaign to clean up and modernise; transforming the old pot banks and coal slag heaps into grassed over hillsides and pleasant walkways. A project that would take many years but would transform that once grimy city into one of greens and parks and lakes and country walks second to none in the industrial north. Ian was happy to see that transformation beginning, his grandson having brought him closer to nature and opened his eyes to the extensive pleasures of the land. At Sneyd Green they turned onto the Leek road in preparation for the delight of the most scenic part of their journey. Once through the market town of Leek they rose above the surrounding wooded landscape, travelling in a straight line over the bleak and threatening yet fulfilling Buxton Moors, often impassable when the snows of winter claimed them; demanding solitude for the land. But it was too early for snow and father and daughter travelled in peace, observing with satisfaction the barren scenery stretching endlessly before and around them. Kathy felt herself in a novel by Bronte, but not the heroine. She was Heathcliffe.

'What are we going to do about Edward?' He asked her, ever increasingly seeking her opinion.

She knew what she would do, but she could not tell her father, the wastrel was still his son. A son in whom she realised that Ian saw traits of his own misbegotten father. Thankfully, she believed, though not with boys, but similar in so many other ways. Unable to disclose exactly what she knew to her father, a little had permeated through to him and for his sake, she could not hurt him more by telling him more.

'I think we should consider letting my Deputy Manager go to Buxton.' Suggested Kathy.

'What! He's a very good man; you've made him a very good man. He'll never work for Edward.'

'I don't want him to work for Edward, I want him to take over as General Manager.'

He looked at her legs, not her face. He saw neither.

'And Edward?' He asked with an indescribably low stomach-sinking ache. He didn't want to lose the boy, no matter what he felt about him. He had lost a father; he didn't want to lose a son.

'Don't worry Dad,' she said. 'I'm not suggesting that we fire Edward; he and you and maybe me too would all fall to pieces. No, we promote him.'

'What!' And this time he looked directly at the profile of his beautiful daughter who could have returned a hasty glance as she drove, but didn't.

'We can give him the job of Marketing Director of both hotels and make them into one company. We give him a seat on the board of the new company; his brief will be to promote our hotels as a joint facility, creating common strategies for the group. His focus will be to market the company on the continent and in America, bringing in a new breed of tourists and businessmen.'

Ian Harris looked at his daughter. No traces remaining of the little girl in pigtails. A hard competent businesswoman. He realised that she had thought it all through while he had been wallowing in doubt, inaction and despair. Edward would love the role; jetting off to the States, to Boston and California and Paris and Rome. And hell, he might even be good at the job! Loving an audience, he was, at least, a capable and enthusiastic speaker. He could indeed attract a new breed of tourists. What a bloody marvelous idea! And so what if he cost the company a heavy pocketful of money? He would cost a damn sight more if he remained where he was and ground the Buxton Hydro further into the dust.

'What a bloody marvelous idea, Kathy!' He said. Then she did look at him and they smiled. A warming reassuring smile, a smile with the tiniest hint of collaboration. Unadmitted, yet evident.

The final half-hour of the journey put the meat on the bones of the idea. They worked well together, father and daughter. She leading, him following. Roles reversed.

9

There had been a frenzy of activity in Bob Castle's bedroom for more than a week. He was collecting. Admittedly a somewhat small and poignant collection, but the most important of his young life. In fact, two distinct collections. The first contained anything remaining of links to his father, the photographs his mother had given him, all she possessed of their African trip save the one of his father standing beside the battered old Land Rover that she had kept for herself. His father's knife, bone handled and long. Bob sharpened it frequently in memory but had never used it, not even to cut a piece of string. The greatest prize of all had been given to him two nights ago and it slept with him beside his pillow. His father's wonderful camera, thirteen years old now, the same age as himself. Tom had painstakingly showed him how to change a film and how to allow for the light and how to ensure the steadiness of the camera when he held it. He explained the different speeds of films and when to use them, how to create different exposures. It was all so exciting, but nothing more so than knowing his own father had held that camera, had pressed his fingers where Bob now pressed his own. He would kill any one who tried to take that camera from him! He would kill them dead, with his father's knife.

The second collection was important too. He wanted to take his best work to Africa to show to his father. Of course he couldn't see it, of course he was dead, but he just wanted the very best work he had ever done to be with him when he went on his pilgrimage, when he went to say goodbye. He chose his prize specimen from his extensive butterfly collection, pinned and mounted exquisitely and entirely by himself. He took his glass slide of a cross section of a queen bee and he took the preserved heart and lungs of the tiny mouse that had survived the owl only to be killed by the family cat. He had done the postmortem himself, surgically removing the heart and lungs intact. It had taken him one and a half very careful hours to perform the delicate surgery and he was proud of his feat, proud that he had not damaged the tiny organs. He took his Boy Scout uniform which displayed his woodcraft badges and his World Wildlife badge, the first in his troop, and his first-aid badge. He took the certificate that proved he had been made a patrol leader, in charge of his little group of little men. He took his swimming certificates that proved he could life-save to a depth of ten feet and could swim twenty lengths without stopping. He took all this and more. Just for it to be with him when he said his final goodbye. Just so that his father might know that he was a son to be proud of. And Bob would make his father even prouder of him. He hadn't told his mother yet, or his grandfather, or Tom, but he had made his decision in life. He would complete his father's work. He had read all of his father's notes and he had read his father's copy of his thesis concerning the creatures in the Galapagos Islands. He had not understood it all, but the photographs of the animals and the birds were magical. Compulsive. His father's short, so short notebook of Africa was devoured too by Bob's young searching mind. It was his legacy. He knew the word, had looked it up as he was trying to grapple with Conrad and Robert Louis Stevenson and Jonathan Swift and Defoe. His father was all of these heroes and none of them for he stood alone, far above the rest in his son's eyes, greater than them all. Bob vowed to follow him, to complete his work. But, as yet, he had told no one.

Then all of a sudden the day came and Tom drove them to Heathrow airport. A very different beginning to Kathy's journey than the one she had made more than a decade previously. Bob tried to be quiet and sombre as befitted the mood he supposed should surround the pilgrimage, but he failed.

'How long will the areoplane journey take? What will we do when we arrive? How far do we have to drive to get to Botswana?'

She had answered all the questions before, but without rancour she answered them all again. She remembered when she had remained awake the entire journey, thirteen short years ago, in the event she might miss something. Now she just wanted to get into that seat and sleep all the way to Africa. But she still remembered her first flight and the terrific excitement and every detail of the journey. So she answered her son's questions each time he asked them with the patience born of love and of understanding. She remembered Robert's desire to touch her privately while they sat on the plane and the insurance agent from down south somewhere watching them. Flashes, as if projected on a shaky aged black and white movie film, of their love-making in the Victoria Falls Hotel returned to her as they drove down the M6 motorway to join the M1, south to London. She was silent, remembering, wondering how many of these flashes she would have to endure on this journey. And it was a necessary kind of enduring, a sweet suffering.

'You all right Kathy?' Asked Tom, 'You're very quiet.'

'Yes, fine thanks Tom.' She touched his hand fleetingly as it lay on the steering wheel, to reassure him. 'I guess it's just a reaction to the rather hectic pace over the past couple of weeks, ensuring the hotel is running well so that Dad doesn't have too many problems while I'm away, especially as my deputy has gone to Buxton now.'

'Will it work with Edward do you think?'

'I hope so, I think so,' she replied. 'He's certainly keen.'

'To travel, to see the world.'

'But he also has a set of objectives to achieve. A number of presentations per week, meetings with travel and tour companies in order to create partnerships and links. Dad has not been soft on him.'

'You mean you've not been soft on him.'

She said nothing. It was indeed her who had drawn up Edward's objectives and given them to her father.

It was indeed her who had linked Edward's generous bonus scheme to the achievement of these objectives. Her father had happily taken them, presented them to Edward who had no alternative but to accept them. His first journey had already been arranged. Three nights in New York, two in Boston, four in San Francisco, two in Florida, three in Hawaii, then home. But in that time he had to show some tangible results. It was true that neither her father nor herself thought he would achieve great things, but you never knew with Edward. If his enthusiasm for life in the fast lane could be channeled into a work related activity, he might come up trumps. He was certainly not a detail man nor a strong operational manager, but he might yet prove to possess some entrepreneurial streaks. And they now had a competent operational manager at the helm in Buxton. All would be well.

There had been no tears of good-bye from her mother or father this time. Wistful looks, but no tears. Kathy was in control, they all knew that. But then they never saw her on those occasions, admittedly fewer these days, when the small watching hours of the night found her awake, staring.

Tom had taken her to dinner to Stafford on the night before her departure, Bob remaining with his Grandparents, yet again repacking his man's rucksack. And she had finally said yes.

'Just a quiet wedding Tom, here in the grounds of the Hydro. Just the immediate family if you don't mind?'

'Not at all.' He was just so grateful that she had finally said yes.

'We'll go away later in the year. I can't leave again so soon after my trip to Africa.'

'That's fine with me. But the honeymoon will not be Africa!' He smiled a warm smile at her. She accepted the sentiment. Provisionally, they set the date for one month after her return, to give her time to make the preparations, few though they may be.

'He will make a very good husband, Kathy.' Said her father as she told her parents the following morning, 'and good for Bob too.'

'Yes,' she replied, wondering why her mother said nothing, didn't cry, simply hugged her and wished her well. Smiling, but somehow not an inside-body smile, a surface one only. Kathy brushed the feeling aside. She had to.

They exchanged a correct kiss at the entrance to the departure lounge for Tom could not be passionate in public; it was not in his nature. Bob shook Tom's hand.

'Remember to keep the camera dust free at all times, Bob,' was his final instruction to the boy.

Bob nodded. Dust free! That camera would be protected with his life!

Then suddenly and anti-climatically they were in the air. They sat in the Executive section of the British Airways 747 Jumbo Jet and within minutes she had been brought champagne and nuts. As the plane droned on, her young companion, the one she had expected to remain alert for most of the journey, the one that was all that remained of Robert, fell into a deep sleep beside her, swathed in blankets and comfort. Despite her own intentions, sleep proved impossible for her. She was still wide-awake, remembering, when the plane landed so many long hours later in Africa. But the hours had not seemed so very long. Perhaps it had been too much champagne or too much wine or too many thoughts. Something had made her handkerchief so wet she had to leave it under her seat as they exited the plane.

BOOK 3

Ndebele

1929–1966

1

Mjanyelwa Mashiane hated war. Despised the loss, detested the sadness, the inhumanity, the futility, the pain. As a child he had sat, assisting in forming a circle on the brushed mud ground in the centre of the compound with other male children of his village, waiting for instruction from their elders. They sat at the ever moving feet of Sibanyou their chief, the greatest living warrior of the village, as he shuffled from one edge of the circle to another, talking, shuffling, admonishing and staring with those great black frightening eyes of his, eyes whose whites were always red, eyes that stared into the very souls of the small children as he told them of battles of long ago. The young Mjanyelwa had tried to seal his ears to the bloodlust sounds, to close his eyes to the bloodstained weapons, which Sibanyou could bring to life, inducing within the small boys' imaginations an ability to visualise the blood that had been spilt, blood dripping still from the weapons' blades and speared heads as he graphically instructed them in ways in which to kill their enemies. Most of the boys loved it, expelled collective breaths as one breath when a particularly gory part of the oft-heard tale was reached, having anticipated the moment with long-held breaths and large round unblinking eyes. Diminutive Mjanyelwa, alone amongst his peers, saw little glory in his savage ancestor warriors, in Mzilikazi and Manala, Ndzundga and the greatest of them all, Nyabela. His heroes were the herbalists, the healers, the spiritualists. The Nyangas and the Sangomas. He revered them for they protected life, they did not destroy it. They possessed great knowledge, cured people, saved life and they, beyond all others, had the ability to communicate with and become possessed by the good ancestral spirits of the tribe, ensuring that the traditions customs and wisdom of countless generations was passed truly down to the present.

Mjanyelwa was not like the other boys; it was seen within one year of his birth. He was sensitive and shy, neither gregarious nor noisy. He kept his own counsel, not sharing, not needing to share. A child apart. As he grew he was often found alone in the veldt, even during the dangerous dusk when animals searched for food and when the great cats owned the land and only the most fearless of the warriors of the village ventured abroad. He would be there, body not tall enough to enable his eyes to peer over the top of the long grass to spy any lurking danger. Mjanyelwa was not afraid of the animals nor ever harmed by them, he was a child apart, protected. His private and happiest games were far away from those of the ancestor warriors; he loved to pretend to run with the lion, to fly with the fish eagle, to swim on the scaly back of the crocodile and to grow as grand and as high and as vast as the biggest bull elephant. And to be as wise. But he was part of the village community and it was not always possible for him to avoid the games of war, serious games, passed from generation to generation, games every young boy was expected to join, every potential warrior for the village. Together the boys were shown how to recreate the legendary mud and wooden fortress of Konomtjharhelo in the hillsides on the outskirts of his village. A fortress that had been so bravely defended by King Mabhogo against the bloody incursions of the hated Boers in 1849 and 1863, then that of the powerful Swazi army one year later. The greatest accolade of all was to be selected by Chief Sibanyou and the other boys to play the role of King Nyabela who succeeded Mabhogo, for he was the greatest warrior of them all. The Boers returned again in 1882, demanding that Nyabela surrender Mampura to them; Mampura was a Pedi chief to whom Nyabela had given protection, a man the Boers wanted to kill by the white man's idea of justice. King Nyabela refused replying that, 'I have swallowed Mampura. If you want him then you must cut me open.' All the boys knew the words, waiting for the time when they would be invited to play the chief, to say the special heroic words. Mjanyelwa was never called, never chosen. He was content that he was never called, for him there was no enjoyment in conflict, no heroism in fighting. Besides, it was all a lie.

The boys only played the story until Nyabela challenged the Boers; they were never given the knowledge of the true history. The proper history that had faded and become lost in a fabricated myth. The reality of the terrible revenge enacted upon the Ndebele people by the slighted Boers, in which the intransigence of Nyabela occasioned the worst suffering in the history of his people. The fearful eight month's siege of the fortress of Konomtjharhelo by the bearded red faced men who had managed to infiltrate Nyabela's food storage areas, destroying them with their European dynamite. The fortress caves in the earth becoming caverns of starvation, disease and death, where barren rock and mud floors could provide no food. Where the people lived like the rats in the earth and the snakes and bats of the cave. But there were no longer any rats or snakes or bats, for the people had eaten them all. Pathetically bloated bodies of small dead children starved to death could not be buried in the caves, for the ground was too hard and the space insufficient. They had to be flung down the hillsides at night, where the animals took them. The distress of the mothers was indescribable, the anguish of the impotent warriors absolute. No, the boys did not play out that part of the history in their games.

Nor did they play the game to its ignominious conclusion, to the capture of King Nyabela, to his imprisonment and torture for the remainder of his life, to the abrupt hanging of his friend Mampura in 1883 when together they were dragged skeleton-like with their dying people from those terrible caves in the earth. Then followed the intransigent revenge of the fearful Boers. The enslavement of an entire people. The once proud Ndebele nation - all slaves. The contemptible Boers of the dreaded South African Republic declared the Ndebele people conquered subjects, turning them into vassals on their own land, slaves working for the red-faced white men in their own ancestral fields, allowed to take nothing from those fields, all the produce going South, away from their land, a rape of their heritage. Those Ndebele no longer cared to live, dying inside and outside as they toiled in their fields twenty hours every day. Toiling in an intense heat, unrelieved by shade and water, save a rest twice a day for ten minutes each time. When they faltered they were beaten, when they died they were kicked aside where they lay. The women were taken by the master and his superintendents when they had the urge, and when the women returned they were dead too. Dead inside. If later they found they had been impregnated with a baby and that baby was born they would take it away and give it to the animals. Such a child from such a father could not be allowed into their village. Their hate was unbounded but their passion was stillborn. This game the boys were not allowed to play, not allowed to know.

But Mjanyelwa Mashiane knew it, knew it all. Knew it from the Nyanga. Every day from the age of nine he completed the chores demanded by his mother, hobbling their animals for grazing wherever some greenery could be found. Their four cows and six goats. He checked the chickens for eggs, watched over his younger brother and sister. Then when he was free, he would walk a little distance from the edge of the village, there to find and to sit at the feet of the Nyanga, the herbalist, Ndimande Mtsweni. It was from this intelligent and gentle man that Mjanyelwa learnt the true history and suffering of his people, the once proud Ndebele people. For the Nyanga told only truths. He told the young boy about the very far off days when the

Ndebele were part of the ferocious and respected Zulu nation, centuries ago. When Shaka and his half brother Mzili, joint kings of the Zulus, jealous of the wealth of the Ndebele clan, of the many cattle they owned, sought to annihilate the tribe. How the Ndebele had bravely escaped to the Transvaal only to be weakened by division at the close of the eighteenth century, the tribe imprudently dividing itself into five sections. How only the Ndzundza and Manala branches survived, the Manala barely. How Mjanyelwa's village was the strongest of the four remaining Ndzundza villages despite, even because of, persecution. The people holding firm together. Ndimande Mtsweni, the Nyanga, did not glorify war, did not welcome discord, it was not his way. In this he was at terrible odds with Sheboi Mnguni, the Sangoma of the village, the witch doctor. And Sheboi was more powerful than Ndimande, for he regularly communicated with the ancestors and the entire village knew that he spoke with them. The spirits of the ancestors constantly possessed him, remained inside him, directed his words. The entire village, even chief Sibanyou, had to listen to him and obey what the ancestors dictated.

Often Ndimande Mtsweni could not believe his ancestors had directed the foolish and warlike words of Sheboi, for the ancestors were not frivolous. He knew, for he too talked with them.

Perhaps not as frequently as Sheboi claimed for himself, but the same ancestors could not say such different things. Could not advise both peace and war simultaneously, could not demand hatred of all peoples, whatever their colour, beyond the confines of the land occupied by the Ndebele people. The ancestors were much too wise to do that, for the ancestral voices were those of the Kings and the chiefs and the medicine men, all of whom had seen so much suffering and were now able to look down upon it all, to have the perspective over vast spans of time, to reach back for centuries and to reach forward to see what further conflict would mean for the Ndebele nation. A nation in danger of self annihilation if guided by the wrong voices. No, Ndimande knew without any possible doubt that the voices Sheboi heard were not the true voices. But, he could do little, he was not as powerful as the witch doctor in the hierarchy of the tribe; his assistance was sought at special times only. Nor could he raise the passions of the people, as Sheboi was able to do. To develop states of trance where the community believed that his deep and powerful words came no longer from his mouth but from that of Nyabela or Mabhogo or Mzilikazi or their witch doctors and medicine men. Sheboi was younger than Ndimande and he had a considerably stronger voice and he could dance and wail all day, even on the hottest day, and he never needed to rest, to take water. So everyone admired him and feared him and listened to him. Everyone save Ndimande and his young student Mjanyelwa Mashiane. Although the villagers listened to Sheboi and feared him, when someone in their family was very ill the villagers would secretly seek out Ndimande, for he was gentle and caring and did not say that life or death depended entirely upon the throwing of the bones, or on the whim of the ancestors. No, Ndimande truly cared and worked diligently to try to find a cure from his vast range of human, animal, insect, bark and ground preparations. He tried to save life with knowledge and care and intelligence. Sometimes he failed and the people returned to the witch doctor, but they at least they knew Ndimande had tried and did not admonish him for his failure. Neither did they applaud him for his attempt, for they must keep their visits secret from Sheboi for they feared his castigation, his deadly revenge. Magic and ancestor worship and the power of the witch doctor was at the very root of all Ndebele life and so, in the good times, when there was no family illness and life was easy and happy in the village, when the beer flowed from the early morning and the people beat the drums and danced and the women smiled as they ground the corn and sewed their beads; in those times the people drifted back to Sheboi. For he was more interesting, more exciting, more basic, more frightening and caused tingles down the back and they were great tingles that went on even when sleeping time came. Many times at the culmination of each of his performances he made you want to make love as if it were an earnest and obligatory cry from the souls of the ancestors. An essential compulsion. The people of the village loved the spectacle and the feeling and the passion. It was grand theatre and it was performed solely for them. So everyone followed Sheboi, especially the chief, especially in the good times. Everyone except Ndimande and his pupil Mjanyelwa.

2

The young Mjanyelwa loved and respected Ndimande the Nyanga in a subtle and more intense manner than he did his own father and mother, and they resented it. More, they worried about the influence the Nyanga had over their son. Was it a good influence or was he turning their son into an outcast as he himself was? The danger was that their son might become an outcast who could bring shame upon the family, more even than shame, perhaps the hostility of the most powerful man in their village next to the Chief, the Sangoma. Mjanyelwa's family feared the Sangoma with a thoroughly primitive fear, a terror of superstition and the dread of reprisal. Mjanyelwa attempted to reassure them, trying to convince them that the way of the peaceful Ndimande was the way of the future and that hatred of past enemies and the glorification of war was the path to destruction. But they didn't listen, couldn't listen, for to do so they knew would invoke the rage of the Sangoma, of this reality they were sincerely convinced. So they began to distance themselves from their eldest son, from the evil that might be latent within him, from the bizarre notions roaming around in his eccentric mind. The ostracisation of their son began when he was but ten years old, his mother weeping softly alone in her hut, his father protruding his lower lip in obstinacy, the boy sleeping ever more frequently in the hut of the Nyanga. But Mjanyelwa was reconciled to this being the way, resigned to his choice, reconciled to standing alone.

Ndimande observed in the boy manifestations he had never seen before. An immediate appreciation and understanding of specific applications of different herbs and their unique composition. He quickly noticed that Mjanyelwa possessed an immediate and sympathetic unity and understanding with the nature gods that he had never witnessed in another man. Never did Ndimande have to explain anything more than once to the boy, he learnt rapidly, understood immediately and completely. In the first months of his teaching, Ndimande set tests for the boy, challenging him to determine which herbs or preparations would have to be used for a particular disease or wound, how the potion should be prepared, how administered. Never once did the boy fail the test. Intuitively he was often able to go beyond the orbit of his teacher's advice, even beyond his teacher's knowledge. In his early teen years Mjanyelwa began to prepare his own compounds, his own medicines; intrinsically grasping how combinations of juices from herbs and juices from insects could together create a healing balm where separately they did little, even occasionally proving poisonous if used solely. By the time he was fourteen, Mjanyelwa was treating almost as many patients as was his mentor, both doing so extremely surreptitiously in order to minimize the hostility directed towards them by Sheboi. At first Ndimande scrutinized the work of his pupil from a discrete distance, available to correct him when he made a mistake or reached for the wrong jar. But Mjanyelwa never needed correction, rarely required guidance. It was not long before Ndimande came to realise that he could learn as much from the boy as he could teach him. Thereafter they became a partnership, a mutual appreciation of ability, no longer surrogate father and son, more mentor and friend.

Then one night, a night without moonlight, Chief Sibanyou arrived at their hut. He came alone in the pitch black darkness, a gloom in which only the lion prowled. He came not as their chief but as a man who did not want to die. As a man who had been told by Sheboi that it was time for the ancestors to claim him. His body had rotted inside and the casting of the bones on the earth had confirmed the sentence. But Sibanyou did not believe it was his time to die, could not accept the words of his Sangoma. He was not yet ready to become an ancestor. So he came in stealth, in the deadest part of a silent night. Ndimande examined his Chief, knew that this time at least Sheboi was correct. It was what the white men called cancer and it was slowly yet remorselessly eating the stomach away. Nothing could be done except to relieve the pain. The Chief would indeed die soon. But just as he was about to tell Sibanyou that beyond all doubt he must make his preparations to meet his ancestors, the fifteen year old Mjanyelwa reached out for his Chief's hand, at first gently leading his Chief away and then settling himself in due reverence beside him. Sibanyou had heard of this strange boy, of this boy that Sheboi wanted to have him send away from the tribe. He had heard all about his evilness and his assumed depravity with the old Nyanga, had heard that even his own family disowned him. But then he felt the boy's gentle hands upon his stomach, hands that pressed lightly and were cool and after some time began to take the searing pain away, hands that remained there, eyes that reassured and lips that smiled of comfort. He lay soporifically as the boy moved around him, obeyed the young man's every request, answered his every searching question, allowed him to undress his sacred body and to feel the most delicate parts, even to explore inside using his small gentle fingers. All the while the boy hummed quietly as he worked, reassuringly, like the gentle red eyed Brubru's wings in flight. Then Mjanyelwa gave his Chief a potion to drink and Sibanyou, totally trusting, did not inquire what it contained. He drank it and the pain was instantly relieved. For the next two months the king came furtively in the night twice weekly, to the hut of the two Nyangas and his rotting body was arrested in its decay. The chief began to lose his constant pain within the first ten days of visiting the young extraordinary Nyanga. Within a month his bowels moved freely and regularly once more. Within two months the unassuming pair pronounced him cured, advised him to keep away from spicy foods and heavy drinking, to treat his stomach as that of a baby's and confirmed that if he did so then he would be sure to live forever. The Chief never forgot his treatment by the young Nyanga, could never admit of it, could never publicly recognize it, but he would never forget it.

When he saw the boy being ridiculed by his fellows, the aggressive youths of the village, Chief Sibanyou would walk just a little out of his chosen direction so that the ridicule would cease as he approached and the boy would be able to more graciously depart. But he could not do it often for fear it might be remarked upon. He did what he could. He silenced his Sangoma when he again asked for the boy to be sent away, citing the necessity for them to retain all the youth of the village. The boy will change, give him time, the Chief said. But the boy did not change, Sibanyou knew he would not change, was grateful that he would never change.

This, the largest of the villages of the Ndzundza Ndebele tribe, was positioned in the midst of a farm called Welteverden in the Denilton district, north east of Pretoria. It had been purchased in 1923 by the then King Mayisha and was now a dispersed and rambling collection of huts possessing little cohesion or apparent unity. It was a little too swollen, a little too impersonal, and a lot too political. Mjanyelwa did not especially enjoy his village, nor was he fond of many of its inhabitants, but he loved the originality and the blazingly bright colours of the wall paintings. Their massive geometric designs, the floor markings in a circumspect reproduction of moving tyre tracks that climbed upwards for as much as one metre from the base of the outer wall. And he loved the times of the competitions, when the women strove hard and long, working from dawn to dusk and sometimes beyond, in the pale light of the moon with the incessant fluttering of insects forever circling their oil-fired lamps; working to be the best, to win the competition, to produce the most ingenious designs. Where their colourful creations suffused deep earth colours merging into the dazzling blue of a morning's sun swept sky, in turn coalescing into the blinding whitewash of a rain empty cloud. Always complimented by the geometry of squares and triangles, parallelograms and circles. Different sizes, different colours reflecting the humour and candour of the paintress and her family. Balances between history, tradition and the sights and sounds of a world barely glimpsed yet modernizing somewhere beyond the boundaries of their insular tribal settlement. A nation reluctantly dragged into the twentieth century by the developing history of an increasingly materialistic world just to be driven backwards again by uncomprehending ancestors and jealous Sangomas.

In his fifteenth year the ancestors came to visit him. They were the same ancestors that visited Ndimande, the quiet ones, the gentle ones, the intelligent ones. They spoke to him of times past, of times to come. They told him he would always be one apart. They told him he must leave Welteverden and travel the vastness of Africa. To find his release, to locate his own soul. Wherever he went they vowed to be with him, to guard and to protect him.

He did not tell Ndimande that he had been visited by the ancestors. He didn't need to.

3

'What will happen, Ndimande?' Asked the boy.

But Ndimande could not tell him, none of the boys could be advised beforehand for fear they would become panicked. It was the rule of the tribe, an inviolable rule, and despite the closeness and the love Ndimande felt for the young Mjanyelwa he could not break the sacred code. The boy was small but he was brave and he could withstand many things, so Ndimande knew he would endure.

Initiation into manhood in the Ndebele tribe must be approached fearlessly, without prior knowledge of the ceremony, the initiates remaining completely uninformed by their fathers and older brothers until the moment of the event. It was the law.

The ceremony took place every four years, so boys as young as fifteen stood with boys of eighteen or nineteen; occasionally there even were boys already out of their teens who had not yet become men because only one son from each family could be initiated during the same ceremony. If, being a younger brother, he had missed his opportunity in the previous initiation ritual, he might find himself at the age of twenty-one standing with a fifteen-year-old, both simultaneously awaiting their moment of official manhood. It was harder on the older boys to have to wait so long. Mjanyelwa was fifteen that year and he was the eldest boy in his family, so there would be no requirement for him to wait. He was old enough, he was ready. Although he did not know the details of what he would have to face, he knew enough to realise that it would be a trial of some nature. He was not a tall boy, not a physically strong boy. He wanted to do his best so that he would not let his Nyanga down, or himself, or his family. Could Ndimande assist him in the preparation to ensure he did not fail?

'I cannot tell you what you will face, Mjanyelwa,' replied his mentor, wishing he could help this special boy 'it is not our way, it is not permitted.'

'Nothing, Ndimande?'

'Nothing.' He paused, 'Save this. Remember all that I have taught you, all that you have also learned by yourself. Take some of our special preparations with you in a small pouch.'

'Which ones, for which ailments?'

'I cannot tell you, Mjanyelwa. You will have to decide that yourself. Perhaps the ancestors will visit you again tonight, perhaps they will tell you.'

Mjanyelwa had never told Ndimande about the ancestors visiting him. He looked at the old man, there was much still to learn from him.

Ndimande motioned for the boy to rise from his squatting position on the floor, he too rose from his ancient three legged wooden stool. The Nyanga laid his hands on the shoulders of the small wide-eyed intelligent fifteen-year-old. They looked hard into each other's eyes. After a moment and out of respect for the older man, Mjanyelwa lowered his gaze until his eyes stared only at the brushed brown earthen floor.

'Do not do that,' instructed his teacher gently 'tomorrow you will become a man. A man looks another man directly in the eye. Look me in the eye, Mjanyelwa, do not bend your head, do not look at the ground. You are a man.'

Mjanyelwa looked up from the dusty brown earth, brought his head higher still until he gazed directly into the kindest, most understanding, strongest, yet most remote eyes in the world.

'Here,' said Ndimande after their intimate and private moment, 'you must eat this.'

'What is it?' Asked the boy, never having seen the preparation before. It had come from the very secret box Ndimande kept by his bed. The box that even the boy, in all his lessons and despite their closeness, had never been allowed to look into. Now, today, the box lay open before him. Ndimande unwrapped a tiny parcel secured within a large old bay leaf which had the consistency of dried yet supple skin. There was no brittleness in the leaf, Mjanyelwa wondered how that could be possible.

From the tiny parcel, Ndimande extracted a small morsel that must have at one time been part of an animal or a bird. Mjanyelwa did not recognise the part. It was grey and dried and small.

'Chew this.' He was instructed.

From a confidence born of love and experience Mjanyelwa placed the dried preparation onto his tongue.

Despite its age and apparent dryness it instantly became alive.

'Do not open your mouth.' Said the Nyanga sharply for he had once tasted the same preparation and he knew that it was fizzing on his pupil's tongue, he knew that Mjanyelwa would feel that it was walking around his mouth like a huge insect and that he would want to spit it out and wash the strange heavy unpleasant taste away.

'Chew slowly, my son,' said the old man. 'Chew slowly, it is from the male lion, it will give you courage and strength. It was taken from the lion as he lived, just a little so that he too would retain all his courage, just a little borrowed from his heart. The lion still lives today, he is still as courageous; you now have some of his power, his strength, his cunning. Chew his heart, chew it well.'

The boy felt the lion's heart in his mouth, alive and pulsing, and it was joining his own body, his own heart. Now they would have to kill him and cut his heart to pieces to find the part of it that was the lion's. He was now both human and lion; for now, for ever.

'Now drink this.' Instructed the Nyanga when he was sure the boy had chewed all of the heart and the lion had entered his body.

The boy did not ask.

'It is from our friend the python.'

The boy said nothing.

'It will instill fear into your enemies and it will grant you the speed and cunning to elude them until it is time for you to strike. If you must strike.'

Mjanyelwa drank the preparation, all of it. The blood of the python mingled with the heart of the lion and the boy, this special boy, became in his fifteenth year, invincible.

Ndimande closed his box. He wondered quietly to himself if it would be for the last time. It was a box he had opened only twice in the last thirty years. Once for his own son, but he had died. Nothing could have saved him, Ndimande had arrived too late. Even the lion could not bring the boy back from the dead. Now, this second time for Mjanyelwa. But he would live, he would return, the ancestors had chosen him.

'Go as a boy,' he said to the small fearless figure before him, 'and return as a man.'

4

Never had Sheboi Mnguni, the Sangoma, appeared more ferocious. Twenty-three initiates stood in a hushed awed group, fearful, silent. There were no heroics, true or false, burning in their stomachs that day, even in the older boys; they were all silent, intimidated. But not the twenty-fourth boy, standing erect, a little apart from the main group. He was calm, untroubled, unafraid and unawed by the machismo of the Sangoma. The ancestors had visited him the night before as he slept peacefully. He knew which preparations to bring in his small pouch although still unsure of what he would have to face that day, why he might have to use them. He felt no fear, how could he? He had the heart of a lion, the blood of the snake and the protection of the spirits of his tribe. He stood apart, watching the Sangoma and his eyes did not roll and his breath was not held and hairs did not lift from his back. He was perfectly unmoved by the practiced antics of the witch doctor. Chief Sibanyou sat on his peacock feathered throne, a lion skin wrapped around his belly and legs and he watched the proceedings, but he also watched this special boy, the boy who had no fear, and he marvelled. The boy displayed less fear even than himself, the Chief. It was as if he plainly displayed an abhorrence of the Sangoma. Perhaps Sheboi was right, perhaps the boy would have to leave the tribe; it was not permissible to show no respect for the Sangoma. But the Chief owed his life to this special boy who was now to become a man. A debt of a life is a heavy debt to repay. He tried not to look at the boy for it was too disturbing, but time after time, magnetically, his eyes returned to watch him. Still uncowed, even apparently bored, Mjanyelwa Mashiane stood unbent; unlike the other boys who were, without exception, in utter stooping trepidation of the man and the day before them.

The largest of the village's impala skin drums beat out a slow solid rhythm. A ponderous beat mimicking the heavy calculated tread of the elephant. Then the insidious throbbing began to increase in almost imperceptible changes as the elephant became the buffalo, the buffalo the antelope, the antelope the cheetah. And as the music increased in speed so too did the dance of the Sangoma and his whirling and his sounds. He made the noise of each animal he danced with and was as fast as they in movement. He whirled and chanted and spun and screamed and it was the scream of the captured antelope, brought down by the sprinting cheetah. Then the music began to slow again, slowing into the rhythm of the cheetah's jaws devouring its kill, tearing the flesh from the bones of its prey; munching, crushing, consuming. The boys could see and smell the animals and the dead antelope, could hear the sound of the bones being crushed by the strong teeth of the mighty animal, could see the flesh and blood as it dripped from the mouth of the Sangoma Cheetah. For the two were one and it was a terrible spectacle to witness. It was something they would remember all of their lives and shudder each time the memory returned. All of them were foully consumed, all save Mjanyelwa. He stood alone, disinterested in the spectacle, unconvinced, unafraid.

The Sangoma came to rest, towering high above the terrified and crouching boys, his top tuft of hair displaying a single bright red bead threaded through a specially grown lock. The bead, as if it were a large droplet of blood, hung down onto the centre of his forehead. Like a large, tear-shaped, controlled drop of blood. He motioned to the boys to release each other from the frightened huddle they had assumed and to sit on the edges of the circle he had described during his fearsome exhibition. The boys crawled in terror to their places. All save one, who walked erect, then calmly sat down. Like a man, like the best of men. The boys sat, evenly spaced, concerned that they no longer held another's hand to give them succour and support against this fearful apparition. Then the Sangoma began the primitive chant of the Ndebele nation. The ancient appeal to the dead. He called upon the ancestors, the Ama Ndlozi, to give them all guidance on this designated day, to give all the boys the strength to endure. Now the boys really became agitated and afraid. What was it that they were to face if the ancestors were being called upon to support them? What was it their fathers and their older brothers could not tell them that would happen to them today? They remembered, a few of them, the older brothers who had died some years before and they wondered could it have been associated with this day for there had never been an explanation of their deaths. The Sangoma held his bizarre atavistic necklace of power in his bony hand. A necklace made from the vertebral column of a male python. On the necklace the Sangoma had attached the tooth of a crocodile, the claw of a lion and a horn containing both crocodile and rhinoceros fats and ground elephant bone. All mixed with the herbs of many plants. He waved the necklace high in the air describing a slow-motion arc, a magical circle. He called upon the spirit guardians and the honoured dead of the tribe. He asked them to tell him if they demanded any sacrifices that day. If so, what form would the sacrifice take? A bird or an animal, or was it more they required to satiate them that day? It was tradition, the ancestors never now requested more than a bird or a small animal, but the boys did not know that and a hush, a completely greater hush, fell upon them. They all looked at the ground, not daring to look at the Sangoma for fear of the answer, for fear they would be catching his eye as the answer came back from the spirits. In case the spirits asked for them. As he appealed to the ancestors, the Sangoma's eyes rolled heavenward and his entire body began to shake uncontrollably. Then the drums began to pound louder once more, as if a herd of buffalo in a charge. Then the Sangoma began to screech hideously; the women far beyond the outskirts of the circle, hiding behind the walls of their huts, praying to their gods, heard the dreadful screeching and they began to wail, a death wail. The boys were mortally afraid. A low moan, a compulsive collective mind association released in sound, unpredictably yet simultaneously, rose up from the throats of the frightened boys, gathering in volume until it became an eerie piteous howl. Sheboi Mnguni felt proud that again this year he had been able to wring such emotion from the boy men. He looked at his Chief for approbation, but his Chief was intensely watching only one boy. The Sangoma had not noticed before, he had been too involved in his dancing and his wailing and his acting to give any attention to individual initiates. But now he did. Now he watched what the Chief watched and his heart stopped and his sounds stopped and as his intonations ceased the other boys looked up from their wailing into the ground. Through their tears of fear they saw the Sangoma staring with a mixture of horror and disbelief at odd little Mjanyelwa. The wailing ceased, the silence became profound. Mjanyelwa was oblivious to their stares as he continued watching his friend the fish eagle as it circled in freedom high above the village, blithely unaware he had become the centre of attraction. He had long before switched his mind from the fatuous movements of the Sangoma and the foolish wailing of the boys. His thoughts were with the eagle and the distance it had travelled to gaze down upon him that day. Where would he be tomorrow, Mjanyelwa wondered? This country called Africa is so immense, so varied, so full of so many things for the fish eagle and for him to learn. New medicines, new preparations from other Nyangas; for now Mjanyelwa was beginning to think of himself as a true Nyanga, despite his youth. Would the fish eagle lead him to these new lands, had he seen them, had he learnt from his friends too? Mjanyelwa's mind had drifted far away from the immediate events in the village compound, from the nonsensical performance of the witch doctor. Abruptly and inevitably he became aware of a different noise. The sound of silence. He moved his eyes from the soaring fish eagle and looked about him. In the intense silence he had felt, Mjanyelwa sensed all the boys and all their fathers who were standing unswervingly behind them looking directly at him and the Chief was looking at him and the Sangoma was looking at him. And there was not one look of friendship in the entire pressing crowd. There were looks variously of wonder, of hatred, even of fear being directed towards him and he had no understanding of why they were looking at him so. He waited. The world of that village maintained its explosive silence and it too waited. There was only one person who could with some semblance of dignity, break the combustible spell.

Chief Sibanyou stood up from his throne. He had no idea what he would do. Must he return face to the Sangoma by publicly chastising the boy, the boy who had saved his life? Or could he make light of the situation? One glance at the Sangoma was enough to display that was not an option. Never had he faced such a difficult choice before, but he must do something immediately, before the moment passed. He held his leather swish in his hand, his ceremonial whip. He walked directly towards Mjanyelwa, hoping the boy would forgive, that the ancestors would understand. He raised the whip above the boy's unmoving head, whispered softly to him to close his eyes so they would not be damaged, and struck him fiercely twice across the face, from left to right, right to left. Deep slashes appeared immediately on the boy's cheeks and nose, slashes that reached to the bone. Blood slowly seeped from the deep cuts on the small boy's face, but he did not move. He opened his eyes and looked directly at his Chief. He gave his Chief a quiet and private pain ridden smile of understanding and forgiveness, and the great warrior Chief withered before the boy's kindly gaze. No-one stepped forward to assist Mjanyelwa, nor did the boy raise his own hands to his face. There would be time later to treat the wounds, time to look after his face after the close of the ceremony. For this moment he must endure, but there would never be enough time or enough special medicine to remove the scarring. They were scars that would remain with him for the rest of his life. Scars he received on his day of manhood.

Slowly, with a smile of triumph on his nauseatingly ugly face, the Sangoma began to take up his circular dance once more and this time Mjanyelwa watched him. No one was looking at the Chief, no-one saw him shaking in his throne. A shaking of remorse, of misery, of wretchedness at what he had been forced to do to the boy man who had saved his life. Shaking as if in trauma from that look in the boy's eyes, a look of anguish and forgiveness. Never he hoped would he see such a look again.

The Sangoma danced to his necklace, danced with his necklace, telling the spirits that watched over him how he had killed the creatures whose parts composed his necklace. How he had used his magic to calm them, to hypnotize them. How he had strangled them, even the lion, with nothing but his own hands. He begged the Ama Ndlozi that they command him to kill again today; to kill a beast as ferocious as a lion or a bull elephant that he alone could secure, even as it was guarding its young. Apparently, the spirits did not require him to kill again that day and he wailed his disappointment to the heavens and he pleaded that he be allowed to kill with his bare hands. But the spirits were resolute in their decision and his wailing gradually died away. This time Mjanyelwa did not look away, did not watch the fish eagle still hovering above. It was not for fear that he did not look away, it was out of respect for his Chief, out of concern for his Nyanga. The moment of emotion progressively passed. The Sangoma grew quiet, he stooped exhausted before his Chief who raised him triumphantly to his feet. The boys also rose as the Chief instructed and stood unmoving in their distended circle. Distended by one.

The Chief nodded his head twice towards the Sangoma, nodding his approval. The Sangoma opened his arms wide in a crucifix of completeness, of contented acknowledgment. The large impala drum began its steady beat once more, heralding the beginning, the time of the Ingoma. The boys' strict initiation into manhood could now commence.

5

The boys who were to undergo the Ingoma, the Abakwetha, the 'chosen ones' all wore the same apparel. A grass headband, the Sonyana, was tied tightly around their heads crossing the centre of their foreheads. Their upper bodies were crisscrossed by white cloth thongs whilst colourful material and grass bracelets adorned their arms. Their genitals were enclosed in a small cupped leather pouch which hung loosely from their slender waists. Some carried coarsely fashioned wooden sticks. A symbol of what, they were unsure, but they carried them just the same.

All the Abakwetha had, three weeks previously, walked together with their fathers to the kraal of Sibanyou, the Chief of the Ndzundza Ndebele tribe. There the fathers had approached their Chief in single file, pointing to their sons and requesting that the Chief accept the nomination of the boy as an Abakwetha, a chosen one, for that year's Ingoma ceremony. The request was purely ceremonial, no-one was ever refused. On acceptance the boys began to prepare for their special day. They visited their grandparents to inform them that soon they were to enter the bush and to become men. They visited the graves of their forefathers, offering drinks they themselves had prepared to the spirits residing there. On the day before the initiation ceremony they made their most important formal visit, that to their mother, to tell her that she was losing a boy, but would soon gain a man. The mothers gave their sons the traditional reply of acceptance, assuring the boys that they would pray to the ancestors to keep the boy men safe during their special day, a day the mothers knew, but could not share that knowledge with their sons, would be immediately followed by a three month sojourn by their boys in the bush. They would pray every day of those three interminable months that their new men would return unharmed to them.

The night before the first day of the Ingoma the boys were housed together in a large hut once belonging to the most revered female ancestor of the tribe; there to commune with her spirit, to seek guidance and support for the trials ahead and encouragement from her and her associates in the spirit world.

Well before dawn the guardians came for the boys and wrapped each one in a weaved grass blanket against the cold. Then the boys were moved in single file through the Chief's kraal to the sacred place at the river's edge. There they were bathed, cleansed of all imperfection before they regrouped to meet the Sangoma.

Once the Sangoma had completed his call upon the ancestors, once he had ensured that intense fear had again been instilled in every boy by his dancing and wailing and that the Chief had given his permission for the initiation into manhood to commence, the guardians regrouped their charges in the single file order of the early morning bathe. The guardians, elder brothers and fathers, carried pangas, heavy sticks and small leather whips. Ominously their purpose would soon become cruelly clear as again the boys were led to the sacred place beside the river. The nervous trembling boys stood in a sombre apprehensive line, remembering the dance of the Sangoma and some also recalling the brutal attack upon one of their number, albeit an unpopular boy, a strange boy. The youths were cold and afraid, no longer having their blankets to protect them from the early morning chill. The guardians stood either side of the snake line of boys, silent, waiting, knowing. Suddenly and forebodingly the Sangoma appeared from behind the large sacred rock, formed by the god of the stone until it possessed the features of a lion. The Sangoma motioned for the first boy in the line, the eldest boy at that day's Ingoma, to go to him. Hesitatingly, the boy slowly stepped forward, encouraged by prodding from the whips and staves of the two men who had been designated to stand either side of him. As the boy reached the Sangoma, standing fearful before him, yet not knowing why the fear was rising within him, the two guardians each took a firm grasp of the boy's arms, holding him fast. The boy did not struggle, his heart was too weak to begin to struggle. The Sangoma moved a slight step forward, taking an ancient unsharpened Okapi clasp knife from within the folds of his garments. With his left hand he abruptly reached down between the boy's legs, grabbing and holding his genitals firmly. The boy could not move for fear, his paralysis making the task of the two guardians that much easier.

'Don't cry,' whispered his guardian father, 'you want to become a man, so don't cry, my son. This is our tradition, we all come from this.' It was all he was permitted to say to his son, so after giving him these words, he stepped slightly backwards, still fiercely holding his son's arm but averting his eyes so he would not see. The Sangoma took the boy's limp penis between the thumb and two forefingers of his grimy left hand forcing back the foreskin. The boy's terror reached his throat but died there, he tried to be the man his father wanted him to be. He bit his lip until it bled, the blood of fear. With the unsharpened old clasp knife held resolutely in his soiled right hand the Sangoma slashed mercilessly down, an expression of wicked joy on his hideous face. He had not connected properly, so he slashed again and the circumcision was complete. The frozen boy's animistic scream reached back to the edges of the village, soared to the highest tree tops, frightening away birds and animals alike. His guardians tried to hold him but the boy collapsed in a trembling heap at their feet. The father, attempting to marry shame with concern was forbidden to assist his son, it was the law. For long moments the boy crouched alone on the ground, silently sobbing.

'Go and wash in the river.' Instructed the Sangoma malevolently.

The boy, the oldest boy in the tribe, now beginning his journey to manhood, lurched painfully to his stumbling feet, held his deformed penis in his increasingly bloody hands and agonizingly slowly made his way to the river's edge. He flung himself into the water, wanting to die just as long as the pain would go away, but the water would not claim him, it bore him up again and gradually, very gradually the bright light of pain became an intense throb. His two guardians pulled him from the water, blood beginning to seep once more from the dreadful wound that they proceeded to pack with salt to clean and sterilize. The boy screamed for a second time as now the salt began to eat into his exposed flesh and the pain was the same as before, biting into his very soul. He curled himself into the foetal position and lay beside the riverbank, sobbing. He had no wish to become a man.

The Sangoma wiped the bloodied knife on his aged leather apron, adding more stains to those already embedded there. He beckoned for the second boy to come to him.

It was then that the fathers and the brothers had to use the whips and the pangas they had brought with them in order to stop the boys from escaping. To force them forward to take their turn, to approach their first trial of manhood. The screams and the moans were now intense and bestial. As baboons scream. As before in every Ingoma, it now required four not two guardians to hold most of the boys when it was their turn for the savage surgery. Much as they wished not to, the boys awaiting their turn could not avert their eyes from the magnetic barbarism enacted before them. Some stared in forlorn hope that something would happen to reduce the pain or that one of the gods might take pity upon him and strike the Sangoma down. But the pain and the screams were the same for every boy and no god of salvation came to strike the Sangoma down. Most of the boys wept openly in their fear as they stood in that

202

pitiful line and none of the boys felt ashamed of their tears, of their fear. None were thinking of shame that day, they were thinking solely of the knife and what it would soon do to them.

There was one boy alone who did not cry, did not moan. Mjanyelwa Mashiane stood assured and firm in his place in the middle of the slowly diminishing line of boys. Calmly he moved forward, waiting his turn. He relived the taste of the heart of the lion and the blood of the snake in his mouth, the very essence of courage and defiance. In his mind he had prepared how he would treat the wound he was to receive. He would not allow them to pack it with salt, not from fear of the pain, rather because he knew his herbs would be superior in their healing powers. Confidently he moved slowly and deliberately forward.

There was panic among the boys now. Their fathers, suppressing their own tears, were beating their children, but the boys scarcely felt the blows, their conscious minds all consumed by the fear within. The ten boys who had already been circumcised sat crouched or lay beside the sacred river, distanced from one another, not wanting anyone to see them or to be close to them in their private shame and suffering.

Then gradually, as in the moment of the dance, a complete and eerie silence began to creep sinuously amongst the boys and the guardians, for the strange one was walking forward, scorning the guardian's grasp, they melting away from his side. Upright, controlled and steady he walked towards the glowering wicked Sangoma, who stood poised, waiting in pleasurable anticipation; calculating how many cuts he could take to circumcise this boy, to ruin for ever his chances of fatherhood, to so disfigure him that no woman of the tribe could bear to touch him, to look at him. Still the boy displayed no fear, although he was aware of much that was occurring in the transparent mind of the evil witch doctor. The elders of the village had never before witnessed a boy prepared to meet this first trial with such absolute and genuine composure. He walked proudly alone, fifteen years of manhood moving calmly forward. The boys beside the river forgot their pain for a moment as they watched Mjanyelwa's deliberate progress. The cowed boys in the tremulous line raised their eyes to watch Mjanyelwa's studied advance. The crying ceased, silence had sovereignty. The small boy stood tranquilly still before the maliciously grinning Sangoma who raised his bloody right hand and his bloodier clasp knife, reaching with his other hand for Mjanyelwa's pouch.

'No!'

The voice was authoritative, young yet strong, convincing.

The Sangoma was momentarily arrested in his downward actions, confused.

Mjanyelwa required only that split second of inaction, he seized his moment, grabbed the knife from the Sangoma's hand. Sheboi the dreaded Sangoma stepped back in alarm, fearing that the boy was going to attack him, to kill him with his own knife. His fear changed to disbelief as the boy, whose eyes never left his own, burning into his very soul, calmly reached into his leather genitals sack, extracted his small thin penis and, still without moving his eyes from the mesmerized

Sangoma, pulled back the foreskin to exactly the correct length and with one deft and accurate swipe, neatly circumcised himself. Without a sound he returned the bleeding knife into the Sangoma's shaking hand and walked self-confidently away; back erect, penis dangling unclenched, leaving a gentle trail of dripping blood on the worn pathway to the river. Hands by his sides, Mjanyelwa Mashiane strode purposefully down to the sacred river to bathe.

In one long coordinated magical moment Mjanyelwa Mashiane had diminished if not destroyed the Sangoma's magic. More, he had elevated his own status to an almost mythological level in a tribe that honoured bravery above all things. No one had ever heard of or seen a boy who had circumcised himself to thus become a man. It was the stuff of which the tribe's great legends were made.

And the boys who followed Mjanyelwa to the Sangoma's knife walked taller, prouder and quieter than those who had preceded him.

6

Three months for some of the youths becoming men during the Ingoma could have been a very long time, but it was nothing when compared to their first day of initiation. Their bruised minds recoiled when they remembered, when they could not force out of their brain, the ghastly images of those first hours of manhood. They recalled with absolute and agonizing clarity the brutal, bloody unhygienic surgery performed upon them, immediately followed by a ten mile tramp into the bush. A walk of excruciating pain and shame. But they also remembered that when they wilted and stumbled in their walk, when they simply craved to stop, to cry, to die, always he would be there and each time he renewed their faith and their pride in themselves. When they no longer wanted to go on they would raise their bowed defeated heads to see where Mjanyelwa Mashiane was walking. The different one, the fifteen year old who was already a man. They would watch him striding strong and fearless and upright and they would join him once again. If he could do it, if he could manage the pain, then they also could. They observed, grew stronger and once more shrugged off the assisting arms of the Guardians. They were men now, they would behave as men; he was showing them the way.

Then, when they stopped after the first ten miles he was beside them, one after another, ministering to all twenty-three boys, treating their wounds with his herbs. Being both a father and an elder brother to them. Even better than a father or an elder brother, for he knew how to treat their wounds. He gave them clean water to wash away the dreadfully piercing salt, he placed a dark cooling balm on their assaulted manhood, all the while calming their minds with his words, helping them to control and accept their pain, to meet it with the strength he imparted to them. And after that first merciless day they started to become men. They had their natural leader, their natural healer, their natural friend. The Sangoma, who never accompanied the initiates on their march into the bush, did not know until later, until it was too late, that the young Nyanga was treating his companions. The Guardians looked away so they also would not know.

It was the first year anyone in the village could remember when none of the Abakwetha died from wounds inflicted by the Sangoma or from subsequent infection. Always one or more of the initiates died, it was expected, even necessary in order to maintain the mystique. The people of the village always accepted the Sangoma's explanation for the deaths. Illness and misfortune, as much as good fortune and good health, were a result of interventions from the spirit world, he would tell them. If a boy died it was because he or his family in some manner had flouted tradition.

Perhaps he had sexual intercourse before the Ingoma, a sin against traditional law. Perhaps the family's blood was bad and the boy was taken to redress the balance, to purify the family. The three months of waiting was a terrible time for the mothers of the Abakwetha. The Guardians, the fathers and elder brothers, were, at some distance, watching the initiates for most of the time and they knew immediately when one of the boys died and which one it was. But the mothers did not know. Every day they would meet together, a grim anticipatory hush pervading their every action. Mechanically they would grind the corn, make the porridge, brew the beer, but their minds were in the bush with their sons. Then the climactic day dawned when their men returned and every time it arrived too soon. They never wanted it to come because then they would know. They would stand together in a forlorn group one mile beyond the boundaries of the village, waiting on the pathway that the boys must take to come home. They knew how many boys had left the village to become men, but they did not know how many would be returning. Always the initiates returned in the first group, the Guardians following one day later, their task to ensure that all traces of the camps and of the Abakwetha who had been taken by the spirits were obliterated, so none could stumble upon them again.

The mothers would stand and together they would count the heads as they began to appear from the short horizon of the bush, checking one another's count. Then, when all the heads were in view, when it could be plainly seen that no more were emerging from the bush, the mothers would know how many sons were dead. Then the awful wailing would begin, for although they knew not whose son was dead for faces and bodies were yet indistinguishable, they knew it might be their own. The wailing and the holding of shoulders and arms and heads gave one another support and solace. The boys were one boy, the mothers one mother. One loss was a loss to all. But this Ingoma, when the boys returned, they would be no wailing. Disbelief only. Mjanyelwa had saved them all. But the consequences of that saving would be harsh for him, for in saving them he had diminished still further the power of the Sangoma who needed one or more of the boys to die in order to prove the mystery of the bad blood, in order to maintain his magic. On their return from this Ingoma the Sangoma would know that now he had two Nyangas in his village, two mortal enemies. It could not be allowed to continue. One Nyanga was old and would die before many more winters but the young one would have to be irreparably damaged, he must be made to quit his treatments, he would have to be taught that his therapy could kill not save. He would have to be made to feel remorse for his activities. On the return of the initiates, Sheboi would know that he must take action to preserve his mystery, his power over the people of the village. As he too saw them appearing from the bush he would know that at least temporally he had lost his power over twenty-three new men of the village. He would know that he must instantly regain it, must act immediately.

However none of this as yet impinged upon Mjanyelwa or his companions as together they began to enjoy the three months of their Ingoma. The pain had gone, the healing almost complete. Now the fun of becoming a man could commence. With their Guardians watching from afar, the Abakwetha began to build their mphandus, their shelters in the bush. It was a time of bonding, not only for the young initiates but also in spirit with their shadowing elder brothers and fathers. Mjanyelwa had no elder brother and his father, after seeing the Chief strike his son and the loathing of him displayed in the Sangoma's eyes, had melted away. He remained alone in his hut, scorned by a wife who left plates of cold food outside his doorway, refusing to speak to him, for the entire three months of the Ingoma. The Sangoma knew Mjanyelwa's father was in self-imposed isolation and was pleased. He did not know what the Chief was thinking, for there was a strange silence from him. His normal ebullient self for reasons unknown to anyone, had taken a temporary holiday. Moreover, he was no longer to be seen carrying his ceremonial whip of office.

With no shadowing elder brother or father, Mjanyelwa was alone in the bush but then not really alone; for although the guardians kept their distance from him and attempted to influence the Abakwetha to do likewise, the initiates could not desert the man who had relieved their pain, had ensured that they would live. As the new men worked to construct their mphandus they sang together the ancestral songs of their tribe, reaching back hundreds of years into the earliest history of their people. At the blazing campfires of the evening, the Guardians were allowed to join so they might pass on the laws of the tribe to the Abakwetha, advising them of all the requirements demanded by their ancestors which they must fulfill, of customs which must be followed, of laws which must be obeyed. The new men began to learn a secret language which only they and the previous Abakwetha of the village may speak together, for now they were men, frowned upon if they were ever to mix again with boys.

For most of the initiates, the Ingoma became a wonderful time, especially the stories, especially the hunts. A change that had, almost imperceptibly, begun when they stood in line that very first day of the Ingoma now took possession of the boys. They no longer reproached Mjanyelwa for his strangeness and although over time some of them listened to the Guardians and began to slowly drift away from his side, none of them ever bullied or berated him again, none of them laughed at his strangeness, all revealed a level of respect they had hitherto never displayed. They did not criticize him when he refused to kill the animals, preferring to collect roots, to study the trees and the bushes, for they knew it was not fear that kept him from the hunt. The marks of the Chief's whip stretched across his face as a constant reminder and they remembered the cutting of the knife he himself had performed. They knew he was not afraid and they knew that his medicines could cure. Sometimes as they hunted they left him alone at the campsite, alone with his work, but always on their return they would bring him food to eat, for he had to live and he had to eat the animals and the birds even if he would not himself be a party to their killing. Primarily he ate vegetables, corn and porridge, but sometimes, simply not to offend his companions, Mjanyelwa would eat the food they brought to him. In a quiet time of the day some of the Abakwetha would go to him and learn about the herbs, how to care for simple wounds, which preparations to use, what to take if they experienced a cramping of the stomach when they had eaten the flesh of a diseased animal, what to do if they were struck by fever. Every day was a good day on the Ingoma, except when the Sangoma made his visit to determine how the Abakwetha were faring, to see who was ill, who were approaching death, on whom he might deploy his magic. His chagrin at their happiness was palpable. His code, his magic absolutely required some to be ill, some to die, some to be afraid, many to hate the privations of the Ingoma. But for the first time in his long and twisted existence he met resistance, competition, and from boys taking their lead from another boy; Sheboi Mnguni the Sangoma was not required! Sheboi Mnguni the Sangoma was no longer feared! He would normally have visited the Ingoma three or four times during the three month sojourn in the bush. To this one, to Mjanyelwa's Ingoma, he came only once.

In the village preparations were being made to accept the return of the new men, every mother wondering whether her preparations would be in vain. Families repainted their homes to welcome the initiate back, additions were built to the homestead to give the new man a place of his own, a place of privacy, for he would be a man on his return and could indulge as a man. Gifts, according to the wealth of each family were arranged for the young man. Mjanyelwa's mother had to prepare for her son's return alone. She repainted her hut and that of her husband without talking to the pathetic man, barely seeing him as she worked. She did not try to make a new hut for her son for she well knew that his nights in that hut would be few, he would be with his new Nyanga father. Her flashing hope that Mjanyelwa might have abandoned the ways of the Nyanga and returned to her home, that three months in the bush would have altered her son, made him more like the others, was a vain one, stillborn and forlorn. She knew her son; he had always been a strange boy. She had heard the stories of the Chief striking her son with his leather whip in front of all the men of the village and that his bleeding face had remained impassive, as if stone. Although she worried for her new man she knew that his extraordinary character would never alter, he was destined for something far beyond the confines of his family's homestead, perhaps far beyond the confines of the village itself. So she did not build a new hut for her son. But she had sufficient money saved to provide him with a new mattress for his sleeping. That she prepared for him, with love tinged with sadness. For she knew the mattress would never be seen by her in his sleeping place in the hut he would share with his surrogate father, a little distant from the village. In time, she vowed, she would find a way to provide him with some goats, even a cow, as so many of the other boys would receive on their return. This in order that they may in turn make them as a gift to pay the lobala, the bridal price, to their future father-in-law.

As dawn broke on the day they were scheduled to return as men to their village, the Abakwetha burnt their shelters, their clothing and their blankets, the last vestiges of their boyhood. Clothed in new ceremonial blankets brought to them by the Guardians, they returned in single file to their village. One mile from the village boundary they passed by their mothers, did not look at them for now they were men. They would meet in private later. As they did not look at them they failed to see the huge beams of relief and joy that lit every face they passed. Maintaining their single-file march they lifted their heads as they had been told to do when they entered the kraal of their Chief, for now being men they were permitted to raise their eyes, albeit with a somewhat contrived respect, to the same level as his. The Chief watched these new men of the village enter his kraal, as he sat on his throne of peacock feathers, his lion skin cloak on his knees, his ceremonial whip absent from his hand. He watched as the boys snaked proudly before him, knowing without looking who would be leading the boys home. Then he saw him, the smallest of the new men, but really the tallest. He came as the first of the new to raise his eyes to his Chief, to be welcomed back to the village as a man. Their eyes locked for a second and the Chief saw the lustrous confident eyes of a mature and knowing man before him, eyes that were alight with wisdom and strength. He saw also the lips of reassurance, the smile of forgiveness appear again on this man's face, this ribbed man's face and almost, almost, the Chief looked down, almost he looked away. But, as if he knew what was about to happen; the new man rapidly lowered his gaze from the Chief he had to protect and stared at the ground between them. The moment passed, the Chief had been saved and no-one had seen. No-one save Ndimande Mtsweni who stood a little distant behind the large Baobab tree at the edge of the kraal of the Chief. He had heard some of the stories of what his pupil had achieved in the bush, of the greatest of all enemies he had made and he was concerned for his charge, his charge who was no longer a boy. He glanced sideways, a non obvious glancing in order to watch the response of the Sangoma to the return of the Abakwetha. As Sangoma it was his responsibility to welcome the new men home, to remind them of their responsibilities to the ancestors, to weave them again into his spells. But on this return, this return led by a young Nyanga, Sheboi Mnguni just stood by the side of the Chief, watching, saying nothing. He allowed all the men-boys to file past him without a word. Visibly he was ostracising them from his medicine, from his protection, unless they came begging to him to take them back. This he would tell the Guardians on their return. Any one of the Abakwetha who did not come to him before the sun set on that day, any who did not come to beg his forgiveness, to seek his protection, would be forever cast out from his care. They and their entire families with them. This he would tell the Guardians. So he stood silent, in hate. Remarkably the Chief said nothing to his Sangoma, did not ask him why he failed to give his customary talk, his usual admonition to the boys. It was as if he had expected the silence, knew the cause, did not wish to interfere.

Quietly and unobtrusively the following day the new men obeyed their Guardians for they did not wish to bring retribution upon their families. Each went and begged forgiveness from the man who had hacked at them with his filthy knife and smiled as he did so.

They begged that he protect them and their families once more and they carried with them or drove before them a considerable part of the wealth of their family in order that the Sangoma would believe in the sincerity of their pleas. Thus, on the Sangoma's acceptance of their apologies and of their gifts, the celebratory feasts to mark their return from the bush and their succession into manhood were not despoiled. One family alone in the village was cursed. It was the beginning of the realisation for Mjanyelwa that his medicine could cause pain, even death. For the Sangoma refused to minister to any of his family whilst also refusing to allow them to seek treatment elsewhere. In time his brother would die from an untreated illness, his sister would never find a husband; his father would wither away in his hut and expire from fear and shame. Only his mother would remain strong, as fearless as her son and she would live to see the death of the man who cursed her family, some would say that she caused that death.

So the new men's feasts began. Twenty-four feasts were planned. Every one of the families of the boys provided a feast for him and the rest of the Abakwetha to attend. Only when this ritual feasting was completed, when twenty-four bloated days had passed could the men return properly to their families, enter their new huts. All Initiates were obliged to invite every one of their companions to their feasts, but that year only twenty-three new men attended each of the feasts. Mjanyelwa did not want to bring the curse of the Sangoma upon any of his fellows or upon their families; it was enough to witness what was happening to his own. When the first feast was over and he had not attended and the Sangoma had been there to watch and check and observe, twenty-three families breathed freer. Twenty-three frightened families breathed more easily again. Mjanyelwa's own feast was held in the hut of his mother, alone save for his younger brother and sister and their mother. Two unhappy children who were beginning to learn how life could be without friends, for none would come to them again for fear of the Sangoma's curse. Mjanyelwa's heart bled for them in their loss; he attempted to comfort them, but they hated him for what he had done to them, for their world that he had so carelessly destroyed. The Sangoma's revenge was beginning.

Mjanyelwa's only relief came when he sat on an ancient three-legged stool, now allowed to be elevated to the same height as his friend and mentor. Looking directly into his eyes, he informed him of the events of the Ingoma. The older Nyanga learned of the new herbal preparations his one time student had found or made; which ones he had discarded and why. Which ones he had retained and how successful they had been or why Mjanyelwa believed they would in time prove to possess curative powers not yet realised. He walked with Mjanyelwa through dense tangles of tropical undergrowth in search of new herbs. He climbed hillsides with him to discover caves where only the lions or the hyenas lived. He viewed through the young Nyanga's eyes the dramatic ravines he had visited in his Ingoma and heard through his youthful ears the deep silences of the forbidding gorges. He sang with this younger lighter voice at the camp firesides and he dreamt the same dreams as Mjanyelwa dreamt when they lay down to sleep. But they never discussed the circumcision and what Mjanyelwa had done that day.

'We have made a powerful enemy, Mjanyelwa,' Ndimande said as the two men lay unsleeping watching the twinkle of a million stars.

'Yes, but why both of us? It is me he hates for what I have done, not you.'

'No, it is both of us. For he knows we both have the power, a power that has now been displayed to so many and in public. Before, it was secretive and singular, now it is public and visible. Now he cannot allow it to continue, he will fight us, try to destroy us.' Mjanyelwa realised anew what his actions had meant. Actions for caring and for saving were actions that had been translated into threats. The injustice of it assailed him but so too did the realisation of his own foolish immaturity in allowing it to happen so publicly, creating so much loss of face to the Sangoma. It would have been possible for Mjanyelwa to have treated the boys privately, not gone from one to the other as they all watched. He could have been discrete in his ministrations. Now it was too late; his family was suffering, Ndimande would suffer. He was a fool!

'We must be careful, Nyanga,' said Ndimande, treating his erstwhile student with a respect the latter knew he did not now deserve. A respect calculated to encourage, to support. But both knew retribution would ensue, that they were powerless to stop it. They could only wait and be alert.

For many nights Mjanyelwa's sleep was disturbed by the vision of the Sangoma coming to them both, then to Ndimande alone, and there was within his dreams a

218

cairn of rocks that covered a body but he did not know if the body was his or that of the old Nyanga. Both awake and sleeping he called to the ancestors for guidance but none visited him during those terrible nights.

7

Mjanyelwa the new man was now entitled to proudly wear his totem Iporiyana, a breastplate made of animal hide. The selection of the skin used to make the breastplate had to be carefully inspected for he was prohibited to wear the hide of his own totem animal, the monkey. The clan Mashiane had from ancient times taken the monkey as their totem. The animal that gave to all men of their clan their agility, speed and adroitness. They were forbidden ever to harm the monkey or to cause it any form of distress, least of all, as others did, to eat its flesh or wear its skin. In just the same way the Mahlangus clan must not harm the steenbok, the Mtswenis the baboon, the Sibanyou clan the guinea fowl. Mjanyelwa knew that in so many ways his behaviour and his fate was irrevocably tied to that of the monkey, he must be as wily and as nimble in both mind and body, know when to stay, when to leave, watch for the many predators that came to assail him. Above all he had to honour the spirits of the monkey with due reverence. Consequently Mjanyelwa's Iporiyana was made from the skin of a wild cat, in itself a difficult animal to capture, wily and fast, living on its wits. Now its skin was transferring these extra powers to the new wearer. Adorning the top of Mjanyelwa's Iporiyana were tiny blue and golden beads woven into the fabric by his mother while he was away on his Ingoma in the bush. On his shoulders he wore a new goatskin cape and on his head a pointed goatskin cap. Mjanyelwa, like all the other boys, was to be given a spear to carry by his father, it was the law. Mjanyelwa's spear had been left leaning against the wall of his mother's hut. The law demanded it be passed to him by the hand of a man but there was no man of his household willing to hand it to him. For Mjanyelwa it was of no importance, he would not be hunting, he would not be fighting, there was no requirement for a spear.

It was only two weeks after the Abakwetha men returned from their Ingoma that Ndimande fell ill. At first it seemed no more than an inconsequential sickness with some cramping of the stomach and so he treated himself with the normal simple preparations. Perhaps the meat that apparently covert friends of Mjanyelwa had brought to his house as a gift for him had been tainted with an animal disease. The problem would soon pass. But the problem did not pass and soon the pains became more acute and Ndimande could eat nothing without the pains intensifying. Mjanyelwa brought him the youngest roots and most succulent leaves, he mixed them with maize and made a gentle calming porridge for the old man to eat, forcing a little of the mixture through the parched lips of his teacher into his dry mouth, but there it remained, useless. The man could no longer chew the preparation, no longer had the will to allow it into his stomach where the pains would increase as soon as it lay inside. Mjanyelwa tended his teacher without sleeping, forcing droplets of water between the old man's parched lips, but it was not enough. Even the flies no longer came to Ndimande. They no longer sought moisture in his mouth, his nose or his eyes, as they did with every other living thing in the village. For he had none to offer them. It was as if Ndimande was drying up from the inside out, becoming waterless. His skin now stretched tightly over easily definable bone, like a skeleton with skin but no flesh remaining. Mjanyelwa tried every preparation he knew to breathe new life into the old Nyanga. Nothing had the slightest effect, nothing alleviated his pain. He tried everything he had been taught, he tried new preparations he had developed during his time on the Ingoma. He mixed the roots of the Buffalo Thorn tree with fruit bat droppings compressed with the bark of the Marula tree. It had worked on the young initiates when some of them had fallen ill with severe cramps and sickness, but it had absolutely no affect upon Ndimande. He was withering away to nothing before his impotent young pupil's eyes. When Ndimande appeared to sleep for a few minutes and when Mjanyelwa did not know exactly whether it was sleep or death, the young man, feeling a man no longer, forgetting how he had led the others from the bush as the first of the new men, cried copiously yet soundlessly beside the afflicted form of his friend. A crying the old man could no longer hear. Mjanyelwa had tried everything he knew, there was only one possible thing remaining.

'I will go for the Sangoma,' he said to the skeletal man, 'I will sit at his feet and bow my head and beg him to come and help you.' This Ndimande heard.

'Do not go for the Sangoma,' whispered the dying man, his voice the lightest croak, 'for it is he that has put this curse on me.'

'Then he can remove it! He has done it because of me, because of my treatment of the other boys on the Ingoma, because no one died, because his magic was not required.'

'That may be so,' replied the stricken man, 'but to go to him is not the answer for me or for you. Moreover, it is my time to withdraw from this world. I am no longer needed. You have my knowledge and you have more. You will take my place, Besides...' His voice had sunk so low that Mjanyelwa had to put his ear to Ndimande's lips to hear what he said, indeed, he felt rather than heard the words. 'Do not beg him, ever. If you beg him, he wins. If you accept my death, take on my responsibilities and treat the people who need your magic, then we win. They will come to you. There is much fear of the Sangoma but there is also much belief in the work of a good and kind Nyanga. You are that Nyanga now. Look well after the people of my village, Mjanyelwa, then forever you are a thorn in his flesh, he can never defeat you. He may try to kill you as he has me. I believe that in the meat he put a poison for me, even for both of us. A poison for which I have no treatment, nor do I know what it is. I thank the ancestors that you ate none of the meat, they protected you. The Sangoma still has some secrets from us so be careful what you eat Mjanyelwa;

223

eat only what you have gathered by yourself, what you have prepared yourself.'

The old Nyanga paused in his long speech. It was time. The boy waited to feel more words, none came for a very long while but he could still feel a gentle breath from Ndimande's mouth on his ear. Then the breath became lighter still and now it contained no pain. Mjanyelwa could feel there was no longer any pain in the old Nyanga's breathing and he was glad.

'I will leave you now, Mjanyelwa,' breathed Ndimande against the ear of the boy he loved as a son, 'my spirits are calling me, so be happy for me.'

And Mjanyelwa did not cry any more. He held the old Nyanga until he felt his spirit fly with the fish eagle.

Mjanyelwa dressed the body of his Nyanga in the purest white. He easily lifted the light bony corpse of his greater than father, better than teacher, closer than friend, in his strong young arms and carried him deep into the bush; to the private rocky gorge he alone had discovered when on his three month sojourn. There he built a byre and laid the old man upon it. He folded Ndimande's arms across his chest and between the gentle dead hands Mjanyelwa inserted the small secret box that had been opened for him. The box that had offered him courage and strength would now offer the same to Ndimande as he entered the spirit world. Chanting an ancestral prayer reserved for the greatest of great men, Mjanyelwa lit the fire.

The new Nyanga of the Ndzundza Ndebele village positioned north-east of Pieterzmariksberg remained with the burning body through the whole of that first night while the old Nyanga went to join the ancestors. He remained with the smoldering ashes through the following day and through the next night, thinking about the last words of Ndimande, thinking about how his life had to be when he returned to the village, wishing vengeance upon the Sangoma, yet knowing that Ndimande's way was the best retribution. Then on the third day Mjanyelwa scraped a depression in the ground with his bare hands, decrying the use of tools and gently placed all of Ndimande's ashes into the depression. Then he collected round flat white stones from his private rocky gorge and painstakingly built a well-formed high cairn of stones above the ashes. It took Mjanyelwa three days to complete the cairn to his satisfaction, ensuring that its geometry and composition paid due homage to his master. He neither ate nor drank the entire time he was in the bush with Ndimande, the entire time he was saying good-bye.

Mjanyelwa Mashiane returned slowly to his village, feeling entirely alone for the first time in his life. He entered his hut, the hut he had shared with Ndimande, now his hut, his man's hut, the Nyanga's hut. He cleaned the hut until there was no dust, he positioned his jars and ointments in uniform tidy ranks on the mud shelves. He prepared the couch on which he would give treatment, the couch that had once been the bedroll of the greatest Nyanga the Ndebele people had ever known. Until Mjanyelwa Mashiane. And he waited for his first patient to come stealing through the night to him.

225

8

Mjanyelwa was nineteen years old when he married. She was sixteen and her name was Esther. She had become a woman at fourteen, displaying her bloodied cloth to her mother and that year was allowed to complete the female initiation ceremonies. Since then she had been saving her body for the right man. Always she had admired the small strong Mjanyelwa, the different one. Her elder brother, on the same Ingoma as Mjanyelwa, had spoken of him in terms of reverence and deep appreciation. One day he had begun to whisper something very special to her about the man and what he had bravely done to himself on the first day of the Ingoma but had stopped when the Sangoma came into view, watching them as they talked. Her brother had never again mentioned Mjanyelwa to her, despite her questions, telling her not to think of him, for to do so would bring the wrath of the Sangoma upon her, but he never explained why. Esther had hated the Sangoma since the very earliest days she could recall, had hated the way he looked at her when a child, had hated the way he looked at the other young girls of the village as they began to develop their breasts, had hated the way he had fingered their bodies when the mothers of the young girls were forced to bring them to him for examination to ensure they were pure and untroubled by the spirits. She had not feared him as had the other girls, she had not cried as he touched her, but she had purposely drunk much water, for her mother had told her what the Sangoma would do, and when he began to touch her there she purposely began to urinate over his hand and he jumped away in disgust and kicked her out of his hut. Her mother had pretended to be ashamed and begged the Sangoma for forgiveness but the two women had laughed together in the nighttime in their hut. They could not tell her father what it was that they laughed about but she had won, the only girl in the village who had not felt that dreadful dirty finger inside her, the only one.

Esther knew there were many stories about the young Nyanga, stories only the men recounted and would never tell the women. She also knew that the Sangoma was feared by all, except one man. She wanted to know that man. She had understood from childhood that the Sangoma was the most important man in the village next to the Chief but that many of the villagers still went to Mjanyelwa when there was an illness in their family. No-one ever admitted visiting the Nyanga. However Esther knew, for as night fell and as she walked alone to the outskirts of the village thinking of the man she wanted to meet, the only one who did not fear the odious Sangoma, she watched from behind trees or dense foliage as shadows surreptitiously crept to the old hut just beyond the confines of the village, the hut of the young Nyanga.

He was different this Mjanyelwa. He did not hunt with the other men, but save for the Sangoma, no-one in the village mocked him, not even the Chief. When, always alone, he walked through the village, as long as the Sangoma was not in sight, the people slightly bowed their heads in respect to this small young man. In respect! He was a mystery to her, a healer not a hunter, a man held in respect yet himself fearing no-one, respecting no-one save the Chief on ceremonial occasions; although he was never welcome to such events, the Sangoma saw to that. Esther knew that she wanted him for herself, wanted to be a part of Mjanyelwa's life. Anyone could get a hunter or a beer drinker as a husband, but a healer, a special man, that was different. She made her plans to ensnare the man she wanted.

It did not take long for Mjanyelwa to notice her. Few women came to him for treatment and then only the old ones or the married ones; no women stood in his path as she did so he might appreciate them, for their families were worried about any overt contact with the Nyanga, a man so despised by the Sangoma. Esther's father was not blind, knew he had trouble, wanted to minimise it, but he also knew the willfulness embedded in his daughter, her fearlessness that was almost that of a man's, but he, like his daughter after him, was a shrewd man. He watched his daughter's antics for but a short time before going to the Sangoma.

'My daughter is a foolish one, but she is simple in the head Sheboi, she cannot understand that what she does is wrong.'

The Sangoma said nothing.

'He has to marry one day and maybe it is best that he marries someone whom the gods have not blessed with intelligence for it means they will have simple or deformed children, it is a just retribution for a man who does not show the respect he should.'

The Sangoma said nothing but he remembered the simple girl who could not hold her water and he believed what her father was saying.

'I want to get rid of the girl, she is a trouble to my family. It is better she goes to a man who will also suffer for her stupidity, who will have to forever live with her problem and her simpleness, a man to whom she will give constant trouble and pain.'

Still the Sangoma said nothing but now he looked up at Esther's father and his evil grin betrayed the pleasure the other man's words were giving him.

'And as a token of our continuing respect of your power and your will, my family would ask you to accept our only cow and two of our four goats.'

Without hesitation, realising he could both personally benefit and cause further distress to the young charlatan Nyanga, the Sangoma nodded his acquiescence to the proposal and said, 'She will forever be cast out from my care as is Mjanyelwa and his family.'

'I accept,' replied Esther's father. He bowed, turned and went to untether his animals to bring them to the compound of the Sangoma.

He loved his daughter Esther, he knew she was the brightest of his six girls, but also the most highly spirited, the most stubborn. He knew he could not persuade her from following the course her mind and heart had decided, but he wanted her to live, wanted the remainder of his family not to suffer for her actions, it was the only way. He himself had been to the young Nyanga, had stolen to him in the dead part of the night, knew what a special and unusual person he was and could see why his daughter was attracted to him. Yet Esther's father could not admit of any of these experiences or thoughts. He had resolved the problem. And he had decided what he would demand from Mjanyelwa for Esther's lobala.

Now it was almost every day that she stood on the pathway to his hut, knowing the times he would venture into the veldt and to the river to gather his herbs and to make his potions. She dressed in her gaudy Isiphephetu, her stiff beaded apron symbolizing her ascent to womanhood, for she was a small woman with a young face and she wanted him to know the truth. She wanted him to know that she was available, ready and a woman. She placed simple beaded hoops around her neck, legs and arms then added a rich smelling tambootic necklace around her slim neck; a necklace that expressed her virtue. He was the only man she had thus appeared to, for she exited her hut at dawn, carrying her garments and adornments with her. As she approached the outskirts of the village, in close proximity to his hut, she would hide in the bushes, don her apparel and await his arrival. On the first day he pretended not to have seen her for he believed she must be waiting there for another man of the village; he knew it could not be for him that she stood there so blatantly offering herself. But when the second and third days came and it was still upon his pathway that she stood so regally adorned, he realised it must be for him, for no-one else from the village habitually used this pathway. There were many easier paths down to the river. He began to look at her more fully; he had never really noticed her during his visits to the village, although he knew from whose family she came. A family whose father, Mjanyelwa believed, was a crony of the Sangoma. Was she being sent to him as some sort of test and was he likely to suffer from speaking with her, being with her? He must always be on his guard; he must not accept food from her. Why had she been sent to him? But he liked her. He liked her size and her smile and her pert young breasts and her calm face.

Hesitatingly on the third day they greeted one another, on the fourth they walked together a little way to the river, on the fifth they sat side by side for the entire morning on the bank of the placid stream and she told him of her family and her young life and that she did not want a man who hunted and killed; but she did not yet tell him that she wanted him. She didn't need to. Mjanyelwa

told her of his work and the herbs he needed to collect and the medicines he had to prepare and she began to love him not simply because he was different and special and had no respect for the Sangoma but also because of his obvious concern and caring for the animals and the people and his inherent basic goodness. He became even more what she dreamt of, what she sincerely desired. He must be hers. Mjanyelwa began to enjoy the companionship of the girl, her brightness, her fun, and then he began to feel stirrings beyond solely companionship. Awakenings that a man should have. He had never yet been with a woman and his arousings occurred every night now, just as he was trying to sleep and they were impressive and they were uncomfortable and he knew he had to relieve those feelings. He thought of her standing beside the road and her naked breasts small and tiny nippled. He did not like the big women of the tribe, was even a little fearful of them. This small woman with the chirpy breasts and the fragrant smell would be enough for him, would be fine for him. He no longer believed she had been sent to him as a test, as a temptation that would lead to problems. She had convinced him that she was there of her own volition, with no one's blessing. He believed her, for he soon began to learn that she could never be fully controlled by anyone without her consent. In their sleeping moments they looked forward to being together and in their waking moments were soon inseparable from dawn to dusk. Sometimes they played as children play, chasing one another along the banks of the river, hiding behind trees. Sometimes they touched and at those times they were not as children any more. Other times they were adult and old as they talked about their village and the future and how to care for the people and the ways of their ancestors and the fear the people had of the Sangoma. Then Mjanyelwa grasped that this little woman was afraid of no-one, like him she did not fear the Sangoma, respected but did not fear her father or the Chief or anyone. And when they were apart they were really together too.

One cow and two goats was the lobala price. It was just. Esther's father's capital replaced. Mjanyelwa's mother gave him the animals, took them from under the putrefying nose of the man who had once been a husband but was hardly a man anymore as he lay prone in his bedroll, drinking his beer from the moment he awoke to the moment he slept again, smelling worse than the animals smelt. The man would not be long with the living and she was glad of that. She was proud to give the animals to her son and she began to love her new daughter-in-law. She would be good for Mjanyelwa, not only from the love that was obvious in her eyes but also because of the strength inherent within her. For their life together would not be an easy life. Nevertheless Mjanyelwa's mother knew they would surmount all problems. Of this she was sure for they had the strength, a strength she herself had once possessed. Mjanyelwa's mother was happy to see them together, it gave her the desire to continue, for now she would have someone to visit, some grandchildren to love.

It was a very small wedding, not the usual village affair and for that the entire village was contented. For that the Sangoma was pleased. Again he felt vindicated. Only one present came to the couple from outside their immediate family. It came at night and in secret and it came with a demand pledge that it must never to be revealed. Mjanyelwa opened the simple wooden box and gazed for many minutes at its contents. Instinctively he raised his hands to his scarred face, touched the black weals still plainly evident there and placed the box containing the ceremonial whip deep amongst his very private possessions, so deep that no-one would ever find it.

There was no traditional wedding for the young couple, they both had the strength to accept that loss. They forwent the three traditional stages of a Ndebele marriage process. The betrothal ceremony celebrating acceptance of and payment of the lobolo was replaced solely by a handshake between father and son-in-law. Their marriage ceremony was attended by her mother and father and his mother, brother and sister only. Mjanyelwa agreed to forgo the pledge usually demanded by the family of the bridegroom that if the bride proved infertile then the marriage would be absolved and the lobola returned. This process was not for Mjanyelwa and Esther, they wanted one another for all time, to be together, to share their lives. If children came to them, good; if not, then that was what the ancestors had planned. On their wedding day they agreed that their initial acceptance of one another had been without conditions, and now that initial acceptance had become final. It was against the laws of the tribe. So many things these two young people did appeared to be against the laws of the tribe. But they had one another, they were as strong as anyone, anything. Or so they believed.

The beautiful fresh bride, pure in body and heart wore a long beaded train, a Nyanga, - the snake. It had been made by herself and her mother, had no backing material, being constructed simply by weaving beads together. It had taken them three weeks to complete it to their satisfaction. Esther covered her bare shoulders with a cape of beaded goatskin and her face with an Isiyaya, her bridal veil. The two beautiful young people stood together as the late afternoon sun began to tumble to the horizon, speaking the words of pledging that the ancestors had taught them. They touched each other's shoulders in the traditional fashion. He presented her to his family, she presented him to hers. And they were married.

It was a gentle evening in the Nyanga's hut. Neither of the young people really knew how to proceed, despite the instructions of Esther's mother to her and the conversations he remembered with his comrades in the Ingoma who had illicitly managed to have sex before their due time. The ones who could instruct the others. Their instructions were vivid and boyish and lacked any finesse, any love. For it was love that lay between and within the young couple who stood together at the doorway of their hut gazing at the same stars that their ancestors had also watched. Gently Mjanyelwa removed Esther's cape to expose her beautiful unblemished shoulders, her firm small breasts, oiled and firm. Her eyes moved to his face when he first touched her and never left it again. She never felt the need to show obeisance by having her eyes meet the floor of his hut as her mother had instructed, nor, she knew, would he ever allow her to place herself below him. They were equals, he had told her so and they would forever remain as equals. She slipped the delicately coloured beads from her neck, placing them beside his mattress. Then they lay down together, side by side, not touching for a long moment, not knowing what to do, not wishing to give the other embarrassment or pain. Then slowly, deliberately, as if another being had taken control of his actions, Mjanyelwa placed his right hand delicately on her small stomach, leaving it resting there for a long moment. Both were unable to speak for the glorious anticipation they both were experiencing transcended speech. In time she led his fingers to her breasts, to her nipples, then down across her firm young stomach and to the private wet blackness between her legs. She gently released his hand, allowing it to wander where it willed. She turned, looked at his beautiful scarred face and, holding his eyes in a grip of desperate love, began to move her own small soft hands upon his young firm body. She reached the hardness between his legs and both gasped and both let their hands most naturally explore. It was as if their hands had been constructed for no other purpose. Implicitly they knew where to travel and at what speed. They touched at first as one would touch a burning branch, with care, lightly, carefully, but soon they both wanted more and the fire of passion consumed the fire of the burning branch until both fused together. Gently he laid his young strong virginal body on her young strong virginal body, fiercely she pulled him into her and she did not cry out. Her mother had warned her of the pain, but for her it was a small pain; a nothing.

Then they slept. Together, locked. Until the dawn.

In one instant, as the sun began its dappled appearance in their new home they were awake together, no gradual awakening. Instant. They held one another tightly, lovingly, as they always would. And Mjanyelwa, the peaceful quiet Mjanyelwa knew that he had found the one thing in life that he would fight for, that he would carry a spear to protect, that he would kill for. He and his friend Ndimande who came to visit him from time to time were both happy at this realisation, accepted the need to protect, the need to fight.

9

The young couple, the different ones, as they were known to the rest of their village, lived in unaffected happiness in their hut. There was a genuine caring one for the other and a patient understanding and acknowledgment of the feelings and needs of each other. They were inseparable. Esther would walk with her man, not behind him as most other women did with their husbands, as he went daily to gather his herbs. She learnt how to mix simple potions, progressing in time to more difficult ones. There were some that as a woman she was forbidden by the ancestors to touch, but this Mjanyelwa explained kindly to her and this she accepted. Within a year their first child was born and Mjanyelwa's mother acted as the midwife, relishing in the absolute love of the task. It was a fine strong boy. Any other family of the village would, as the law permitted, have paraded him within the first week of his birth, displaying their pride in him as a future warrior of the tribe, a new hunter to feed hungry mouths. But Esther's and Mjanyelwa's first born was paraded before no-one, he was simply loved and cared for because of who he was. The second year brought the couple male twins. Again Mjanyelwa's mother officiated, although Mjanyelwa was in truth a little sad, for he had wanted a girl child for his wife. To be like his wife. They extended their homestead, the little old hut remaining their home, as, they thought, it always would be. They added two fresh new huts, built by their own hands, for none in the village would assist them. One hut for the male children, another for the girl that would eventually come, Mjanyelwa knew she would come. He had already chosen her name, Francina. He awaited her arrival, but in that third year of their marriage, she did not come.

Because the young Nyanga now had a wife, it was quite proper for the men of the village to allow their own wives to visit him in the dark of the night, alone with their problems. For the men knew that Esther would always be present during the examination and the treatment, and they knew of her reputation and her strangeness; her jealous love for her Nyanga husband and her potency. Esther learnt many of the skills of her husband, how to treat small wounds, broken bones, diseases of the body, even of the mind. She loved the capable small man and the gentleness he constantly demonstrated to her and to all who came to him. She kept her own family away from the Sangoma, away from his influence, away from his evil.

Mjanyelwa decided to use the wasps to help him make a girl child. Amongst the most skilled Nyangas of the Ndebele tribe, there had been a select few who could affect the sex of an infant at conception, wasps were often the key. Ndimande, Mjanyelwa's predecessor, despite his many abilities, had not possessed this skill. Mjanyelwa

238

did not know whether or not he had been granted this special power by the ancestors, but he determined to find out and to do so within the confines of his own family. For days he scoured the countryside, seeking a fresh wasp's nest, which he eventually found on the second level branches of an ancient Baobab tree some three miles distant from his hut. Carefully, without destroying the construction of the nest, he covered its entrance with a clean goatskin cloth to keep all the inhabitants trapped therein. This he did as dusk fell when all of the wasps had returned to the nest, for he required the maximum number of inhabitants to make the magic work. Slowly and with infinite care he gently prized the complete nest away from the branch of the tree, lowering it to the ground by means of a large cowhide pouch tied with string. With both firm hands cupping the pouch he walked carefully in the moonless dusk so as not to stumble on a hidden branch, for the attention of his eyes was fully focused on the precise balance of the nest, in order to disturb the sleeping wasps as little as possible, treading deliberately, he returned to his hut. In the corner where roof met wall above the mattress on which he slept with Esther, on the mattress where he made love to Esther, he had prepared a mixture of cow dung and water, molding the mixture into the prepared place. He held the nest against the compound until it had dried sufficiently to support the nest. The drying, to Mjanyelwa's satisfaction, to his belief that the nest was now firmly secured in its new home, took six hours. He held the nest high above his head for the entire six hours, dismissing the ache in his arms, for he was making a daughter.

If the wasps continued to live in the nest above their bed in the hut, if they did not sting his wife whilst they lived there, if he had remembered the correct prayers and if, above all, the ancestors had granted him the power, then their next child would be a girl. For the first few days Mjanyelwa caught himself trying to count the wasps, attempting to determine whether their numbers were holding firm or diminishing. Were they all returning every evening as dusk fell or were there a few less every day? If so, the nest would soon be empty and there would never be a girl child, a wasp child. Or perhaps he did not possess the power? Doubts assailed the young Nyanga. Then as the days turned into weeks even he had to admit that all the wasps were returning and Esther had not yet been stung. Then the month came when she did not bleed and he believed the magic had worked, that the ancestors had indeed granted him the power.

On the first of October 1950, a daughter was born to Esther and Mjanyelwa. They called her Francina, but she was known to everyone as the wasp child.

The years passed with little dissention for Esther and Mjanyelwa. He was never tempted to go with another woman or to take a second wife. It was allowed by the ancestors but not required by this Nyanga. He was discrete when he practiced his profession, often with his wife and daughter by his side, disappointed that none of his sons yet seemed interested in learning the skills of the Nyanga; afraid that his eldest son thought only of the ways of the warrior and spent too much time with the other youths of the village. Those who would play with him when the Sangoma was away, or those he would watch and track and be an appendage to when the Sangoma was present. It seemed the Sangoma did not protest too much at this wayward boy, realising it was not the wish of his Nyanga father that he be so employed. For this the Sangoma was delighted; it was yet another punishment for Mjanyelwa to endure.

Mjanyelwa never competed with the Sangoma, never publicly displayed his abilities, never questioned the powers or the practices of the witch doctor. Only once did they come close to conflict when Mjanyelwa administered to his first born, much to the boy's own chagrin, during his Ingoma. He could not allow his son to die as had two boys already that year and the boy, without his father's ministrations, would surely have joined them. Mjanyelwa knew he was flouting the law as he had done on his own Ingoma, but he also knew that the Sangoma had targeted his son during the circumcision, an evil act he had witnessed for himself, a deliberately awkward slicing, designed to give maximum pain, maximum likelihood of infection. As a father, despite the fact that he was also the Nyanga, Mjanyelwa was entitled to treat his son. This he did, not with the conventional bathing and packing of salt, but with his own medicines, his own preparations, administered as surreptitiously as possible. The boy lived and the Sangoma knew he should have died, knew that some special power had kept him alive, but because the father had been so discrete in his treatment the Sangoma could prove nothing, could take no further retribution. It was sufficient to relish the certainty that the boy would never be attractive to a woman; yet another burden to inflict upon the boy's father, the Nyanga. The boy began to hate his father for what had happened to him, for his disfigurement. He would rather have died in the Ingoma than suffer the shame of his useless tool and his single remaining testicle. He wanted to kill, wanted to be a warrior, desired to be everything his simple quiet cowardly father was not.

The boys talked a lot about the white man during Mjanyelwa's first son's Ingoma and that the time was coming for the black man and how they had to regain their heritage, their lands, their dignity. How Africa was black and should always have been black and should be black again. The boys all wanted to kill the white men, the men who had raped and plundered the land of the Ndebele nation and made them slaves. The men who even today from their tall white cement huts in Pretoria were plotting to send the Ndebele people away again from the homes they had established, homes to which they had been dispatched so many years before. They wanted to send them away to an unknown area where the land was poorer, the animals fewer. Sent away to establish a new homestead. Once more driven from their land like so many cattle. And when the Ingoma ended, Mjanyelwa's son brought home to his father the wonderful tales of the ZANU and the ZAPU parties, the creation of the African National Congress, the mighty warriors who would drive out the white men, drive them from the land, forever. And with reverence Mjanyelwa's son reeled off the names of the new leaders, the men offering salvation to the enslaved people of Africa. Joshua Nkomo of Rhodesia, Motsamai Mpho of Botswana, Sam Nujoma of Namibia and others, so many others. Mjanyelwa's son wanted to be like them, wanted to follow them, wanted to kill the white man, drive him from their rightful land forever. As Mjanyelwa sat and listened to the froth of volatile hatred spewing forth from his emotional son's mouth, he realised his world was no more. The world of the caring, of the attentive, of the kind. The new Africa was a world he no longer recognised, a new world of the fierce, the bloodthirsty, a world of the warrior. But a different type of warrior than before, a warrior with a single impossible target. There was no likelihood at all that they would be able to defeat the white man; for he was too strong. His weapons too powerful, his friends in the other white countries of the world too numerous. It was inevitable that they would be defeated. There was insufficient synergy, insufficient agreement amongst the various tribes for them to hold together in the same way as the better disciplined white men would hold together. It was hopeless, he tried to tell his son it was hopeless.

'You are old, you are a coward! All the men of the village know you will not fight, that the Sangoma's words are the words of truth, that you are not to be respected, that you have married a mad woman and that you will never fight. Coward, coward, coward!'

Mjanyelwa looked at his sixteen-year-old son, seeing nothing but hatred and loathing in his eyes. He felt like crying for him, for all the young men of the village. When they most needed the best guidance of the ancestors, they listened to the charlatans. When they most needed the way of reason, they listened to emotion. Their way would be the way of death. He felt like crying for all of the black men of Africa. For their stupidity, their lack of reason. There had to be a balance in the world, the white man was superior, the black man provided that balance. For long moments the two men looked at one another, one in hate, the other in despair. The small woman who had been sitting by the side of her husband quietly listening, slowly stood up, walked towards her eldest son who now stood towering emotionally above her. Swiftly she drew back her small strong arm bringing it fast and furiously forward with an open palm that smashed against her son's unprotected cheek like the crack of white water breaking on the rocks of the rapids in the river. Her son staggered back at the force of her blow, her husband stood still in bemused admiration.

'Return to this hut only when you are prepared to apologise to the man who lives here, the man who is worth ten of the Sangomas of any tribe. The man who is my husband.'

The small middle-aged couple stood sadly together as they watched their first born march stiff-legged from their hut.

Fifteen families of the Ndzundza Ndebele village north east of Pietermaritzburg lost their new men within one week of their return from that Ingoma. Mjanyelwa's first born son, spurred on by the Sangoma, led the exodus away in the stillness of the night. Fifteen young men deep in passion and heightening revenge for all the woes of their world began stealing northward to join the parties of liberation, the leaders of the new Africa. Their meticulously painted new huts lay abandoned, their mothers weeping at the doorways of the unused homes were ignored, unopened presents spilling from their arms. The boys' fathers uncertain whether to be sad or proud of the actions of their sons, new men, now freedom fighters. Should they follow and if they did what would they do? Should they attempt to make the boys return or should they join them in their travels north? The moment of their challenge passed whilst they debated and then it was too late for the boys were too far ahead. And perhaps they had spun out the debate in order that there could only be one decision, apathy. Indolence. Or fear. In time the boys became heroes, some of them even became martyrs as news reached the village of their deaths in battle. It was all such a waste, young lives wasted for nothing.

Esther and Mjanyelwa did not cry when they heard of the death of their son. They simply held one another, remembering the good times with him, the growing up times when he was too young to care for anything save love and excitement of the new day, the times they swam together in the safe areas of the river far away from the crocodiles and the hippopotami. The times when they camped in the bush, listening to the night sounds of the animals, this and so much more. They knew they would not have liked the man he had become, so they grieved for the boy he used to be and they buried him in their hearts.

Even before the news of his death they had talked long into the nights, wondering what was to become of their family, their people; knowing that the way of conflict was not the way for them, was not a life they could be a party to. They knew that the white South African government would come to their village, would move the people, would destroy the huts. They realised that more and more of the youth of the village would leave to join ZANU or ZAPU or SWAPO or the ANC or whatever new terrorist groups might be created. Maybe it was the only way for Africa, but it certainly was not their way, not the way for the Nyanga and his remaining family. What was this fight for freedom anyway? To live as you wish with whom you wish? Mjanyelwa had that already. His family had that already. It was only the white governments or the black terrorists who could take that away from him. Make him believe he did not already possess it, enter and despoil his mind with their lies. He could rise at dawn and walk where he wished. He could gather herbs from the veldt and the riverside and from the animals whenever and wherever he wished. He could return to his warm loving home when he became tired, eat when and what he wished. He already possessed freedom, true freedom. But would his children think of it as freedom? His dead son had not thought of it as freedom. Did the twins think of it as freedom, did his daughter who was so naturally like her mother that they were sisters in thought and action, think of this as freedom? Was freedom to them something else? Was freedom the ability to visit the great cities and to go where they wished in those cities without restrictions? To be able to ride in white men's cars, wear white men's clothes, go to white men's schools to learn the history of the white man, the songs of the white man? Was that what they thought freedom was? No! Better to remain as we are, to feel a quality of living. If necessary, better to go away where the evil white men and the evil black men cannot harm them. Better to go away to a peacefulness and to begin again. Deep away.

A new beginning, a new homestead for his family alone. A peacefulness and a love together, no opportunities for the white man's lies and the black man's lies to despoil the minds of his children, upset the harmony of their existence. This village does not need me anymore. In these increasingly troubled times they are turning more towards the Sangoma, listening to his emotion, hearing his words of bloodlust. I will take my family and go. I will take my family away and I will protect them. I will teach my children and their children about the love of the gods and the love of the ancestors and the ways of the Nyanga, and tell them about the trees and peace and gentleness and love. It was a very long speech in the mind of Mjanyelwa, but when he had completed it, he knew what he must do.

On the day of the fourteenth birthday of his beloved Francina, Mjanyelwa Mashiane and Esther his wife gathered their few belongings together, loaded themselves and their two sturdy almost sixteen year-old boys and their courageous daughter, and began their journey, their quest for a new life.

10

The malevolently loathsome grey bodied Whitebacked vultures circled impatiently, waiting to swoop on a dying animal or perhaps a human, it was too distant to see.

Mjanyelwa and his family had been travelling for many months. At first they had struck generally northwards, away from the fast developing troubles for the black man in racist South Africa; far away from the schemes being hatched in Pretoria. Schemes constructed by white men to move black men. To move them anywhere, as long as it was as far away and as out of sight as possible. It was not only the Ndebele people who were thus afflicted, in time this policy would affect all the tribes. All the black men. In his journeyings Mjanyelwa had to be careful not to run directly north and into the fierce arms of the surging black freedom fighters, for they too would pose a threat to his small defenseless family. He had heard the stories of their indiscrimination and he feared them as much as he feared the white men.

For their first few days, Mjanyelwa and his family travelled in familiar countryside. Trees, pathways and landscapes well known to him from his many forages collecting herbs and roots and from his time as an initiate in the bush twenty-one years previously. A land and a time he would never forget. A land that still displayed an unmarked cairn of rocks, undespoiled by animals or man, a sacred place. An innocent time when the world and his companions in that world were so much purer then the world that now assailed him. A world he was not sure he even wanted to attempt to understand or to come to terms with. He preferred to hide from this new world; to hide and to protect his family. His family which had lost its first born to the new world.

Mjanyelwa watched the twins as they walked on before him, always wanting to be in the lead, always wanting to be the first to see something new, then speaking, almost chanting in unison as they always did, to tell the smaller-framed trio who followed them what to look for, what they had seen. Mjanyelwa did not mind, he loved to walk with his two women on either side of him, both loved by him with a passion transcending all else in the world. He watched the two broad backs before him as they moved resolutely ahead, carrying the family's home upon them. He loved them too but in a far different way than he loved his two girls, for they were men and they could protect themselves and they were courageous and strong. But the women needed him; his devoted wife Esther, his enticingly bright daughter Francina, both needed him. He knew that one day he would have to find a very special man for Francina, the wasp child, for an ordinary man would not be enough. She was too much like her mother, had so much ability, too much spunk for her to be able to accept an ordinary man. Francina's husband would have to be very special indeed. Sometimes Mjanyelwa worried that he might be denying his daughter if they travelled too far from other habitations, for how would she then find her special man? Every now and then with her close cropped hair and her slender athletic body she looked like a boy, but her little breasts were developing a fullness which may even become greater than her mother's. Before leaving on their journey, she had seemed blissfully unaware of the effect she had begun to have on the older boys of the village. As many of the girls of her age were preparing themselves for marriage, selecting and coquettishly enticing their chosen man, she preferred to play with her brothers, to run with them, to hide with them, to talk with them, to hunt with them, to be a part of their world. She had as yet no interest in the shallow world of the young virgins making beads, smiling at boys. She was enjoying her own freedom, taking her own time. Perhaps he had been right to take her away for who was there in that village who could possibly be good enough for his daughter? He had to find a stranger for her, a man she could respect, a man who could manage her. As yet he had not met one, but one day he would, one day he would meet that special man and when he did he could give his Francina away. But for this moment both father and daughter enjoyed their mutual companionship in the bush. It was as if she were undergoing her own Ingoma, the only woman in the world to do so. A time when she was being taught the ways of survival in the bush; which plants to eat, which small animals to snare and how to best prepare them for cooking and which herbs to use. Best of all for Mjanyelwa was the realisation that daily she was developing a genuine interest in the work of the Nyanga. Rarely could he go to seek the ingredients for his preparations without her being at his side. There she would remain until he had completed his work for the day.

The first month was a wonderfully exciting time as they journeyed far beyond the territory known to Mjanyelwa, discovering new herbs, new lands, new birds and animals, new trees, new rivers. New people. However, the new people were rarely friendly, always suspicious, frequently defensive, sometimes openly aggressive. In time Mjanyelwa and his family learned that discretion was the best policy, that it was sensible to avoid settlements and thereby ensure no possibility of conflict. So whenever they detected signs of other human beings in their vicinity, they subtly altered their direction to ensure no meeting would occur. Or sometimes they would conceal themselves deep in the bush as a group of warriors went by. Mjanyelwa's family posed no threat to the people or to their lands or animals, but the people did not know that. Far too many mistakes were being made in those days in Africa, simply due to fear. Mjanyelwa did not want his family to suffer from a mistake.

The family soon determined a rhythm to its journeying. One week of non-stop walking was too much, not only for the women but also for the men. For they had to walk and to carry the belongings of the family; they had to hunt or scavenge for food to fill the bellies of the wandering band; sufficiently nutritious food that would ensure they were all able to proceed in full strength the following day. Their backs ached with the weight of their burdens, their feet were sore and sometimes damaged by the thorns and rocks in the underbrush, their eyes stung from the shadeless perpetual sunshine. So Mjanyelwa devised a pattern to their walking, knowing that his family would have to travel for weeks, perhaps months, before they found the special place that was awaiting them, somewhere in the heart of the country he loved. For six days they walked then for two days they rested. Mjanyelwa had a vague notion that north and west would lead them to the land they sought. Even he did not know why he felt so convinced, perhaps the ancestors had enlightened him in one of his dreams, he could no longer recall; but he was convinced of the route they must follow. He knew he must never go south, for south was the white man and the troubles; he knew he must not go east for east had always been unlucky for the Ndebele people. When the great movements of his people a hundred years before had taken them on pathways with the sun beating on their right shoulders and their chests, always there had been fighting and death and famine. No, his family would keep the sun on their backs and on their right shoulders in the morning and on their left shoulders and chests in the afternoon and there would be safety and they would find the shielded secluded land that awaited them. This Mjanyelwa knew.

So the family maintained a pattern in their walking, in their search for a new and better life than the one they had left behind, in their search for a life without fear.

They arose with the dawn, eating a frugal breakfast. They collected their bundles, faced away from the rising sun and began to trek westwards. When the broiling sun reached its highest point in the cloudless sky, they adjusted their direction by again placing their backs to the sun. Thus north westwards they walked. For six days. Then they rested for two days. Six then two then six again. When the moon became full and round and shone its light like a night-time sun upon the land and they could see all the shapes around them and none were fearful for all were plainly in view, the family sometimes remained for more than two days at that campsite. They lingered until the moon's light diminished, until it became smaller again. Thus, at a particular time every month their stop was longer than two days and at each of these longer stops they wondered whether it would be the final one. They scoured the land immediately in the vicinity, they discussed whether there would be enough water, enough food, plentiful herbs for Mjanyelwa to collect, to continue his work despite the lack of patients, for there was always research to be completed, always new preparations to discover. But they never found that special place; there was always some feature of their monthly campsite that proved elusive, unsuitable. So they journeyed on anew, northwestward in search of their home. They continued to walk for many months. Through the Transvaal they roamed, keeping the sun on their backs whilst also trying to follow the watercourses. They gathered food; Esther cooking vegetables and herbs together with the meat that the boys brought into their temporary campsites. The two young hunters, relishing in their

253

task, brought Impala and Kudu, Puku and Red Lechwe. Esther added fruit from the Motopi tree and dried the roots of the same tree to make a sturdy strengthening porridge. Francina and her father gathered their herbs and soon she became as competent as her father in many of the preparations. The family ate well, there was a plentiful supply of food for them and they grew stronger as they walked and they became more united, but still they could not find the home they sought. They moved from the Transvaal into Eastern Botswana delighting in the plentiful supply of the luscious mangosteen and fruit from the numerous Motsaodi trees. They avoided the settlement of Francistown, walking alongside the riverbank until they came to a beautiful large lake. Game and special health-giving trees were in abundance here and Mjanyelwa began to feel for the first time that perhaps they were reaching the end of their journey. They remained in this camp for one month and he began to make plans for a more permanent stay. But it was not to be. Early one February morning, jealous Kwena clansmen appeared, they wanted no-one to enjoy their lake other than themselves, it was their lake, it had been so from the beginnings of time. Mjanyelwa tried to reason with them. It was a mistake.

It was a cold morning beside the lake and despite the protection of goat and antelope skin coverings, Mjanyelwa and his family were chilled. These were the only possessions they had been allowed to keep. The Kwena men had stripped their camp of every other meagre piece of their property. It was pointless to try to fight nor was it worth losing life over bedrolls and cooking pots, water containers and utensils, weapons and food, or even the many herbal preparations that Mjanyelwa and Francina had made together. That morning, Mjanyelwa's family were stripped of all the possessions they owned in the world, everything save what they were clothed in. The theft was completed swiftly and dispassionately, clinically and menacingly. But at least no one was killed, no one injured. The Kwena men passed swiftly on, advancing to kill the white man that their false political leaders were now so foolishly believing and negotiating with. It was madness. The cry of these men was a cry from the very souls of wicked ancestors. It was a time to kill, not a time to negotiate. To kill well they needed to eat and to have weapons and tents and food and medicines, even if they took items that they knew not when and how to use. So as they travelled to kill the white man they took from anyone weaker than themselves, it was only right, only fair. They were the chosen ones to wreak retribution for all; it was only reasonable that all had to contribute to their crusade. So they took from Mjanyelwa and his family, they took everything.

Then the hardship really began.

For a full ten days Mjanyelwa and his family walked non-stop away from that dreadful place. They had only leaves and grass and roots and berries in their stomachs to sustain them. They walked for two hundred miles with no weapons to kill game, no knife to fashion a weapon, nothing to defend themselves with; hiding from everything that moved in the long grass of the bush, making lengthy detours to avoid contact with people, possessing no containers with which to carry water, no cooking utensils to prepare food. But they kept on walking. On the eleventh day Esther became ill from the impurities in what meagre food she took and from the water they drank and from fatigue and from sadness. She collapsed in front of her husband, immediately before the man who had brought them to this place to die. But she never complained, never looked at him with other than devotion on her sallow face, in her misting eyes. Mjanyelwa picked her up, tried to carry her, but his weakness too was great and so the two fitter young men of the family carried their mother between them, sometimes on their backs, at other times in a chair they made by interlocking their fingers and arms together. They carried her for a further two days. Then Francina also fell ill and they could not carry both their mother and their sister for even their remaining strength was fast ebbing. Both the mother and daughter had the fever and both had the sickness and both became unconscious for times then awoke again to the urgent slapping of their men folk on their yellow faces. Mjanyelwa knew he must replace the potions the Kwena men had stolen, potions with which he could cure both his wife and his daughter. Without them he knew they would die. He would have to leave his family to find the herbs, travelling more swiftly alone, to cover more ground in his frantic search. He spoke to his twin boys; for his wife and daughter were now beyond hearing, beyond understanding and he remembered the old Nyanga dying in his arms and he shuddered. He would not let them die, he knew this time he could save their lives, if only he could collect his preparations in time. He had to go quickly. He spoke to his boys as if they were men and now they were men for they had to protect their mother and their sister; they had to hide them and stand guard over them and gather stout branches as weapons and try to find food, but never were they to leave the women alone. It was a terrible charge to put at the door of two boys not yet through their Ingoma. But Mjanyelwa told them that their trekking through the country had been their Ingoma, that the catching of the game and the evenings in the campsites had been their Ingoma. They began to feel as men should feel, to think as men should think, to act as men should act. Now he really believed he could leave them all and feel certain that the new men would protect his women.

Mjanyelwa hid his family as best he could by the river's edge on the south-eastern extremity of the Okavango swamp. A vast alluvial delta whose river is known as the water that never finds the sea, disappearing as it does into a maze of channels and lagoons; the water eventually evaporating. There he left them and went desperately in search of the healing herbs, the nutritious roots. He had to strip the medicinal bark from the Marula tree, the roots from the Mothono. Then somehow to boil them together to make the first part of his treatment, the relieving porridge that coated the stomach walls in preparation for the strong medicine to follow. Then he must catch the snakes to use their gall and their blood. Together these preparations mixed with special river herbs would save the life of his wife and that of his daughter. Without them they would die. Soon. He found the trees within the first morning of his search, that afternoon he collected water-lily flowers and prickly bamboo-like reeds, he caught three different snakes on the rocks while they slept in the heat of the sun and he opened their bodies with sharp stones and he collected their juices, but he needed one more. He needed the Black Mamba snake, the snake that made its home with the Hammerkop bird, constructing its nest with two compartments, one for itself and its young, one for its protector the snake. The Mamba was thus given a secure home high in the branches of a tree. In return, the Hammerkop and its family were afforded protection from the predators who sought the eggs and small chicks. A symbiotic relationship that had been for all time. But the nests of the Hammerkop were infrequent and always in the highest branches of the trees. At dusk on his first day away from his family, Mjanyelwa spied such a nest, attempted to climb the tree but failed. He tried again but failed. For more than one hour he attempted to climb that tree but there were no low branches and he could not hold his legs tightly enough together on the sun polished bark to gain sufficient purchase upon the trunk to pull himself upwards. He realized his own strength was ebbing fast. He left the tree, despising the darkness of the moonless night, for he could not see into the high branches above him. A Mamba might be waiting there but he could not see him! Unsleeping, impatiently waiting, he cursed the darkness until the very first weak rays of the dawn began to light a darkened sky. Even before any portion of the sun was visible he was again scouring the countryside for the nests. He knew that if he did not find one soon, if he did not kill the snake and take its life-giving juices back to his women, then they would die. He had but hours remaining. The sun reached the heavens and began its descent, still he had not found a snake. In the middle distance he could see light smoke from a fire. He had nothing to lose, maybe someone there might help him, might tell him where such a Hammerkop nest existed. If they were frightened and killed him it was no great loss, for his women would soon be dead. But if they could tell him, if he could return to his family before the dawn broke on yet another day, he might yet save them. Soon he reached the settlement and it was not a settlement of the Kwena people. This was the region of the Tswana clan, a gentle people, a people in many ways not too dissimilar from his own Ndebele people. Hunters and lovers of the land, knowledgeable of the ways of the earth that gave them life, deep reverence for their ancestors, never seeking conflict. He entered the homestead with due respect, calling out well before he came into full view, reassuring them that he

was one man alone, not to be feared, a man seeking only help from friends. The people did not threaten him as he entered their village, they could immediately see that he was no one to be feared, that he seemed to be close to death, so emaciated did he appear to them, to these people who ate well from the river and from the land. Their own Nyanga was one of the first to greet the stranger. He was a man whose face had been beaten by the rain and the sun and the wind. And by other men. A broken face but still a powerful one. Mjanyelwa told the Nyanga what he was searching for and the old man informed him his search was over, for he had the exact preparation Mjanyelwa sought. The old Nyanga went quickly to his tiny hut on the outskirts of the compound and for a moment in his weakened state Mjanyelwa believed he was with Ndimande once more and that the old man and Ndimande were one and the same person and now all would be well. He wanted to lie down on the ground and sleep as he had done when he was a boy and Ndimande would cover him with a blanket and his rough smiling face would be reassuringly there when he awoke.

'Come, we will go to your family,' said the old Nyanga.

'Yes, Ndimande,' answered the weakened man, 'but I must travel quickly to them.' Mjanyelwa knew that Ndimande could no longer run for his legs were old and bent.

'I will travel as swiftly as you.'

And Mjanyelwa looked into the face of Ndimande and saw it was not Ndimande and believed the old Nyanga.

The two Nyangas, thirty years apart, clutching their life-saving secret preparations in their clenched hands ran together through the bush land, racing back to Mjanyelwa's family.

The old Nyanga was as true as his word. He ran as fast as Mjanyelwa, faster even, for Mjanyelwa was weak and tired. The old man forced the pace. And now Mjanyelwa was racing and he no longer felt any tiredness or any pain. He was racing with Ndimande and it was as if they were boys together and they were racing somewhere, but why were they racing and where were they racing? It did not matter for the race was everything and he must not allow Ndimande to win the race! He must try to beat him. And so the two men separated by nothing raced into the night.

It was very quiet at the place where Mjanyelwa had left his family. Emerging from the bush he could see no evidence of them at all. It seemed quiet and deserted. His family had hidden themselves well, his sons protecting the women. Mjanyelwa called, there was no reply. He called again. Silence! Frantically he searched for his family, looked where he had hidden them, but they were no longer there. He could read the signs of a scuffle in the grass close by the hiding place and further away the movement of many feet, running, catching, and then blood in the pathway and he groaned aloud to the ancestors for what they had allowed to happen to his family. He saw his sons' tracks, easily recognizable to him, and then the tracks of four men. Were they the tracks of the Kwena men, had they returned? The old Nyanga attempted to calm him, but Mjanyelwa was beyond calming. The old man followed the tracks, the signs of the fighting. And while Mjanyelwa was beating the bushes in a frantic attempt to locate any member of his family, the old man found the boys. He found their bodies and he found their heads, separated. He turned to beckon to Mjanyelwa, but did not do so. He listened as he cried out the names of his family as he desperately tore into a camel thorn bush, disregarding the thorns that were ripping his flesh, the blood that was covering his fingers. Oh gods, thought the old Nyanga, not the women too!

But they were alive, Mjanyelwa could see their tiny emaciated chests slightly rising and falling with their shallow breathing. Somehow Francina had been given the strength to pull her mother deeper into the protective spikes of the camel thorn bush when the

261

tribesmen came close to discovering them; when she saw what they had done to her brothers and knew they would do the same to her mother and herself if they were discovered. She had remained completely silent. Her poor mother, already unconscious, made no sound. There was no noise at all to betray them where they lay. The boys had seen the tribesmen coming, knew that this day they had to be the men their father expected them to be and had raced to meet the tribesmen with their wooden branches held aloft in their young protective arms, racing quickly away from the secret hiding place of their mother and sister so they would not be discovered. The twins did not suffer long. The tribesmen needed to kill, the bloodlust was upon them. They had to kill someone, anyone. The rough beer they had stolen that morning coursed through their veins, took command of their senses. They had

lost all control of their reason but not of their basic animal urge to kill. This they knew they had to practice, their leaders had told them to practice so that they would be completely fearless and utterly swift, deadly and accurate when they finally met the white man in battle. There were two youths menacing them, two youths not of their tribe, they were ones provided for the practice, it must be so. Swiftly they cut them down, drunken machetes slicing through the air. One head severed instantly, neatly. Perfect! The other requiring three blows for it hung on the shoulders after the first blow and the second missed the neck entirely splitting the skull. They would have to practice more, this kill had not been perfect. They saw no one else to kill, so laughing, slapping backs in appreciation of their good work, they went on their way.

The murders had occurred only two hours before Mjanyelwa returned. The old Nyanga could see it had not been long for the bodies were still fresh and the vultures had not as yet appeared. He went to assist Mjanyelwa with the women, there was nothing more to be done for the boys. The two men knelt together, forcing moisture and the snakes' gall and blood through the barely conscious lips of the young girl and the apparently dying woman. They tried to revive Esther so that she could swallow the medicine, but the two Nyangas failed.

'We must carry them quickly to my village,' said the old Nyanga, 'we can care for them there, we can treat them there. The girl will live but we must work very quickly to have a chance to save your wife.'

'But I must find my sons.'

'I have found your sons,' said the old man in sadness, he closed his eyes and slowly moved his head from side to side. Immediately Mjanyelwa understood.

'Where?'

The old man pointed, 'But we must go now to save your wife, there is nothing you can do for your male children, they have left us to be with the ancestors.'

'I will go and say good-bye,' said Mjanyelwa very quietly, saying it for both himself and his wife, going to say good-bye to the last of his male children, no-one now to continue the work of the Nyanga.

'No! You should not see what there is to be seen, I will go for you to your sons.'

'I will see my sons, I will say good-bye to my sons.'

And the older Nyanga did not try to stop the small quiet man, for he was correct. It was his charge, his responsibility.

Mjanyelwa was away but a short time. He returned with nothing of his boys, nothing save the knowledge that he alone had killed them by taking them from the security of their village. He returned with nothing but total and absolute despair.

'We have no time to take care of them?' He pleaded.

'No.' replied the old man sadly.

But Mjanyelwa could not leave his boys for the animals, for the hateful hyena and the terrible vultures to feast upon. The old Nyanga understood his feelings, did not wish to witness more suffering.

'Your daughter is stronger now. Care for your boys. I will leave now with your wife, you will catch up with me on the trail.'

Saying nothing further he picked up the frail tiny Esther, noting the thankful look in her husband's eyes. He carried her as if she were a new born goat, cradling her in his arms. With a rolling jogging motion, he began the journey back to his village.

Francina stirred as her father gathered branches and dried grass for the fire. Many branches, much wood. But she knew not why he gathered the branches, in her sickness she had forgotten. She dozed again into a kind of unconsciousness. A smell of burning awoke her and it was not a smell of wood burning. She saw her wonderful peace-loving gentle father alone in the hazy middle distance, standing like an old man stands. Standing beside a large fierce all consuming fire. Then she saw the shapes in the depth of the fire and she smelt the roasting. Then she remembered and sobbed and sobbed and sobbed.

In time the man she knew as her father, the man who now looked as a grandfather looked, returned to her side. There were no tears remaining on the face of this gentle man, no tears remaining anywhere within his small frame. His soul had shed them all. Then Francina cried aloud, crying for both of them, crying for her dead brothers, crying for her dying mother, crying to be the only one left alive. Her father picked her easily from the ground, she tried to smile at him but the smile would not come. Gently he placed her across his shoulders, feeling no tiredness of the body, no pain of the flesh. His mind completely weary of life. His conscience destroying him. There was only Francina remaining now, only himself and Francina. He would return to the village, bury his dear wife and then go away to die. There was nothing else to do. His burden, feeling to be no burden, slept fitfully upon his back as he reluctantly went to where he would find the body of his wife.

11

But Esther lived. Mjanyelwa's family became three again, but only three. His trek to find a new life for his family a complete mistake, for he had killed his sons, all of them, all three. In not stopping the first born when he could see what was in his mind, in not being strong enough to force him to remain in the village, cowed again by the Sangoma. He had killed the twins by deserting them but he had to leave them in order to save the women. But he should not initially have placed them in that terrible position. It was he and he alone who had killed his three sons and to live with that knowledge was unbearable. However he had to live, he had to do the best he could be for his two women. He had to protect them, provide for them. He had to do a better job than he had done in the past. And if necessary, he must fight for them. He must form weapons to fight for his remaining family.

The old Nyanga invited Mjanyelwa and his family to remain in the village. They had told him their story, he knew they would never find their perfect land, a land safe and distant from all troubles. There were always some troubles to be faced in life, he told them; you cannot go away and hide from them all, they will always find you. Better to remain here in this small compact peace-loving community. Besides, he said, within a not too long time, the community would have to find another Nyanga for he had but few summers left to him. The small community acutely depended upon the Nyanga for there was no Sangoma; there were insufficient people to merit a Sangoma. Mjanyelwa would be able to practice his profession without restraint and he was needed there. He would be performing a service to the small village if he remained. It did not take long for the old Nyanga to prevail, for Mjanyelwa and his women were tired of travelling, tired even of life. They had need of a permanent home, they also needed people who cared for them and for whom they could care for. So they stayed.

The quiet and calming remoteness of the world's largest inland delta began to weave its spell on the shattered spirit of Mjanyelwa, gradually began to work a healing balm. The Moreni uninhabited wilderness veldt contrasted with the teeming birdlife and animal wildlife of the inner delta. After he had nursed his wife and his daughter back to health, Mjanyelwa went alone for days at a time into the remote peace of the delta, attempting to come to terms with his life and with himself, debating, considering the mistakes he had made and suffering alone because he wanted to suffer alone. He needed to suffer alone, it was not a grief or a responsibility he could share. Sometimes during the time he was away he felt he would go mad, often he did not eat and sometimes forgot even to drink. During his first time alone he returned to the ashes of his boys, and, as he had once done so many years before, he scraped a shallow ditch in the earth with his bare hands, inserted the ashes and collected stones to make a cairn. But the stones were few in that place and they were not round or of good quality so the cairn he made for his boys was not a high cairn. It was a cairn made with love and sadness but it was not a cairn of the same quality as the one he had made for Ndimande and for that he was ashamed.

Most times he borrowed his new friend's mokoro, a dug out canoe made from the Kigelia tree. Using a straight pole of Mogonono wood he pushed the canoe along its silent slow passage through the reeds. By the end of the rainy season in April many of the small low islands he had walked upon some weeks earlier alone and troubled were completely covered by water. Only to be exposed again when the summer drought began to enact its penance from the land. However, he could still slide his friend's mokoro into the mud at the edge of the larger islands of Madinare or Letenetso to sit there all day by the water's edge. And listen. And think. The choking reeds and papyrus afforded welcome cover for him as he watched the strutting African Jacanas, the graceful Kingfishers and Hornbills, the truly magnificent Goliath Heron and his friend the powerfully pretty Fish Eagle.

Beside him, unharmed by his complete still and silent presence ventured the antelope, the Sitatunga, the Red Lechwe and the Reedbuck. He remembered his boys killing these animals and bringing them back to the campsite so that their family would live and have strength to move on. But they had not kept the family alive, these animals. He, Mjanyelwa Mashiane, had seen to that. He would never kill these animals again nor eat of their flesh for he had failed them too. Their deaths had been in vain. He sat silently in his favourite place by the water's edge on the south side of Letenetso Island, quietly observing with some fascination the equally unmoving family of hippos that he had adopted. So peaceful, so certain of themselves, a prey to nothing in all the world. Completely satisfied and unafraid. Always they basked in the same location in the mud at the edge of the largest canal in the delta. Their huge heads resting for comfort upon one another's backs, wholly at peace. Or when requiring cooling as the heat of the day came visiting, they would enter the water until only the tiny black stones of their eyes were visible, and then only to Mjanyelwa, for he knew exactly where to find them. To all others they were a fearful danger if inadvertently disturbed, if either man or animal encroached upon the territory of this normally peaceful family, the lords of the river. Some days when the melancholy was not eating into his soul too badly, Mjanyelwa would begin collecting his herbs once more or he would gather the purple-bottomed leaves and the pink and white blooms of the water lily and roast their delicious root stalks together with the leaves, adding them to mangosteen and Marula which he collected from the ground where he sat. These were the better days and they were becoming more numerous now. He was compartmentalizing his grief, coming to terms with his loss, knowing he should spend more time caring for the remainder of his family, helping them

269

in their grief. But it was a difficult thing for him to do while he still felt the pain himself, the responsibility, the shame.

Sometimes a wandering herd of elephant, upwind of him, would come visiting to drink from the stream and to shake the nuts from the large palm trees close by the water's edge. He watched them in their gentle fury, their trunks wrapped firmly around the trees. Sometimes they shook too hard or sometimes the tree was too old or too young and they uprooted it from the land and then the tree would die. They selfishly protected the tree they had killed, tearing at its succulent leaves, allowing no other animal near until they had completely stripped the bark and the leaves. They protected their own with a noble ferocity. As he should have done. As he, Mjanyelwa, should have done. Best of all Mjanyelwa admired the warthog, for it was the only animal that made him smile on his bleak and desolate days in the delta. The almost blind, always comical callused beast. Vertically tall when disturbed, running swiftly but always at a pristine trot or gallop, like a charging ballerina. Hopeless animals, yet survivors. However hopeless they were, still they survived. He must too.

The tiny Tswana village housed only six family groups, seven now, including Mjanyelwa's decimated family. Mjanyelwa and Esther called the old Nyanga, Elder Brother, for he and his medicine had saved the lives of both Esther and Francina and was thus closer than a friend. Francina called him, Respected Uncle. For a short while, until their own hut was completed, Mjanyelwa's family lived in Elder Brother's compound. Mjanyelwa and Elder Brother shared the same hut while Esther and Francina went to the hut of the wives. Mjanyelwa and Elder Brother talked the talk of men and the talk of herbs, deep into the night. For Mjanyelwa it was as if he was with Ndimande again and the healing of the mind began in that hut. Mjanyelwa was satisfied with this arrangement for he could no longer look at his wife's face or hold her in his arms or touch her passing body without each time feeling he had killed her inside, just as he had killed all her sons. Betrayed her. The guilt drove him further and further away from the woman he loved. But Esther did not feel these things, her emotions were in tighter control than those of her husband. She had been part of the decision, she told him so many times. She knew him to be a good man, one who could never harm another, never wish to give distress to another; she told him so many times. He could not hold himself responsible for the deaths of his children, it was the will of the ancestors; she told him. They wanted these good young men to join them, they could not survive if only the elders of a tribe joined them in their heaven, they needed young people to talk with, to understand, to ensure that they were providing for all of the people in their tribe, not just the old and infirm. Mjanyelwa so wanted to believe his intelligent wife, but the ancestors did not come to him any more and so he could not ask them and thus he could not believe. Not yet. And while he did not believe, Esther lost her man. She lay together with her erstwhile strong small daughter in the hut of the women, two lonely small women sobbing together in the night. Every night.

By the end of April and the beginning of the dry season that would last for many arid months especially on the land away from the reviving waters of the delta, their new hut was completed. The men of the village had assisted Mjanyelwa in constructing the circular wooden frame of sharpened poles angularly driven deep into the earth. The framework of the roof had been added, interlaced branches prepared to accept the thatching of reeds which had been collected and dried in the sun. The women of the village helped Esther and Francina to mix red clay with the dung from their animals, plastering the mixture between the wooden supports, ensuring the hut would be cool in summer and warm in winter. Their new home began to grow. Thatching for the roof was cut into uniform lengths and bound with thong by the women. The men heaved the bundles to each other and fixed them securely onto the prepared latticework of the roof. Esther wanted to paint her new home with the animal and plant dyes of her tribe, for it was the very first new hut she had ever owned. She wanted to decorate her hut in the colourful geometric designs of the Ndebele people, but Mjanyelwa would not allow this.

'We live with the Tswana people now, Esther. We must respect their customs, their ways, our colours may offend them.'

It was uncommon for Mjanyelwa to deny his wife anything she desired, but this time sadly he must. Moreover, he thought, reminders of the village he had forced them all to leave despite the problems they may have faced there, would be too much to bear.

So Esther did not paint the outside of her house, reluctantly agreeing with her husband. But when it was almost completed and when he was away for three nights and two days, searching his soul in the midst of the soulless delta and not finding it, she defied her husband as she had never done before. She had to reassert herself or she too would go mad. Hiding their work from most of their other new friends, Esther and her tenacious daughter mixed their vivid colours and in the light from burning torches placed at intervals inside her new home, they created the most wonderfully bright and decorative patterns filling every inch of the inside walls. Great sweeps of red parallel lines, bright blue and white circles, triangles of yellow and orange and brown, squares of pink and green and purple. It was a miasma of blended colours, a shouting of spirit. A cry to live once more, to be alive again. When Mjanyelwa returned from his aloneness, while the women remained a little distant from him, he entered unknowingly into his new home. He did not emerge for a very long time. They waited, wondering if this small changed man would be so altered that he was even now destroying their work. Or perhaps he would come out shouting at them. For a long time they waited. Then Mjanyelwa emerged from the hut. He looked at his two women who stood holding one another, not advancing, waiting. He paused for a moment, looking at both of them, then he opened his long-yearning arms and beckoned them to him. As the smile they used to know adorned his scarred and beaten beautiful face, the women raced to see who could be first into the arms of the best man in the world. And they were a family again. The true healing had begun. That night, that first night in their new home, Mjanyelwa and Esther held each other closer than ever before, fusing together. Both cried together; they cried and held and sobbed and fused and the emotion was a deeply tangible thing. Francina, behind her curtain on her bed of straw wanted to go to them, knew that they would take her in their loving arms, but she didn't go to them. She gave them the gift of their long moment of private grief and sorrow. There was much they needed to heal between them, she was not required that night. It was too private even for her to join them. No-one that night in the new hut in the Tswana village in the Okavango Delta in Botswana slept for one minute. But in the morning three reconciled smiling, touching and holding and renewed people emerged into the sunshine of the first day of the rest of their lives.

'May we make a trip together, Father? Just for a few days, just to explore?'

Their lives had been placid and caring for many weeks now and Mjanyelwa had not journeyed alone into the bush again. When he went to gather his herbs and make his preparations he was always accompanied by one of his women, most frequently by Francina who loved the gathering and the learning. When she was not with her father she would be sitting at the feet of Respected Uncle and learning from him. Mjanyelwa looked at her and saw himself at the feet of Ndimande and was glad. He had been talking for some days about making a longer trip, a trip of two or three days, to travel father afield, to look a little more at the countryside around them and to see what it may offer him in knowledge and new medicines. Francina felt that this time may be her opportunity. She loved her new village but she was young, she needed to explore, she needed to experience something new. She realised that her father now hated to be alone, hated to be lost within himself. Required company as if it were a drug to keep the innermost reaches of his soul from ever reappearing. It was her opportunity.

'I could gather the herbs with you. I want to learn more. I want to be a Nyanga!'

Mjanyelwa looked at his little girl, no longer little. Soon to become fifteen years of age, only five months away, knowing that she had already passed through her childhood and now had to care for herself monthly, had become a woman. And a beautiful woman, a beautiful virgin. But there was no man in the tiny village for her, none. She didn't seem to care, she wanted to be a Nyanga! She wanted to be a man!

'It is impossible, Francina. Only a man may become a Nyanga. There has never been a female Nyanga.'

'Then I shall be the first one!'

He smiled at her tightly pursed lips, at her flashing eyes, at her petulant boyish stance. Hands on slender hips, small breasts with defiantly erect nipples pointing directly, audaciously, towards him.

'Why not?' He thought to himself. Perhaps she is destined to be both the daughter and the son of our family, 'why not?' but he said nothing to her, he simply smiled.

'If your mother will allow Francina, we will travel together for four days, no more; we will find new herbs, but my daughter, you cannot become a Nyanga.'

She looked at him with the love and knowledge of a daughter who knew when she had successfully made her point, she knew this wonderful small man as he did not sometimes know himself. She would argue no further with him that day. She nodded her head three times, deliberately, challengingly but sweetly, a kindly yet convincing nod from a smiling face. Mjanyelwa turned away, allowing the back of his head to disguise the broad smile on the front of his face.

Father and daughter loaded the Mokoro together, took advice from the old Nyanga of the safest route to travel, a route that would be sure to keep them away from people but close to the best herbal hunting grounds. North eastwards through Moreni for one whole day, then to turn directly northwards to where the Khwai joins the Chobe river, journeying along it for the second day, then to turn around well before the outskirts of the village of Kasane, to be certain not to enter the turmoil of Rhodesia. A four day trip. A four day adventure of father and daughter. A time of controlled, peaceful though still wary travel. A bonding time of two people already so very close. A first time for them both to be alone with each other. But it was to be a bonding beyond family, a bonding in transferred knowledge. A new Nyanga was being created. And they both knew it.

12

He didn't know who he was or where he was, but he knew he was in a dangerous place. It was pitch black and he was standing in water that lapped against his naked stomach. His head throbbed with an excruciating pain. He reached up to touch it, to hold it and his hand met a copious sticky mass that he knew was not water. His other hand held the hoof of an animal. Only the hoof. His entire body was soaking wet. He began to shiver in the cold of the night. He began to remember. He had been in the water, dragged along by something, holding on to an animal. It was important that he hold on to the animal. Then he was released, but he couldn't remember how. He waded to the river's bank, pulled himself ashore still grasping the hoof and lay down to rest. Totally exhausted. With strenuous efforts he pulled dry branches and leaves over his shaking body and immediately fell asleep, only awakening as the warmth of the sun began to steam the mud beside him and the morning calls of the birds assailed his ears. He was thirsty but knew he should not drink water from the river. How did he know that? He reached again to his head where the blood was now deeply encrusted and in which the intense pain had become a dulling thud of constant ache. He knew he should clean the wound to avoid infection. How did he know that? But the only water available to clean the wound was the river water and that he knew he must not use.

Where the hell was he? It was so hot and still only early morning, he could tell this from the position of the sun. Then with a desperate and creeping dismay he realized he had nothing at all in his life except his damp shorts and the hoof of a small animal. Nothing.

He did not even know his name.

He looked at himself, explored his body as if for the first time. It was a strong body, a young body. It had many scratches on the chest, deeper lacerations on the arms and two fingers that wouldn't move on the left hand. But they didn't give him any pain, not unless he struck them against some hard object. All the cuts had stopped bleeding, but they too required cleaning for the dust and mud of his night's sleeping had entered them. Then he realised the absurdity of not using the water in the river. It was where he had been, where he had come from. All his cuts had been penetrated many times by its water. God knows how much of it he had already drunk. Who was God? The sun was warm on his back as he reentered the water, submerging his head time and again as he painstakingly separated the blood-matted strands of hair on his head. When the sharp pain returned, he knew he had reopened the wound, but at least it was clean now. Dirty water clean. He carefully washed his arms and chest and there was a little pain but it did not compare in intensity with the new pain in his head and so was easier to bear. Despite the agony he was beginning to feel refreshed and capable. He had to protect his head from the sun and the insects. Think, think! He returned to the land and gathered large leaves and reeds. He wove them together into a kind of head dress with leaves at the top and reeds making a length which he could tie under his chin. A reed and leaf bonnet. He re-entered the water and could feel the large wound bleeding once more. So again he washed it and again the pain was intense. He carefully washed his bonnet, ensuring it was as clean as the river water could make it. Then he tied it to his seeping head, firmly and securely. It was the best he could do. The pain began to recede, reassuming its familiar throb. But now he felt tired once more and decided to take a brief rest in the short savanna grass that would also dry his body.

He slept the entire day.

As dusk began to creep its way from the treetops to the grasslands he roused himself, the chill of the evening air beginning to eat into his bones. But he was clean despite retaining his consistent throb and he was very hungry. He realised how much of the day he had wasted unproductively and was angry with himself.

Momentarily a deep fear gripped him. He had no idea who he was, where he was, which way to go. No idea about anything whatsoever and it was frightening and he felt he might go mad if he thought about it too much, better to do something rather than to think. There was only one thing to do and that was not to think about it but to do something practical, something to keep warm, find food to eat. Afterwards he could begin trying to put the pieces together. The task now was survival, whoever he was. In the distance, just in front of the dwindling horizon he saw a herd of elephants sedately crossing the river to a small island where they would be spending the night. And so he knew that he must be in either India or Africa for where else are there any free-roaming elephants? How did he know all that? But he did. He looked around him, having no idea at all which was the best direction to walk, but decided to remain close by the river, at least there he would have water to drink. But as dusk became night and again an absolute darkness pervaded, unrelieved by moonlight, he worried about walking alone and aimlessly in the night. What would he stumble across, what would find him? Men do not walk carelessly in the night in Africa. He had convinced himself he was indeed in Africa. He had always wanted to be in Africa, he knew that. How did he know that? So it must be Africa. Animals hunt at night in Africa. He would be safer if he were hidden, he could go one more night without food, he would find food in the morning. He would be safer too if he made a fire, but he had nothing to start the fire with. Two sticks, friction? Then very dry, very wispy grass, then twigs, then wood. Again knowledge, from somewhere. He would be all right for if he could remember these small things then soon he would surely remember everything. He would be alright! And this thought gave him cheer and his terror receded and his practical ability automatically began to take ascendancy. He squatted with two sticks, a small pile of dry grass, twigs and larger branches at his feet, all was prepared. He vigorously rubbed one stick against the other until his hands hurt, especially the two fingers on his left hand, but nothing! Perhaps it had to be a special wood, perhaps there must be no bark upon the wood. So he selected two new pieces of dead wood, stripped the bark from the wood, checked that the wood was dry and then began again. For ten more minutes he rubbed the two sticks together. At one point he thought he saw a little wisp of smoke but it could have been his imagination for the darkness consumed all. Hopefully he held the dried grass to the sticks and furiously tried again, and again. Nothing! He threw the sticks away in disgust. In a fatigued and hungry state, knowing he must not venture abroad into the dangers of the night, he lay in temporary defeat on the grassy floor, covering himself with old brown palm leaves and branches as he had done the previous night and tried to sleep.

But sleep did not come easily to the man that night. He was cold and shivering and although his eyes were closed he could see the huge flat head and the razor saw teeth of a monster. He was holding on to an animal and the animal was only half an animal, he could only see the bottom half of the animal, but still he held on, grabbing the leg, holding desperately on to the hoof. Then drowning in the water and knowing he was dead, being dragged ever deeper, down, down. Drinking the water and drowning and dead. Then the saw teeth abruptly snapped the bone cleanly through and suddenly he was released, leaving him with only the hoof and at last he could escape and he rose surprisingly quickly to the surface. Then foolishly realized he could actually stand up in the water and it was only as deep as his shoulders. He looked around him and there were no flat heads and no half animals and he was alive!

But as he waded into even shallower water he looked down at his body and there was blood everywhere, it was streaming down his forehead and seeping from his chest and his arms and he was a bleeding corpse so he thought he should really die and decided to let his body slip back into the water and die. But each time he went into the water the absurd water spat him out again and he knew he couldn't drown if he could stand and if he held the top of his head it seemed that the blood flow was not quite as great and anyway he wanted to live and what was the nonsense of remaining in the water and he should stop floating and walk to the shore. So he did. But he still held the hoof in his hand, he would not let that hoof go, ever. Then a woman came to him as he lay under the leaves and the branches. She had large breasts and no face and she came to hold him. And the breasts were of no colour but they were large and reassuring and just as he reached out to hold them a huge foul smelling mouth came out of the breasts and grabbed his hands and snapped them off at the wrist and he had no hands, just arms, but they did not bleed, they were simply gone, and so too were the breasts and so too was his mind. But the mouth remained and it had his hands inside it and yet it was already full with the feet of countless animals and then the mouth came towards him again and this time it was claiming his bleeding head and he screamed. He screamed himself awake. Shivering with distress and cold. He could sleep no more that night.

With the morning's sunshine came new hope and for a time his spirits lifted. He loved the dawn, he loved Africa. He walked alongside the river, going with its flow, the morning sun warming his back, meandering southwards with his friend and saviour the river. His head did not feel so bad today, but he did not try to remove the bonnet, he knew that to do so would probably start the bleeding once again. He wondered at the difficulty of removing the leaves and reed bonnet that was now also encrusted with the dried blood, and he knew it would be a problem. But he did not want to face the problem at that moment. He wanted food. He saw a number of small game antelope, he knew each variety of them. How did he know that? He knew that the golden brown Sitatunga live almost permanently in and around the water, that they are related to the Bushbuck and the Kudu and have splayed hooves allowing them to move easily in the mud. He recognised the striped horned Red Lechwe wading in the shallows seeking the nutritious aquatic plants to feast upon. He knew the Impala with their dainty black ankle straps and the black lines on their rump and tail, and he recognised the red coloured desperately shy Puku grazing anxiously beside the river, too nervous to enjoy their food. He knew them all, every one, but still he did not know how. It would come back, this is a beginning, it will come back. The animals convinced him he was in Africa but he did not believe he was an African for he knew they were black and his scratched body was white. But who was he?

The pain of hunger and the desire for food transcended all other body and head pains of the walking man. The sun beat mercilessly upon him and so, like an animal of the bush, he rested in the shade of the large trees by the water's edge. And like the animals he knew that he must find food by the dawn of the next day if he was to have a chance of survival. But how could he compete with the animals of the veldt and the bush? He could not run as fast, he could not kill with his nails and his teeth. What could he do? Could he make a spear and throw it accurately enough to kill a moving animal? He doubted it. Indeed, how to achieve the correct balance, how to throw it? Fish in the river! How to catch them? He had absolutely nothing except his shorts and the animal's hoof that he had strung around his neck with plaited grass, his talisman. Could he eat the foot, was there any flesh remaining on it? He brought it to his mouth but it was covered in dust and there was nothing except the hoof yet he sucked it, searching for nutrition, but it was dead and hard and had nothing to offer him. Even if he managed to catch an animal or a fish how could he cook the meat without a fire? He could eat fish raw, so they would be his best plan. About one hundred yards away from where he stood he could see a Buffalo Thorn tree, so he went and tore a sturdy branch from its trunk, a branch which tapered to a thin yet still strong end. He removed his talisman from his neck and tied the plaited grass rope to the thicker end of the branch. Then, close by the water's edge he dug his fingers into thick black mud finding beetles and eventually the small grey grubs he was searching for. He pinned six of them onto separate barbs of the branch, ensuring that their wriggling bodies held securely on the makeshift hooks. Then he cast the branch into the river, watching it play just below the surface, watching the wriggling grubs offering their dying bodies to the succulent fish. He saw an immediate flurry, pulled on the rope that was his line and rescued the branch from the boiling water.

He jerked and pulled wondering how many fish he had captured. The branch emerged dripping from the water, naked barbs laughing at him. But the system worked! He had simply to pull at the precise moment a fish took the bait and then he would have it and then he would eat. The hunger pains were heavy now and he knew he was beginning to become light headed. But he baited his hooks once again and with great optimism cast his line into the water. Again an immediate boiling, again he jerked, faster this time and again his branch emerged from the water, dripping and naked.

For over three hours he baited the thorns, he threw the branch and line into the water, he jerked and pulled but not one fish did he catch. They defeated him, they laughed at him, and he swore at the fish and he cursed at the fish and he heard his voice for the very first time as it shouted at the fucking, damn fish! It was a strange voice and low and rough. Then the voice began to speak constantly as if it had suddenly found a life of its own and it was talking to the branch and to the river and to the fucking damn fish and then apologising to the family of grubs that he had so decimated. The voice tried to explain to them that it was necessary and that it was the law of nature but the grubs did not believe him and so he became angry with them also and careless of how many of them he killed. He frequently tore the skin from his fingers as he inserted the bloody stupid grubs that couldn't catch the fucking damn fish and then the breasts came back again and this time there was a lot of hair and it was flying in the wind and then there was laughter and the breasts and the hair and the laughter and the grubs all came together and then all fell apart.

When he regained consciousness the branch and the plaited grass had gone but the hoof still lay beside him. He quickly and with increasing expertise made another plaited grass rope and replaced the hoof around his neck and told it that it would remain there forever and apologized that he had removed it and hoped it was not angry with him. He offered it water to drink from the river and it spilled the water on his chest for it was not a very good drinker but that was OK and he loved that hoof and so they drank some more water together. He began to eat the dark green grass that grew beside the river and it tasted very succulent and he liked the dark green grass. Then he tried crushing the newer palm leaves and gnawing them and they were not too bad either. He frightened a group of baboons who were feeding on the husks of nuts fallen from the palm trees and he went and sucked the nuts where the baboons had sucked and he thanked them for leaving him some flesh. But they were ignorant and went away without replying when he thanked them, so he felt quite justified in eating these impolite animals' food. He would have shared it with them, but they had decided to leave; their loss. On the fifth day in his rambling wanderings, weak from the loss of blood, ill from the water of the river, alternately eating grass and leaves and filthy nuts and finally the grubs he had attempted to lure the fish with, then vomiting the mixture up again until his body was racked with pain, he came across the Moshu tree. He saw its green seeds and they reminded him of green rice and he knew that rice was good so he took a handful of the seeds and began to chew them. He drank the water from the river as he chewed and it was delicious and he did not vomit the mixture from his body. It remained in his stomach to begin its work. Within two hours the poisonous prussic acid in the seeds began to invade his weakened system, preventing oxygen absorption by his body cells, making its ponderous but dangerously insidious journey to the brain. His breathing became laboured, his limbs began to tremble. He collapsed beside the water's edge. Slowly but inexorably paralysis struck his lower body then reached to his arms. The sun beat overhead and the bareheaded broad-winged, heavy-billed Lappet-Faced vultures flew to the surrounding flat-topped trees above where he lay. Patiently waiting. They would not have to wait very long.

13

They saw the vultures from their mokoro, waiting like salivating dogs to sweep down upon their kill. Francina and her father could not yet see the kill, but they knew it must be close by the water's edge for that was where the trees were that held the waiting vultures and they surely would never be far from the feast to come. They were not circling so the time of their meal was fast approaching. There was no need for them to be circumspect, their prey was unmoving, unseeing. Within moments they would swoop. Their heads constantly moved round, eyes scouring the surrounding veldt, searching for predators who might still, in these final moments, rob them of their legitimate feast; but as yet they saw none. They did see the canoe but knew that man was not a rival for their food. Moreover, they were content to see the people and the canoe for it would have the affect of keeping competitive predators away for they would not visit whilst man was in the area. The two humans were also content to slide past the kill, unhindering the law of nature, but they were curious to see what it might be, what small medicines it may yet have within it to surrender to the Nyanga and his apprentice.

They were now in their second day and must turn their mokoro before dusk to begin their homeward journey. Southwards again to the Okavango Delta where Esther and the new family to which they now belonged, awaited them. They had successfully collected many of the herbs they would require in the coming months and marked the places to halt on their return journey to gather others. The land around this bounteous river was rich in its stock of herbs and plants they required to make medicines for themselves and their new family. Francina saw her father positively coming alive once more as together they searched for the health giving roots and bark and flowers and leaves. They talked with affection of her lost brothers for now they could talk of them without tears and desperate pain. Best of all she was learning so much from her father, loving the learning. Mjanyelwa in his turn delighted in teaching his intelligent wasp child daughter, the special one and it was no longer important that she was a woman. Perhaps she was right, perhaps she would become the first female Nyanga of the Ndebele nation, for although they now lived with the Tswana people and perhaps would always do so, they were still Ndebele and would always remain Ndebele.

They were gliding slowly and contentedly under the trees on which the awful vultures perched when Francina saw the man. He seemed to be dead. No movement at all, head at an awkward angle to the body. She pointed silently and then her father saw the man too, saw the white man. Mjanyelwa assumed he had been caught and killed by terrorists from Rhodesia, but then if so, why was his head still attached to his body? Nevertheless, it was time to turn around, the freedom fighters were obviously closer than he believed, there was no point in tempting fate yet again. But the healer within him could not simply turn and retrace their path without checking the corpse. His daughter's generosity of spirit combined with his, willed them both shoreward. With a complete mutual understanding and no requirement for words, they maneuvered the narrow mokoro to the bank of the river, pressing its bow into the mud at the water's edge. Slowly and together they walked to the man. They had heard of the booby-trap mines that were sometimes attached to dead bodies, but they did not know what a booby-trap mine was or where to look for it. They did not speak. For long moments they looked down at him, the vultures now circling and annoyed; were they to be denied? The two Nyangas could see he had the face of a young man although his hair was completely white. They could see the deep red wound in the centre of his skull, but it was not a wound of blood, it was a long moving gash of red ants from the trees. Feasting. Some were moving down his face from the skull and entering his open mouth and nose, seeking moisture and food there. They hung like blood droplets from a bleeding nose. The man was almost entirely naked. There was a ragged cloth which had become little more than a belt around his thin waist, a limp penis showing below it. Despite its covering of ants, young Francina was blatantly fascinated to observe that it was somehow very different from her father's penis and the male penises she had seen in her village. It was like a child's penis, but much larger, with a small sack on the end of it. And she wondered why this man had not yet become a man. His chest was little more than bone, the ribs well defined, little meat remaining upon them. Around his neck there hung the hoof of a young Impala, seeping black flies. At one time this man had possessed strong arms and legs, the definition was there but the muscle sadly wasted. As she looked at him she saw his eyes blink once, just once. She stepped back as if she had been physically struck then immediately she wondered if she had seen it at all, whether it was simply imagination, for the man seemed dead. But Mjanyelwa had seen it too and believed and the great little Nyanga bent to his task.

He opened the man's mouth, inserted his nose and smelled deeply into the man's body. Immediately he smelt the poison, knew instantly from where the poison originated and knew that it almost always proved fatal. He dug his fingers underneath the man's tongue, moved them around his teeth and brought out the confirmation, tiny pieces of the deadly Moshu seeds. There had been no terrorists, the man had eaten of the seeds that kill. He must be a very strong man, thought Mjanyelwa, not to already be dead. If he was not dead then it meant he was still alive, and to the healer that was all the impetus he required. Not dead meant he could at least try to save the man. For he knew that in the herbs he and Francina had collected there were antidotes he could use in his attempt to save the white man. But the man was unconscious and it would be difficult to ensure he swallowed all the medicine Mjanyelwa would have to prepare. The medicine which could unfreeze the body and restore life. The only way would be to cut him and insert the thin paste directly into his blood so it could quickly be carried to the brain and heart and begin its work. It was the only way. He had never attempted this operation before. He had mixed the paste twice in the past but his patients had both been able to chew it and besides they had eaten only one or two of the seeds; this man had consumed so very many that chances of recovery were in any event extremely slim. He took the herbs and roots, selected the correct mixture to mould into the antidote paste. He then heated it on the fire that Francina had prepared until the mixture bubbled blackly. Then he took the knife which had been a present from the old Tswana Nyanga; the knife that could easily slice elephant hide and with it he firmly cut into the man's wrist where the blue coloured river rose in its channel above the skin. As the blood began to freely run he took the scalding hot poultice paste and worked it into the river of blood, dismissing the pain to his own fingers as he worked. The body twitched as he first slapped on the paste and a low deep moan of the dying came from the man's mouth. But it was not a moan of the dead, not yet. The blood flow had been cauterized by the poultice whose contents should now be on their journey to the heart and the brain. But the man required still more. Mjanyelwa added water from the river to the heated paste and boiled them together until the paste became liquid. He allowed the mixture to cool to below boiling point then began to force it between the man's lips. At first the liquid fell down the white man's chin, but with the help of his apprentice, Mjanyelwa forced the man's head as far back as he could, easily raising the emaciated chest above the ground on which he lay. Mjanyelwa held the man's mouth open, his hand forcing the tongue to the floor of the mouth while Francina pored the liquid slowly over his hand and down into the man's stomach, working her hands upon his chest and belly to assist the passage of the liquid. Then they began to massage the man. They worked together on every muscle of his body, willing the medicine to find its way there, preparing the muscle to receive it. They took turns to blow some of the air from their own healthy bodies into that of the inert man, filling him with the unsullied air of life. Then they prepared a fresh supply of the mixture and they cut his other arm and stemmed the blood with a second hot poultice containing their antidote and they forced him to drink the residue once more. Into the dusk and into the night the two small black Nyanga's worked on the tall thin white man. Then as the intense blackness fell, Mjanyelwa knew they could do no more. He covered the white man with blankets and took his exhausted daughter a little distance away.

'He will stand when the sun's first light comes to the land, or he will be dead. There is nothing more we can do for him Francina. You must sleep now.'

The apprentice Nyanga looked at her father. She could not remember ever being so tired before. Her body ached with the exertion and the emotion consumed whilst treating the white man. But she could not sleep. He might need her in the night. She wanted to see him when he awoke, be with him. He must wake! He must live! Proprietarily, Francina remained awake the entire night, watching her first patient, willing him back to

293

life, fighting off the sleep until it finally claimed her just a few minutes before dawn.

As she slept the peace of the just, her patient's dreams were no longer of flat heads and lost hands and half animals. They were peaceful dreams of floating and music and white clouds and lovely large enveloping breasts. There were coloured beads and sandals floating in the air and a woman all in white and laughter. A woman he always saw only from the back or the side and never saw her face. But now he knew the breasts belonged to that woman because sometimes she was in the dress and sometimes she was only halfway in the dress and so the breasts were there to welcome him home. So the breasts were home and the woman was home and he was home and floating and he tried not to float because it was eerie floating above the earth and then he was on the earth and couldn't coordinate his movements but he wasn't floating any longer for he was awake.

He could see an old black face with a small black beard looking down at him. He could not get up to greet him but he felt no fear, simply extreme lightness. Then he saw a young face beside the old face and the young face was all eyes. The biggest blackest eyes in the entire world. Then he realised that the eyes had a black face too and that the face was a lovely face, the blackest face in the world, black like a night without stars or moon. Then he saw the light behind those big black eyes, but it was not truly a light, it was a kind of light but not a light and he did not know what it was but he did not care what it was because it was peaceful and warm and it was home. Then the teeth in the lovely head flashed with a smile and they were kind teeth, flat teeth, white teeth. Eyes and teeth with a big strong light somewhere behind them in the head that looked down on him with love. The head was not so big so the light must be very intense to be held in such a small head and to shine so brightly and he was at peace and perhaps this was the woman with the breasts. But they were black and in his dream the large full breasts had been white. At least, he thought they had been white. Then he began to float again and the eyes floated with him. Every time he opened his eyes he saw the same face and the huge eyes and the light. Young and black and white and with red gums and the light. Sometimes it was moving and the clouds were moving above it and the water was flowing, and sometimes it was standing alone and there was a blackness behind the blackness. Then there was blue and he panicked because the black light was gone, then it would return and all would be well once more. Then there were many black faces but only one had the inner light and when that one was not with him he knew he would die and he tried to move and he panicked because he could not move and because he was dying and his body was wet and dry and wet again. And he knew he would go mad without the light. Then the eyes with the inner light returned and he made it promise never to go away again and he became calm and he knew he was alive again.

For three entire months Mjanyelwa and Francina nursed the white man. He did not stand that first day as Mjanyelwa had promised. He did not walk for many weeks, the poison and his injuries had ravaged so much of his inner and outer body. But he was recovering and he would walk again. However, Mjanyelwa could read the signs, he could see that the poison had irrevocably destroyed some of the brain of the man, for much of his mind was missing. He did not know who or where he was. A man without a history, without a family or friends. The old Nyanga advised Mjanyelwa to send the white man away as soon as he was able to walk again but Mjanyelwa had seen too much death in his lifetime, he did not want to be responsible for more. He had seen too many young men being prematurely taken by the ancestors who no longer spoke to him, and it made him wonder whether they were truly honourable ancestors. Colour of skin did not matter to Mjanyelwa the Nyanga. Here was a young man, even with his white hair he was young, just slightly older than his own first-born would have been. If he could save him, if he could stop him going to his ancestors before his time, he would do so. He and his young apprentice Nyanga would do so.

After one month they knew they would be successful, they knew the man would live. He was their responsibility and he was their substitute for the sons and the brothers they had lost. He belonged to them, them to him. Frequently Francina wished her father would leave her alone with the white man so she could bathe him whilst he slept and then she would be able to discover the real secret difference between him and the Ndebele men. For there was a difference, but why and what was it for? Why was he still a little boy down there, why didn't it develop in the same way as those of the men of her tribe developed, growing out of the holding skin? Was it only black men that grew like that?

The curiosity of an almost fifteen year old was fully aroused; she had to know the answer.

Then the day came when her father had to travel for the entire day, away from the village with the old Nyanga to replenish some special herbs, which were to be found only at a place a half day's march away. So she was left alone with her white man. She watched her father leave the village, waited a while. Looked down at the sleeping man, made certain that the medicine she gave him would make him sleep peacefully for many hours. She lifted the coverings and she looked. But looking was not enough, it told her nothing at all. Carefully she went to the thick curtains covering the doorway to the hut, closed them, but then realized there was insufficient light to see what she needed to see. She reopened the curtains slightly. Besides, it would have been unnatural for the door to be closed during the day and some one might come to discover whether there was a new problem with the white man. Better to be slightly open, not creating interest, no one able to see within, yet sufficient light for her examination. She stood for a moment in the doorway marking where the women of the village stood or squatted, counting heads to ensure she had accounted for them all. She did not bother with the men for she knew that among the men only the two Nyangas ever visited the white man.

She went back to her position beside her patient, taking a wet cloth to attend to him. She rubbed soap into the cloth so that if by chance any of the women did approach the door they would see her bathing the invalid. She began to rub the cloth gently between the legs of the white man. As she washed him she watched

297

with fascination as he began to grow. He was not like a small boy any more. The man slept on. She watched, enthralled, unafraid. So weak in all of his body except there; so strong there, how could it be? As it grew and grew Francina dried it carefully, gently, moving the cloth slowly along its length. Caressingly. Not touching him save through the cloth and still it grew. Tall and strong and firm and then suddenly the skin at the top erupted back by itself and she dropped the cloth in awe and then she touched the man and held the very hard skin and pulled it a little more to assist it and it came back still further. Now it began to resemble the ones she had seen before, though all those had been resting, not grown like this. Now it was similar for it no longer had its protective pouch that had disappeared like those of the men of the village disappeared as they became older. Perhaps that happens with the white man, perhaps his pouch only goes away when he becomes firm, not as he becomes older. She had discovered the difference between the black and the white man! She realised she was still holding the pulsating rod, and she held it without fear. It was big and pink and deep red at the top and like the stem of a beautiful large flower. She felt the entire length, moving her hand from the top to the base, then the base to the top and back again and it felt pleasant to touch all of it, so long and firm and strong. Then she squeezed it tightly to feel all the power within, to feel the secret of the white man. As she squeezed the full power came and it jerked and pushed all by itself and suddenly, like a small hippo pushing water joyously from its mouth as it bellowed its joy in the river, a milky fluid flew from the rod and immediately he

298

cried out, his eyes opened wide and he looked directly into Francina's face. She dropped the hard hard flesh, staring into the deep brown eyes of the white man in an absolute paroxysm of fear and panic and fled in terror from the hut. Immediately outside she stopped. It would not do to run from the hut, the other women would see, they might even now have heard the groan made by the white man and be coming to investigate and they would see what she had seen and they would see the milk and they would know. What had she done? What had she taken from the man? Would the loss of that strength now mean that after all their hard and dedicated work, he would die? Was all the medicine her father had given to the man now spread over his legs and stomach? Oh gods, what should she do? She had to return to the white man, she had to clean him, care for him, so no-one would know, so he would live again. She must go back into the hut!

The man was asleep again as she reentered the hut. Peaceful, his face unlined, his lips placid, gentle, as if smiling. His entire body relaxed and calm and breathing normally, and somehow he seemed stronger, more of a man. There was no fever and no sickness apparent in him. Carefully and lightly she cleaned his sleeping body, ensuring the most minimal touching possible of his sleeping stick in case she brought it back to life again. She softly wiped it where it lay. Then she sat demurely and lovingly beside him. She had not killed him. Indeed, had she given him new strength in some unknown way? As she looked at him and as she remembered in every absolutely vivid detail what she had done to him she realized she too needed the cloth.

She wiped the heavy musky moisture from between her legs, unsure of what it meant but as she dried herself she knew she enjoyed the feeling and was not ashamed. But she knew she must ensure she alone washed that cloth, the cloth with both of them on it.

Francina gazed at the white man for the remainder of that day. Then the next and the one following. She helped to clean him but never down there again. She fed him and she gave him medicine, but somehow it was different now. And he was no longer a white man, he was whatever colour she wanted him to be. Into the nights and sometimes alone, she sat beside the man she had saved. Her man.

14

After three months he became sufficiently strong enough to join the few men of the village in their simple daily tasks. Communication becoming increasingly easy for he had no memory shackles to cast off, no biases to remove and he had an excellent, intelligent and patient teacher. A teacher with the biggest eyes in the entire world. Like a child he learnt their language and their dialects. Open mindedly willing, possessing no preconceived restrictions, no intellectual restraints. In time he belonged to all of them in that tiny village for his personality charmed them all and his knowledge of the animals and their ways gained him much respect. He helped with every task his strength could manage and in time nothing was too difficult for him to assist with. He learnt to sing their songs and one evening as they sat around the fire in the centre of their small village, he sang a song to them in his white man's language. As he sang, he faltered and moistly, but still as a man, tears appeared in his eyes, ran down his face. Francina wanted to brush them away, to kiss them away, but the magic of the song enforced immobility. He brushed them away himself as the song ended and it was as if he had killed them, killed something. The villagers could not see into the soul of the white man as he attempted to remember where the song had come from and how he knew the song. And how, in this failure of remembrance, he felt so unutterably melancholy. They had seen him cry and they knew that he must be a good man for only the best men can be made to cry by the emotion of a song. Francina went to him and held his hand while he cried and all the village saw her go to him and hold his hand but no-one said anything.

Although he belonged to the entire village, he belonged in Mjanyelwa's family. He was their son, their brother and their friend. Together they helped him to build a hut for himself, for he had no-where to go, knew no-one outside the village. His experiences and the poison had destroyed his memory so totally that everything in his life was within their tiny village. They did not wish him to leave, for the world outside their private secluded village would kill him. Even the old Nyanga agreed that the white man must remain. If visitors ever came to the village then they would hide him, so all would be safe. This they agreed together. Then the villagers brought the white man to them and told him of their decision. They told him that his name would be Nnyaa Leina, in their language meaning 'no name', the man with no name. And then the white man did a very strange thing. He kissed them all; all of them, women and men and children, then abruptly he strode away alone to the river bank, away so that they could not see the tears upon his face. But she knew they would be there.

He squatted beside the water and gazed into its depths, the depths from which he had come and he tried to remember. But nothing came. His life and all of his life was in this tiny village with these gentle kind people. But he wondered about before. Sometimes he heard the laughter and saw the breasts and the woman all dressed in white but she came less frequently now and sometimes she had her own breasts but the face of Francina and sometimes it was only Francina and the woman had to turn and go away. He looked into the depths and saw his long white hair and his long white beard and he wondered who he was. He looked for long, long moments and then he made his decision.

'I am Nnyaa Leina' he told the river quietly in his new language. 'My name is Nnyaa Leina, *Nnyaa Leina*!' he shouted to the trees. He was content and he drove the woman in the white dress from his mind and told her never to return for now he was Nnyaa Leina and he had a family and he had friends. And he had Francina. There could never be any distance between himself and his family; he could never allow there to be any distance.

He collected bark from the Mokabe tree, combined it with bark from the Mophane tree and added leaves from the dark red-brown Mogotlho tree. He gathered black mud from the shallows beside the river and began to make his paste. With his fingers he kneaded the dark brown, almost black paste into his body, layer after layer. He allowed it to set in the heat of the sun, then he went to the river and gently washed the top layer of paste away, until all that was left was the dark brown wood die that clung tenaciously to his skin. He repeated the treatment four times. The task consumed the entire day. As dusk fell he reentered his village, beard trimmed with the knife that had saved his life and been given to him by Mjanyelwa, his entire body shining with a dark brown blackness. The seven family groups came into the central compound and walked around him and no one laughed, not even the children. But many were smiling and all would remember this greatest gift the impoverished white man could give to them. The denial of his skin, the desire to be like them. To be entirely one of them. Mjanyelwa took his hand and led him away from the other families, took him to his own hut and in time honoured tradition said to the new family member. 'Tsena!' - come in. It was not simply an invitation to enter the hut, but an invitation to enter their lives and to remain.

Nnyaa Leina went into the hut and sat cross-legged a little distance from the smoky fire. Saying nothing, asking no-one's permission, the small Francina, the now fifteen-year-old daughter of the house, pulled in her little stomach, pushed out her small rounded breasts whose nipples grew larger in audacity, entered the hut and sat down on the right hand side of Nnyaa Leina. She had made her claim public. Esther and Mjanyelwa dismissed the difficulties, accepted the situation, knowing that their daughter had always needed a very special man. She had found him. No-one knew what life would give or what life would take away. They and their family, above all others, were the proof of that. But what they did know was that happiness and love, even if possessed for only a short time, transcended every other possession or emotion the world could offer. They were happy for their daughter because she was happy.

Francina and Nnyaa Leina were married that year. The ceremony as simple as the one her own parents had completed; simple, loving, caring.

Nnyaa Leina held his new bride to him in the darkness of their new home and she did not know what to do, but she remembered the day she had washed him and he remembered the day she had washed him; the day he had faked sleep for a few erotic moments. Her mother had spoken to her and she felt no fear. There was nothing to fear in Nnyaa Leina, the man who could cry, the man who would paint his body black to be as she was. There was nothing to fear from this man. She made him lie down, she remembered the touching and the stroking and he was big again. But she did not want it to be quickly over as it was before, so when it grew to its greatest length, when the sack jerked back and the huge red snake head proudly rose, she took her hand away. She straddled her small young body over his larger, more muscular frame and she made him lie entirely still. She sat on him and she too was absolutely still and the brief pain of his entry had gone away now but still she sat unmoving upon him. Then he began to feel what she was doing to him and it was with her internal muscles only. Neither of their bodies moving, only the muscles inside her, just as her mother had told her, the special gift some women had to give to their man. It was an exquisite anticipatory feeling of pain or of pleasure, he knew not which. He cared not. It was impossible to accept without moving but she told him he must not do so. She was in absolute control. For although small, she held him down and if he moved at all, even slightly, she would stop and wave a finger sideways at him and not begin again until he lay unmoving once more. It went on and on and he thought he would have to scream with the exquisite torture but she would not allow that either and so he groaned and it was not the groan of the dead or the dying but of the very alive, a groan of incredulity. There never seemed to be an end, a conclusion; for if she felt it close by, she would desist in all movement for long seconds until she felt certain it was safe to proceed. He was ascending and drowning at one and the same time and how did she know to do this for no-one could have taught her? Was it because she was a Nyanga, the first female Nyanga and the ancestors had given her this special power? But he did not really care from whence she had the power, it was enough to be the beneficiary. Then finally, after the longest time in the world, she allowed him relief and when it came it was like the floodwaters breaking through a damn and he threshed with joy and he cried aloud with relief and everyone in the tiny village pretended not to hear.

Nnyaa Leina loved his child woman with an intense passion. He loved this woman who had saved him, brought him back to life, given him so much pleasure, a joy in living, in exploring, in learning the ways of her people and the ways of the trees and the plants and the animals. He was entirely happy and did not think of before. For there was no before, there was only now.

BOOK 4

Homecoming

1979......

1

Kathy awoke to the all-pervading odour of insecticide. It was not a smell she had associated with the Victoria Falls Hotel during her first short sojourn there some fourteen years before. But she had been in love then and there had only been one smell she had recognised, only one smell that had been important. His smell. She lay completely still for a moment, remembering. It could even be the same room. The view was similar, drawing the eyes down the valley and past the sweeping manicured lawns to the black iron boundary gate. Then on beyond, through the constantly suspended spray of the smoke that thunders, to the bridge arching over the mighty Zambezi, the bridge to Zambia. Kathy had no need to rise from her sleepy prone position on her lonely bed that had been designed for two people, now containing only one, in order to gaze from the verandah window at the timeless view. She knew it would be there and she remembered what it contained. And as she lay there, quietly reminiscing, alone in the bed designed for two, the face she had so successfully buried for so long suddenly reappeared with a burning clarity. The tousled black hair, hair thick enough to cling to in the heights of passion, the broad courageous smile and those eyes that reached to the very depths of her soul, eyes that had always caused her to tingle with anticipation. Oh God, those eyes! She blinked rapidly, attempting to clear the moisture which she unsuccessfully pretended was the morning moisture; blinking frantically to chase away that face, the face she had not seen for so many years but still was able to recall in such detailed intensity! And the sight of it, the plain and detailed sight of it, filled her with fear.

She allowed herself another few self-serving reflective moments before moving the hardened businesswoman she had become from the too large bed to the too small bathroom. She removed her long ivory coloured Christian Dior satin nightdress preparatory to stepping into the shower and stood objectively transfixed before the full-length bathroom wall mirror. She stared at her body. What would he think of it now? She wondered. She had attempted to keep it reasonably trim, but long hours behind her desk and countless business lunches had taken their inevitable toll. He had last known a twenty-four year old body, young supple and strong with breasts that required no support, with thighs of straining muscle. As she gazed at herself she accepted the reality. It was indeed the body of an approaching forty-year-old woman with more than muscle at the thighs and with breasts she now had to cup with her hands to stem their natural droop. But still it was a good body with little fat around the middle, a reasonably firm stomach. It was just those damn thick thighs and sagging breasts. What would he think of them now if he could have lived to see them? Would he still have loved her body or would his eyes more constantly become distracted by a woman fifteen or twenty years younger? Would she have kept him? Would he have strayed? He was too much man, too much man for one woman. Hell no! She would have kept him! She was strong too; he would still be hers. For a sensual moment the fingers of each hand rested on each nipple, beginning to describe a deliciously sensitive circle around the aureole. She looked at her reflection in the mirror as her nipples hardened and she thought exclusively of Robert Castle. It was a long moment. A sad reflective sensually long moment. Then the guilt came and she thought of Tom and Bob and their future together and she abruptly stepped into the shower. To wash it all away.

Bob was outside her bedroom door at eight, impatiently knocking, desperate to begin his first day's adventure in Africa. Then, breakfast dispatched with alacrity, he restlessly waited as his long drawn out mother sipped her second long drawn out cup of tea. Whilst sipping, the hotelier within Kathy gathered her surroundings through tutored eyes and senses, then processed them in her capable business brain. Only fourteen years before she had noticed nothing, now she could tell them what was good and what was bad about this hotel. She could advise with absolute authority how to improve their service, reduce costs and increase profits. And she had only been there one half day and one full night. It was instinctive within her. She recognized that major faults lay in the training and motivation of the staff, attitudes requiring improvement. The reflection of their care level displayed by the less than excellent scale of general cleanliness, speed and quality of service. She bet herself that the manager was an older man, a person who had been in the job for many years, for too many years. The hotel fell well below the standards she would have accepted in her own five star hotel. The natural happy smile endemic of most African peoples seemed to have been battered away in many of the staff. Probably by a combination of impersonal, even uncaring management attitudes enhanced by dissatisfied brusque tourists, especially from South Africa. Whatever originally had created the lingering attitude of apathy enveloping the entire hotel was now beginning to attain the extraordinary prominence and negative distinction of a quasi art form. Customers do not return to unhappy hotels. Customers, especially holidaymakers, do not spend money at unhappy hotels. They seek for and will eventually discover happy restaurants and happy bars, returning only to sleep in the hotel. The problem was compounded by the sombre ornamentation and associated lack of cleanliness. All seemed old, shabby, colonial without the possession of the splendour and grace once associated with colonial living. Unwelcome seediness had crept invasively into its solid frame and, once having established a tenacious ownership, become difficult to remove. The hotel required a refit of surroundings and decor and most of all, of mind set. It needed smiling helpful dignified staff in an atmosphere of elegantly understated spotless refinement. Such an investment would reap returns, a probable pay back of capital costs within twenty months assuming that excellent marketing complimented the retraining and refurbishment plan and that occupancy reached and was maintained at seventy or more per cent. Kathy found herself calculating costs and time frames in her head, programme planning as if it were an hotel she had herself acquired or been appointed to manage. She pulled herself up short, looked at her impatient unsmiling son and laughed aloud.

'Busman's holiday!' She said, replacing her empty white cup in its small white saucer. There ought to have been a thin gold stripe in the too frigid virginal design, she thought.

'What?' Asked Bob. 'Busman?'

'Nothing Bob,' she smiled at the boy she adored, and she saw Robert's face looking back at her. Oh, how many times would his father's face return whilst they were in Africa, how many? 'Let's go.' She said, rising, blocking.

She stood with Bob where she had once stood with Robert and realised, arms around each other's shoulders, that he was now almost as tall as his long dead father. And almost as handsome. But there was a delicate seriousness within him, which his father had never possessed. She did not mistake determination for seriousness for in that quality they were just the same, as brothers. But Bob was more serious than his father, more calculating, more prone to consider the alternatives before making his move. Had he inherited that quality from herself, She wondered. He planned before action, did not dive headlong in, was not as impetuous or as foolish as his father had been. She loved them both for what they are and what they had been. But she loved Tom now too and it was only Africa that kept bringing Robert back to her. He was dead, dead,

dead! She couldn't have him any more, she had Tom now. Be satisfied! But she was not in Staffordshire, she was in Africa and there had only ever been one man in Africa. Oh God, had it been a mistake to come back? She had made her commitment to Tom. This dreaming, this hankering after the unattainable must cease, now! Slowly, so as to cause no offence, she physically detached herself from her son, as if in so doing she could also detach herself from his father. She tried not to analyse whether she had succeeded for implicitly she knew the answer. She looked instead at the mighty falls.

'I wonder what that place is called?' Bob asked, pointing across the gorge to the Zambian side where water powered down a cataract seeming to issue forth from the gaping mouth of a small palm fringed island.

'Stairway to Heaven.' She immediately replied, instantly knowing, not having to refer to her guide map. As she spoke she recalled what Robert and she had done on that tiny beautiful island. Christ! That could have been where Bob was conceived! On that very island. She stood stock still.

'Are you all right, mum?' Asked the concerned boy.

'Yes, fine,' she replied, but it was not the truth.

She gazed again at the island, that strip of earth and grass with five swaying palm trees where Bob Castle had been made by two young people so much in love. Tears poured down her face, tears washed by the spray from the endlessly churning cataract. Tears of joy mellowed with years of sadness. And she was glad she had come again to that place.

Bob saw the tears and his maturity registered the smile and the overt sentiment accompanying the tears. He asked nothing. He felt a presence. He felt his father. He knew that she did too. He smiled intensely at this seemingly helpless small crying woman who smiled bravely back at him, depending upon him. He held her tight until all the crying had ceased, until the tough strong mother he knew had returned. Neither had spoken a word to the other through the tears. But both knew his presence had returned, if only for a moment, just to be with them. Just to weld all three bodies one last time back into the one they had once been before.

There was a complete stillness and silence of soul. The water raged around them, colourful wild birds shrilly circled and spray erupted, dispersing in ragged clouds. But within them there remained a complete stillness and an absolute silence of soul.

2

Although visually magnificent, at times enchanting, especially when the powerful afternoon sun created an impressive vividly-hued rainbow as it struck the cascading spray of the timeless waterfalls, Bob was anxious to move on, to move further into the interior. Further towards that site he had been told about but was still unsure he really wanted to see. But knew he could not miss.

They moved from Victoria Falls to the Cresta Lodge at Chobe, there to hire a jeep and driver for two day's safari in the Chobe national park game reserve. To see the animals, - the lions, rhino, elephants, buffalo. To see the birds, - the vultures, eagles, herons and hawks. To see the place where the land and the water of that land and the beasts of that land had claimed his father. As they rose at dawn for their journey into the park their mood was sombre. Today was the day when they would finally be able to say good-bye. They hardly spoke at all to one another, but they touched each other from time to time and once, for a long moment, they held hands. They both needed the comfort, the reassurance.

They mounted the open-topped vehicle and sat in their seats high above the road, a wonderful vantage spot. A togetherness, alone. But, within minutes of entering the park their mood began to change as the reality of Africa assailed them on every side. Breathless, Bob watched as the magic unfolded before his young impressionable eyes. Scenes he had not believed possible. Nothing compared with those he had seen on the cinema and on the television for this was reality and around him were the animals of his dreams. All around him! Kathy too was drawn into the delight of sharing the fantasy with her son, but it was not a fantasy. Again she began to remember and through her son to feel once more what *he* had felt. To relive again. Despite her previous visit it was as if it were all new to her, as if the previous experience had been shuttered out from her mind, the pain consuming all. Now, it was as if it were the first time and she shared the spell with her son. But she was in charge; it was her expedition too! Her rental jeep, her driver, her money. She was the leader of the expedition and she needed to see it first, whatever it was, so that she could assume ownership and point it out to her enthusiastic son. Enthusiasm bordering upon ecstasy, just as it had been with Robert. Every sighting meticulously checked for correct identification of species, every entry neatly logged in a script legible to future generations. Date and time of sighting. Sex, habitat, distinguishing marks noted for future re-identification, current activity of the animal. Everything painstakingly recorded and supported where possible by a photograph taken by the camera that had also visited this park before.

The two people openly revelled in one another's enjoyment of the scenes unfolding before them, at times almost looking away from the latest discovery as if to close the curtain so that they would be able to open it again in order to watch yet another show. Always moving towards the top of the bill act but never reaching it for everything was top of the bill, everything totally entrancing. Their first sighting of a menacing pride of lions chomping through a baby buffalo they had taken at dawn that morning, their first viewing of the graceful flight of the exquisite fish eagle swooping to gather its kill, the stately unhurried progress of two giraffes as they went to seek shelter from the ever rising sun. The frenzied squawking of a small bird they were unable to identify and felt chagrined in their incompetence, until the next delight came along to gather their attention. It was simply the best time they had ever shared together in their lives. They were as happy as mother and son, as very special mother and son, can ever be. And it kept getting better.

Until they came to the riverbank.

Kathy was astonished at how untouched, how unaltered it all seemed to be. This area of her previous visit she now recalled in uncanny detail. She knew exactly where the tree was where they had seen his blood and the marks of him being dragged to the water's edge. She would not have been surprised to see the stains now brown, still lying where she had first viewed them when they had been red. Everything was so precisely as it had been on that day. Almost as if it were a protected shrine. An eerie unacceptance crept within her, insinuating its presence. She could have been here but yesterday, throwing herself and her unborn child into that river, at exactly *that* point *there*! Her mind screamed. She had to remove that presence now! It was Africa and these things happened in Africa for it was the land of superstition and voodoo and she must get the thought out of her mind *now!* The thought of racing down to the water again, one last time, to find him again, one last time. It was magnetic and fearful and strange and frightening and she had to turn away from that river, turn away or die! Then she saw her son's face and he had read the anguish in hers but said nothing, was in total control. And she was glad now that she had been unsuccessful in her suicide bid, for her greatest pride in life would have been denied her. He stood silently beside her and he was strong, as strong as ever his father had been. Had she killed herself, she would have missed him, missed seeing this boy grow, watching him becoming a man. He too would have missed his opportunity in life. It was a compellingly awful thought. She looked at Bob, she looked no more at the river. She did not wish to go down to its water's edge, to see the tree, to see again the marks. Neither spoke as they stepped down from their vehicle, one staring at that special place in pain, the other staring away in anguish.

Bob carried his small rucksack to the bank of the river while Kathy sat at some distance on the fallen branch of a large old Marula tree, out of hearing though never out of sight. That river had taken one of her men, she would not let it take another. Bob unpacked his rucksack, book by book, certificate by certificate, explaining each one to the river, pretending modesty.

Failing. He sat for a long time by the river's side letting it see each page of his collector's album, each word on his certificates, every badge he had gained; first in the cubs, then in the boy scouts. The butterfly he had mounted, the slides he had prepared. He explained everything. Just once, just as he always had everything explained to him. Kathy looked at the broad strong back sitting beside the river and it could have been *him*! He was entirely his father's son now, but he would never know it. At last the young man repacked his rucksack, his cheeks dry again. His ghosts had been exorcised, he had finally said good-bye.

They met by the jeep. They met in silence. In a strength of silence. Now, in their own different ways they had both said good-bye. They were both free to continue their safari. To continue their lives and to accept their new commitments. As they raced away in search of leopard, Bob realised he had not taken a photograph of that place by the river. And he was glad.

The fifth day of their holiday together, for now it was truly a holiday, the pilgrimage over, was to be their first day deep in the stunningly attractive simplicity and solitude of the mutely vibrant Okavango Delta. It was there that their travel advisor had promised the round-eyed Bob the most exciting part of the entire trip. For here mother and son would be camping with their guide in the very depths of the interior of Africa, on low-lying natural islands surrounded by countless tributaries, streams and small lakes where game came to drink at sunset and where thousands of rare birds hunted by day. They arrived on the ill-constructed landing strip at Delta Camp at noon, their one hour flight from Maun completed in a small noisy five-seater Cessna aircraft whose pilot obligingly swooped from the skies to reach closer to heavy herds of elephant, fiercely charging buffaloes and gently swaying giraffe families all making for the best pasture and the next watering hole, all spotted by the South African pilot from his singular vantage point beneath the wispy cirrus clouds. Bob was exhilarated by everything he saw, with all he was able to record in his notebook. Stronger than ever before he felt the pull to complete the work his father had barely begun, to assist in the preservation of these magnificent animals and their natural habitat. Stronger than ever came the conviction that he knew it was the proper decision for his life. He would tell his mother soon, perhaps within a few days whilst they were under canvas together; away from the world, away from the hotel she so wanted him to take from her one day. It would not be enough for him; he had to make her understand. Here was the best place to force that understanding, where she could feel it for herself, could smell it, could touch it. She had to understand. But he must be so very careful, he never wanted to hurt this woman, this woman who pretended to the world a strength that sometimes she did not possess. For he had been the one to see her, the only one to see her in the unguarded moments at home, moments when even she did not realise that his sensitivity was sufficiently honed to be able to collect the information on her face and in her body movements. He would have to be so very careful. He had thought most of it through. He could explain how the hotel management life was so rewarding to many and an occupation to be proud of. This he could readily express to her, but she had to try to understand that the pull of the animals, the enormity of his father's ideas, the need for committed people to do what they could to save the animals, save the land, would be something in and of itself that she could feel pride in when she talked about her son and his work. And that although the magnet of Africa pulled him today he would tell her, one never knew, perhaps one day he could return to the family business and take it from her if that was still her wish. No, he'd better not say that, for it was bullshit and she had promised him she would never give him bullshit as long as he never gave it to her. They had a long discussion about it last year and she had used the word, just like that, and she didn't mind, despite what granddad said, for Bob to also use the word. As long as he knew what it meant and as long as he never gave it to anyone. No, he wouldn't tell her he would return to manage the Arlaston Hydro one day, for that would be bullshit.

They spent their first night in the Delta Camp compound, becoming familiar with the people and the procedures. Not a camp in the way that Bob understood the word, for it was a collection of well-constructed rush and wooden-poled huts with pull down palm-matted windows and doors to discourage the marauding local baboons from taking a fancy to the personal items belonging to the human inhabitants of the huts. Larger animals infrequently visited the camp for it was surrounded by lights and there was always a fiercely bright fire burning in the centre of the compound. As sunset bathed its reflective orange torso in the shallow water lapping at the shoreline one hundred yards from the newly lit log campfire, Kathy sat reflectively, watching a family of four elephants. Trunks holding tails as they would in a circus, they passed by on the horizon. In the foreground the water, on her shortened horizon the elephants framed in the huge orange ball of the setting sun, all reflected upwards again from the still gentleness of the water. In her hand Kathy nursed an effervescing glass of first class South African Champagne, at her side sat her peaceful, quiet, smart fourteen-year-old son, he too being allowed the champagne. She looked at him and it was so easy to guess what he was thinking. He didn't have to tell her, she had known for a long time, she had known for ever. They sat in silence and they both loved everything around them, everything they saw and felt. But she knew that if she did not hold herself fiercely in check, if she did not bite down upon her lower lip, if she looked again at his handsome profile silhouetted in the African dusk, then tears would come. Tears expressing emotions derived from the awareness of nature's perfection and from the loveliness of memories. When words are no longer adequate for they had not yet invented words expressive enough to illustrate those very special emotions that come but once in a life, and then only to the favoured few. Kathy knew that she had never before felt the desire to cry at beauty. Had never before been moved to tears by perfection. Nor was she in any way ashamed of the tears that could so easily come. Bob might misinterpret, so, although wishing to cry, she held herself in complete check. Perhaps in so doing she was also ensuring that she too did not misinterpret her own tears. Dusk fell, the elephants sedately passed by, the sun already visiting another continent, the new moon barely displaying itself. An apology for a moon. Yet she was reminded of Peter Pan and his flying and the stars and the simple sweet story and it seemed to her that she had become the Wendy that Peter had brought to this place and that he would suddenly present himself to her. Collect her in his powerful and fearless arms and together they would fly to the moon and to the stars and she would again know happiness and love and romance and excitement and..... then she remembered she was forty years old and she thought of Tom. Never a Peter Pan. She thought of home and commitment and her floating flying mind picture sharded into a thousand tiny irretrievable impotent pieces.

'Beautiful' was all she quietly breathed to her son, it was not enough, but it was all she permitted herself to say. He did not reply, he nodded but he did not reply. He also knew that 'beautiful' was not enough.

In the morning and as soon as there was sufficient light to enable them to enjoy the sights developing around them, they took two mokoros on their gentle journey along the narrow Boro river. The first mokoro was loaded with their camping equipment and moved more quickly ahead to the prearranged campsite on the north western tip of Chief's island. Its owner, contracted from one of the small local villages, propelling his craft with an instinctive expertise possessed by all the people of this peaceful place, where vehicles and engines were banned. He would erect their tents and prepare the site for their arrival, ensuring safety from foraging animals and disturbing snakes, both seen and unseen. In their mokoro their guide was a newly baptised Christian and his name was Paul. He smoothly moved them along the river singing quietly in a low melodious baritone. As they travelled along water pathways barely distinguishable to the two English visitors, Paul identified the birds and animals they passed so closely and quietly by. Save for their scent, the scent of man, they would not even have disturbed them, gliding silently by, offering no threat. Frequently the English couple could not see the tiny birds Paul was able to distinguish from their surrounding camouflage, but for his sake they pretended more often than not, to have seen them. By noon and before the searing heat of the day could encompass them and dissolve their will to continue on their journey, they reached the campsite. Paul had timed it perfectly, as they knew he must have done so many times before. Their tents were already erected. One for Kathy, the second for Bob, a third for the two guides. Looking at them and remembering, Kathy wondered with anguish how she could ever let her son sleep alone in his tent that night. Even with him beside her she knew she would not have slept, would have had to remain on guard lest he display any desire to step outside the tent's protection at any time of the dark dreadful night, before the blessed safety of the dawn reappeared. She wondered at her foolishness in agreeing to her son's pleading to be allowed to camp in the bush. It had all seemed so easy and safe in the travel agent's office in Stafford, but now and here was the reality and it was an awful reality and she knew she would be awake and distraught for all of the night and she knew she was mad to have allowed this to happen. God!

'I will pay you double to remain awake all night, Paul,' she said to the strong solid smiling guide she had taken a little distance from the others. 'I want you to build a very large fire, to keep it going all night, to stay awake all night. You can sleep during the day, I don't mind, the other guide can help us then.' There was a beseeching in her voice that struck deep into the newly Christian soul of the tall competent man standing beside her. For he hated to see any frightened or wounded animal, let alone a terrified woman.

'Madam,' he replied with his own particular unassuming pacific authority, 'please do not worry about the night. Even asleep I hear all the animals. I will protect you and your son. You are my charges. I will never let you down. You must have complete faith in me. But if it is your special wish that I remain awake all night, then that I agree to do. I shall look after everything, I shall maintain a good fire. But you must not pay me more. I am here for you, all the time, to look after you, to protect you. And God is with us too; you cannot come to any harm.'

Chastened by his reply, Kathy said nothing more to the deeply committed young man. A man she knew she would want to have on the end of her rope if she was ever left dangling from a cliff face, for he would pull her up to safety or die in the attempt. This she knew and so she questioned him no further. But deep within her she remembered another confident young man she would have wanted on the end of that rope and she knew that still, despite the assurances, she would be unable to sleep that night.

As the heat of the afternoon slowly began to disperse and as the languishing sun began its descending journey cooling the windless African savannah, Paul suggested a two-hour walk into the hinterland of the island. Bob was by his side in a second, pulling his lethargic mother to her feet with large imploring not-to-be-denied eyes.

'O K, O K!' She laughed. Was it Africa, she thought, or would those eyes inevitably have become *his* eyes over time?

'Why don't you carry a gun?' Bob asked Paul after they had been walking for but a few moments. He carried his father's knife. Was that all they possessed in order to protect themselves?

'It is not allowed now in the Delta,' replied Paul. 'We carried them until a year or two ago but it is now agreed amongst all the guides that our task is to preserve, never to kill. We are taught how to keep ourselves and our charges safe. You must not worry. People who carry guns, use them. We do not need to use them. It has been decided.'

'By whom?' Asked Kathy, 'who has made this decision, who is in control here?' She asked out of interest rather than from concern.

'By Nnyaa Leina and Mjanyelwa Mashiane.'

'Who are they?'

'Our leaders. They care for us, educate us, teach us your language. They instruct us in the ways to protect the animals, care for our peoples, not to kill, not to fight. They are our leaders, our chiefs, our healers, we must obey them in all things. They are very good men.'

The trio walked in a companionable silence for one hour, punctuated occasionally by Paul's sighting of a particularly interesting bird or mammal. For now the creatures really had to be special. Kathy and Bob were on their sixth day in Africa and had already seen so much that although still charmed and interested, they were no longer excited by sightings of common elephants and zebra, giraffe and impala, buffalo and warthog. Bob much less frequently than before finding it necessary to log a newly identified species in his note-book. Now he sought the more evasive creatures, the great cats, the white rhino, the Goliath heron.

'I will show you three leopard cubs tomorrow,' said Paul to the entranced boy. 'Tonight we cannot go near for the mother will be in the lair with them, but tomorrow in the early morning she will be hunting to find game to fill their little bellies, and if they are still where I saw them three days ago we will find them and you will be able to witness one of the great gifts of God to the world.'

Kathy smiled with appreciation at his honest faith, his intensity of belief. This part of life, this important part of life had somehow passed her by. Her world was not as simple as his. Was that of her own making or had it been inevitable from the beginning? Why was her world not as simple as his, as honest as his?

Night blackened the sky, further intensifying the diffused light from their campfire around which four people of two races sat in quiet congenial silence, each deep in his or her own special thoughts. As the night sounds of the water and the land rose to chorus the trees, Paul began to sing. Not the songs of Africa but the songs of his new-found faith. Onward Christian Soldiers, Abide with Me, Love Divine all Loves

Excelling. His powerful baritone rang with joy and conviction and the love of Christ. Kathy found herself singing with him, recalling the memories of her days at the lovely old Arlaston Church. Then, with emotion bordering on awe she realised that her son Bob, the boy she had rarely taken to church, was singing every word along with them, in an intensely unique tenor, a voice she had never heard before. He knew every word and every tune of every hymn. Where had he learned them? With whom? It must have been her father. That lovely, tough, angry, soft, wonderful grandfather. She wished he were with them tonight and could sing with those Christian soldiers onward into war, with the cross of Jesus going on before. Even though she no longer believed in any God, she sang at the top of her lovely voice and her son sang with her and as they sang Abide With Me Fast Falls the Eventide they held hands, all four people in a completed unity of expression in the dark African night in this awful and wonderful world and all loved where they were and who they were and what they were. And even if they no longer believed in God, they still loved him.

3

As Paul had predicted, they discovered the leopard cubs just after dawn had risen. Silently, enticingly slowly, he and Kathy and Bob had stalked the family lair, desperate to ensure they neither frightened the cubs nor exposed the hiding place of these still vulnerable animals to the predators of the delta. Three humans gazed down in protective wonderment as three sets of inquisitive pinprick eyes stared up from the depths of an old warthog hole which was now their home, eyes curiously watching the two-legged intruders. Black button noses wrinkled the air as the cosy animals attempted to differentiate and categorize this strange human odour, one they had never smelt before. It was not one of the smells that so far in their brief cautious lives they had been taught by their mother to be wary of, so, more confused than afraid they sought advice, but there was none to be given for their mother was away hunting for food. She had left at dawn to make her kill and was yet to return. It was the same every day, she was sometimes absent until the sun swung round to pour heat into their home and it became necessary to exit the burrow and play in the shade of the tree, for the burrow was too narrow to play in, too hot to remain in. But that time of the day had not yet arrived. For the moment they were content to watch the two-legged animals while the latter delighted in the reciprocity of observing the cubs.

'I hope they come out, Mum.' Said the gentle fourteen year old who, even before coming to Africa, had loved all animals and was now unsure how he could ever leave the country. Or if he must, how to manage his life to return to its allure in the shortest possible time.

'How long will their mother be away?' Asked Bob.

'Usually no more than a couple of hours,' replied Paul, 'for the cubs are still very young and she will not want to leave them alone for too long. We must be gone soon for if she sees us here, despite her natural fear of man, she will attack to protect her cubs.'

'Just ten more minutes," pleaded the boy, enraptured.

Paul could not deny this boy who felt for the animals as he did.

But it was ten minutes too long.

The female leopard had seen them from half a mile away, had seen them standing above her tiny vulnerable family. Abandoning the chase of a small male impala she rapidly retraced her tracks until she stood, out of sight of the intruders but within range to be able to rapidly pounce. Her cubs were in danger but they were three large animals! Which one to take first? The largest, the oldest of the herd for then the others might run away? Or the smallest, for then the others would follow to try to save it and she could lead them away from her cubs. She had but seconds to decide. Her mighty shoulders hunched in primeval power as she made her choice. She prepared to leap, she waited for the movement of the animals so that she could best judge which way they would attempt to escape and thus which way she should jump.

'Stand absolutely still!' Came a booming shout from her left side down wind. So concentrated had she been upon the kill she had failed to see another family member creep up beside her. For a moment she was disorientated. Which threat to immediately deal with, the one close to her, or the one close to her cubs? Her hesitation was time enough for the man, he moved towards her.

'Now, move away from the cubs,' he instructed in a quiet authoritative voice. As the frightened trio began to slowly move from the old warthog's hole, the man advanced upon the leopard. The leopard was confused, no animal ever advanced upon her, ever threatened her in this way. If she disturbed an elephant or a buffalo or a lion they would attack out of reflex action, but none would stalk her in this way. Her confusion was absolute and with the confusion came a little fear, for she had never experienced this stalking before. The same fear she created in others she now felt within herself for the first time and, although snarling defiance, she began to retreat. The man moved nearer, she retreated further and then suddenly he stopped, he stood absolutely still, he threatened no longer. Momentarily the leopardess stole a glance at her lair, the animals were gone, were her cubs unharmed? The man no longer threatened, the pull of the cubs became the greater pull. She snarled at him once more, just to let him know she was not really afraid and then slunk quickly down the slight rise to find her family.

'Who is he?' Breathed Bob transfixed, watching the man whose power, whose bravery surpassed anything he had ever seen before in his young life.

'Nnyaa Leina' Answered Paul. 'Now I shall be in trouble, for I put you into danger and you are my charges and he will admonish me.'

'I'll say it's our fault,' said Kathy, 'I won't let that old man harm you, Paul.'

'Oh, he would never harm me, Mrs. Castle, he would never harm anyone or anything, it is just the look in his eyes that I do not want to face. His eyes can kill or can inspire. I just don't want to look into his eyes!'

Kathy watched as the white-haired, white-bearded old man came towards them and there was something very special about him. As he approached she could see that his body was not the body of an old man. Muscle, health and strength cried out from its every inch. He walked with a surety of purpose. He walked as only few men walk, as only one man walked. And she began to feel the hairs lift on the back of her neck and on the calves of her legs. She knew it could not be, that it was Africa doing it to her again. He had white hair and a white beard, but the hair was thick, it had always been thick. Now he was close to them and it was *his* body, but it could not be his body! It was Africa that was doing this to her, Africa! And then he was standing in front of her and he was taller than she remembered and his body was not as dark as the native African's body but it was dark nevertheless. The body was too dark and the hair was too white and then he looked at her and the eyes were the same. Dear God, the eyes were the same! And she looked into the eyes of Robert Castle and she knew it was him and the strength went from her body and she fell into a desperate haunting faint at the feet of the man who was known as Nnyaa Leina.

It was mid afternoon when she awoke but it was as black as night. There was a young woman sitting beside her as she lay on the ground. Her throat was dry and she realised she was in a native hut and she wanted a drink but she needed the dream to go away first. The white-haired dead man who had stood over her and tried to take her life with his eyes and then the leopard had come and the man held the leopard in his hands and the leopard was dead or the man was dead. One of them was dead. Then they were both alive again and both of them should be dead and how can they be alive? *How can he be alive?* And then she remembered and she sat bolt upright and she looked about her. Was it really Africa that had done this to her or had she really seen him? Whatever it was, it could not have been him! Dear God! It could not have been him! She dared not move but she had to move, she had to see. Who was this woman beside her and she was smiling, what the hell did she have to smile about? Then she was giving her something to drink and it wasn't water but it was good and it was sweet and it made her throat pain go away but not the pain in her mind, the disbelief in her soul. Then she saw a tiny glimmer of light and it came from around the curtain at the doorway and she reached out and could touch the curtain; she drew it open and the woman did not move. Then she saw him again. Dear

God, she saw him again and he was squatting with her son, Bob. Her son, his son, oh Jesus! Our son! He was talking to him and they were both animated and she could not hear their discussion but it was the discussion of one soul in two bodies. The woman beside her could see it too but she did not know. No-one knew. What was he telling his son? And why on God's good earth had he not come back to her when he had been here, alive, all the time? It must be him! There is no-one else in the entire world who has those shoulders or who could sit like that. And if it was him then why had he not returned to her? But how *could* it be him? It could not be him for he had been taken by the crocodile, everyone knew he had been taken by the crocodile. Her racing heart began to slow as she realised it could not be him, that it was indeed Africa playing its games with her again. That it was a man who looked like him. They said that somewhere in the world we all have our double, but why here in Africa for Heaven's sake, why here in the place where he had been killed? It was a crazy thing but it was only a crazy thing, it was not reality. Nevertheless she wished her father were with her, just for a moment or two, just when she felt so vulnerable, so much like his little girl again. What was the white-haired man saying? What the hell was his name again, Leina? What the hell sort of a name was that for a man? And now Kathy became angry at that white-haired charlatan. Who the hell had given him permission to look like the only man she had ever loved? Yes, damn it, admit it, the only man she had ever loved. Who had given him the right? Sod him! Bloody savage! Who the hell did he think he was to take a dead man's eyes? Bloody impostor! Exhausted, she sank back into her rush mat, lying with eyes open, looking up into the face of the blackest prettiest woman she had ever seen. She felt ashamed for her stupidity.

'I'm sorry,' she said.

'I'm Francina,' said the girl. Kathy laughed at the absurdity.

'No, I'm Kathy,' she tried again.

'I know,' said the woman, 'your son, he told us. He is with my husband, you must not worry.'

Kathy had to ask, she knew it was nonsense, but she had to ask. 'Your husband?'

'Nnyaa Leina' replied the girl quietly but with intense pride. 'Our leader, our Nyanga, my husband.'

'The white-haired man?'

'Yes.'

Francina looked down at this lovely sad white woman and the gods spoke to her, but she did not understand what it was they were telling her. She did not truly understand when they told her that she knew this day had to come. Did not accept their words. She dismissed the gods, told them never to return, they were false gods anyway. Paul and his preachers and the others told them now of the true God and she liked the true god for he had nice music and he was a kind god and a forgiving god and he had died for her and now she believed in the new god and she no longer listened to the old gods when they came to speak to her. The new God had not yet come to speak to her but she knew he would do so one day. It was only a matter of time.

She looked at the woman lying on the ground and she did not know what she felt, for the emotions chased one another.

Kathy had to ask, she knew it was absurd, but she just had to ask.

'Is he from your village, your husband?'

'He is now.'

'And before?'

Francina was quiet, something was happening that she was not in control of, not even a party to, but she did not know what it was, only that it harmed her and Nnyaa Leina and their son. But how could this helpless woman harm her? The gods were wrong!

'He came to me many years ago, he came to me from the river's side, he came to my life, to fill it, to give me love, to give me a son. He came to lead our people and to do good work for our tribe and to educate us and to fight for us against the white man taking our land and our animals and he came to save our little village and we all love him. He is mine!' She was wearied, it was a very long speech for her in the language of her husband, in the language of this woman.

Kathy's nails bit into her palms as she attempted to hold her emotions in check, as she watched the pathetically beautiful face of the threatened girl sitting motionless beside her.

She asked the question, the question that would separate them forever.

'Was he a white man when he came to you?'

Francina did not look into the face of this beautiful woman now sitting beside her, but she felt her power, a power merged with compassion. No-one had ever taught Francina to lie, she could not lie now, but what would the truth mean for her? She could not speak but she nodded her head and looked down at the floor. Lost.

Kathy felt surprisingly calm. No longer in anguish. It was him, she accepted it was him. She accepted, she did not understand, but she accepted. She put her arm around the girl, the girl who knew the gods were never really wrong, the girl who knew that one day this day must come. The girl who was dying inside.

It was a long moment that the two women held each other, then Francina began to speak and it was as if her voice came from far away, a voice she did not recognise as her own.

'He was almost dead, lying beside the river. Something had almost killed him, he had been fighting in the water with something and he had a huge wound on his head, much bruising, many cuts and the fever had come and that had almost taken him away. My father and I, we brought him home and we saved him and he lived again, but....'

Kathy did not press the childlike woman, all would emerge in time. She was chillingly calm, controlled.

'But he could remember nothing, his mind had left him; he did not know who he was, where he was from, what his name was.' She sobbed, Kathy stared straight ahead. Oh God, those wasted years!

'So we called him Nnyaa Leina, which means in our language, *no name*. For he had no name.' Francina's voice trailed into a silent black abyss.

Kathy released the girl who discovered the dignity to cease her sobbing. She walked to the doorway and gazed out at the sight of Robert Castle talking to his son. Then she realised there was another boy with them, smaller than Bob but close to the same age and the two boys were talking and they were laughing together and they were listening to the white-haired man in reverence as if he were a god. As indeed he was to them.

'Your son?' Asked Kathy in anguish of her soul. Francina beside her nodded again,

The two women looked from the doorway of the hut and saw their husband and saw their sons. The women, separately and together, recognised the trio's unambiguous kinship, the boys' unmistakable parentage. Neither said another word to the other. They never again spoke another word to each other.

Francina left the hut in a rush of speed, running beyond the compound, running into the bush.

'Francina,' called her husband, 'where are you going?'

But the woman who would always be a girl, did not reply.

Kathy walked towards her husband, no idea in her mind what she would say. He looked up from his spirited chatter with his sons. He looked up at her with those eyes.

'Sorry about that,' he said, 'my wife is not accustomed to white woman strangers.' He smiled at Kathy. With those eyes.

Dear God, *I am your wife!*

'Are you feeling better now?' He enquired. 'It must have given you a nasty turn, being so close to the leopard, I've had a quiet word with Paul, he is most terribly sorry.'

It was his voice, dear God, *it was his voice*. But he didn't know her. *He didn't bloody know her!*

'I'm fine now,' was all she could manage to choke.

Inane, screamed her mind, *bloody fucking inane!*

'It's been a long time for me to talk politely with white people,' he said, smiling broadly, smiling with a face she remembered despite that awful huge white beard. 'Normally I am shouting at them for pointing their guns in the wrong direction or for trying to build roads through our lands.'

Our lands!

'Your son is very intelligent and seems interested in our work, I was just telling him of our latest projects.'

It was like Alice in Wonderland, at the mad hatter's tea party, and she was the maddest of them all. Christ! It *is* Robert. But he doesn't know me, he can't even see himself in his own son, for God's sake! He's too damn interested in his own bloody crusades for the people and the animals to see beyond his bloody white-fringed nose!

She began to laugh and it was the laugh of the insane and the laugh of the lost and the mad and the unhappy and the crazy and it went on and on and then the tears came with the laughter and then she found the strong arms of her son holding her and the laughter subsided and she saw how Robert and his chocolate-coloured son were talking quietly, looking away from her in embarrassment at what she had brought to their village. If it had not been for the strong arms of her loving son, mentally she would have gone over the edge that day. He pulled her back and he held her and she loved him. But she could not tell him, she could not tell

340

anyone. It was all so much nonsense and so much pain and so crazy and she wanted to go home and she wanted to remain with him for ever, for he was just the same as he had ever been and he made the world come alive for others. She would even share him with Francina and no matter that her skin was black and her son was chocolate and his beard was white and those eyes, dear Christ, those eyes! She had come home, but she could not call it her home. Poor Francina, she thought. She knew, she must know. She could see Bob and she could see her husband in Bob, and knew she could not fight, so she had gone away. Kathy knew she must find her and bring her back and all must be well, for there is only one life for us all. Robert Castle was exceptional, he had been granted two lives and had made two families so happy, two sons so proud. He truly was too much man for one woman. But she would never tell anyone, ever!

Francina returned with the dusk and all was entirely still as she went to sit by the side of her husband as he lit his first pipe of the evening, a long thin clay pipe that she had filled for him. She looked at Kathy and their eyes locked and their souls cried out in anguish, but both knew they would never break the confidence, never tell the man they both loved. For what is gone, is gone.

'Can we stay tonight, Mother?'

'I'm afraid you will have to, Mrs. Castle,' he said, 'it is too dangerous for you to travel back to your campsite in the night. Paul has been informed. In fact, for him it is a bonus, he can be with his own wife and family tonight.'

'So can we all!' Thought Kathy as she watched the man she loved but did not know, accepting another filled pipe from the woman who was his *other* wife.

The woman came to him again that night as he slept. She had not visited him for many years but she came to him again that night. She came in white, a blinding white and he held her breasts in his hands and they were large breasts and full breasts and he knew he had seen those breasts recently but he could not remember where he had seen those breasts. But now they were lying with him and he was drowning and the water took the breasts away and then he was walking, carrying a child on his shoulders and he knew it was not his own child. He was singing and it was the song he had sung to the villagers and he was crying again and then she was there and she was black and she held him and all was well. Then the monster with the tiny eyes and the large teeth came again and it dragged him under and he held the leg and then the leg came away in his hand and he screamed as he held only the leg and then abruptly he awoke.

She lay beside him as she always did, peaceful, breathing quietly so as not to disturb him and she was like a child and he loved her. For her simplicity, for her charm. He was no longer tired and so arose from his mat and walked into the closed compound, safe from marauding animals. Then he saw her and she was outside the compound, carelessly sitting in the dark star-spangled evening and he liked her shoulders and somehow he knew exactly what her breasts were like and he wanted those breasts but he must not have them for she was a white woman and there would be trouble.

But he was a white man too! At least had been, although he never now thought of himself as a white man. He wondered what it would be like with a white woman, he wondered whether he had ever before had one. Would this one hold him inside unmoving as Francina did or would she be charging like that leopard today, yesterday, whenever. He had never had a white woman, he wanted one. He walked towards her.

'It's dangerous here,' he said.

She turned her head to see the approaching man and he loved what he saw in her eyes. But he did not know what he saw. Was it a gentleness, a strength, a need for no-one? Whatever it was, the analysis momentarily melted his desire. No longer did he need to possess her, rather he needed to understand her. How could this woman who fainted at the sight of the approaching leopard and laughed aloud like a mad hyena so suddenly be so unafraid of anything as to sit here, distanced from the security of the compound and the huts, uncaring, unconcerned about her own safety? As if almost willing the animals to come and take her. What sort of a woman could do this? He sat down beside her.

They were silent for a long time. Silent together. At last she spoke, for his magnetic animal presence was pulling fiercely at her soul and she had to calm it, to calm herself.

'Tell me about your work.' She requested.

He realised he wanted to, wanted very much to tell her about himself, his work, his plans, his life. He began to tell her of the charge he believed he had been given, of the responsibility he had assumed.

343

'In 1954 the government erected the Buffalo fence, they called it the Veterinary Cordon Fence,' he began, 'It was supposed to segregate the wild buffalo herds from domestic free range cattle and stop the spread of foot and mouth disease. The problem is that it not only prevents contact between wild and domestic animals but it also prevents the wild animals from migrating to water sources and good pasture ground.'

He was back! The old Robert was back. His work for the animals transcending all. It was wonderful and sad to see the old Robert back. Wonderful to watch him fight his crusades, sad to know that no-one, not even Francina, not even herself, could ever fully possess him. But she loved to hear him speak for his cause. He continued.

'Some animals become entangled in the fence, whilst others die of exhaustion trying to find a way around it. Whole herds, entire species are decimated. We have to get the damn fence removed or, at least, some substantial part of it knocked down so that natural migration of the animals can take place, so that they can find water and pasture land.'

Passionate! My passionate Robert. She touched his hand, he did not seem to notice. She held his hand more firmly, still he seemed not to notice.

'And then the bastards are looking to dam the Boro river to provide water for Maun and the other towns, all at the expense of local animals and small village farming communities like ourselves. Bastards!'

He was back. No, she was back with him. He had never been away. It was she who had deserted him. She should have stayed, searched harder and longer and then she would have found him and become part of his new world, the world he had always wanted, always needed. It was her own damn, fucking fault! Now she held his hand in both of her hands and she brought it on to her lap and if he wanted to take her now, tonight, under the stars and in sight of the whole damn fucking camp, then he could take her. Please Robert, take me, please!

But he never even seemed to notice her hands or the cry from her body's depths as his words and his passion were all consumed by the need to help his people, his animals.

'I must stop them from damming the river, I must get them to open that bloody fence. They must understand that they have to involve the local communities in natural resource management, teach them how to conserve the animals, offer them benefits from increasing tourism, change from hunting to photographic safaris, this they must do.'

But she was no longer listening to the words, just the exciting animal tone of his wonderful voice and if he would not take her, then she would damn well take him, just as she had done when they were students together. He still had that bloody thick hair and I want to hang on to it, dear God, I want to hang on to it and feel him come inside me, just one more time, PLEASE GOD!

And then Francina was beside them and she gently lifted Kathy's hand from that of her husband and for the first time he noticed where the hand had been. But it was too late. Proprietarily Francina pulled her husband to his feet and she led him, without a word, back to their hut. The white woman, the lonely unprotected crazy white woman sat alone in the African night and her sobbing could be heard by all the animals and all the humans awake in that dreadful dark.

4

Paul arrived with the telegram around ten the following morning, the morning when Kathy had decided to tell Robert the truth. She had fought for him once, she would do so again. She had only one life, she now knew that into that life she could accept only one man. She was sorry for Francina but it was not really a marriage anyway, how could it be a marriage? They had not been married in a church. There was no church. They had probably not even registered the marriage. No, he was hers! Had always been hers, legitimately hers. Legally hers. They could not deny it, no-one could deny it. In time his memory would return and he would be wholly restored to her. It was the only way. She could give him his platforms to fight from, audiences to listen to his words of concern for the animals and the villagers. She would organise it all for him. She had the resources now, she had the skill and she had the money. Nothing could stop her. They could not continue to live here of course, they would have to return to Staffordshire, certainly for the time being in order to sort out their lives and her business and for him to be accepted again and to fulfill his new roles as husband and as father. Even whilst she made these plans and talked them through in her head, she knew she was not thinking straight; that he could not return, that he did regard Francina as his wife and his other son as his son. She understood all that but she could not accept all that, for to do so would be to die again and she did not want to die again. So she had to change the world and his world and her son's world, she had to tell them everything and they had to accept; they must accept. She was accustomed to being listened to, to being obeyed. Like her father she was not to be denied when she had made her decision and she cared nothing for others at that precise moment. She was all and he was all, and that damn white beard had to go and he could become young again. She lay on her mat in the hut reserved for visitors as she thought all this through and she knew it to be wrong and hopeless and horrible, but correct. Yet still hateful. And she began to sob once more. There was no-one, no-one in the whole of the great big world who she could tell of her plight. No-one. Why not die here, for how could she continue to live with what she knew, with what she felt?

Then Paul brought the telegram to her hut.

Come home stop accident stop father and Edward stop little hope stop come home stop Mum stop

Oh God, how much more do you want me to take? Father, father! She ran from the hut, all other thoughts thrust from her mind.

'Bob!' She shouted, 'Bob!'

He came to her, he came with his new friend, his half brother, Ndimande, but he did not know Ndimande was his half brother. He came smiling and laughing for they had been tracking together and he felt it was a wonderful life and he never wanted to leave his new friend and he never wanted to leave the man who was his new friend's father, Nnyaa Leina, who knew everything, who could teach him everything.

Bob read the telegram, silently showed it to his half brother who immediately ran to inform his father. Kathy was lost, what to do, how to return? Speed was vital. Who to help her?

Then he came to her.

'I have a short wave radio, Mrs. Castle,' he said

Mrs. bloody Castle even now, Oh Christ!

'I will call Maun straight away, they will send a plane to meet you at Delta Camp then decide how best to get you to an international airport on the first flight to England, leave it to me.'

Kathy needed to kiss him, to hold him, but *she* was there, ever watchful, ever knowing.

'My two strongest men will take you swiftly back to Delta Camp by our mokoros, one for your son and one for yourself, it will be faster that way. The plane should have arrived by the time you get there.'

'Thank you,' was all she could say. All she could say to this man who should be holding her and comforting her and returning with her. Damn it! She's not going to have it all her own way. Kathy grabbed Nnyaa Leina, the man she had known as Robert Castle and she held him close to her and she hugged him and she whispered, 'thank you, Robert my darling,' in his ear. Then he was gone to make the radio call. Gone in bewilderment.

Twice she had been to Africa; twice she had left in distress, in the depths of despair. Bloody Africa!

She stood in the international phone booth in Maun airport trying to reach the same number, probably from the same bloody phone that she had used fourteen years before, nothing had damn well changed and that is why it seemed like only yesterday and not so many years ago. It was a continual nightmare and nothing had happened between her two greatest nightmares. All her progress in the business, all her building of the reputation of the hotel, her son, everything, must have happened to someone else. It must have done so for she was the same lost person who had stood here before, trying to make the connection. Nothing had altered, nothing had grown or developed, the world had stood still, the pain forever there.

'Hello?'

It was her mother's voice, strained and tired, defeated.

'Mother, it's me, Kathy.'

'Oh, thank God, Kathy, thank God, are you in England?'

'Not yet, mum, I'm still in Africa, but I'll be on a plane within the hour and home by tomorrow morning.'

'I'll get Tom to meet you at the airport.'

No, not Tom, I couldn't face Tom, not now, not yet.

'No mum!' She said quickly, too quickly. 'Don't do that. I'll hire a car or a small plane if I can get one. Leave it to me.'

'Alright, Kathy,' agreed the woman who never argued with her husband, who never argued with her daughter.

Kathy did not want to but she had to find out.

'Mum?' She asked, 'how are they?'

There was a long silence at the other end of the telephone. Then a voice which was a no person's voice because it was a sigh and a gasp of pain coupled in one, began,

'Edward's gone, Kathy.' It said

Kathy's knuckles grew whiter still as she held tightly to the phone.

'He was driving and the steering wheel crushed his chest.'

Bloody, bloody, mad driver! Bloody, bloody mad car! Was all that Kathy could hear in her head.

'And Daddy, how's my daddy?' She cried, begging for different, better news.

'He's still in intensive care. He was thrown from the car and that saved him, in a way.'

'What do you mean, in a way?'

And then the brave little woman a thousand miles away began to sob and it was in between the sobs that Kathy heard the words that wrenched her soul.

'His back was broken in the fall, Kathy, he will never walk again, he's paralyzed at least from the waist down, maybe from the neck down, they can't tell as yet. Oh Kathy, there are tubes all over him and into him and he can't speak Kathy, and he doesn't know me Kathy, and he won't want to live like this! Kathy come home to me soon, help me Kathy, Kathy...' The line went dead. Whether her mother had purposely broken the connection as emotion encompassed her or whether it had been lost above the African continent, no matter, it went dead, as dead as Edward.

I'm sorry you're dead Edward, she thought, but damn you, damn you! Why did you do this to my father and to my mother you worthless shit, with your stupid bloody car! And she cried for her father and she cried for her mother and she cried for Edward and, most of all, she cried for herself. Her life destroyed again, by men, by worthless bloody men. The only good one amongst them lying fighting in a hospital, fighting for what? So he could be wheeled around like a vegetable and not able to do anything for himself, not able to clean himself, to pee on his own. Christ! He would be better off dead, she knew he would prefer to be dead. Hell, her dear strong mighty father would prefer to be dead than to live like that. He could never live like that. She prayed, standing alone and cramped in that telephone box in Maun airport, she prayed that the god she no longer believed in would take her father rather than force him to live the life of a helpless cripple.

Please take him!

When she saw him in the hospital room the next day with her broken mother clutching on to her arm and her son beside her and Tom waiting in the car outside, Kathy again prayed that he might die. The kindest thing. Tom sat in his car not knowing why she did not want him with her to console her, why she had hardly spoken a word to him. Perhaps it was grief, perhaps it was something else, perhaps nothing. He thought he knew Kathy, but a different woman had returned from Africa to him. Even, and as if in sympathy, her son was closing ranks with his mother. Displaying a detachedness, as if he, Tom, was now not good enough for either of them. Or was it his imagination? She was deep was Kathy, he had always known that, but now her depths had become unfathomable. He felt that somehow, in so short a time, he had lost her. So he sat, smoking, unwanted, in his car in the hospital car park whilst the woman he loved prayed that her father might die.

It was Bob who was in control that day. He was thinking of a man he barely knew and how he would take charge of the situation, how he would have been calm and controlled and capable. As courageous as when he saved them from the leopardess. He consciously tried to act like he knew that man would act and to take control, to take charge, to take responsibility as the leader. His mother gazed in distress at Bob's grandfather, lying there, incapable of movement, not even the eyes opening although flickering slightly beneath the lids just to prove to them all that he was still hanging on. The fighter that had hung on through the war, the thruster who had rebuilt the Hydro. This was not a warrior who would give up on life, even if confined to a wheelchair. Bob knew his grandfather really would not give up on life. Bob felt that at this moment he knew his grandfather better than anyone and he tried to explain the essence of the man to his mother, to his grandmother. The essence of this man whom he both loved and respected, the second man he wished to be like. Bob told his mother and his grandmother that, without any doubt at all, Ian Harris would live; he convinced them that Ian Harris would want to live. The boy gave new spirit to the women, gave them hope. On that day in that quiet hospital room Bob Castle shed his boyhood, just as the snakes of Africa shed their skins.

5

It was three months before Ian Harris was allowed home and it was Bob who collected him from the hospital in one of the hotel cars driven by one of the hotel porters. Ian Harris had not wanted his wife to assist him from his bed to the wheelchair, had not wanted his daughter to wheel him from the place in which his life had been given back to him. He wanted his grandson, the new man of the family, the man who had talked with him at his bedside every day for the past three months, to assume that responsibility, to take that pressure, that pain. For Ian Harris knew Bob was now the best equipped of them all to handle it. They were able to meet as equals, despite the youth of one and the disabilities of the other. They met in that small hospital room as equals and they left from that small hospital room as equals.

'I don't want them to choke me with kindness, Bob. Do you understand?'

'Yes, Granddad, I won't let them do that to you.'

'I still have my pride, son.'

'Yes Granddad.'

'You can call me Ian when we are alone, Bob, just when we are alone. I would like that very much, will you do that for me please?'

And the boy looked at the man he loved and fought back the pricks in the side of his eyes and the mist that was threatening to appear within them and he said, 'yes Ian, yes Ian, I can do that. I would like to do that very much.'

And the two men embraced as they left that hospital room and a new chapter was born in the young man's life.

'I don't want to talk about me, Bob,' said the older man as his grandson lifted him into the car. I want to talk more about you and what your thoughts are of Africa and what you want to do with your life. You've worried your mother you know. She's changed too, Bob, she seems as if she's crying more again, like she did when she returned from Africa the first time. She tries to conceal it from me when she visits, but I've seen it before, I know what to look for, she can't hide it from me. When she thinks I'm sleeping or dozing it comes back to her, in wave after wave'

And because Bob lived in the same house as his mother and because he slept little at night due to his waking dreams of Africa, he knew this observant man to be correct, but he said nothing. His grandfather questioned no further.

'So the African bug has caught you too, Bob?'

'Yes, Ian' he replied and the word was not alien to him, it was the most natural thing in the world. He looked at the man he loved and wondered how he could tell him.

'How much have you discussed it with your mother?'

'Not so much, Gran....Ian, she refuses to discuss Africa, she refuses to discuss the trip with anyone and we had such a wonderful time and we camped and the stars were magical and the animals were wonderful and we met these marvelous people and they love the animals and are trying to preserve the environment for us all and....'

'Slow down for Heaven's sake!' Chuckled the old man, loving the boy's passion and knowing that life was still good if he could listen to such enthusiasm, even if he had to now live an active life through another and he hoped that it would be a long time before this boy went away. He knew Bob must leave some day to become his own man. He had good genes this boy, a warm and loving mother, a courageous, even foolhardy father, but both exciting people, strong, their own people. Shit, he has my genes too! How can I ever think of giving up with those genes, mine and his genes, coursing through our bodies. Despair or failure are not acceptable thoughts for us. Ian Harris knew Bob Castle possessed superior genes and that he had to fulfill their challenge. But Ian Harris hoped the boy man would not be leaving for a very long time.

'Your mother will want you to take over the business from her, Bob. I'm just about out of it now. She'll be made Chairman at the board meeting next week. I'll be there. It'll be my role, my proud role to propose her. She wants you to take over from her, Bob. To learn the business, to study at university. It's a great business. You can be Hotel Manager by the time you're twenty-five, probably Chairman by the time you're thirty-five or forty. Good money, a great life.'

But deep in his soul Ian Harris realised his hopes were stillborn.

The boy was quiet for a moment, he heard his grandfather's words but could not read his grandfather's thoughts.

'What do *you* want me to do Grandfather?' The Ian was momentarily in suspension as the young man prepared himself for the disciplinary advice he knew he would be bound to follow. Advice that could destroy his dreams, his life.

His grandfather was a long time in replying. Ian Harris was thinking of his own father whom he had despised and who had brought the business to its knees. He thought too of the early days of his own stewardship, of the business he had built. He thought of his daughter and what she had done, of the excellence they had created together, an excellence that she would now maintain. He remembered how important he had always believed it was to uphold the family tradition, to keep the business exclusively in the controlling hand of the family. Why? Why did he believe that? Was it for himself that he believed that? Was it because he had always imprinted that belief into the mind of Kathy and his dear dead son Edward? What was it all for anyway? He had loved the hotel business and so did Kathy. They did not love it because they had been told to love it, they loved it because they felt it, they lived it. It was intuitive within them, an essential part of their very make-up. They loved the work and the people and the growth and the challenge and, even if it had not

358

been a family business, they would still have loved it. At last he realized, at last he could admit that he had done it not for posterity but for himself. He had not built up a business in order for his children to take it over from him when he was gone or no longer capable of managing it, as he was now. He had built up the business, because he, Ian Harris, had wanted to do it for himself. And he suspected deep down, his daughter felt the same. She was not building the business for her son, she was building the business for herself, because she loved it; loved the authority, the status, the power, the buzz. All the things he had loved, and, whether she had a son or not, she would do it all just the same. It was gross arrogance to pretend they had built the business for future generations. They had built it for themselves, for themselves only. So what if the business was no longer managed or owned by the family, they both had achieved what they wanted to achieve in life. Be honest Ian Harris, be honest!

Bob waited, he had the patience to wait, he had a stalker's patience. At last his grandfather spoke.

'I want you to do what *you* want to do with your life, Bob. Not what your mother wants you to do, not what I want you to do.' The old man paused for a long moment, then said: 'Anyway, I suspect you have already made up your mind what it is you want to do and whatever I say, whatever your mother says, will be politely listened to, but in truth is likely to have little effect upon your decision.'

The old man fixed the young man with an impish fun-filled glare as the corners of his mouth moved imperceptibly upwards, breaking into a wide smile.

Then came a laugh from the man who but one month before had believed he would never laugh again. He reached out to the boy he loved and embraced him, held tightly to him. Knew he would really want to die if anything bad ever happened to this boy. After a short time they released one another. The hotel driver had not looked into his mirror for the entirety of that embrace. It was not his place. God, it was good to see the old man back again! He would be able to tell them when he returned to the hotel that the old man was alright. They would all be there waiting for his return, waiting to hear. He knew they would all be there. He would tell them that the old man was back, but he would not tell them what he had overheard.

'But let's think how we shall tell your mother, Bob. We have to be so careful how we tell her.'

'She hates Africa.'

'No, I don't think so. I think deep down she hates what she lost in Africa, not Africa itself. She has to find something again, something to cling on to. It's not Africa, it's the people she lost whilst she was in Africa. She cannot lose them again, they are gone now, she can only find something, or someone new.'

She's broken with Tom.'

'I know, she told me, but she didn't tell me why.'

'He was not man enough for her. She realised it just in time.' Replied the youth with a perceptiveness that again proved him to be the person his mother and his grandfather had come to respect as well as to love.

His grandfather nodded. He understood. Poor Tom. How could he hope to compete with Robert Castle, or with Bob Castle. Or even with Ian Harris? He was on a loser from day one. Poor Tom.

'I want to work in Africa, Ian, I want to work with the animals.'

His grandfather said nothing, offering the encouragement of silence.

'I want to work with some people we met there, to help in preservation of the big five and the other species.'

It could have been his father speaking, thought Ian, feeling a slight shudder of foreboding, but he simply said;

'The big five?'

'Lion, elephant, hippo, buffalo, rhino.'

'Ah.'

'I want to do something with my life that I can be proud of, something for the good of humanity.'

'And the hotel business is not that?' Asked Ian with a mischievous but unagressive grin.

'I didn't mean that granddad, I didn't mean...' But then the boy saw the twinkle in the eye of the older man and felt the light punch on his arm. Thank God he felt the punch, at least Ian could move that arm. It was good to think of him as Ian, it was natural.

'I'll study hard first. I want to get a degree in Zoology and then I'll go out there. They'll listen to me more if I have that qualification, don't you think so?'

His grandfather nodded, loving the boy, but now beginning to feel just a little fatigued. He hoped they would soon be home.

The boy picked up on the tiredness. Damn, thought his grandfather, he misses nothing.

'You're tired now, Ian, I won't bother you more at the moment, but when I'm ready, I'll come to you to discuss it further.'

The old man looked again at the young man and he saw something there he remembered from so many years before, a stubbornness, a set of chin, a belief in self, a man he should have admired rather than disliked, a man whom through his son he now had a second chance to know and to admire. And Ian Harris was grateful.

6

'From what you tell me, Mrs. Castle, I can only suggest it's some form of post-traumatic amnesia.'

'Can you explain more to me, doctor? I understand the words but tell me more about the condition.'

'Well, you have to understand that all I'm doing is making an educated guess. Not being able to examine the patient means I'm flying blind but, from what little you can tell me, your husband suffered extremes of trauma in a fight with a crocodile as well as a major head injury. Either or both could have created the conditions conducive to complete memory loss.'

'Will it ever come back, his memory?'

'Who can say? What I can tell you is that it really is a little unusual for there to be no memory recall at all, even subconsciously, often in dreams or flashes. In the few cases I've seen and those I've read about, the memory begins to return after not too long a time. There may, in some cases, never be a full memory recall, especially concerning the event leading to the loss but usually within months, in most cases within a year, much of the pre trauma memory is recovered.'

'Then why not in my husband's case? It's been 16 years now.'

'I really don't know.'

'Guess.'

'I'd rather not.'

'Please!' I'm paying you enough you bloody man, she thought in despair, stop talking like a lawyer and give me a bloody good psychiatrist's guess!

He was silent for a minute, gazing out at the quietness of the street, for it was the dead time of the day, almost always at eleven in the morning, almost always for only twenty minutes. Why was that? He looked directly at the aggressive, far too wealthy woman, belligerently questioning him and edge-of-chair sitting in his upper class leather clad office. She did not flinch for one moment in his gaze. No wonder the poor bugger wanted to forget, she'd be a handful for any man to manage. Why not give her a guess? He had to say something and what the hell, she was paying by the hour, this'll cost her another hundred, because one guess will lead to a host more of questions that will have to be answered, consuming time that will have to be paid for. What the hell.

'I can only suggest, Mrs. Castle, that his mind either wanted to shut out what occurred in his life before the trauma, because he no longer wished to follow that life, or that the new life he has discovered post memory loss is so attractive to him, so fulfilling, that he is not searching to reactivate the pre-trauma memory.'

'I can't believe that.' Is what she said. I won't believe that, is what she thought.

They sat in silence for a while. He didn't mind, silence was chargeable too. Kathy wanted a better answer, she needed more time to digest, to be given alternatives, to be offered hope. At length she asked the same question, but differently.

'Explain exactly the condition to me again.' She demanded. 'Explain what possible treatment exists.'

Dr. Anderson sighed; she was becoming tiresome, he had no answers, he had only his considerable training and experience to fall back on. She had been told he was the best, he probably was, but who the hell can do anything without the ability to see, to hear, to examine the patient? This would be the last try, he said to himself, her money wasn't everything. Why didn't he like this woman? She was attractive, smart, wealthy, she was everything; so why the hell didn't he like her? Was it because she regarded herself as his equal?

'Think of the brain as a computer,' he began. 'Memories are filed there and when the correct command key is pressed, the files open up again. It's only a matter of knowing the password, the right key to press and any memory filed there has a good chance of being re-instated. But, if the memories have become too confused to store or if they are hit by a virus, then they may never return, or if they do, they are likely to be unintelligible. If there is a virus and if it can be isolated and destroyed, then the memory file can be opened again, but only if the correct key is pressed, the correct command given. It's just a matter of knowing which command to press.' He paused, he said nothing, he watched her digest his words, waiting for her next question.

'And the possibility of randomly discovering the password or the correct key, the right command?' She begged

'Remote.' He replied, trying to temper his harshness, maybe she was hurting so much inside that her apparent strength and belligerence was all a facade. 'Perhaps he will find it on his own, perhaps something will trigger it off, a sight, a sound, another trauma, who can tell?'

That was all he could tell her, she knew that was all he could tell her. She would not wipe her eyes in here, in his presence. She rapidly placed her glasses back onto her face. He noticed, said nothing, felt the slightest suggestion of pity and remorse. It soon passed.

'Please send your account to me, Dr. Anderson, here is my card.'

He glanced at it, he read 'Chairman', he was not surprised.

Kathy walked into the brisk cool sunlit spring morning of the London street, deriding a cab, walking from Harley Street to Hyde Park, walking, walking, and thinking.

'Dear God, it isn't me he's blocking out is it? Please God, tell me it isn't me!'

She sat alone on a bench in Hyde Park until the afternoon shadows turned into an early dusk. She fought through the self-recrimination, through the self doubt and she came out the other side, stronger, resolved. The Kathy Castle known to her employees re-emerged. It could not be her, she reasoned, for theirs had been a wonderful albeit desperately short time together. It was as Dr. Anderson had said. Bloody Robert was so tied up in the care of the animals and his new, easy going unchallenging family and damn pretty young wife that he had blotted out everything else save his work. That was the answer! He needed a shock to bring him back to himself. Was it too late now, would he ever come back? How the hell could she manage to work on him now? She had the entire business to run, her father had passed all responsibilities to her. She also had to assist Bob to achieve his goals. Alright, so he wouldn't run the business after her. What her father had said to her about the business being theirs for their own sake made sense, she hadn't liked it, but she had accepted the undeniable logic of it. If it was not to be Bob's life then who was she to object, to attempt to change things? She had always done what she wanted in her life, why not Bob too? And yes, she hated the thought of him going away from her, returning to that dark continent, but it was only dark in her mind, only dark because of what it had done to her. It was not Africa itself, there was much beauty in Africa, she internally admitted. They had been correct when they said it was not Africa. She knew he would return to the Okavango Delta, she knew he would seek out the white-haired man and work with him. Maybe it was only right, father and son working together, enjoying one another, despite the fact that neither would know how closely related they were. She had debated at length within her mind, within her soul, whether to tell the son that his father was alive, whether to tell him who his father was. But in the end she had calmly decided against it. For she knew her main reason for telling him would be because she wanted Robert for herself, and in the telling the pressure would be upon him to accept her and to accept Bob as his son.

But without a memory how could that acceptance ever be genuine? The memory must return by itself and if it did, then everyone would know the truth. If it didn't then their separate lives must forever remain separate. Without memory there could be no genuine affection, without memory there could be no love. It had been sixteen years, how the hell could she expect any change to occur now? It was too late. Close that chapter, Kathy Castle, she said to herself as she shivered, unaware of her shivering, on that lonely bench in the cool spring evening in Hyde Park. Close that chapter. You have the business you love, you have the son you love, you must let him have his head. Let him go in order that you may keep him. To attempt to stop him now will surely mean that you will lose him. You know that, Kathy, do what you do best and let your son go.

She drove slowly from London to Arlaston. She never stopped once. But she drove slowly, as if not wishing to return, as if knowing that when she put her foot through the doorway of her hotel for the next time, she would be leaving her past behind forever, her decision irrevocable. But until she put her foot through that door, there was still the slightest, the very slightest of chances for something to happen. So she drove very slowly from London to Arlaston, hoping, waiting, for something to happen.

7

But nothing did.

So that when she put her foot through the doorway of her hotel she left her past behind forever, her decision irrevocable.

The three years Bob spent at university were years of some interest and great frustration. His lofty academic standards, higher than either his mother or father had achieved, left him constantly at variance with a system that worked at its own pace and not at his. However, he possessed his mother's discipline and a determination to complete the course, to attain the required degree that would enable him to pursue with authority the career he had chosen. Never once had he deviated from the decision he had made during his trip to Africa, never once, despite the constructively structured arguments of a mother attempting to dissuade him from such a course. She had never resorted to the ploy of tears, simply the reasoned argument of security, financial return, job opportunity, people contact. But as his final year drew to a close, the arguments ceased. She had at last accepted that there would be no way to alter his mind. His anticipated First Class honours degree in Zoology, his quiet calmness and authority, his generosity of spirit and his maturity all combined to finally persuade her what she had known all along. He was his father's son and he was his mother's son. There would be no stopping him, no changing his mind. As Bob's exceptional final year performance came to its conclusion, Kathy and her father prepared for their day on the vice-chancellor's lawn.

Bob had remained in letter contact with Nnyaa Leina and his son Ndimande. In his final years at school and during the first year of university, the letters had been spasmodic. Friendly, passing news from one to the other. But as his second and third years in university progressed, the letters became more intense and more relevant to their disparate lives and hopes. Bob found himself able in the university library to spend free time researching ever deeper into animal and land conservation projects throughout the world. He surfed from Africa to the Antarctic, from Peru to the jungles of Indonesia. He researched government opinions and political stances. With this superior access than theirs to what was happening in the world, he was able to suggest to his two friends new ideas for conservation projects and ways of lobbying and appealing not only to local governments but also to world-wide humanitarian and wildlife organisations. In turn they supplied him with information, photographs and reports on their current activities, allowing the young student to apply his earnestness and intelligence to the task of raising general consciousness for the endangered species of the Okavango Delta. The need to resolve the conflict between man and wild animal, ensuring the maximum preservation of the latter. This Bob did not only among his friends and the relevant associations of his own university, but also with inter-university groups and internationally recognised and prestigious organisations. The National Geographic Magazine agreed to consider a full length feature article, which could become a film if they were sufficiently excited by the material Bob supplied. Bob undertook to complete the project within six months of his arrival in Africa. This contact with Africa, his friends there and his own contribution to their work, made the relative dullness and lack of challenge afforded to him by university life more bearable.

Then came the day of his graduation. All he could think about was Africa, all Kathy could think about was the pain of her own graduation day some twenty-three years before and the knowledge that he was still alive. The fact that her son, their son, was in contact with him; the fact that he did not know who she was, would never know who she was. Ian Harris, proudly upright, looked healthier than a man of seventy-two years of age confined for ever to a wheelchair was entitled to look. He had bought himself a dapper dark grey suit with just the suggestion of a light red stripe flowing self-consciously through it. He had gone to the best tailor in Stafford and been held upright by his daughter and two shop assistants while the manager had measured him to ensure a perfect fit. What the hell if he could never stand or walk to display the perfection of the fit, *he* knew it was perfect and his grandson knew it and his daughter knew it and they were all that mattered in this world. All that mattered now that *she* had left him so suddenly last year. Never a day's illness and so suddenly to have gone! A massive single heart attack. He had mourned his wife of forty-six years with the intensity of passion of a young bridegroom. Thank God they had come so much closer together in the final years. The accident had been good for them, realised what they might have lost, made every single further day count. Days together in their garden or rides in the car in the countryside or high tea in the tranquility of the winter garden of the Arlaston Hotel. Or sitting together in the brightness and warmth of their cosy room with the log fire blazing and their reminiscences of long ago. Living their lives once again through their memories. She would have been so proud to have seen Bob today, so proud. As he sat stiffly in his wheeled prison his misty eyes remembered her, intensely. She would have liked the suit too. He wore a red handkerchief in his top jacket pocket, his flouting of individuality. As they sat right at the very front of the large town hall being used for the conferment of degrees, he waited for the name of Bob Castle to be called. He didn't have to wait long, for there were very few Firsts that year and none were students whose surname began with A or B. Bob Castle was the first graduate to be called. The first and the best. Ian Harris had to use his red handkerchief, unnoticed through the applause, save for the young woman beside him who squeezed his hand and shared his tears.

She knew her son resembled one man only as he, thick black long-haired, walked calmly and resolutely to receive his award from the Chancellor of the university, his first brush with royalty. As Kathy watched him move, she clung tighter to her father's hand, not to give him succour and support, rather seeking it for herself. Somehow her marvelous father knew, his comprehension and concern shifted to her and he became dry again as he sought to comfort his little girl.

Kathy did not accompany Bob to the airport, he didn't want that, nor in truth did she. But she did drive him to Stafford station where, on that never changing platform, she said good-bye to her son. She did not know for how long. And although she feared for him in Africa, feared what it might bring back to her, she somehow knew that he would survive. Moreover, she reasoned, if Robert Castle could survive and he was going to join Robert Castle, then surely his son would be fine too. She had lain awake almost all of the nights for the entire week before he left, debating whether she should tell him. He was going to work with him, live with him, surely he should know that he is his own father! But if his father could not remember, could not acknowledge him, wouldn't that be an even greater pain than not knowing? There was no pain associated with not knowing, no pain at all. The pain only came with knowledge. Why give him pain? He was joyfully travelling to meet friends, going to work with them on the projects that set his youthful mind on fire, able to contribute at a very meaningful level. He had the agreement letter from the National Geographic Magazine in his hand, he had the experience of his many talks on the issue of preservation, he had enthusiasm. Together with his father they would be an unbeatable team. Momentarily she wished she too could have been a part of that team. But that life had now passed her by.

The Chairman of the Arlaston, Buxton and Matlock Hydros embraced her sturdy son on platform one of Stafford station and then watched him board his train for Africa. Just as she had done.

'May God go with you,' muttered the small woman under her breath, the small woman who did not even believe in God.

8

'Ndimande and Bob are like brothers. They get on so well, understand one another so entirely despite their different backgrounds, their different upbringings. It's remarkable.'

Francina sad nothing as she listened to her husband; as she watched the two young men diligently studying the latest reports of lion sightings on Chief's Island. If she could so plainly see it, then why did the gods not give him the power too? She had returned to her own gods, she had totally rejected the white man's gods. The ancestors had come back to her too, they were speaking with her again. They were telling her to be aware of the new white man in the village for he could bring her harm and she believed them. She had asked them if the new white man was truly the son of her husband but the gods would not tell her, did not give her a response, they had remained silent. So she could not answer her father when the old man asked her what ailed her. Why she was so reserved and quiet since the young white man had come to them. To the now almost sightless Mjanyelwa, Bob Castle seemed a good man, a pleasant man, and he was contributing significantly to their work. He came with the ideas of the white man, the ideas that had been tried and proved successful. The fight was the new generation's fight and Bob would help to lead that fight, he and Ndimande. Mjanyelwa could not believe her when she told him that the gods had warned her against Bob, that he could bring problems to their village. Mjanyelwa did not believe her. Besides, he had little time for the gods these days, he was doing what work he could for the project, but his eyes were poor now, he had difficulty in distinguishing the features of the people he knew, he could identify their voices, but sometimes not their features. He spoke to Nnyaa Leina and told him of his daughter's fears and as always the clever, once white man, understood. Understood that what she perceived was the threat of the unknown, the threat of the first white man to live with them since he had arrived so many years before. He understood, he would ensure all was well. The old man believed him, the old man waiting his call to the ancestors, waiting to be reunited with his wonderful Esther, preparing for that day not long hence, absolutely believed in Nnyaa Leina and all he said and all he did.

The project group was now four. The three men had been joined by a South African student, Jane McEwan. She simply arrived one day and stayed. Backpacking around Africa, avoiding responsibility, avoiding university, avoiding her overbearing Afrikaans parents. She had become captivated by the work of the trio and captivated by the man from England who had such an enthusiasm for life, for everything he did. An enthusiasm mirrored by the leader and she was fascinated by the mystery of it all. The mystery of the old white-haired man who wasn't really old and had such a good body and looked at her sometimes in the way she wished Bob would look at her, until his wisp of a wife joined him, managed him, removed him. Ndimande, the leader's son, so similar in so many ways to the two white men, all so similar to one another. The younger men possessing the same intelligence and grace and fun and love of Africa and the animals and the work they did together. And the singing, oh God the singing! Such voices that could make your hair stand up rigid on your back with the songs they sung. The songs they taught her of Africa and the hymns of England. Music to make you cry, voices to make you weep. And their very closeness, the bond of all members of the project became in and of itself a constant harmony. She began to join in their work too and the day she saw the baby impala coming out of its mother, still in its sack, was the very first time she cried at beauty. Then the day she sat with Ndimande and Bob and the lions let them sit there, no more than twenty feet from them; that day her fear transformed to wonder. Then the day when she was terrified by the charging elephant and the way that Nnyaa Leina had with peals of laughter and a zig-zag run saved her and so she ran to him and how she held him and how she felt his manhood through his wafer-thin garments and how she had almost responded, but then she thought of Francina and she thought of Bob and knew that she wanted to remain there and if she allowed him to take her as she knew he wanted to, then it would destroy everything. So she had released the hold and walked on to the village. Leaving him standing, wryly smiling in the bush. A man alone.

'Who will give the talk?' Asked Bob. It was to be their first public meeting, hosted by The Scientific Research Association of America. The venue Cape Town, the conference one at which ten papers were to be given to almost seven-hundred delegates.

The three men and the one woman sat together in the evening's stillness around their bush campfire, more aware than ever of the enormous chasm existing between their lifestyle and the opportunity now offered to them. Here they were in the bush, next month they would be accommodated in one of the best hotels in the continent of Africa. Were any of them ready for the ordeal, were any of them competent to unfalteringly and convincingly deliver the paper? The choice was between two men. But could the older achieve what was needed to be achieved? He had only been as far as Victoria Falls and the town of Maun in the last twenty-four years! He had no suit to wear, no resources to purchase one. He had an ancient tie that was wrapped around one of his mixing sticks and a faded blue shirt and old shoes he wore with his jeans on Sundays when occasionally he attended the small Christian church in the village, but they would not be satisfactory for the meeting. Bob had little more that was really suitable. In his packing he had not considered the necessity for a suit. But Bob had something that none of the others possessed.

He left quietly the following day, telling no-one where he was going. It took him two days to reach Maun. It took him two hours to make the connection to England and it took him ten minutes on the reverse-charge call, ten minutes of loving mutual concerns and updates, before he could begin to describe the requirements of his group. He had never doubted his mother for a moment. There was even something childlike in her willingness to help. It took him a further two days to return to the village. Jane grabbed him as soon as he appeared, she grabbed him from the fear of losing him for it was the first time he had ever been away from her. He looked down at the blunt-nosed, stringy girl and realised he too had missed her. He held her as he had never held her before, as she had always wished he would hold her. Nnyaa Leina watched the young couple, felt his jealousy transform into a happiness for them. Francina watched them, understood, but did not know what she felt anymore.

'I was able to raise some capital for our venture,' he began, lying for security, not knowing why. 'There is a nature organisation in the UK that is willing to fund our trip to Cape Town and willing to provide us with whatever we require to make a good presentation.'

'Including suits?' Asked Jane, jokingly, and Bob realised he was still holding her hand.

'Including suits!' He replied and he loved his mother but somehow needed to protect her. He could not explain why, even to himself.

Still the question of the presenter had to be decided. They talked long into that exciting first night of their heightened awareness of their own importance and the presentation began to devolve into two separate sections. There were the statistics necessary to convince the audience; the reduction seen since the 1979 census of twenty-five per cent of the Zebra population throughout

Botswana, of a massive forty per cent of wild buffalo, sixty-five per cent of hartebeest and the saddest of all, seventy-five percent of wildebeest. The only success story, the only animals to beat the iniquitous fences strung across the shattered heartland of Botswana were the elephant, powerful enough to travel where no man could stop them and so their numbers had risen by a welcome thirty per cent. These and more were the statistics, these should be presented by a man with the authority of learning, of research competence and of academic authority. This section of the presentation fitted exactly into the area of Bob's ability, played to the intellectual earnestness he could display to the invited audience. Section two would be an appeal to emotion and to action, an explanation of what the threats of poor water management meant to an increasingly drought prevailing countryside. The illegal hunting that was decimating the herds and those damn fences that were not fairly coping with the constant conflict between the needs of the people, of the cattle and of the wildlife of the region. An appeal to the senses from a person with an authority derived from first-hand knowledge of years of experiencing the situation at first hand. A person with the passion to get the message across, to tear at heart strings. There was only one choice for this task, only one man of the group who could carry that emotional message. So, as night became dawn the tiny group determined their responsibilities and it was a sharing of abilities and of strengths and of acceptance and they all loved what they were doing. They retired to sleep a few short hours before the thrill of their trip, before the preparation of their speeches again began to consume them. But neither Jane nor Bob slept that night. They had found something else, something momentarily transcending their work. They lay in each other's arms for hours, unheeding the brightness of the dawn. Their lovemaking was gentle and ardent, earnest and controlled. He was inexperienced. She knew this and she also knew she wanted to keep him. She would show him the other things later, did not want to display to him what she had learnt during so many times before. This was now the only time, this was the best time. She wanted this man, she would keep this man, she was proud of this man. When they emerged from their hut it was already noon and when they came to join the others in their preparation for Cape Town, everyone smiled at one another and all were contented, for the match was a good one. It would remain, as long as Africa and animals and conservation remained.

It was the longest journey of his remembered life and he realised now that he was not simply embarking upon a journey, he was embarking upon a new lifestyle. He enjoyed his companions, their youthfulness, their intelligence, their challenge. Their excitement at what lay ahead. He was happy he had made the decision to leave Francina and Ndimande in the village, they had desperately wanted to come but they could never have coped with this. The segregation of black and white on the trains, on the buses, on the very beaches of South Africa. But what a beautiful place! The rolling waves of the frightening ocean, the waves that had visited other continents, perhaps even the land of his birth. The land he assumed to be England as English seemed to be his native tongue. This exposure alone with Bob and Jane and with the white people in South Africa made him want to reach out to find his own roots, before it was too late. Somehow in the Delta, deep in the heart of the Delta with Francina and with Mjanyelwa it had not seemed important but now, in this modern cosmopolitan city, it was important. Poor Mjanyelwa was dying now and so it was also a good decision for his daughter and grandson to remain with him. It was good that they had not come. Nnyaa Leina loved being with Bob and Jane. They looked so good together although her nose was awful, well not awful but small and squat, but she had good breasts too, for such a skinny girl. Too? As well as who? Who was it that had the good breasts? She had not been to visit him for quite a while now, for some years now. Perhaps she was also gone? He felt she held a key for him, whether she had been real or merely a fabrication of his imagination. He believed she had existed and sometime again she would exist, of this he was sure. But he did like to watch the young people together. And he did like to think of the breasts.

At first Nnyaa Leina had felt awkward in his new suit, but the awkwardness passed and if he looked anything like his companion, then he must appear very handsome indeed. He liked appearing handsome. There were some very smart young women walking in the streets of Cape Town and on the beaches and many of them had large breasts and some of them did not cover their breasts. He retained a deep appreciation of their sensuality. He trimmed his beard for the speech, he considered removing it entirely, but both Bob and Jane told him that it made him seem distinguished, emphasized the fact that their message transcended generations and so, he kept his beard. He wondered what his face would look like without the beard, probably ugly. He didn't want to appear ugly, so he kept the beard.

Theirs was the penultimate paper to be delivered on the final day of the conference. They listened in patience and understanding to the other papers, none had quite the depth of study and deep local knowledge that theirs would be able to display. He realised that was attributable to Bob and the research methods he had learned whilst at university and employed in the Delta. However, he felt he had contributed too. When they had compiled their handout for the conference delegates and they had composed it together with juxtapositions of photographs and text, it had all seemed very familiar and very easy to him. And he wondered why it had felt so easy. That camera of Bob's, despite its age, provided wonderful photographs. In their quiet times together, Bob never spoke of his father, the previous owner of the camera; somehow he needed to speak little, for the loss was easy to understand, difficult to bear. But there was the compensation of his work and the friendships and their life together and now, of course, now there was Jane. Nnyaa Leina felt so very close to Bob, almost as close as he felt to his own son Ndimande, and he enjoyed that closeness.

He could not understand his complete lack of nervousness as he rose to address the audience, following on from the brief but detailed presentation by Bob. It was as if all of his life he had been waiting for this moment of challenge and that all of his life he had prepared for it and knew he could do it. The power of the moment swept over and around him as he looked out at a sea of expectant faces. He looked down at his notes, he saw nothing but a blur of passion, he felt nothing but the certainty of the moment. He put his notes back into the inside pocket of his new suit, he did not need them, he spoke from his heart. His voice rose to the ceiling of the crowded auditorium as he challenged the governments of Africa to cease in their wanton destruction of their national heritage. He fixed his eyes on every blurred face in that audience making them all feel he was speaking directly to them and to them alone as he berated the governments of Africa for blatantly and carelessly issuing hunting licenses to men who were allowed to murder with importunity. He shouted down the gun lobbies of the world, the fence builders of the world and he held that huge audience in the very palm of his hand. And when he had caught them he kept them and then he told them what they must do. How they must turn hunting tourism into photographic tourism, how they must encourage the making of wild-life films and projects that allowed the local people to benefit financially from the wild animals, so that they no longer fought for small fenced-off portions of grazing land for their few cattle. He demanded the re-allocation of monetary resources to water preservation projects that would transcend this century and be available for the next. For the children of the next generations, for the animals of the next generations. He proposed the maintenance and the policing of an open wildlife corridor between the Okavango - Kwando - Linyati - Chobe complex in the north of Botswana, a corridor desperately and clearly required for the long-term maintenance of the wildlife resource of the great continent they were all privileged to live in. As a passionate Nnyaa Leina completed his speech there was a profound silence in the hall, a profound silence that lasted for long seconds. Then the applause began and the delegates rose to their feet and Nnyaa Leina knew that something momentous had happened in his life. Bob Castle looked at the man he knew as Nnyaa Leina in wonderment and in awe. He had now heard what Nnyaa Leina could do, what he was capable of. He knew the man, and yet did he really know him? What was it about him today that made him appear in such a different light? Wearing a suit, presenting a long, powerful and authoritative speech in English? And then he knew what it was. This would have been how his father would have acted had he lived. This is exactly how he would have sounded. He knew it. He felt it. Then he felt something else, questioned something else as he watched Nnyaa Leina basking in the applause, standing tall and proud. But before he could begin to analyse it, even to capture it Jane was beside him and Jane was kissing him, there, right there in front of all those delegates and they all saw and he did not care and the intuitive question of a moment before was eliminated from his mind.

Right at the back of the hall, hidden by the enthusiastically applauding sea of delegates stood a small and beautiful woman. She had cried quietly to herself when she felt her husband's passion bouncing from one delegate to another, she had cried happily to herself when she saw the warm loving embrace her son both received and gave to the fine-looking girl who had so impulsively, so unashamedly leapt on to the platform at the end of his father's speech.

'Bully for you!' She had shouted and no-one had heard her above the din of applause. 'Bully for you!' And she was shouting her appreciation at all three people who now stood together on that platform, standing together in their glow of success.

The beautiful, sad, happy, lonely woman hurried for her cab to return to the airport for her solitary flight back to the UK.

9

The success of their trip to Cape Town and their unqualified achievement remained for a long time with them. The organizers of the conference assisted them in opening a bank account to receive the many donations, which were sure to come their way once the delegates returned home and spoke with their own individual organisations, talked with their government agencies. The crusading quartet would soon be cash rich, the organizers had seen it before, it would happen again with them. They required a name, they required registration as a charity to which tax-free donations could be made. They needed to put their plans together so that they could inform the donors how and where and when their contributions would be spent. They required this and so much more. They were told all this as they left Cape Town to return to their small village in the Okavango Delta. It was a new experience for them all, one to savour, one to wonder about, one to manage. It was then that the two men stood apart as Jane came into her own, as the canny Afrikaner, so accustomed to wealth but decrying it for its own sake, displayed her abilities to control finances, to manage a set of accounts, to plan what could be done, which investments to consider. And the two men were grateful. One the scholar, the other the adventurer, both requiring the practical manager of money. They discovered that quality in Jane and now she too realised how well she could contribute to the team, the small and happy team. At first the money arrived in tiny amounts, but within a month there were more than twenty thousand pounds and twelve thousand dollars sitting in their two external accounts in Cape Town, unconverted into local currency. For Jane wanted to ensure they did not suffer any currency exchange charges or future governmental restrictions that could have the effect of locking up local currency and not making it freely convertible until they were certain how and where the money was to be spent. Then, on the last day of their first month after the momentous Cape Town visit, they received notification via their post box in Maun, that there had been an anonymous donation of one hundred thousand pounds into their account. Unable to cope with the magnitude of the largess, the men passed the problem to Jane. It was a problem she relished, an opportunity she knew how to manage. For more than one week she secretly and quietly made her notes, performed her calculations, spoke little to her friends, not even to the man she loved when they lay awake tired and happy after their passionate love-making in their special hut in the family compound. In the hut that had once been reserved for visitors but was now their own. A gift from Nnyaa Leina, the first gift the young couple, as a couple, had ever received. And now, in the depth of the African night, she had taught

Bob many of the things she had learnt and he never asked her how she knew them, he just enjoyed. They took pleasure together and always it was as if it was the first time and always he was so very caring and so very careful, but still she did not tell him of her plans.

Then the day came when she was ready and could tell them all. They had a feast that night for also it was her birthday. She was twenty-one years old and that was a special birthday for the white people and so her new family also made it special for her. There was chicken and lechwe, hare and eland. There were the special vegetables prepared by an increasingly distant Francina who now believed that the white people were taking her husband away from her. She could not understand any longer what it was they were doing to him but he seemed so far removed from her now, so rapt in his work and she knew he would never return, never return to the simplicity of their love-making in their hut and the life she had planned for them as they came into their second age. She believed she would probably now enter that age alone, for she felt herself becoming old just as, simultaneously, she witnessed him becoming younger. The work, the excitement of the young people had brought back his youth and he became as she remembered him in the early days. He now appeared closer in age to his son and to the other young people than he did to her. So she sought solace with her gods and now they spoke to her every night and they told her that they would accept her when she was ready, for she informed them this life now held nothing further for her. Her father was dying, her son and her husband seduced by the fame of the moment, a fame granted by white men. They were lost in the work they pretended to perform for the animals and the people but really they were performing it for themselves for they loved it, in and of itself. At least that is what she told her gods and her gods agreed with her and they were ready for her. But still she prepared the vegetables for the feast and she wished the white girl well, and then went to her hut to talk with her gods. No-one missed Francina, the team were awaiting the proposals from Jane. Their work all-consuming.

'There are two things we must achieve.' She began. 'One is to interest people in what we're trying to accomplish by showing them at first hand what the problems are that we're facing. To interest them in the plight of the animals, to encourage them to take their knowledge home with then and to become our ambassadors in their own countries.'

'And the second?' asked Ndimande, the man she loved as a brother.

'Is to take our challenge to the highest level of government, to visit many of the major governmental and nature conservationists of the world to put our case to them, to obtain their support.'

So far she had them with her, for they had purposely drunk but little of the maize beer provided at the feast; there would be time for that when discussions were over.

'So,' here goes, she thought, hesitating, hoping she would be able to take them all the way with her, hoping her financial calculations would stand their scrutiny, especially that of the man she loved, the smartest of them all.

'So,' she began again, 'this is what I propose. We will build a unique safari operation that will take committed supporters with financial resources into the Delta for periods of two to four weeks at a time. Small groups, up to a maximum of ten. I will manage the camp, Bob will give talks to the people on the work we are doing and encourage them to work with us for the weeks they stay here. He will plan their activities, gather their information, provide them with training. Ndimande will lead the parties into the bush and handle the camping in the bush. This way we can take two parties at one time, one based here in an extension of our homestead, the other actually working on projects in the Delta. We will be careful who we allow to come and work with us and they will pay all their own costs and we will together plan how they can become ambassadors for us when they return to their home countries. Ambassadors to both enhance awareness of our situation and to assist in fund raising for us.'

Nnyaa Leina had sat silent through all this, but he felt he must now speak, this was his work and she was taking it from him, she was to manage the operation, his son the tracking and camping, Bob the planning and execution of the field work. What was remaining for him to do?

But Jane McEwan knew him well, read his body language, caught him before he began to speak.

'And for you, Nnyaa Leina, is the most difficult work of all. You must leave us and travel to the countries that must hear you. You must speak to the audiences as you spoke in Cape Town. We now have the money to send you, to support you. You and you alone can put our project on the map of the world, deliver it to the consciousness of the influential, to raise the funds we shall need to continue to be successful.'

She had finished. The conversation began to buzz, all talking at once, all seeing the problems, all seeing the opportunity, all moving along the learning curve that she had worked through some days before, and all, in the end, as she hoped they would, agreeing that her plans were sound. Even her costings for transport and building materials and tents and safari equipment and economy class travel twice a year to and around America and four times a year to Europe with hotel costs and taxis went unquestioned. The minutiae of the detail she had incorporated into her proposals left them with few questions to ask, fewer points to raise. Bob was proud of his woman, had not realised how far her capabilities extended and began to think of a permanence for them both. They had their project, they had their life together, they had their hut and their work, but he, as a corollary of his disciplined life, knew he had to have more.

Kathy received her son's letter as she opened the morning mail in her company house that she shared with her ever outwardly cheerful father. In fact the old bugger was becoming more and more of a nuisance these days, again wanting something to do in the business, his mind as sharp as ever it had been, needing something to stimulate him mentally. What to give the old devil? She thought with affection. Maybe I'll pack him off to Africa too, all my other men are there! Then she saw the letter, recognised the handwriting. She rushed it to her room to read alone. To savour it. She would be a few minutes late for her busy daily schedule, but some things were more important than her work. She read of the success she had witnessed unseen in Cape Town, she read of the anonymous donor with a smile of modest delight; she read of the plans they had made and the pride that swept through the words as her son told her of the woman who had made those plans and then she read her invitation to the wedding of her son. A wedding to be held at Delta Camp, the place where she had seen the elephants of Africa, trunk to tail, and she remembered the champagne and the sunset and the beauty that had caused her to cry. It was so perfect and so right and of course she couldn't go and of course she must go. Then she read that her son had invited Nnyaa Leina to be his best man at the wedding and she laughed aloud at the absurdity of it all and she loved the absurdity of it all and of course she must go.

'Father!' She called as she left her room, 'Father!'

Ian Harris decided he would not go to the wedding. It would be too much hassle and he hated travelling abroad anyway, always had done. There was something else too and they both knew what it was but neither admitted it to the other. It was only as the date became closer and the plans had to be made to ensure the hotels would function well in her absence that he played the card they both knew he would play.

'If you don't object Kathy,' he said, with the twinkle in the eyes that she believed had almost been lost but now was there once again. 'I'll look after things for you while you're away. You haven't had a holiday for years, it'll do you good. I'm not too old, too senile or too immobile to keep an eye on the place, don't you worry.'

She loved this ruffian of a man. He was totally shameless. He lived for the hotels, he would live until he was a hundred! She didn't argue, she offered direction only, direction with a smile.

'I'll expect eighty-six per cent occupancy, my man. We are entering the holiday season now you know, and I also want catering costs reduced. We need zero point sixty-five per cent higher margin in the F&B department over the next month.'

He looked at her for a moment, nonplussed. Then both father and daughter smiled their broad knowing smiles at one another. She moved to him, they held one another and he chuckled deep within his chest.

'Unbeatable!' Was all he said.

10

For Francina it was reminiscent of the old times, when together they would roam in the bush searching for her medicines. The early days before he became so obsessed by the need to protect the animals. They had always been there, they would always be there, what was the need to protect them? The whole thing was crazy and now there were more people coming to her village, the white boy who may be his son and the white boy's woman. She had heard their plans and soon there would be more people and they would all be white and they would work their magic on her husband and he would be leaving her. How could he return to her after he went to the countries of America and Europe, after he saw their ways, after he saw their women? Francina felt that her life was over, her life with Nnyaa Leina. Her only life.

It was a dazzling morning, the sun's rays shimmering upon the Boro River as the two mokoros silently glided upon its surface, disturbing its tranquility but little as they slithered through the bending reeds. Whitefaced ducks vied with Egyptian geese for the better shady areas, and lost. Sparrow Hawks competed with Brown Snake Eagles for the best food, and lost. The red-eyed Brubru watched in protective peace as the strangers passed by, they would not be able to reach her nest, could not disturb her young. Reedbuck and Red Lechwe non-competitively munched together at the water's edge observing the passage of the mokoros, always one of their number posted as sentinel, just in case. A serenity of calm imposed its welcome grip on Francina's innate placidity. And they would take it all away, their plans would take it all away!

Ndimande and Bob took turns in poling the mokoro, both loved to do so, for that extra few feet of standing height above the water level whilst others sat in the gliding craft, made every difference to what could be seen. Heads above, rather than in the reeds, meant that animals on the land could be observed as they variously sought food or shelter, animals unnoticed by passengers forced to sit still on the waterline to ensure the correct balance of the craft. The day's full beauty, the charm of the birdlife, the gracefulness of the various antelope breeds invaded all their minds, all their senses. They spoke little, merely pointing at a new sight for others to enjoy. They were a unity bar one, and that one was becoming more and more distant from them all. Nnyaa Leina felt it more harshly than the others, but had no answer, knew that the life he was now leading, the challenge he was now embarking upon, was what he had been created for. There was no turning back.

Their quest this trip was to find a pride of lions that had been sighted three days previously on Beacon Island off the southwestern tip of Chief's Island. They wanted to find the lions, record their numbers and determine how successful this year's breeding had been, for it was still drought conditions and difficult for the cubs to survive unless they remained constantly close to the water, where they would be in the path of all larger predators visiting to drink, as well as in danger from the large vicious reptiles lurking at the water's edge.

They made camp as the sun began to soften its position in the sky. They left Francina alone to begin her preparations for the evening meal and they went to look for the lions. The land was still baking from the day's heat of the sun and soon they could feel the warmth seeping inexorably through their footwear, until in places it became too hot to walk. Then they would stop for a while, bathe their feet in the shade of a tree and continue on. While they stopped they searched around with binoculars and with the naked eye, but still they could not find the lions. They saw the zebra and the wildebeest and the elephants in the distance, crossing the shallows of the river, returning to the greater area and greener pasture of Chief's Island. They saw the buffalo on that larger island, but none were charging today, the heat had temporarily overcome them. It had been ambitious to believe that they could have encountered the lions on their first day so, only a little disappointed, they returned to their camp, hungry, anticipating their evening meal.

But there were no signs of cooking in the camp, no signs of Francina. For a moment Nnyaa Leina and the others were concerned, but then they heard a splashing and a singing in the water a little distance from the camp.

'Stay here, I'll get her,' said her husband, 'maybe you could begin preparing some food.'

Nnyaa Leina walked away from the camp to where he could hear the singing. He was about to call his wife when he saw the dying sun's rays glance off her smooth oily skin and decided to watch her for a moment, concealed like a voyeur. She was still beautiful to look at was Francina, her tiny breasts still pert, her waist still small, unfattened by food or childbearing and she was enjoying herself. Childlike she jumped into the air then went under the water to come up again laughing at the fun she made for herself, like a baby impala playing unhindered for the first time in the welcoming coolness of the water. She was a joy to watch and he remembered why he loved her and he felt guilty at what he was now doing to her, what they were all doing to her. She was such a pleasingly simple girl, like a young child still. How wrong it was to destroy her life, her dreams. How wrong. Yet as he watched her and despite his love for her he knew there could be no going back for him. He loved her well enough but he silently admitted that he loved the tasks before him more. If he analysed it truthfully, it was the act of lovemaking he enjoyed the most with her and her lack of fixedness, lack of decisiveness. Her devotion to him and her compliance only to the shifting winds with which she drifted or which were directed by him. He watched for a minute more then left her alone in the dying sunshine, alone at play, knowing that if she realised his presence it would destroy her moment of childlike joy. He returned from the innocence of Francina to the intellectual stimulus and the challenge of his work now emboldened by three thrusting young people waiting for him by the campfire.

It was as he was approaching the campsite that he heard the screams. They shattered his soul. Cries at first exactly like those of a wild animal. Then he realised that the shrieks were coming from the river, from exactly where he had left Francina playing in the river! He raced back to where he had seen her but a few moments before and as he came abreast of the river he was met by thrashing and screaming and the head of a huge Nile crocodile and in that head, clamped in those jaws, were the breasts of his lovely Francina and she was screaming and one of her breasts just seemed to be hanging loose by a thread from her chest and she was screaming. He dived into the river and there were voices on the bank, voices yelling on the bank and he did not hear the words. He saw only those breasts he loved and the waist he loved and those naked legs and they were moving away from him. He dived for the legs and he held onto the legs. Then he was pulled down and at tremendous speed they moved away from the shore, the trio locked as one, the crocodile his wife and himself. Francina was still threshing in the water but weaker now and all he could do was to hang on to her leg. He was almost losing his grip with the power of the beast pulling her away from him and his body was searing along the bottom of the river and wounds opened up along the entire length of his body but he felt nothing. All he knew was he must hold on to that leg and all would be well. Now he was drowning and the water invaded his body, rushed down to his lungs and he struggled for air and still they sped along. It was only the ankle he was holding now for the leg must be somewhere else and where in God's name was the leg? Where was Kathy and why was this river trying to kill him? Francina Kathy where are you and why am I dying and why did we come to Africa. Your father was right Kathy! All I have to show for my trip is this hoof, this hoof foot this foot hoof this....

For two days the young people treated him. He lay semi-conscious. He had fought his battle with the crocodile and it was a tremendous battle, and when the first battle had ended always the second began again. There were two battles, two rolled into one. And his screams were pitiful to hear and sometimes Jane could not bear to hear those screams and so she went a little apart from the hut where he lay. Sometimes she visited the pitiful site where they had burnt all that remained of Francina. Her tiny leg, her tiny leg that looked no bigger than an animal's hoof, not even a leg, more the foot only. Oh God, and did she want to remain in Africa now?

Bob sat by the bedside of Nnyaa Leina and listened as he called his mother's name. At first he thought he had misunderstood, but the calling became insistent, unmistakable. Clearly Nnyaa Leina called out for Kathy and clearly now everything made sense. Nnyaa Leina had not been acting as his father would have acted when he stood in front of that large audience in Cape Town, he *was* his father! And if he was his father then why had his mother not seen it when they came here so many years ago? Then he realised she had seen it, realised that the man with no memory had not remembered her. 'Oh mother, oh my poor mother!' The anguish that must have eaten into her soul, the torment that she could control only by burying herself in her work. All the nights of tears he remembered when they had returned from Africa. Oh mother! He cried for his mother, he cried for his father and he cried for what they had all lost and what they had all found.

Ndimande felt no jealousy, he felt only loss. The loss of a mother, the perhaps losing of a father and despite the words they used together, he and his now brother Bob, he believed that in the end he would be the loser of everything. He felt no anger, no jealousy. He could not direct such vile emotions at the two men he loved. He had the advantage over Bob, he had had a father for all the years of growing, for all the times of play and of learning. Bob had not had a father, he had been alone. How could he feel jealousy or anger? He felt only pain.

On the third day Nnyaa Leina emerged from his black hole of despair and of illness, the fever had passed, the wounds were beginning to heal on his strong body. The first face he saw when he awoke was the face of his son, but still he was not certain it really was his son.

'Bob?' He asked.

Bob Castle reached over to his father, he held the weeping man in his strong young arms and he kissed his cheek.

'Yes, father, I am your son, I have your name.'

They held one another for more than an hour. They said nothing. There were no adequate words to express the emotion of their moment.

Ndimande and Jane sat a little distance from the hut. They held hands, they needed one another's support. For the moment, they did not exist.

Robert Castle went alone to say good-bye to his African wife. He did not go to the small secret place where they had burnt the foot, he went instead to the river. He went alone in his mokoro canoe and he was away for three days. He talked to her as he sat beside the river, he talked to her of the love they had known together, of the very early days when she had saved his life and claimed him and he did not know who he was, did not want to remember who he was. He talked to her of the birth of their son and he promised her that he would always love Ndimande, would never forsake him, would always care for him. He promised her that he would care for her father until his final day that now seemed such a short time away. He reminded her of their walks together in the Delta, their evenings in the bush, their love-making which was so new to him and so special. He did not weep as he talked to her in the river, for she had been a happy girl for almost all of her life and she hated to see sadness and to see tears, especially in a man, especially in her man. It took him three days to tell her everything he wanted to tell her of their life together, of the feelings he had for her, of the happiness she had given to him, of the promises he would keep for her. Then he went home to be with his sons.

In his father's absence Bob thought of his mother in England, of the life she had given him despite the pain of her own. The debt he owed her was incalculable, she had always been there for him, she had always supported, she had never tried to falsify anything. Yet she had known, at least for the last eight years, she had known that her husband was still alive, and she had borne it all by herself. That was why she had removed Tom from her life, that was why she had never taken another man, always living in hope that one day he might remember, he might return. He thought deep into the night about his mother, he thought deep and knew that there was something he could now do for her. He borrowed Ndimande's mokoro and stole through the dawn to be at Delta Camp as it awoke. They had access to a telegram service. He thought of the words he should send, then he realised that there were only a few required, a very few. He dictated the words and was told the telegram should reach his mother in England within twelve hours. That was time enough he thought. She has been waiting for twenty-three years, twelve hours is not too much time.

Dear mother stop my father stop your husband stop has come back stop all my love and understanding stop was what he said in his telegram to England.

11

The wedding was only three weeks away now, they had postponed it for one month in respect to Francina. She had been dead for almost eight weeks and the pain was lessening, the work all-consuming. But Jane missed the attentions of another woman to aid her in her preparations for her special day, the assistance every bride requires. What to wear, how to look? She only had herself to depend upon.

Bob and his mother exchanged long letters in the interim period and Bob and his father talked long into many nights, always asking Ndimande to be there so as to involve him in their discoveries. Slowly Robert Castle began to piece together the remnants of his life, his sons, especially Ndimande, intrigued to learn of his work in the Galapagos Islands. Bob still kept the thesis at his home in England and if his father wanted it, he would ask his mother to bring it with her to the wedding. When he spoke of his mother, Robert Castle grew silent and reflective, as if fearful, as if afraid. Yet he spoke lovingly of their time together and their wedding in Arlaston and the absurdity of his dress on his wedding day. But he never talked of the Impala nor did he ever talk of the day when Francina was taken. The boys loved to hear the stories of his life. They also had stories of their own to recount. Robert learnt how his son had developed without him and the role his grandfather had played and he felt so grateful to the old man whom he had never known, simply disagreed with. An old man he wished he had known. Almost every night they talked together until the woman of the camp decided she had had enough and she needed her man, she didn't need his father and his brother and Kathy Castle in her hut for the whole of the night! So she shooed the other men away and took Bob to herself alone. She understood their need, but she had needs too.

There had been no communication between Robert Castle and Kathy before the day of the wedding, none at all.

He emerged from his hut and he looked twenty years younger. The beard had gone and it was as if in removing it he had shed one persona and stepped into the arms of another. He was truly Robert Castle again and as he stood beside his son, preparing for their short journey across the river to Delta Camp, it was as if two brothers stood together. Faces so similar, so handsome, so strong. Ndimande too stood with them and joked that he was equally as handsome, in addition he was a better colour. They laughed together as only the greatest of friends can laugh together. Jane awaited them at Delta camp. She had gone there the day before to be alone from her man, to prepare for her day. She had found an extraordinary woman waiting for her in the camp, a very special woman with an exceptionally beautiful white dress that had not seen the light of day for twenty-four years.

'It is yours to wear Jane, if you wish it. It was mine on my wedding day. It is yours if you wish it.'

They had hugged one another for a few seconds, they knew instantly they would gel together as mother and daughter. Jane shrugged away the sadness associated with her own home life, the despondency of not even wishing to inform her parents of their only daughter's wedding. The moment she saw it and touched the exquisite material Jane wanted to wear the dress, prayed it would fit. But Kathy had thought of that too, had hired a dress-maker from the village together with her antiquated treadle sewing machine, so what little alteration necessary was soon completed. Then the two women sat in the setting sun, drinking South African champagne together, talking about their lives, talking about their men.

They stood together, groom and best man, father and son. From the rear as they stood in their dark Cape Town suits they could not be told apart, save for the give-away white hair on one of their heads. Except for that there was no difference, they were of the same build, the same breadth of firm shoulders, the same upright stance. They stood under the gaily decorated, flower-bedecked archway, constructed the day before, constructed to accept the flowers the graceful English lady had packed into the small light aircraft she had chartered from Maun. Bringing her, the Christian minister and the flowers. They stood and looked out at the bend in the Boro river that had brought them each so much happiness and so much pain. They looked, not talking and they waited.

A small battery-operated organ keyboard began to play and the untrained powerful voices of Paul and of Ndimande reached out to the Delta and informed all the birds and all the animals that the bride was coming, she was here. The two white men shifted their glances from the water, looked briefly at one another and, with one accord, swiveled their heads to see the bride coming down from the wooden chalets to meet them. It was as if there were two brides and both as lovely as one another. A stunningly white clad young beauty followed demurely by a simply elegant bridesmaid in captivating blue, the colour of the African sky. Kathy was holding the train, carrying the drifting material above the dried mud of the riverbank. Each man had eyes for only one woman. Both women were smiling, then all were smiling and Robert Castle felt fear no longer. His son was holding the right hand of his bride and his wife was standing on the left side of the bride but he was standing beside his son and he could hardly push them all aside so that he could see Kathy and go to her. He damn well couldn't see her, yet she was only a few feet from him! Shielded by the others. Then the minister began to speak and the moment was gone. The hymns of praise rose to the sky, 'All Things Bright and Beautiful' sang the lusty male voices and the sweet female sopranos of the campsite and their village and all the villages around. For today Nnyaa Leina's son was getting married. They all respected Nnyaa Leina and he needed some happiness in his life now that his wife was gone and his father-in-law was gone. He was a good man and he would bring work to the villages and he would look after the people. So they all came to the wedding and they all came to the marriage feast. They brought little presents of food and large presents of themselves and the love they had for Nnyaa Leina and all his family, his old family and his new family. The singing and the feasting and the pleasure went on well into the night. Sometimes one of the feasters would stop for a moment and see Nnyaa Leina deep in conversation with the white woman. The conversation seemed so very deep for a wedding night and too serious, so they would go to him and stop the conversation for they wanted him to be happy that night and not to be solemn. He was probably working for them, discussing his projects, but tonight was not the night for such discussions. They wanted him to enjoy every moment, so they broke up the conversations when they seemed deep or serious, tonight was for fun and for drinking and for eating and for happiness.

Kathy's wedding gift to them was a pair of round-the-world Business Class air tickets and vouchers for hotels in the Galapagos Islands, New York, London, Hong Kong, Bali and Australia. They needed that time to be away, that time to be alone together, to enjoy one another, to find one another, away from the closeness of Africa. It was the best gift she could have given them and they accepted with exhilaration.

It was difficult for the two of them to talk together that night, it was difficult for them to know what to say, how to say it. They were different people than they had been more than twenty years before. She so assured, so much in command, so sophisticated and competent and in control. He, in contrast, wearing the only suit he possessed, the suit he now suspected she had provided the money to buy; about to embark on a lecture tour which he now suspected her money had financed. What to say, how to say it? Their only common bond their son and, in a way, he was now leaving them for another life, albeit a life still in Africa. Robert would often be able to see him but somehow all was topsy turvey when it should be falling into place. Her life was in England, his life was partly in Africa, mainly on the road travelling from country to country, from meeting to meeting. Their son and his wife to be based here. It was all disintegrating. And here was the best place and all of them knew that here was the best place, with the animals and the tranquility and the birds and the placid people and no stress and just love and simplicity, here was the best place. But they could not talk about it, could not express it. There were too many people and too much singing and too much drinking and too much happiness to spoil the evening, so they could not speak about it. They talked as if they were only friends, only good friends.

'When is your first lecture, Robert?' She asked.

'The day after tomorrow.'

'Where?'

'The Victoria Falls Hotel.'

They were both silent for a long time. They watched as the newly married couple danced together in the glow from a hundred torches. Abstractedly Kathy saw that the hem of her wedding dress, their wedding dress, was dirty from the soil. It did not matter, it would not be used again.

'I think I would like to hear your lecture, Robert, if you don't mind my coming. I could do with a few day's holiday before I return to England and Vic Falls is as good a place as any.' She attempted to keep the catch in her voice from betraying her. She almost succeeded.

'Not at all, Kathy, I would love you to be there. I leave tomorrow.'

'Perhaps we can travel together, I still have a plane for the next day or two. You can hop a ride with me if you wish.'

How the world had changed! He thought to himself. And then there was no more time for them for they were split again by the villagers and forced into the dancing area. Forced to enjoy themselves.

It was a small aircraft and they sat very close to one another. They were the only occupants save the pilot, their thighs touching. And then for a moment he thought he felt a pressure which was more than a simple touch and he responded but the pressure had gone and she was looking out of the window and pointing down at a herd of elephants and her voice was unnaturally loud and her speech was hurried. For she was so afraid. Oh God! It would be so easy to give herself again to this handsome virile man, so easy. And he wanted her, she could feel it. It was no different than twenty years before. It was no sodding different at all! He was so strong and so animal and so beautiful and he smelt so good up close. He *was* so close and could easily reach out to touch her, to caress her. There was no insurance agent from somewhere down south, she thought with a wry smile. Oh God she was frightened! When do we land, pilot? When do we land? Can you please make it soon for I dare not give myself to him again, it will all come out wrong again. It will, I know it will! They landed and they had not even held hands.

His lecture was a success, his lectures would always be a success, for he had the twin benefits of knowing his subject in absolute detail and the ability to express his message in true and believable emotion. He was a powerful man, a powerful speaker and as she applauded with the rest of them she felt so proud of the father of her son. So proud of the man who had once been her man.

He knocked on her door as she was emerging from the bath, she knew it was him, she knew it was his knock. He came in like a boy, like a sheepish boy. She could not leave him in the corridor, she wore only her bathrobe, she had to invite him in.

'Room 208.' He said.

Yes, that's this room, *my* room,' she replied with smiling menace.

'You know, my memory for detail has returned almost better than I think it was before.'

'What do you mean?'

'I didn't think you would remember.'

'Remember what?'

'This was the room where we stayed in1965.'

'How the hell do you know that?'

'I remember.'

'You're making this up, it's too much of a coincidence for me to be given the same room again, you're making this up.'

'It's not a coincidence at all, Kathy. I remembered and when we checked in, I asked that you be given the same room. I gave the desk clerk ten dollars, probably your dollars, and he allocated you this room.'

The bastard was back and it was as if he had never been away. He was just the same. A simple arrogance, an inability to be anything but a rogue. But a lovable one. So what the hell if he had made up the story? It might be true, it just might be true. If it were, then it was better still, poetic justice. Then she began to laugh and the laugh chased away twenty-four years of pain. It *was* this room! He took her as she stood. He lifted her to the bed. She tried to struggle through her laughter and it was not really much of a struggle and anyway she was too weak to fight him. He could have taken her anyway, so why struggle? All of a sudden she did not want to struggle. She began to burn with the passion of a lost youth, of so many lost years. Her hands tore into the clothes she had bought for him. She shredded them on the floor by his feet. She was naked and then he was naked and he was so big and strong and so powerful and so hungry and such a giant among men and he entered her. It went on and on and on for ever and he never came until she came and when she had come and when they had lain sweating together for but a few minutes he began again and it was what she remembered. His gentleness, his caring, his touching and his caressing in every part of her body. She remembered his touch and her body responded just as it had done so many years before and it was the response of the found, the response of the needed, the response of the loved.

They did not leave room 208 for two days, food was brought to their door, towels and sheets remained unchanged. They didn't want them changed, they wanted the scent of one another, the scent of their love-making to pervade and pervade and forever pervade.

And they talked. But as they talked they could see no way forward for either of them. This was but a moment in time and when the moment had gone it was all that there had been, just a moment in time. Their lives were too different, too fixed. Her life was her work in the hotel industry, his life was the preservation of what little part of Africa he was to be honoured with. There was no future for them together. Although they spoke of it they could hardly believe their own words, for they were the words of convention. They had already lost so much time together, it was senseless not to remain now, to continue to enjoy one another for whatever time they had remaining to them. Life was not a try-out, it was all there was and now they had one another and they must not lose one another. The business was nothing, it was only money and position and power. She could surely give it up for love and for him? He argued with her, and when they were not making love some of the time they were fighting and it was ridiculous that she did not put him first and come to join him in his work and live and love and be near their son, it was absurd! She could contribute too. It *is* absurd you stupid bloody ignorant man to think that I would live in your hut with you. In the hut that you shared with Francina. A place with no furniture and no real light and nothing! It was a ridiculous idea! Then she would cry and then they would hold one another and then they would make love and when they were exhausted they would realise again that their lives were too dissimilar. Then they would pretend that one day, when he was out of Africa making one of his lecture tours they might meet again and that something might be different and that they might find a way to come together. But that too was absurd, for he would never permanently leave Africa, never leave the country that had given him his purpose in life. She in her turn could never relinquish her hotels, never abandon her anchor, never give up her hard fought for security, she could never lose everything again.

They said good-bye at Victoria Falls, as the spray misted above their heads, dropping to moisture on their clothes. They said a tender, heart-rending, sad good-bye.

12

He was beaming with the delight of new life coursing through him as she greeted him.

'Why are you back so soon, I was having a great time!' He said.

She laughed at her father, she laughed with him. He looked so bloody good.

'You look so bloody good, you old rascal.' She told him.

'I'm loving it Kathy, I'm really loving it and I'm on track for your damn occupancy rates and catering cost reductions, so you can't sack me yet!'

She loved this man, this man who would go on forever, no matter what assailed him. He would simply go on for ever.

She suddenly realised it was not enough for her, the three hotels were not enough for her. Her father had done much to ensure their success then had passed them to her. She had brought them into the last decade of the twentieth century and they were powerful and strong and slick and well managed. The Chairman needed to do little else to ensure success for she had chosen her senior staff well. She had always chosen her senior staff well. The Chairman was a convener only, a strategist, no longer hands on. There was not enough challenge remaining for her she now realised, and she was not yet ready to retire.

It was peculiar, he did not ask about Africa, he did not ask about the wedding, he did not ask about Robert Castle, he did not even ask about his grandson. It was as if he did not care, or that he cared too much to ask. Or maybe, he knew it all already. Suddenly and with complete conviction she realised exactly where Bob and Jane had made their first port of call on their world-wide trip.

They sat together in front of the fire and it was as if they had always sat there. Companionably, in total understanding one of the other. Ian Harris waited his moment. It had to be right, unhurried, casual, a worm to catch a fish.

'I've bought another hotel.' He said casually, addressing the glass of port he swirled in his hand.

'You've done what? What did you say?'

' I said, I've bought another hotel.'

' You daft bugger! You can't damn well do that, I'm the Chairman, I decide on our investments.' Kathy was instantly livid. Her father was no longer the lovable old rogue. He was an irresponsible idiot. In his bloody dotage! Senile!

'I can and I have.'

'We'll see about this!' She said rising, her Chairmanship challenged. She knew she was in the right.

'Sit down Kathy and shut up.' It was years since he had spoken to her in this way. 'Just shut up and listen.' He paused. She sat. 'It's nothing to do with the company, I've realized all my personal holdings and purchased a hotel, that's all. I used to be in the hotel business, I loved it, I don't see why now that I'm approaching my late seventies I should give up what I enjoy. So I've bought myself another fucking hotel!'

She stopped mid breath, he never swore, not even when he was angry, he never swore. She looked at the strong sturdy young old man sitting beside her, solid faced, resilient, unbeatable. She smiled at him, they smiled together, then she laughed at the nonsense of life and the sense of life. She laughed at the need to carry on, the need to do what you did best, what you loved to do. She began to clap her hands together and she rose to her feet and she stood above the crippled giant of a man and she applauded and applauded until her hands hurt.

'Good for you, you silly old bugger. Where is your fucking hotel?'

'Realistically I know I can't manage it day to day, Kathy. I want to put in a competent manager and watch it grow. I want you to find that person for me Kathy.'

'How many bedrooms?' She asked, the proficient hotelier taking over.

'Probably two hundred, maybe two hundred and fifty, I don't know.'

'You don't know!' She was incredulous.

'It was a good price and it has tremendous potential. It just needs the right manager and some refurbishment and a plan to get the tourists in. It requires a theme for its improvement, for its business growth. A theme relating to its place in the world, its position in its country.'

Her breath stopped. No, it wasn't possible. She had to ask.

'Which country, father?' She asked, quietly, sitting down in her favourite chair. Her chair of safety.

His eyes twinkled the Harris twinkle and he poured himself another port from the heavy glass decanter beside his left arm.

'It's quite an old place you see Kathy, and it needs a fresh touch, new ideas. It will need a very active and shrewd manager. You'll have to choose well. In my experience, there are few people up to the task. I know even I would find it difficult to manage. It's an old colonial style hotel and needs bringing up to date but also must retain its aging sophistication, its elegance. An elegance matched by its obvious potential'

Slowly and deliberately, as the unbelievable matured in her mind, Kathy asked calmly, although her heart beat loudly in her ears.

'Where in the world is your new hotel, Ian Harris?'

He looked directly into her beautiful green eyes. A look of love, a look of everlasting respect, of endless love.

'It's in Africa, Kathy, it's at the Victoria Falls and it needs the best hotel manager in the world to pull it around.'

Kathy had no words, none at all. Like a child she ran from the room. She ran out into the cool darkness of the night and she looked up at the sky. It was the same sky, the same stars that held the same dreams, the same hopes, of people continents away.

Postscript

There is an hotel at the Victoria Falls in Africa and it is called *The Smoke That Thunders Hydro*. It is an hotel that caters for all travellers; calmly, restfully, luxuriously. But do not ask for room 208 for it is permanently reserved.

About the
Author

Howard Ingram has lived in Africa, the UK, Cyprus, Hong Kong and Singapore and now makes his home between Thailand and Korea, where he is constantly living the detailed research that is a hallmark of his novels. He is both a businessman and a writer and has, in his time been an actor, a sailor, a business consultant, an entrepreneur and a world traveller. He is unlikely to settle down anytime soon.

Printed in the United Kingdom
by Lightning Source UK Ltd.
123822UK00001B/1-9/A